METAGAME

SAM LANDSTROM

PUBLISHED BY

amazon encore

Published by AmazonEncore
P.O. Box 400818
Las Vegas, NV 89140

ISBN-13: 9781935597162
ISBN-10: 1935597167

This book is dedicated to everyone who lived one hundred years ago who couldn't have dreamed of our world today and to those of us now looking forward to a big, big surprise.

CHAPTER 1

Games within games, that's all life is.
And God is keeping score.

—Minister A_Dude, archives, "From the Pulpit"

Sitting in his shower bowl, D_Light slumped over and retched again. The pungent vomit turned light pink as it mixed with the EasyClean SaniRinse™ and then disappeared down the drain. His body trembled, and his tears were swept away. Crying and vomiting, he muttered, "OverSoul, please help me."

He was ashamed before the words had even escaped him. It was not as if the OverSoul—the creative intelligence that guided the billions of beings of this planet and others—had the time or inclination to bother with the pitiful pleas of one insignificant baby blubbering in his shower. But he had lost his perspective. Despite the hot, viscous, exfoliating, bacteria-laden water pounding down on him, he was trembling uncontrollably. This was unprecedented. Maybe he *was* having a reaction to one of the drugs in his system. Perhaps he was dying. A voice in his head told him he was not.

Master, your vitals differ from your personal history, but they are well within the normal parameters of your species. According to all available data, you are in no danger of termination at this time. The soothing voice of his familiar pressed gently into his mind. *Master, would you like me to give you a downer?*

D_Light's familiar, a jet-black cat named Smorgeous, sat quietly next to the shower, his eyes fixed impassively on his human master. Like any good servant, he worked tirelessly to anticipate his master's needs. *Mountain Sunset is on sale, 343 points per dose. You have been using 11.3 doses of this drug per month. Averaged over the last six months—*

Smorgeous, not now! Just be quiet! D_Light sent the message back without a word. A gentle ping echoed in his mind, indicating that Smorgeous understood and would not initiate communication with his master unless an emergency transpired.

Familiars were able to read and write to their masters' minds, and although this was designed to be useful, it was sometimes irritating to D_Light, especially when he desired silence. Unfortunately, D_Light had had the interface kit installed in his brainstem fairly late in life, making it difficult for the telepathic input from his familiar to mesh naturally with his own thoughts. This was in sharp contrast to people he knew who had received their kits at birth. For them, the voice of their familiar was a part of them, essentially an extension of their consciousness. But there was nothing natural about how D_Light perceived his familiar. To him, Smorgeous still felt like an alien entity living inside his head—an alien who tended to invade his private space. This was particularly bothersome when D_Light just wanted to be alone, like now.

D_Light attempted to quiet his mind by going into a relaxation trance, concentrating on the rhythm of his breathing and the sensation and sound of the shower as it pulsed over him. *One, relax...two, relax...three, relax...* Like a slow drumbeat, he recited the mantra. It was a simple and effective way to unwind without a drug boost, a technique he had learned long before his familiar implant. Although maintenance drugs were almost always in a player's system, spiking a drug to get a desired effect, called boosting, could lead to a violation of his health contract if done in an abusive pattern. Lately, he had been taking too many of these drugs, and although Smorgeous had not yet warned him of any contract violations, D_Light felt it would be wise to lay off for the next couple of days.

D_Light began rocking back and forth as he sat huddled and naked in the shower bowl. "I'm sorry. I'm so, so sorry." The hiss of the shower took his words and drowned them.

It took several minutes of this routine before D_Light was able to calm himself to some degree, at which point his nausea subsided. Only then did he attempt to fix this emotional hitch in his mind—not that all feelings were to be avoided. Anger, fear, even jealousy could embolden the human spirit when it needed a kick or could instill a healthy measure of prudence when warranted. However, D_Light suspected that not all emotions were of equal utility. As best he could tell, the emotion he felt now was remorse. Remorse. How could he have remorse for making a bold and excellent move in accordance with the Game? There was little room for remorse on the path to immortality, and unjustifiable remorse was surely useless. Worse than useless, it was detrimental.

Of course, this was not the first time D_Light had experienced a disadvantageous emotion, and his favorite way of dealing with them was also the most expedient—good old-fashioned suppression. D_Light liked to imagine taking a big iron box, putting the emotion inside it, and then sealing that box in another one. He would repeat this process as necessary. He had used this mental trick many times, but it was not working now. It was as though the negative feelings were wisps of dark, incorporeal threads that escaped out through the seams.

Suppression not an option, D_Light decided to try some simple desensitization exercises. This required more time and was more painful than his box technique, but it tended to be more reliable. He began by picturing the corpse in his mind. The girl's eyes came to him first. Her eyes—eyes that had been arresting in life—were merely large glistening marbles in death, vacant and swiveled downward at the floor. He held the memory for a few long moments, inhaling a few slow, deep breaths. He then silently called upon Smorgeous to execute a gradual uploading of the entire corpse into his consciousness. He wanted to see her in detail.

At first he studied her with great unease. Her jet-black hair was glistening, sticky and matted with coagulating blood. The good side of her face—the side not mangled—was facing up, and the perfect lines and arcs of her face made up an olive-colored stone mask. Next, the image panned out, allowing D_Light to see the scene in its entirety. There was a lot of blood—blood on the face, neck, and pooling out across the stone floor. He focused in on her lifeless hand until the entire image blurred. Slowly, he felt the dark threads slackening as the grisly image became less painful to him, and by the time he finally dismissed the archive, he did so with only the slightest tinge of relief.

Out of the shower, D_Light picked out a lightweight skinsuit, the lightest one he had. It was summer, after all, and he hoped to get outside today and feel the sun. The selected skinsuit was stark white, and it shimmered slightly from the countless microlenses that were embedded in the fabric. Since he was going to a church service this morning, he mentally asked Smorgeous to upload something a bit more formal than one of his common selections. *Okay, Smorgeous, we can talk again. I'll wear the suit from, um, from the play I saw the other day.*

D_Light's recollection of that particular memory was enough for Smorgeous to determine which suit his master had requested. *Yes, master,* the familiar replied. *The suit model Divine Fate costs 630 points per use.*

The specifications were uploaded to D_Light's skinsuit, and the optical lenses immediately rendered the blue slacks, shirt, and sport coat, all of which hung on his body perfectly, as only an illusion could. Looking himself over in the mirror, D_Light wished he could also change his hair. It was getting long and unwieldy, a blight on an otherwise strikingly handsome man. However, that sort of change was out of the question. Changing one's natural appearance using holograms—even just the style of one's hair or the hue of one's skin—was a transgression.

He took a long minute and studied himself carefully in the mirror. Not a blemish or wrinkle on his face. He, like everyone he knew, was locked into the same body he had attained in his early twenties. He was so young—only fifty-four years—and yet he did not feel like it this morning. He did not want to go to church. There would be a lot of attention, mostly positive he imagined, but he still did not relish the thought. And yet, it would be a good thing to get out of this room. A very good thing. Involuntarily, he looked over at the floor near his chamber door. He felt his stomach lurch slightly, thinking he could make out a faint bloodstain. *Naw, can't be. The cleaning bots don't leave anything behind,* he thought. Still, he made a point to avert his gaze as he opened the front door to leave. If there was a stain, real or imagined, he wanted to miss it.

D_Light stepped out of his chamber into the castle hallway. As D_Light punched into the general house skin, images of the girl were washed away from his mind by the swirl of images at his feet—visuals skinning every conceivable surface. Even the floor displayed text messages and static pics of people he knew, places he wanted to be, and products he liked. The walls and ceiling featured a variety of video feeds, but the floor did not. D_Light's skin settings prohibited video on the floor. He found it disorienting, as moving images on the ground incited vertigo. This was doubly true for him when on peps.

"Morning breath?" The voice came from beside him. A man, looking far too much like his bio-father to be coincidence, smiled broadly at him. The semitransparent, tenderly smiling man waited to see if D_Light showed interest and then shifted naturally backward down the hallway as D_Light ignored him and advanced.

"Remember when Icy_B gagged and nearly threw up in her mouth when she kissed you?" Although that incident happened many years ago, the avatar did not need to elaborate. D_Light remembered.

His bio-father, rendered as true as life by the skin software, winked at him and asked, "How's the breath this morning?" It did not wait for an answer because only a n00b talked back to advertisements. "Too busy owning the Game to rinse? Get a booster of FlavaPhage™ today! Just one boost a month and—" D_Light shifted his attention away from the ad, which automatically cut off the auditory feed.

As he continued walking, he scanned the walls for something interesting. Burger_Fling™ reminded him that he had accumulated enough "Customer Love" points to get a free TerriBurger™ with his next visit. The Divine Authority suggested he visit a reproduction representative to see about a progeny permit. Saucy_Dice, a girl he perved a few weeks back, had posted yet another message for him. Saucy's freckled face grinned at him mischievously. "What's new, D? Give me a blink when you get a wink." D_Light rolled his eyes. No doubt the skin software, called SkinWare, thought the message from Saucy and the message about getting a reproduction permit were related, which is why the messages were displayed near one another. As if D_Light would repro with a girl with freckles! D_Light frowned down at Smorgeous, who strode beside him, and sent, *Smorgeous, I'm not interested in perving with Saucy ever again, much less having a child with her.*

Smorgeous pinged confirmation. The familiar should have known better, D_Light thought. D_Light had no patience for poor message targeting. D_Light then thought about a fragment of a church hymn that he really liked: *"To be a top player, optimize your input."* In response to that thought, the SkinWare finally gave him something useful. Huge 3-D letters appeared on the ceiling above him:

House Tesla Top Scorers in the Last Twenty-four Hours:

1. D_Light
2. Beensa Sardanaha
3. Speedy_LeeA
4. Down_to_ChinaTown
5. GloverAce
6. Mona_Love

Irritated, D_Light wondered why this wasn't the first thing he saw when he punched into the skin. Not that he obsessively monitored the house ranking, but he was currently number one!

Master, the score tally was published 4.1 seconds ago. Smorgeous answered the question before D_Light even thought to ask it.

Under normal circumstances, D_Light would have basked in his glory. He would have just stood there on the stairway and smiled to himself. After all, there were over eight thousand members in his family, and he had won the day. Of course, his top position must be from a projected score, as the points from his win the night before had not officially been transferred. The points would be official soon enough, that is, after the ritual.

The cathedral was immense, inspiring, beautiful. Such splendor was not wasted here, for this was a place of renewal, a place that exuded zest for the Game. The walls arched, curving in to meet at the center of the sprawling ceiling. The dome was supported by huge pillars that were garnished to look like towering trees, complete with fine stone branches and ornate leaves of every shape and size. The sunlight of the summer morning filtered through large stained glass windows, creating the effect of a magical forest.

D_Light, perched high above on a branch of a faux tree, watched over the pews below. This was not meant to be a viewing point (stone leaves obscured much of his view), but it was private, allowing D_Light to observe the congregation unnoticed.

At the front of the congregation, Minister A_Dude was leading morning prayer. The music was just starting to crank. A morning service always started in this way. The music, which made up the backdrop of the service, always built up gradually. This provided routine for service members and a sense of anticipation. A thundering bass track was throbbing with a *thump, thump, thump, thump, thump, thump*, which looped over and over. A female voice track glided over the bass, almost too softly to hear, but was building in volume. "Welcome, OverSoul...wel...wel...welcome, OverSoul... wel...wel...welcome to our feast." This track also looped, but the warp of the voice varied with each iteration.

The congregation consisted of people in a wide array of attire, accompanied by their equally diverse animal-styled familiars. Through the chiseled leaves, D_Light could see LuckyB. The woman boasted a tall hat—impossibly tall—and a huge, splaying dress of fluorescent green; she bobbed and swayed toward the front with the greatest confidence. Luck loved to dance. Her familiar was styled as a baby leopard with unrealistically large blue saucers for eyes, making it permanently adorable. The leopard was up on its haunches, bobbing along with its master, mimicking her every move. If D_Light didn't know better, he would have thought it was mocking her, but familiars were designed to be in sync with their masters, so this was expected behavior. D_Light had always admired Luck's carefree attitude. She didn't give a clip about anything or what anyone thought. With any luck, one day the two of them would get hooked up by MatchMaker™.

D_Light's three favorite siblings were stationed toward the back in their usual spots. TermaMix, C, and K_Slice were swaying to the music in their routine, repetitive, and unimaginative manner. Of the three, K_Slice was the best dancer, but that was no surprise since she was a girl. Still, she didn't hold a candle to most of her gender, especially not to a girl like LuckyB. K_Slice had a linear and inhibited mind, so while she might be technically good at performing dance moves, she had no style of her own. TermaMix and C, both geek males, simply had no style.

The mere thought of abandoning his perch was agonizing, but they were all expecting him. It would be an insult to the congregation not to show, for it was customary for the fragger to bear testimony for his deed. He had delayed too long as it was. A few noticed him as he descended the sharp-angled stairs of the long dais that led down to the congregation floor. He kept his head high and his chest puffed out, perhaps a bit too much. Word spread silently through the familiars, and soon all eyes—robotic and human alike—were on him.

"At last, our man!" shouted the unthinkably rotund minister, who grinned widely and laughed with a rumble.

K_Slice immediately sprinted up and sprang on D_Light like a windup toy, wrapping her arms and legs around him tightly. Having lost his footing, D_Light staggered a bit, but fortunately his old friend was a lightweight. "Alive and still walking!" she shouted, pressing her cheek against his.

The pulse of the beat quickened. The ritual was beginning. K_Slice unlatched herself and splayed out her arms, palms pointing toward D_Light. She waved them back and forth. Her torso bowed, and her hips gyrated in sync with the beat.

"Deeeelight!" the minister boomed. "Show us your hands!"

D_Light put his palms up and began swaying back and forth in rhythm. He knew he needed to look natural, to feel the beat, but the music was not suffusing him and he felt stiff. He needed to show strength. Oh, how he wished he had hit an enhancer before coming down here. To hell with his healthcare contract! He needed to be *up* at times like this. In response to his wish, Smorgeous sent out the required electromagnetic signal that unlocked the nanocontainers in his bloodstream. Still, it would be several seconds before D_Light would feel the effects of the drug.

No one seemed to notice his discomfort as the congregation cheered and closed in. There were hands, chests, and shoulders all pressed around him now. In unison, they swept back and forth, falling down and pulling away like giant breakers massaging a beach. As they moved back, D_Light had room to dance, which he now did with wild abandon. The pep administered by his familiar had taken effect, and he felt the blood rushing everywhere it needed to go.

"Yes, to play the Game well is divine," A_Dude intoned with a throaty growl. The minister was dancing as well, but his skipping back and forth across the stage more closely resembled a pacing bear crossed with a crazed monkey than actual dancing.

"And today, right now, Deeeelight is fine!" the minister bellowed. His words were perfectly timed with a frenzied blast from the AI-composed music.

The congregation had been waiting for the moment to uptick the intensity of their celebration. More impassioned cheering ensued. The flock pressed tightly into a circle that enveloped D_Light so closely that few had the room to dance anymore. In their confinement, motions became upward and downward bobs or, for the more energetic, high jumping. D_Light heard the slithering sound of his skinsuit's optic lenses running up against the lenses of other suits. An outrageous feathered boa draped around the neck of a nearby dancer swung realistically into D_Light's face, momentarily blinding him with the color pink, but being only a hologram, it passed right through him.

I'm alive, and I'm a winner! The sound of D_Light's laugh was doused by the celebration. *Soul, thank you for the blessings you've bestowed upon me!*

TermaMix, impatient by nature and capable of as much violence as the most belligerent flake, thrashed his way into the center of the circle. He shouted into D_Light's ear, "Congrats, Brother!" TermaMix, an engineer who was fanatical about his work, did not even bother to come dressed. His skinsuit was unadorned by any illusionary clothing. Wearing a skinsuit without a skin had come somewhat into vogue. It was sort of a "what you see is what you get" (also known as WYSIWYG) fashion statement. However, D_Light knew that TermaMix paid no attention to fashion trends. TermaMix was just being TermaMix, devout and ignorant of everything but the Game.

The wave of flesh swept out again. D_Light now had room to use a move he had kept in reserve for just such an occasion. He began to undulate fiercely, appearing as a snake standing up as though about to strike, simultaneously swirling and whirling about. It was not a very acrobatic move, but it required good muscle control and was at least original.

From the circle around him, some laughed while others cheered, but it was evident that everyone was entertained. No doubt that move would be up on the Cloud in a matter of moments. Another hymn fragment entered his mind: *"Nothing ventured, little gained."*

D_Light recited this as he attempted to enter the right trance for the task at hand. He wanted to be focused, yet free to improvise.

"Ah yeah, dive down deep into the depths of the sound. There ain't nothin' in this world but the dance o' life," the minister intoned. He had a toothy smile, and his thick hands clapped hard in rhythm to the music.

The dance of life! D_Light thought. *For the chosen, the beat will never stop!*

The shadow of the dead girl was receding from his psyche like smoke blowing away on a blustery sunny day.

D_Light began transitioning out of his "starky snake" dance and moved over to a more popular favorite. Gradually, the circle closed back in and he found himself back in the sea of limbs and warm breath. Most familiars stayed out of the throng, being no larger than medium-sized pets. With AI on board, even the most primitive familiar was smart enough to avoid getting crushed by an excited mob.

The music intensified, perhaps in response to the mood of the congregation. The female voice echoed with "ooooh" and "ahhhh," intertwined with a faster and louder thundering beat. Some hands caressed D_Light, some groped, and others punched. K_Slice, eyes shining with glee, managed to weave her way back in front of him and then slapped him hard across the face. Of course, it was impolite to reciprocate. People were supposed to express their feelings to the victor in whichever way they liked. D_Light, however, preferred less painful well-wishing, and he twisted away from her to avoid additional congratulations.

Another punch—this one well delivered—slammed into D_Light's side. Naturally, the most violent ones always managed to push their way to the front. And like a shark testing its prey with a few tentative nibbles and now finding it safe to feast, the blows began raining down on him.

The seconds ticked by as a disharmonic blur of thundering music, chaotic movement, and hurt. No caresses, kisses, or congratulatory shouts could drown out his pain receptors as he was struck repeatedly. From outside the throng, Smorgeous sat on his haunches and sent signals for pain reliever deployment into D_Light's bloodstream, but they proved inadequate. Such a shame. As much as he tried to keep his poise, D_Light figured he looked like a n00b as he got the wind knocked out of him and crumpled over in an involuntary heap.

Mustering his drug-induced reserves, he got up quickly and began dancing as fast as he could. A moving target was harder to hit, but he knew he couldn't keep up that pace forever. Then, as if reading his mind, the music suddenly stopped, the dancing ceased, and there was only the sound of hundreds of the faithful panting for breath.

CHAPTER 2

The great families did not spring up overnight. Like the evolution of most social structures, it was gradual. It started in the time of the Second Jeffersonian Era of the United States. There had been a long-standing strain between those who supported homosexuals' right to equality under marriage versus those who stood by "traditional" family units.

This long-standing strain, which was one of several battlefronts of the so-called "War of Moral Values," came to a head in the Second Jeffersonian Era. The legal status of marriage was dispensed with completely in favor of civil unions. It was argued that marriage was a religious institution and therefore violated the principle of separation of church and state. Therefore, marriage would no longer be recognized by the government at all.

After this, marriage remained a private religious ritual, but now it conferred no legal status. All property rights— including rights to offspring—were determined by civil unions. All civil unions were legally the same, regardless of the genders of those in the union. However, it was initially limited to two consenting adults. This limitation seemed arbitrary, and so a few court cases later, civil unions were extended to two or more consenting adults. Furthermore, these adults were no longer required to be physically intimate with one another.

The lifting of these restrictions gave birth to the Great Families, which at first grew slowly until they became viable alternatives to corporations. With families, risks and rewards were shared more equitably, and members found a positive psychological component as well.

There used to be a saying that went, "You can choose your friends, but you can't choose your family." Well, needless to say, that is now history.

—Excerpt from Dr. Steely_Flame's lecture series, "The Second Jeffersonian Era"

D_Light was aching all over, but he stood up straight anyway. And although his lip was swelling up and bleeding, he managed a rather convincing smile. However, nagging at him more than anything was the intense pain in his groin where someone—probably well intentioned—had squeezed a bit too hard. Tattered, the hero of the day stood in all his glory, covered in sweat and a little blood. Members of the congregation regarded him with the full spectrum of emotions evident in their stares.

"Now for the real fun!" bellowed the minister, his voice exploding through the relative quiet of the great room. "Let's see the story! Deeeelight, can we hear it straight from the source?"

Back at his podium, A_Dude was smiling with his unnervingly large mouth. He was perhaps the ugliest man in D_Light's family. The minister must not have had any genetic engineering in his background, or if he did, it had obviously not gone as planned. Really, there was no excuse for such homeliness in this day and age, but everyone loved him anyway. Perhaps his unique appearance, although grotesque by conventional standards, was at least distinguishing.

Master, there is a request from A_Dude to broadcast your archives captured yesterday between the hours of 20:04 and 20:34.

Although he wished he could ignore Smorgeous's message, D_Light knew that was not an option. He hated the testimony, dreaded it even more than the violence of the opening hymn. But tradition was tradition, and when a player accomplished an exceptional deed in the Game, it was customary to bear testimony of that deed. To do this, one did not tell the tale in the player's own words; instead, the events were shared by broadcasting one's personal archive so that everything could be viewed exactly as it had occurred. This was a far more accurate way to recount the story, not to mention a lot more entertaining for the congregation. Since players' familiars recorded every sight, sound, smell, and surface thought of their masters for possible later retrieval, sharing experiences was quite easy.

D_Light's smile faded as he telepathically replied to Smorgeous, *Fine, I grant permission for a public feed between those hours.*

A moment later, the minds of D_Light and all the others in the cathedral were submerged in the sights, scents, and auditory experiences of D_Light at 20:04 on the previous day. As D_Light saw the first scene of his archive, he was immediately thankful that it was no longer in vogue to include one's personal thoughts in testimony feeds. A certain amount of privacy was a good thing. However, the thoughts archive was still available to D_Light, should he desire to relive the whole event in its entirety. He was not sure he was ready to remember it all just yet, still recovering from this morning's wretched display of weakness. What if watching the archive feed inspired another performance by his rebellious stomach? Still, he had to admit to a twinge of morbid curiosity, or perhaps it was an insatiable need to revisit an old wound, like picking at a scab against one's better judgment.

D_Light closed his eyes, revealing the usual wall of blackness. Moments later, as his familiar began streaming the archive, the darkness quickly swept aside to reveal his own vision from the night before. Everything appeared exactly as it had—the ever-present specter of the outline of his nose, a few rogue hairs from his bangs that had managed to find their way into his peripheral vision, and the girl from last night, appearing exactly as she did at 20:03.

It was hard for D_Light to peer through his own eyes without having control of where they looked. It was like traveling back in time, but with no free will. The die had already been cast, and he was now a mere spectator of his own life. All that he did—everything he said, all those decisions he made—was done hours ago. Also troubling was the fact that even though he had reviewed countless hours of his own archives in the past, he still found hearing his old thoughts played back on top of his current ones rather disconcerting. For this reason, he could never handle watching his own archives with the thoughts turned on for very long. It was maddening.

The D_Light of 16.2 hours ago set his eyes on Fael's face, a face that now filled the vision of the entire congregation. One look and it was obvious that she was descended from the Murmos line. Although she had the telltale olive skin, jet-black hair, and angular face, it was actually the eyes that gave away her lineage. Voluminous green eyes, not cold like those of his cat-styled familiar, but warm and sensuous. Her voluptuous lips were naturally pink and plump, painted with a sheer, glossy finishing product that seemed to beg for kissing.

The whistles and catcalls started up immediately. Although immersed in the archive feed, D_Light could unfortunately still hear the congregation. "Go, D-bone!" "MaximumAss™!" "Light that up, D!" It was juvenile, but just the sort of outburst that was appreciated during a communal replay of a frag archive.

Fael's narrow nose lifted slightly at the tip, not enough to see the nostrils, but enough to give a youthful perkiness. This type of nose was in style long ago, and apparently one of Fael's ancestors had gotten one. Although it was well sculpted, it was not at all unique, and so while Fael would certainly be considered beautiful to people of previous generations, she did not stand out in a contemporary crowd. D_Light recalled how, on a previous date, Fael had lamented her common nose, saying how she wished she could have it redesigned. Of course, it was a minor transgression for players to make such modifications. Such an act would fall into both the categories of "wasteful vanity" and "false advertising." Besides, males and females of the Murmos line profited from their classic, albeit predictable, beauty. Nine out of ten Murmos males and females played royal grinder games, and royalty demanded a certain traditional aesthetic look from those who served them.

While her nose might have been unremarkable, Fael more than made up for it with her keen ability to work the fashion angle. Her shiny black hair, for example, was styled playfully. Long black pigtails sprung up at forty-five degree angles and then drooped down behind her shoulders. Her clothing was always trendy and unconventional, and she tended to accessorize with small living creatures or the latest genetically engineered plant life. Given her affinity for bizarre fashion, one would think she'd have a field day with footwear, but Fael preferred her feet bare. She insisted that there were too many fantastic toe rings, ankle bracelets, and retro toe tattoo designs out there to cover them up with shoes.

For this date, Fael and D_Light had planned to attend a comedy downtown, making a playful look an appropriate choice. D_Light's appearance was not playful. In fact, he felt a bit stuffy in the presence of Fael, old and unimaginative. His hair—dark, coarse, wavy, and mid-length—did not permit much in the way of styling, and it tended to succumb to entropy despite attempts to tame it. For a man, making a fashion statement was pretty much limited to clothes and hair, and since the hair was out, perhaps he should have done something more creative with his illusionary clothing. Next to Fael, his loose red silk shirt and dark slacks made him look more like her father than her date. Of course, he could render a new outfit at any time, but that might be perceived as a sign of being self-conscious. Not attractive. On the other hand, perhaps he could make light of the situation by asking her to help him come up with something more fun. Yes, that's what he would do, should the conversation dry up and need a punch.

"Beloved brother," the woman said while bowing ceremoniously. Although it was their third date in as many months, they still greeted formally.

"Lovely sister." D_Light bowed also, allowing his gaze to rove over the rest of her curvaceous body. The delicious creature was wearing a perfectly formfitting emerald green suit that left little to the imagination. His breath stopped, a common reaction of men who suddenly find themselves in the presence of a Murmos woman.

Back in the cathedral, the whistling and scattered laughter continued. Had D_Light known he was going to have to publish this archive to everyone he knew, he might not have ogled the girl so thoroughly upon first sight. Ironically, the D_Light of those previous hours had thought himself clever and discreet by looking over the woman during his slow, formal bow, but Fael had noticed immediately.

"Oh, you see!" She beamed as she took note of his inspection. "It's an organic. It's designed by PrimeFlavor™. Breathes as though you have on nothing at all." She let loose a curt laugh, extended her arms outward, and then twirled to show off her suit.

D_Light's hand shot out compulsively and stroked the top of her jewel-green sleeve. The skintight plant had an undulating ribbed texture, a pleasure to his fingertips. He could feel the warmth of her body radiating through the living fabric, and it enticed him. He commented, "I really ought to get one of these someday. Expensive?"

D_Light nervously continued to watch the archive feed, noticing that his left eye had been twitching while chatting with Fael about her suit. That mutinous left eye! It always acted up when he was anxious or excited, thwarting his attempts to portray a cool and casual appearance. D_Light bit his lower lip and hoped the congregation did not notice his wild eyelid snapping about.

"Oh, it's a PrimeFlavor™, so it set me back a few days in the Game," the girl answered. "But you have to live a little, right? Wait a minute, you've never worn a PrimeFlavor™? Ever?"

D_Light shook his head, noting that his date was making excessive references to the brand name of the suit. *No formalities there,* he thought. *She's feeling comfortable enough to name-drop. She must like me.*

Name-dropping, more commonly referred to as just "dropping," was the common practice of casually promoting products in conversation. Merely mentioning a brand name usually earned a player a point or two, but if the conversation resulted in an actual sale, you stood to make much more.

"Oh, shut up!" she shouted. "You have to wear one! Feeling it from the outside is nothing, *nothing* at all. Right now I'm tingling all over. Oh Soul, it's like being in the shower all day long!" She rolled her shoulders from front to back and did a seductive little purr.

"When will it die?" D_Light asked without thinking. *Snap, is it impolite to ask about the death of one's garment so early in a relationship?* D_Light wondered.

Polite or not, Fael didn't seem to mind. "I bought a three-week lifespan. I'm sure I'll get tired of the color before then anyway, although I heard if you switch up your diet the fabric changes hue. Anyway, it's not like I can wear it every day; it wouldn't be proper. What would the other girls think? I would if I could though," she said with a naughty laugh. "You know, even though Lyra started the trend and—" The girl abruptly ended her mile-a-minute chatter, smirked, and looked guiltily at D_Light. "I'm sorry, enough babble. Bottom line is I love my PrimeFlavor™, and I'll have to buy you one if you're too cheap to buy it yourself."

They continued walking down the wide castle hall. D_Light was only jacked into a lightweight skin, just so he could see in the dark. He didn't want to distract himself with ads, bulletin announcements, and the like while on his date. Without the Skin-Ware rendering anything over it, the walls were bare—merely large blocks of granite cemented together with ivory grout. Two men strolled ahead silently, their bird familiars deftly riding their masters' shoulders while staring into one another's eyes. Smorgeous took the liberty of grokking the men, looking up their identiy by searching for their faces on the Cloud. The men were brothers of the family, but no one D_Light knew personally. Only marketers of relatively low level.

"So, what's new with you?" Fael asked.

D_Light actually preferred to be the listener in a one-way conversation, but he shrugged his shoulders and replied, "Grinder games, unfortunately." His voice was apologetic. "Yeah, I've been pepped for three days straight," he continued. "The game finally timed out like two hours ago." He lowered his head and tapped his foot a few times on the floor beneath him.

Fael smiled sweetly. "Three days? Phew! So, what? Are you still pepped?" she inquired.

D_Light let out an exhausted sigh that he feared was a little too dramatic. "Yeah, haven't slept yet. I'm starting to feel it though. I took some Kick_n_Go™. Good stuff, no real side effects, but my neck's a little stiff." He placed his hand on the back of his neck and briefly worked at the tense muscles.

Now I'm whining like a little bitch! D_Light thought. The indignity of that last sentence was not worth the three points he just scored for using the brand name Kick_n_Go™.

"Sweeeet™, you didn't crash out and flake our date!" she exclaimed. "You get extra points for that!" Fael reached over and scratched the back of his head like a good dog. D_Light threw out a half-cocked smile as he caught a whiff of her inviting perfume, an exotic blend of sandalwood and ardonna flower. However, he was quickly distracted by an ad forwarded to him by Fael that stated, "You need some R&R at Defraggers Spa and Luxury Resort™." The ad included a construct video of Fael, sporting a skimpy bathing suit, beckoning to follow her as she bounced toward an immense, white sand beach.

"So, what was the game?" Fael nonchalantly slid her fingers down the side of his face, playfully bouncing her hand off one of his wide shoulders and then returning her hand to her side.

"Oh, it was a free-for-all. Four teams with three days to slap down as many points as possible in any way we could think."

Fael raised her eyebrows with apparent interest. D_Light continued with a tone of sarcastic smugness. "Yeah, your man here made all the difference. It was a cheap move, but I punched together some avatars that scored enough to win us the game. As a matter of fact, it was your mistress who paid the most for one of them."

"Mother Lyra bought one of your avatars?" Fael hopped and clasped her hands together like a happy toddler on her second birthday. "Small world!" she exclaimed.

D_Light noticed that Fael often summoned a great deal of enthusiasm for the smallest things. But he supposed it was better than dates he'd had with players whose weary souls could barely summon a smile for anything.

"Small world?" replied D_Light. "Not really. The game was closed to everyone outside the castle. There are only a couple thousand people here. But yeah, I suppose it's an interesting coincidence."

"Perv me, I'm getting soft just listening to this shit!" someone in the congregation shouted. More laughter.

My Soul, this is embarrassing! D_Light had never taken pride in his small talk skills, but normally his failures were more private. He had to wonder if anyone in his family would date him after this.

Not missing a beat, Fael did a little skip, seemingly unconsciously. "I guess my mistress has good taste then. What avatar did she buy?"

D_Light lowered his voice and muffled his answer. "Oh, it was a creature, a monster really. Part seagull and part—"

Fael interrupted. "You didn't! You created SeaGuy™?" She raised both hands to her mouth and gasped with disbelief.

"You know my work then?" D_Light's voice was elated.

"Oh, my mistress has been parading that monstrosity through her chambers for the past two days!" Fael's eyes widened, and she clasped D_Light's shoulders and shook him violently. She then pushed him back with mock disgust. "It's disturbing, really! I mean, the seagull's head…its beak is constantly dripping with blood, its eyes are demonic green. Its voice—its voice is straight from hell!" Fael laughed.

"Yep, that's why I knew someone would bid high for it. It's got local appeal." D_Light did a quick little dance consisting of a few slides of his feet coordinated with the tilting of his head. This was a shortened version of what he liked to call his "victory jig."

"Living on the ocean, we do have our share of flying rats." Fael paused, pursed her chiseled lips, and then punched him hard in the shoulder. "D_Light, you're sick! Flip, I ought to resubmit for another date right now!"

"But we won," D_Light reiterated, resisting the temptation to rub his now throbbing shoulder. Fael was as strong as she was beautiful.

She nodded. "Anyway, what are you doing grinding away on productive work? I thought you engineers were all hopelessly addicted to spank games." Fael put her hand on her chest, which she puffed out imperiously. "Personally, I don't need spank games. I'm a handmaiden of the royal court, so I have plenty of palace intrigue to amuse me."

D_Light nodded. "Oh, I'm plenty addicted, but I know how to control myself—er, at least a little. I try to play just enough to keep in shape and to unwind, but it's really easy to go overboard." D_Light raised his eyebrows as though he was about to give the girl an education. "Take my friend C. He just got off an eight-day binge. Even the peps weren't helping. He was actually starting to hallucinate! And you say I'm sick?"

"Yeah, domination baby!" D_Light recognized his friend C's voice in the distance.

"Sure, I already called you sick, and I meant it," Fael replied with a playful smirk.

"Yeah, I *am* sick," continued D_Light, "because I actually felt jealous of poor C. Jealous he had all that time to spank while I was grinding. If I let myself, I'd be there too, letting it suck me up. And then what? Spank games don't pay out enough, and I'd end up getting demoted a level." D_Light shook his head and looked to the side.

"And then you'd be in an even worse dating pool than you are now," teased Fael, sticking out her tongue at him in a lighthearted manner.

Fael strolled ahead, bouncing slightly as she walked. "Seriously though, present company excluded, if the dating pool was any worse, I think I'd have to frag myself."

D_Light laughed genuinely. "So true! I've been on nothing but stinkers lately. You know, the dating program should be pretty good. I know one of the lead software engineers—a sister of ours, actually—and she's a good player, a real high scorer. I think she's even nobility bound."

Fael turned around and walked backwards, facing him while she talked. "Sometimes I wish they'd just let us choose, you know?"

"Sure, but you earn more points if you play MatchMaker™," D_Light reminded her. "Besides, it's not about whose company you prefer, it's about what's best for you. Humans are notoriously stupid when it comes to knowing what's best for them in regard to the opposite sex."

Fael pouted. "Hmm, well, you need to ask your software engineer friend how she knows what's best for me, unless her program is trying to teach me the lesson of futility. In that case, tell her—"

Their conversation was suddenly interrupted by an ear-piercing wail of sirens. Instinctively, D_Light spun around quickly and took a brief but thorough look at the other players in the hall. Presently, there were only the two marketers nearby. Both men had turned to face Fael and D_Light. Their eyes were wide, and the color had already drained from their frightened faces. Fear was good. That was safe. The shrieking siren died down after only a few seconds and was then replaced by a low, rhythmic pulse. Over the audio a sharp female voice intoned, "House Rule Number Seven is now in effect. All house players are now available for termination."

"Oh, Flip_It™!" Fael squeaked nervously. "Guess the hunt is on."

Back in the cathedral, the excitement was palpable. A male member of the congregation shouted, "Game on, bitches!" This was accompanied by cheers.

"I say we sit this one out," suggested D_Light to his date.

Fael looked over with sarcastic coyness and replied, "Your place or mine then?"

Whistles and catcalls erupted from the congregation.

"I'm closer, I think. Follow me." D_Light waved for her to follow, and Fael eagerly complied.

As was usual during Number Seven, the SkinWare soon shut down. Without a skin showing you the way, the castle was pitch black at night. To mitigate this, white-burning torches placed evenly along the walls flared up with a glow that, under other circumstances, might have been romantic.

D_Light led the way running, not at a full sprint, but certainly faster than a jog. Others were running too, some of them in a panic, like frightened rabbits, making them tempting targets. As he came across other players in the hallway, he presented his hands to them, palms up, and they did the same. Each made a point of making eye contact and nodding in a reassuring fashion while skirting around one another.

Up the spiral staircase they scrambled. D_Light hated winding stairs, as they limited visibility to only a few steps ahead—a likely ambush point to be sure. Perhaps there was a flake waiting on the steps, blade raised. He quickly erased the thought from his mind and focused his attention on the task at hand.

Strategically, he kept to the outer wall, almost flat against it. He wanted to move quickly, but he did not want to run headlong into the wrong player. With a quick thought, he ordered Smorgeous to go up ahead. It was against the rules to use familiars as scouts while Rule Seven was in effect, but he had always worried about this staircase. Hopefully, his little cheat would go unnoticed.

D_Light twisted slightly, bumping into Fael's familiar, a tan and white creature stylized as a fox. The familiar looked up at him with its big, pale, dispassionate blue eyes. It was constantly shifting its attention all around, its head swiveling unnaturally, like a cannon in a turret. A few steps below stood Fael. D_Light smiled down at her and touched his index finger to his lips to indicate quiet. She smiled back, or at least that's what he thought. Perhaps it was just wishful thinking and it was really nothing more than a twitching of the corners of her mouth.

They waited there for only a second, and he took that brief moment to find the key to his chamber and clasp it in his sweaty palm. Distantly, echoing through the stone corridors, there was shouting and screaming. Smorgeous gave the all clear, prompting D_Light to whisper with a hiss, "Okay, run!"

D_Light bounded up the steps as fast as he could, momentarily catching up to his familiar. The door to his chamber was near the top of the stairs. Across from his door on the hallway wall hung a painting of a lone, jagged rock under siege by savage green ocean waves. D_Light had used his door countless times before, but since so many of the castle halls and doors looked alike, the memorable painting offered a welcome confirmation that he was indeed at the right door. Soft, glowing light filtered through a nearby window. The moon, perhaps. He did not have time to look or care, as he was intent on the lock. Jamming the key in the hole, he opened the portal. He turned his head just before throwing himself in, and as he did so, he saw something that made his blood turn to ice.

The torches played tricks with light, for sure, but D_Light thought he saw something down at the end of the hall—something hideous that moved fast from one wall to the next with inhuman speed. He stifled an unmanly yelp and pulled Fael into the chamber with him.

The door slammed shut, and the two stood motionless, breathing hard. As they caught their breath, with the sturdy door between them and whatever was on the outside, the weary duo soon found themselves at ease enough to laugh. The familiars made no noise, but merely watched, taking it all in.

Fael rested her hand on her heaving chest. Her smooth forehead glistened slightly with sweat. Eyes wide, jaw dropped, she asked, "Did you see that thing?"

"What, down the hall?" D_Light inquired.

"Yeah, just as you opened the door, I saw what I…I think it was a man. Or not a man," she whispered between breaths.

D_Light nodded. "I thought I saw something, but just barely," he said with uncertainly.

Fael blinked hard, rubbed her eyes, and said, "I just saw the face, er, mask. It looked like a lion or something truly ghastly! I just got a glimpse, but it was enough."

D_Light chuckled. "If you're trying to get me in the mood by scaring me, well, you don't need to."

With that, she grabbed his stomach lightly and squeezed. "Hey, you're the ghastly beast, D_Light. I'm serious about the lion. I'm a very serious girl. You'll see." D_Light, a bit ticklish, recoiled from her menacing fingers and smiled wryly.

"Yeah, serious is the first word that comes to mind when thinking of you." D_Light took in a deep breath and let it out slowly, still recovering from the frantic race to his dwelling. "Okay, so it was a mask? How do you know it was a man?"

"'Cause it had the body of a man, kinda fat too." She poked at him again.

D_Light parried her poke and lunged at her flank with two fingers. "Okay, so there's a fat guy running around my hallway with a lion mask on?"

Fael gave a strong confirming nod and replied, "Yeah, pretty hot, huh? Maybe I should invite him in?" She made a mock motion for the door, giggling like a child.

"This sucks!" yelled someone from the congregation. "Get it on, already!" yelled another.

"Yeah, now we're having fun! I've always thought that getting hunted in my own home would be a great icebreaker with the la-dies—just never had the opportunity to test my theory until to-night!" Without thinking, D_Light put his left hand up on the door as though he meant to block her exit.

"Well, your theory *might* be correct." She squealed and slapped his hand as he managed to prod her in the ribs with a finger from his right hand.

It was about then that D_Light realized that he probably hadn't looked all that cool running around like a frightened rabbit out there while Number Seven was in effect. Worse was the absolute silliness of this poking and prodding dance between himself and Fael; obviously, his techniques of wooing the ladies had not changed since he was a young boy. *Soul, I really should take some time to come up with some new moves*, he thought while redirecting his attention back to the subject at hand.

"So, I s'pose the mask is meant to frighten the wits out of any-one he gets the jump on," mused D_Light as he made a mock lunge at his date, abandoning his earlier notion that his physical flirtations were lame.

"Sure, when you turn your back to run, it's easy to get a knife stuck in it," replied Fael, retreating from D_Light's tickling fingers. She sank down into a spongy moss chair that conformed perfectly to her body. Fael, a forty-eight-year-old woman with the body and skin of someone less than half her age, suddenly looked even younger as she slouched back and casually draped a long, lean leg over the arm of the chair. D_Light felt something stir in him, and while reveling in the feeling, he nearly failed to notice that the luscious creature was again speaking to him.

"Truly, anyone who actually participates in Seven is already a bit dodgy, but someone who uses a mask, actually employs props? Now that's downright sick!" She crinkled her face in disgust and relaxed back into the chair.

"With the psychos out there, I guess we're just stuck in my room for…a whole hour."

Wow, that wasn't very subtle, D_Light thought.

Fael laughed. "Yes, your rather…er, depressing room." Fael surveyed the chamber with her dark, sculpted eyebrows raised high. "You know, I'm not trying to be rude or anything, but your room could use a little color, don't you think? I mean, I know you want to keep that naturally drafty castle look and all, but um, I don't know, maybe a little artwork?"

D_Light forced a mock smile—lips pursed tightly—and gave Fael a look to indicate that he was indeed listening, but not particularly pleased with what he was hearing. He liked his minimalist surroundings. He had all the essentials—two chairs, a desk, a table, and a bed. As a bonus, he even had a few plants to make the room smell nice and provide nectar snacks.

"And yes," Fael continued, "I think our only option is to hide. After all, I left my sword in my chamber. I realize plebs get rowdy at comedies sometimes, but when I left my chamber this evening I didn't expect I'd have to shed any blood!"

D_Light took another decisive step toward her. Now standing between her spread legs, looking down at the woman sprawled out on his favorite chair, D_Light took the opportunity to thoroughly check her out once again. Nope, she certainly wasn't carrying a sword. *Not a lot she could be carrying at all,* he thought.

There was a moment of silence in the archive. A congregation member yelled out, "Go, Deee!" There was more whistling, but the cathedral quickly grew silent. No one wanted to miss what seemed to be imminent.

CHAPTER 3

Why are spank games, games of entertainment, required by divine law to include physical activity? Why can't we play spank games lying still in our beds as past generations?

Sloth is a sin for a reason. Inactivity has a price. Although modern medicine is capable of keeping anyone fit regardless of their activity level, it costs more to keep the slothful healthy than it does to keep the active man so. Thus, the sideliner can opt for lazy virtual reality spank games, but those of us in the Game, we have to play by the rules.

—Excerpt from "The Rules: A Life Primer"

"Rule Seven is beastly, don't you think?" asked Fael. "I mean, I have heard the reasons—that it provides an outlet for aggression, that is helps bring in new blood, provides incentive for players to be more civil to one another, but...I don't know."

"Yeah, on that last point, SirRuthless—I don't know if you knew him—got fragged about a year ago?" D_Light asked.

Fael looked at him blankly, so D_Light continued. "Anyway, he was a real bastard to everyone, and so when the opportunity came, he got fragged. You think twice before you disrespect a player in this house 'cause you could find yourself on the wrong side of a knife after the bell rings."

Fael's eyes flipped up momentarily, often a sign of communing with one's familiar. "Oh yes, I did know SirRuthless. You know, he wasn't so bad. I saw the archive of his fragging. They ganged up on him. It was terrible!"

D_Light scoffed, "Sure, I bet he was a real pussycat to *you*. No handmaiden of Mother Lyra is going to get disrespect."

Another from the congregation, possibly C, shouted, "N00b, get on with it!" The exclamation was followed by laughter throughout the congregation.

Fael's voice was sober. "Ha, you'd be surprised. Anyway, I don't buy any of those reasons for Number Seven."

"Just entertainment, eh?" D_Light smirked.

Fael nodded. "Something like that."

Her eyebrows furrowed momentarily as though she had just remembered a troubling thought. Then, without warning, she all but flung herself out of the deep-cushioned seat and turned her attention to the chamber again. Ivory flames licked out from torches in each corner. Flickering light and shadows battled for supremacy on the rough-hewn walls. There was a single window nearby, and she walked over to it. "My, you have a view—of the ocean, no less! You must be a pretty good boy around here." Her voice sounded like it was meant to be a purr, but there was stickiness beneath it.

D_Light thought about asking her to stay away from the window for her safety, having heard hunters going out on the roofs during Seven. On the other hand, the window was locked, and it was made of high-quality plexi. Even a modern weapon would be hard-pressed to penetrate it, and fortunately modern weapons were against divine law, a full-fledged sin, in fact. Even royalty could only carry "classic" weapons.

"I do okay," D_Light stated evenly.

"Indeed," replied Fael, turning away from the window to face him. With the moon shining through the window behind her, she was little more than a silhouette. Although the pigtails curved downward—not up—they reminded him of horns. The light of a nearby torch caressed her face just enough to see her glimmering eyes and moist, voluptuous lips. "I imagine you have a few spare points lying around," said the horned temptress.

D_Light knew exactly what she was suggesting, or at least he hoped he did. It was a transgression for humans to be physically intimate without first buying the proper permit, and although acquiring a permit was not a big deal—a simple electronic transfer of points to the OverSoul via one's familiar—it was expensive. In the Game, sex was not to be taken lightly.

Although Fael was legally his sister, she was not genetically related. Indeed, numerous mothers, fathers, and siblings who shared this house had chosen to be a part of the Tesla family, and most were not related by blood; rather, such familial titles merely conveyed relative status in the Game. For example, D_Light, who was an accomplished player for his age, was already the "father" of several of his biological brothers and sisters and seemed likely to soon become the legal father of his own biological father.

Indeed, genetic relation had little bearing on one's sex life anymore. After all, the taboos against incest were, from a pragmatic viewpoint, built upon the drawbacks of inbreeding. However, no female player in her right mind would *allow* herself to become pregnant. It was much more convenient and safe to have the fetus grown by professionals, a fetus whose parentage had been approved with a repro permit. In this way, sex and reproduction had long ago been separated from one another, and along with it, the messy ethical considerations.

D_Light himself had perved four of his own bio-sisters. Although he initially found these experiences to be an engaging experiment, akin to self-exploration, he now did his best to avoid such encounters. For whatever reason, it felt a bit creepy to him. Perhaps he was old-fashioned, but nowadays he only perved bio-relatives to be polite or when it was absolutely necessary to exert his familial dominance.

Fael took a few steps forward, her hand sweeping along the top of his unassuming chamber bed. She was smiling at him ever so sweetly. She stared through him, full of purpose. D_Light couldn't help but liken her to a lioness—irresistible, powerful, and perhaps even dangerous. No, not dangerous, for the girl was clearly unarmed. He set his eyes upon her. It would be rude to look away, and indeed, he didn't want to. In fact, it was all he could do to divert the slightest amount of his attention to his familiar.

Yes, master, Smorgeous echoed in his mind in response to the unspoken summons.

Still moving ever so slowly, Fael ran her tongue across her upper lip and said, "I checked up on you. You're of the Anadar line. They say your people are animals."

D_Light smiled wolfishly while issuing a mental command to his familiar. *Smorgeous, does Fael Rami own a license for poisons?*

Yes, master, the familiar replied. *It was issued 6.3 months ago.*

Sweep the air for poisons, D_Light commanded.

I do not have a license for that version of airborne chemi detection software.

Buy it, ordered D_Light.

Yes, master. That will cost—

Buy it! D_Light interrupted.

D_Light tried to hold his smile, but it was weak due to a distracting suspicion of the girl. *No need for this,* he thought. *Fael's not a killer. Her profile said zero frags.*

"Yeah, I might have a few points," D_Light said in response to Fael's intimacy permit invitation. "There are some things that are worth any cost, right? But, um, I think I'd feel more committed if you had some skin in the game, so to speak." He did his best to sound seductive as he negotiated the transaction.

"Ooooh, not very romantic," she said with mock scorn. "But I s'pose I could meet you partway—say, fifty-fifty split?" She did two little kisses in the air and waited for his reply.

"You're too good to me. And with the way you look right now, I'll go ahead and put up sixty percent—you know, to be a gentleman."

She laughed. The laugh, D_Light thought, was a bit too sharp for the girl.

Fael was now within a foot of him. She looked him up and down like a piece of meat. "I'm not going to argue with a gentleman," she replied. "You know, since we're still just getting to know each other, what do you say we start with just a twenty-four-hour permit?"

Master, I have detected traces of three different poison-classified compounds in the air, said Smorgeous.

"Bless you!" D_Light shouted aloud, waving his hands in no particular pattern. He knew he must look like a fool, but he didn't know what else to do to cover up his shock and dismay. *Poisons!*

Fael's eyes widened with surprise, and she had herself a good laugh while dancing and twirling about his room. Meanwhile, D_Light was feverishly communing with his familiar. *What kind of poisons? How are they deployed?*

Smorgeous replied, *Xanelpheno—*

No names, just what they do! Summarize fast!

Chemical #1 is injected or ingested. When active it paralyzes the muscles of the subject but is usually not fatal. Tasteless and odorless. Onset two to five minutes. Chemical #2 is normally injected. Fast acting, taking full effect in ten to twenty-eight seconds. Fatal. Chemical #3 can be injected, ingested, or absorbed into the skin. Onset forty-five seconds to one minute. Fatal.

D_Light, overwhelmed, responded, *One of them can be absorbed into the skin? Contact poison! Does she have it on her?*

Smorgeous knew what he meant. *The concentration of detected molecules is too dilute to currently be exposed to the outside air. It is likely contained in a secure vessel at this time. Using similar data, I deduce that the other poisons are likely to be contained as well.*

Closely monitor those poisons, ordered D_Light. *If the concentration goes up, I want a red alert.*

Yes, master.

Fael recovered from her laughing fit and declared, "You're hilarious!"

D_Light shrugged. "Hey, I always give thanks to those willing to sleep with me."

"I appreciate your appreciation, but don't you know that getting a girl into a dark, cozy bedchamber with faceless killers prowling just outside the door is a surefire way to get lucky?" She giggled again.

D_Light grabbed the backs of her wrists as tenderly as he could, given the adrenaline that was coursing through his system, and affectionately turned her palms upward. Her hands were soft, smooth, and empty. *Empty hands are good,* he thought. *Maybe I should just ask her about the poison. No, laying out my cards like that could be very risky. Besides, everyone has a right to be armed. The poisons are contained, and bringing it up—talk about not romantic.*

Fael gently twisted out of his grasp. "I'd kiss you right now, but rules are rules," she said. She then bounced over to the bed and sat on the corner. Sitting on its haunches a few feet away was her fox familiar, its eyes fixed upon her. She looked over to it to open a line of communication. Speaking out loud to her familiar, she commanded, "Paxos, spend forty percent on a twenty-four-hour intimacy permit with co-owner D_Light, er, what's your full name again?"

"Smorgeous, send Paxos my full identification," said D_Light, also speaking to his familiar aloud. A ping signaled in D_Light's mind to confirm that his ID had been sent.

"Smorgeous, complete the purchase of the permit." D_Light, not accustomed to speaking out loud to his familiar, stammered over the words.

Master, the permit is authenticated. Your permit partner has no known pathogens communicable by use of this permit under terms of use. Would you like to learn more about your partner's intimacy permit history before finalizing this purchase?

No, D_Light answered in his mind. Learning the *who* and *when* of Fael's personal life was far from a turn-on to him.

His familiar pinged confirmation and replied telepathically. *You have purchased sixty percent of intimacy permit #29483723201DC for a cost of 1,342 points. This permit will expire at 20:23 tomorrow.*

Transaction complete, D_Light planned to meet the girl at the bed, but she was too fast. With her seemingly boundless energy, Fael sprang up, crossed the room with one long leap, flung her arms around his neck, and kissed him passionately.

Beyond the archive feed, D_Light could hear a general clamor of approval. Apparently, the congregation really liked where this was going.

"Forget the lion outside," Fael whispered. "I've found myself a lion in here." She purred in his ear. D_Light thought the line sounded rather cheesy, but he liked it just the same.

Fael led D_Light to the foot of the bed and knelt down on it. She then began fumbling with the back of her suit. "Let me help," offered D_Light, a bit too urgently. He had no idea how to take off a living garment, but he thought it only polite to try.

"Yeah, please." Her voice quavered. Her breath quickened.

D_Light ran his sturdy hands along the sides of her heaving torso and gently stroked the silken fabric while making his way to the back of the suit. He pulled her closer. Starting just behind her ear, he allowed his lips to travel down her long, supple neck, and she trembled with excitement. The girl smelled sweet, delicious. She was a present for his unwrapping. Nearly forgetting his offer to assist with the removal of her clothing, D_Light looked over Fael's shoulder to see what he was working with. It was just then that his senses were flooded with Smorgeous's presence. *Master, red alert! Poison concentration has jumped 31,245%.*

D_Light twisted his head toward Fael. Only a few inches from his face, her smile was gone. Her breath was warm. *My Soul, she's going to cash me in!* D_Light realized with a shock.

Adrenaline dumped into his bloodstream, enabling D_Light to twist out of the girl's grasp with lightning speed. She took a swipe at his face, a dark patch of glistening liquid barely visible on her sleeve. The sleeve narrowly missed his face, and only the girl's nails nicked him. In one fluid motion, D_Light spiraled away from the bed, pulled a throwing disc from a fold in his suit, and threw it at Fael with a great arching of his arm. Once released into the air, the disc's six spring-loaded blades popped out from the outer edge and sent the weapon rotating.

D_Light had aimed low, having anticipated her to be on the bed, but she had already jumped up; the disc struck her in the thigh with a muffled thump. She did not make a sound. D_Light could see that she had something in both hands, something that looked like long needles—spring-loaded syringes. Like most people, Fael was ambidextrous. If she got close enough, there would be no way he could prevent one of those needles from sticking him once. Just once would be all she needed.

Fael leaped from the bed at him. Wounded, the move was slightly awkward, allowing D_Light to sidestep out of reach. The blades of D_Light's disc were long and should have sunk deep into her flesh, but they had barely penetrated her muscular quadriceps. The living fiber of her suit must be tough indeed, for his throwing discs were very expensive, designed to penetrate even armor.

Smorgeous, attack! D_Light ordered telepathically.

As a rule, familiars were not designed for combat, but they certainly could distract or slow down an opponent. However, Smorgeous was already latched onto Paxos's neck, trying to trip and pin the other familiar. Apparently, Fael had already ordered Paxos to intercede on her behalf. To D_Light's benefit, Smorgeous's AI was advanced enough to take the initiative to counter Paxos. The two familiars spun and flipped in a frenzy, each trying to gain the upper hand.

It was clear to D_Light that his first objective was to stay out of range of those needles, so he immediately maneuvered to get the table between himself and his attacker. He then proceeded to throw at her everything at hand—decorative books, glassware, a potted plant, and even precious trophies of which he was quite fond. Between throws and desperate grunts, he maneuvered as fast as he could to keep the table between himself and the onrushing woman. She was definitely taking a beating, but she was also resilient and, despite her wounded leg, quite fast.

Deciding that he needed to up the ante, he forcefully threw his plexi desk chair at her. Although she was struck solidly, throwing the bulky object slowed D_Light down, allowing her the opportunity to close most of the distance between them. With no time to withdraw, D_Light flung himself under the table and rolled, coming up on the other side. She was rushing him again, but he had just enough time to retrieve another disc and throw it. The disc struck her in the face, and because she was unprotected there, the weapon reached its terrible potential. A gurgling scream came from her as she dropped the syringes and grasped at her mangled cheek. A torrent of blood was spilling out, streaming between her fingers as she tried in vain to contain it. She had been sliced from the back of the jaw to the lip, and through the gushes of blood he caught a glimpse of gums and teeth.

Assuming nothing, D_Light ran backward a few steps and readied his next disc. Fael scrambled for the door, a deep spatter of blood marking her passage. He threw his last disc, this time putting all of his weight into the throw. It gouged into her back, pierced the tough suit, and stuck into her firmly. She arched her back and let out a short, garbled scream.

Still, his date kept on her feet and continued on. D_Light was breathing shallow and fast, and his heart was beating so hard that it felt like it would split open his chest. Feeling dizzy, nauseated, and somewhat disconnected from reality, he hurried to his closet and pulled out a crossbow. It was always loaded.

Fael stood at the door, crazily fumbling at the lock while making a terribly disturbing noise that was difficult to classify—crying, perhaps, or the sound of a badly damaged windpipe. Her one hand fumbled uselessly at the lock while the other, slick with blood, slipped on the door handle. D_Light rushed up to only a few paces behind her. He was a pretty good shot, but he wanted to get close, not trusting his trembling limbs. He could not risk a miss. She did not turn to face him when he finally pulled the trigger.

CHAPTER 4

When the time came that you could buy a genetic engineering kit as easily as past generations could buy an erector set for their children, you knew a pandemic of monumental proportions was just a matter of time. In fact, the genesis of the TerriLove virus was traced back to a disgruntled seventeen-year-old suburban boy. Unlike other angry youth of history who went on killing sprees of varying magnitude, Justin Flairon ended up killing four out of every ten human beings on earth. He himself was the first victim of his monster.

The social aftershocks from this culling were nearly as bad as the virus itself. Death begot sorrow, desperation, and anger, which in turn begot war and anarchy. And so when the OverSoul came to humankind and offered her guidance, it was the answer to countless prayers. The Authority promised shelter—shelter to a people who had gone from a post-scarcity economy where famine and poverty were history, to a raging nightmare. The OverSoul, in her divine wisdom, fulfilled her promise with the Game—a system of rules and an economic framework wherein everyone, nearly regardless of their talents, could find security, prosperity, and above all, a purpose. Indeed, through the Game, one could conquer death itself.

—Excerpt from "Musings of an Immortal," by Dr. Stoleff Monsa

D_Light turned off the feed, as the congregation would be bored with additional footage anyway. His obligation to them was met, and the rest was no one's business. No one needed to see how, after leaving her body there, unable to look at it, he had leaned into his window and stared into the darkness for what seemed like an eternity. No one needed to see the cleaning bots dispose of Fael's body and the fluids that had spilled from it. And most importantly, no one needed to see how D_Light took a mega dose of tranquilizers and went to sleep.

The congregation's curiosity was satisfied, and the mood became more tempered. There was no music. Despite the cathedral holding over three hundred people, it was almost quiet. Almost. There were always a few who couldn't abide silence—D_Light's friend, C, being one of them. C did a low hum and murmured, mostly to himself, "That was clean, eh. Sure, that was a clean frag."

With the testimony over, the rest of the service was a mere formality. The congregation confirmed unanimously that the frag was clean, at which point 825,445 points—one-fifth of Fael Rami's net worth—was deposited into D_Light's profile. It would have taken him several months of nonstop grinding to accumulate that many points, so by any measure of a mortal player, last night turned out to be very profitable indeed.

He went through the motions of giving a speech, but no one really cared, and so, interspersed between cliché inspirational statements, he name-dropped. "Fael would've topped me had it not been for Supa_Sniff™ chemi-detection software. Sure, it costs a few points, but what's your life worth?"

Although it felt cheesy to do so, he continued. "By the way, that PrimeFlavor™ organic suit of Fael's was perfect. I'm sorry it all went down like it did 'cause she had great style. Comfort, protection, and chic? I'm ordering one today. I'm getting one in honor of Fael."

D_Light considered ending the pain there, but he couldn't pass up the opportunity for one last drop. "All right, enough of my prattling. I'm gonna go kick back with a Gd_Lookin™ hyperbeverage and relax."

The last statement was a little off topic, but surely no one in the congregation was going to blame him for milking it a bit. It was not every day a player had such a large audience. Besides those in the cathedral, his testimony was streaming live up onto the Cloud. Presently, a green flash in a corner of his consciousness relayed the bounty points streaming in. Just the brand name exposure from the dropping was worth a good fee, but his referrals had already resulted in three orders for the detection software and five for the organic suit. Excellent.

After a good score, D_Light liked to celebrate in his own quiet way, which was more of a reflection and introspection. And so, without his usual after-service chatter and gossip, he bolted straight to the exit. It was midsummer and the sun beat down mercilessly, but the castle was on the sea where there was always a breeze. Good, salty wind that always gave him a twinge of childhood memory the way that only smells can. He strolled down to the boathouse where he kept his sailboat. The craft was ultralight for her size, so with a little sweat, he was able to slide her out of her cylindrical storage capsule and carry the still folded vessel down to the water's edge unassisted. Kneeling down, he quickly unfolded the hull, mast, and stabilizers. The components of the vessel snapped into place with a series of unambiguous and satisfying clicks. It was similar to assembling a well-designed kite—a huge, waterborne kite.

Terralova, as the vessel was called, cut through the waves cleanly. Her hull was bulletproof strong, but ultralight with just the right amount of flexibility to make the best of the liquid terrain. D_Light sat comfortably in his harness, Smorgeous lying on his chest. D_Light did not bother with a harness for the familiar, as he had infallible balance. He looked down at the catlike creature. The outer surface of his body was soft, and his synthetic fur was convincing. His organic computer chips gave off heat, furthering the guise of a mammalian creature. All Smorgeous needed to do to be a perfect cat-machine was to purr, but D_Light prided himself on being too utilitarian to download worthless kitschy software that enabled familiars to do things like purr, meow, or nuzzle.

D_Light pointed *Terralova* straight out into the infinite blue. The vessel surged forward as her living filament sails made the most of the wind. It felt like she wanted to get out of there as much as he did. There was the familiar slosh and hiss of the water just beneath coupled with the slight chill as the occasional wave managed to break above his harness and soak his protection suit. No games. He had pulled in enough points today. Just water and sun.

D_Light did as much of his grinder gaming out on the water as he could. Because of this, he tended to ante into games that did not require his physical presence somewhere, unless that "somewhere" happened to be nearby and accessible by sea. Luckily, most of the grinder games he played involved creating or debugging software, so it could usually be played virtually. Grinder games allowed you to interact with the Game virtually, without having to be there physically. On the other hand, spank games—games designed primarily for entertainment—did not allow this. From the perspective of the Game, sloth was a sin, so if you were going to play a game with no productive value, then the least you could do was work out your body.

The wind gusted and the roar of the air rushing past his ears drowned out the sound of his breath as he let out a deep, contented sigh. *I'm alive and I'm free!* The thought was as forced as the smile he coerced onto his face. Real or not, a smile always made him feel a little better. And why shouldn't he be happy? With his recent score, he could afford to take a few days off—enough time to do some island hopping. There were sideliners on some of the more remote islands. *That could be a real vacation*, he thought. *Log out of the Game and live old-school for a day or two. The sideliners could show me how they do it.*

Master, there is a summons from Mother Lyra Ramanavi.

D_Light had ordered Smorgeous to hold his calls, but the familiar knew his master would want to take this one. Smorgeous did not fully understand human social hierarchy, but his pattern recognition software was adept at making connections like this. House nobility was a high-priority contact.

There was no call, just a message. A summoning. *Damn!* he thought. Anyone else he could blow off, but Mother Lyra was nobility and, as such, was not to be kept waiting. Nor were nobility to be called back. If she had wanted to speak to him remotely, she would have done so.

Mechanically, D_Light pushed the tiller and, with some readjusting of sails, spun *Terralova* around and pointed her bow back to the castle.

D_Light had mixed feelings about meeting with Mother Lyra. On one hand, of all of his mothers, D_Light was most fond of Lyra. First, she liked his work, especially his avatars, so she actually knew who he was. Secondly, on the one occasion they had met, she was kind to him. But what D_Light liked most about Lyra was the sheer magnificence of the woman herself. To say that Lyra was beautiful was a gross understatement. Almost everyone had enough engineering in their line to be easy on the eyes, but Lyra was a step above. Her ancestors were among the last to be engineered before direct modifications to the germ line were banned, post–Bottle Neck. By then, doctors were doing their best work, particularly in the area of physical attractiveness since those attributes were easy to measure and improve. Mother Lyra had inherited the legacy of that final push for perfection, and it showed.

D_Light had heard Mother Lyra speak several times at annual services, and she had always done so with easy confidence and abundant wit. As a rule, D_Light doubted the merit of nobles, who inherited their titles from birth rather than through the Game. However, Lyra, as soon as she spoke, brushed such prejudices aside as though to say, "You love me because it is right for you to love me."

This being the case, D_Light could not help but feel some thrill at being personally summoned by this magnificent woman. Of course, there was the messy business about D_Light having fragged—less than twenty-four hours ago—one of Lyra's handmaidens. Obviously, the summoning was related to this incident. Although the frag was perfectly legal and done in self-defense, he did not imagine that praise was on this meeting's agenda.

CHAPTER 5

For years video game developers have had psycholo-gists on staff whose sole purpose is to help make their games addictive. And the results are in. Just last week the president of the United States called for a "war on idle distraction." Indeed, by some estimates, over 16% of our gross domestic product is piddled away playing games of no economic or social benefit.

But games needn't be idle or unproductive. I propose we harness the addictive aspects of entertainment games and apply them in the workplace. Aspects like clear, measurable goals with frequent and tangible rewards, transparent scoring and competition, gradual increase in difficulty of tasks as the player progresses in skill, and so forth. We can build this abstraction over mundane employment using software.

Until we take the "work" out of work, world labor will not meet its full potential. Making the tools to do this will be a lot of fun...and make us a few bucks!

—Excerpt from "Introducing the Grinder Game," as pre-sented by Tyler Alison, Software Developer Conference, 2016

———————

D_Light scratched the scalp under his thick, dark hair and inquired, "I don't suppose you saw the archive? You know that she tried to frag me first, right?"

The guard, who Smorgeous said was named Brian, glared back at D_Light and said nothing. Instead, he tensed his biceps and rolled his shoulders forward, like an animal presenting a threat display.

D_Light returned a smirk. *I can't let some palace guard intimidate me,* he thought.

Finally, as though he could no longer control himself, Brian hissed back, "I'm sure you deserved getting fragged." His greenish eyes then twinkled a bit, and a subtle grin spread across his face. "I wish I had been there. Oh yeah," he exclaimed. He breathed in deeply through his flaring nostrils. "Had I been there, you'd have had to answer to little Tiffany here." He caressed the hilt of his mace.

"Seriously? You named your club?" D_Light asked incredulously. And then he laughed. "My Soul, you've got to be a human! Only a human would name their weapon. A security product would shut up and do their job."

"Mmmm." Brian smiled. "One tiny tap on the skull with *Tiffany* here and you'd be meowin' like your little kitty there." The guard looked down at Smorgeous with disgust. Smorgeous stared back indifferently.

"Meowing, huh?" D_Light asked as he raised his eyebrows. In response the large guard grabbed the hilt of Tiffany hanging from his belt.

Why am I provoking this guy? I'm gaining no advantage from this, D_Light thought.

D_Light took a step back and put up his hands in what he hoped was a diplomatic gesture. "Look, I know I'm enjoying this as

much as you are, but I was summoned here by your mistress, so..."
He cocked his head, giving the guard an expectant look.

Brian gave no reaction. He just stared at D_Light as though
daring him to take an unauthorized step. The guard was muscular,
even for the modern day, and he was wearing a full suit of armor,
which for House Tesla guards was a yellow and black skinsuit. The
nano-enforced fabric was not much thicker than a normal skinsuit.
However, when forcefully struck—say by a weapon—the fabric instantly hardened and then pushed back in the region of impact,
counteracting the blow. This guard didn't adorn his armor with
anything. Some guards projected medieval armor or even normal
clothes.

After a few seconds D_Light continued. "Look, brother, you
liked Fael? Well, I actually liked her too. A good, sweet, and smart
woman. It's just, you know, during Rule Seven, ShipIt™ happens."

"Yeah, maybe I should go flake. Then I could bring the ShipIt™
to you!"

D_Light knew House Tesla guards were not allowed to participate in Rule Seven. In fact, they could not even be ordered to
frag another during Rule Seven unless it was in defense of a client.
Due to this restriction, it was common for guards to quit that game
and become a flake. A flake was a member of the Tesla family who
specialized in Rule Seven. Since a person always took a fifth of the
points of anyone he or she fragged, it was just about the fastest way
to get points in the Game. Indeed, most flakes didn't even play
other games. They simply trained with their weapons, memorized
the labyrinth hallways of the castle, sized up their rivals, and then
waited for the siren to sound them into action once again. Appropriately named, flakes were called such because it usually wasn't long
before they were fragged by another flake and ground up into fish
food. Since anyone who wasn't a flake took cover when Rule Seven

was in effect, flakes were typically left to hunt down each other. Needless to say, it was a dangerous undertaking.

Perfect. Now I have this psycho fantasizing about fragging me. Smorgeous, alert me if Brian Roffenbach ever revokes his guard status. His thought was followed by a ping from his familiar.

Several more minutes passed in silence as D_Light shifted his weight between one leg and the other. Although D_Light was prepared for the worst from this meeting, he decided it was particularly ominous that he was getting flack from the sentries outside the waiting room doors. *It's like I'm wearing a ring of toddler heads tied to my belt,* he thought. *I mean, who is this guy? I'm not a flake. It's not like I enjoyed fragging her. Ignorant plebs like that don't even try to relate to anyone else's situation.*

D_Light reminded himself that he should not let people get the better of him. Nor should he dwell on the past. He was being soft. *Nothing matters but the present.* He had Smorgeous repeat this mantra in an infinite loop over the top of one of his favorite songs for such occasions, a peppy little track called "What's Done Is Gone," by Real_Deal. He let the custom music wash over him as he let the minutes slip by.

Finally, without a word, Brian nodded his head toward the doors to indicate that the visitor could enter. Typically, guards opened the doors for visitors, but it didn't take a genius to realize that Brian would skip this courtesy. D_Light pushed his way through the heavy doors as quickly as possible, brushing against Brian's shoulder as he passed.

The doors led to the actual waiting room. It contained no chairs, simply beds canopied with semitransparent curtains of purple and gold. Only one of the dozen beds seemed to harbor a resident, a lump of a man who appeared to be sleeping. Prismatic colors from an unseen source oozed and undulated over the walls, ceiling, and floor. The rays of light also filtered through the gossamer bed curtains, creating a hauntingly beautiful 3-D effect. There was no receptionist here, only a pair of tall and ornate double doors that commanded the wall in front of him. A low, rhythmic hum pulsed all around him. D_Light's skinning software was not rendering anything, as the room was a designated dark zone—an area where no SkinWare-facilitating nanosites covered the surfaces of anything. D_Light chose a waiting bed and sat on the edge, legs dangling. The softly shifting light patterns, more entrancing than an ancient lava lamp, were as real as the low, rhythmic, pulsating sound that filled the air. Despite his best efforts, D_Light fell fast asleep.

D_Light woke with a start. "*Haw, haw, haw,*" the SeaGuy™ called out. The seagull-like head was cocked sideways, regarding D_Light with one bulging, pink eye. The torso, pelvis, and legs were those of a nude and impossibly muscular man. Tufts of white feathers interspersed with patches of curly black human hair shot out haphazardly. The ankles of the monster faded into the webbed feet of a seagull. It had great seagull wings in place of arms, which it now splayed out wide. The creature quickly waved its gigantic feathered rear end back and forth a few times, at which point it tipped up its beak and yammered out another call. "*Haw, haw, haw!*"

D_Light couldn't help but chuckle a bit at the avatar he had designed for Mother Lyra. *Man, I really nailed it with this one*, he thought.

"Oh, D_Light, have you any fishies for me?" Blood and orange-colored ooze streamed out of its beak, running down its mottled chest as it spoke. The voice was guttural with raspy undertones.

D_Light supposed that this bizarre reception was par for the course. Mother Lyra seemed to be one of the few nobles with enough confidence in her position and enough of a sense of humor to not take herself too seriously—or anyone else for that matter. He decided to respond in kind.

"Um, no fish, but there's a guard out in the hall you can have." D_Light jumped out of the waiting room bed and bowed formally to the gigantic holographic birdman. A lynx, which D_Light assumed was Mother Lyra's familiar, stood only a few paces behind. Certainly, the familiar was projecting the holographic avatar at Lyra's command.

With a sweeping motion of one of its wings, the seabird motioned for D_Light to proceed through the double doors ahead, doors that had apparently opened as D_Light slept. He bowed to the beast and passed through the opening into the formal entertaining room.

The entertaining room was colossal, leading D_Light to the safe conclusion that Mother Lyra must truly be a favorite of House Tesla. A nondescript man was sitting in a chair to D_Light's left. D_Light did not recognize him, but the man's crest indicated he was a noble. He stared at D_Light as though he had nothing more interesting to do. D_Light knew better than to stare back at his father. Lyra, pacing back and forth like a caged jaguar, was clearly multitasking, distant and preoccupied, evidenced by her fixed, vacant stare. While D_Light knew that part of her brain was being used to control the birdman avatar, he could only imagine what she was doing with the other part. Whatever it was, however, must have something to do with why he had been summoned here, and that was unsettling to the slightly anxious D_Light.

The birdman pointed a wing toward some high-backed chairs and ordered D_Light to take a seat in the corner. It then proceeded to hop over to the mute nobleman who still stared meditatively at D_Light, protracted its beak out towards his ear, and did a low *haw, haw, haw,* each *haw* repeating in rapid succession like a machine gun. D_Light suppressed a chuckle, intrigued by Lyra's use of SeaGuy™ for the purpose of taunting. He was also impressed with Lyra's lynx familiar, how it was capable of projecting its auditory output to seem as though the sound was coming from the bird beak. Very polished.

Clearly, the nobleman was doing his best to ignore the persistently irritating avatar, but D_Light imagined the man would grab the birdman by the throat and throttle the life out of its deranged body had the creature been anything more than a projection of light. Of course, if he did lose control and go ballistic on the monster, he wouldn't be the first human alive to thoughtlessly attack an avatar. D_Light almost wished he would, as it would provide him some much-needed comic relief.

The birdman, appearing to be bored with tormenting the nobleman, parted with one last goading *haw, haw, haw, haw.* It then ambled—a combination of hops interlaced with waddling—over to D_Light, its absurdly long penis swaying back and forth as it approached. Upon reaching D_Light, it turned its head so that one devilish eye was facing him, inspecting him with intent. It stood there momentarily and then said, "I'm so rude! I forgot to ask if you wanted a little something to eat. I have these chocolate truffles that are to *die* for!" It spoke the word "die" with an extra raspy flair. "You must be famished after a long night of snuffing out my handmaidens!"

Oh, here we go, D_Light thought. *I was wondering when she'd cut to the chase.* D_Light was not entirely sure how to react to the comment, but he did like chocolate and wasn't about to screw up that offer. "Yes, please," he replied with a nod.

The birdman then took a hop closer, twisting its head and beak around to regard D_Light with its other eye. The creature just stood there, staring at him with an unnerving and unnatural rigidity that D_Light first found discomforting and then amusing. Remembering that he was actually interacting with Mother Lyra via this creature, D_Light decided to return the gaze for a while and then eventually mustered the courage to wink at it playfully.

D_Light was now feeling downright cocky and was getting ready to compliment the bird on its fine plumage—especially on its backside—and its lack of fishy breath. Fortunately, he was interrupted before he said something he'd later regret. In walked a tall, well-built man carrying a round stone tray. The man, dressed in a long, dark, flowing robe that dragged behind him with a faint brushing sound, bore a dark circle tattoo in the middle of each cheek like a classic clown who had gone gothic. These tattoos indicated that the servant was a product, a living organism based on a human template that was engineered to serve a human master. The servant smiled politely and bent down to present D_Light with a truffle. He selected one that was dusted with a shimmering golden powder.

"Ah, curry coconut," squawked the bird, "my favorite! Take another, we can always make more."

D_Light, having confirmed with Smorgeous that no poison was detected, decided to take two. They *were* to die for, at least metaphorically. Not that D_Light was truly afraid of being poisoned, for outside of Rule Seven it was a sin for anyone—noble or otherwise—to murder another human, even a common player like D_Light. Still, the truffles could be drugged. The recent sniffing software Smorgeous had downloaded could detect many drugs, but not all of them, especially since new drugs were being invented every day. Calculating the risk and deciding that the benefits outweighed them, D_Light reached for yet another. After all, this was top-notch gourmet chocolate that was prohibitively expensive for anyone but nobility. It also seemed to contain a chili powder or some such substance that inflicted an addictive and satisfying burn.

D_Light was about to remark that these chocolates were even better than Cweet™ gourmet chocolates when he caught himself. Nobles themselves never dropped brand names, and it was rude for others to drop on them. Unlike nobility of past eras, the powerful of today were distinguished largely by what they *did not* say. By refraining from name-dropping, a well-to-do player was telling the world, "I needn't the trivial point scraps for which lesser players prostitute themselves."

Until now, Lyra had been completely committed to pacing between the fireplace on the west wall and the fireplace on the east. Presently, she began advancing toward D_Light, her eyes bearing down on him. D_Light, halfway into a truffle, swallowed the contents of his mouth and silently debated whether or not it would be rude to pop in the other half while she approached. In his indecision, the delicate chocolate melted between his fingers. He ended up not only popping in the other half, but licking off his fingers as well. *Good one, D_Light*, he thought. *Why not just blow your nose on your sleeve while you're at it!* He glanced up at Lyra and gave her a quick and innocent, "Oops!"

Mother Lyra was unusually tall for a human female. Like most humans, she was pandectic, a descendant of a rich mixture of many different races, making her skin a deep tan color. Her heart-shaped face was softly sculpted, the skin smooth and flawless, like polished stone. Long, jet-black locks of loosely curled hair were amassed on the top of her head and hung haphazardly about her face, encircling her cheeks and eyes. She wore an organic bodysuit, similar to the one Fael had worn last night, but Lyra's suit was blood red. Power red. Although Lyra was not very muscular, the formfitting bodysuit revealed a lean, fit figure. Over her bodysuit a semitransparent cloak of sea blue hung on her like a whisper. She was the godmother of many, and she definitely looked the part.

D_Light had been in Lyra's presence before, and aside from the noblewoman's carefree manner, there was one thing about her that fascinated him more than all else. It was her eyes. Striking green emeralds that nearly glowed against the otherwise dark shadows of her countenance, a trait engineered by her ancestors. As would be expected from someone of her station, her eyes were fearless and determined, but there was also some wilderness that hid behind them, a feral quality that somewhat belied her elegant composure. It was a contradiction that D_Light found most intriguing.

I want you to know that I harbor no ill feelings toward you with regard to the matter between you and Fael. Lyra's voice was transmitted telepathically, using Smorgeous as a security intermediary.

This was completely unexpected, both the message and the method of delivery. It was highly irregular for members of unequal social classes to blink one another. Lyra's lynx familiar had locked eyes with Smorgeous for optimal communion. D_Light was caught off guard by the blink, but he promptly gave a telepathic reply. *Thank you, Mother. I never intended—*

I do not want an apology, Lyra interrupted. *I watched the archive. You did what you thought sensible, and it appears to have paid off well. Clearly, Fael underestimated you. It was her own ambition that was her undoing.*

D_Light sent the next thought that came to him. *Mother, if you saw the archive, then you know I did not have to frag her. I could have let her go.*

D_Light immediately regretted the response, wondering why he was insisting on apologizing when she had expressly stated that she did not want one. He silently chastised himself for his pathetic behavior.

Lyra smiled at him shrewdly. *Well, I'm sure you know that if you had let sweet Fael live, every girl with a pretty smile would think she could get a free pass. And then what kind of player would you be?*

A dead one, D_Light thought, although he kept this superfluous thought to himself.

Lyra's eyes softened and the taut skin of her face relaxed as she turned away from D_Light. *I like that you felt something for her, D_Light. Watching the two of you together...* Lyra hesitated for a moment. *Well, I would say she was fond of you as well. Sure, she was willing to cash you in, but that does not mean that under other circumstances you two could not have been friends. Or more.*

As she sent that thought, she turned and looked directly into D_Light. His heart seemed to stop for a moment as he became simultaneously afraid and thrilled by her intense green eyes.

"Lyra, what are you doing?" The nobleman in the chair looked back and forth between Lyra and D_Light. His tone was not one of urgency, but of mild curiosity and possible irritation.

"Just making our new friend feel at ease," Lyra said aloud. As the blink terminated, D_Light felt as though something warm had just fled his mind. He lamented the loss of their private telepathic communication.

As though taking a cue, the monstrous birdman flew up onto one of the arches high overhead. It then perched itself, swinging its giant webbed feet under the rafter while contently watching over the room.

"Djoser, this is D_Light, level eighty-three player and resident of the upper east wing of this little pile of stones," Lyra declared.

Then, gesturing toward the nobleman, she said, "D_Light, this is Father Djoser Townsend, third son of the First Grandfather of Townsend." D_Light stood and bowed low to the confirmed noble.

Mother Lyra brought her hands together and interlaced her fingers. "So now that you are comfortable, properly introduced, and stuffed with fine chocolate, let me tell you why you were summoned here."

D_Light felt a slight knot in his stomach. He bowed to his mother and then stood alert.

"Our house has been selected for this month's MetaGame," Lyra said. "Father Townsend and I have been invited to be the players. According to the rules, participants in the game are allowed to bring along an advisor. I was planning on taking Fael, as I always do, but due to recent events, I thought it appropriate for you to take her place."

D_Light stood dumbfounded, half wondering if he had heard correctly. MetaGames were reserved for nobility and their closest entourage, and he certainly did not qualify as either. He hesitated before responding to make sure that he did not speak over Lyra. "Mother, I am at your service," he declared. Another bow.

"Have you ever played a MetaGame before?" inquired Djoser, making no attempt to mask his skepticism.

D_Light assumed it was he who was being addressed. "No, Father," he replied.

"What makes you qualified to advise anyone playing a MetaGame?" Djoser barked at him.

"I, um...I do not know for sure, Father. From what I understand, every game is unique." D_Light had no idea what to tell the man, for he was just as surprised as Djoser.

"Lyra, is this a joke?" asked Djoser while looking at her severely. "This is a high-stakes game. If you are going to invite a pleb, at least choose someone useful!"

"He will be," Lyra answered, her voice cool and unaffected.

"Really? What did you say he does? Makes avatars like...like that thing?" Djoser pointed up at the birdman in the rafters.

D_Light felt his gut wrench, for in actuality he designed and built all sorts of software, not just avatars. He hated it when people wrote him off as a designer of useless toys and tricks. However, D_Light knew it imprudent to correct his father. Besides, the man was probably right that his day-to-day skill set might not be all that useful in a real-life game.

A brown hawk with gray flecks swooped down from a high, dark marble fireplace mantle and landed directly across from Lyra's lynx; it was the nobleman's familiar. The two creatures locked eyes, and for several minutes the nobles discoursed silently, punctuated only with a variety of eye maneuvers (rolling eyes being the most common), hand gestures, sighs, and occasional laughs of contempt.

Finally, Lyra turned to D_Light and said, "We shall see you at sixteen hundred tomorrow. The game starts at sixteen thirty. I trust you will be prepared."

"Yes, my lady," D_Light confirmed. He bowed once to each of the nobles and did his best to back out of the room gracefully. He nearly tripped.

CHAPTER 6

Grinder games, which underlie the major economic activity of the Game, are firmly grounded in twentieth-century psychology. Rather than simply furnishing a framework for "productive work," grinder games are designed to facilitate a state of "flow" in the player. Flow, first proposed by positive psychologist Mihály Csíkszentmihályi, is a state of consciousness where you are so immersed in your activity that you lose yourself in the "doing." You lose your sense of time, replacing it with a state of energized focus. People who experience flow later report a sense of well-being and accomplishment.

Spanker games, by their very nature, send players effortlessly into flow, while it takes everything from sound psychology, engineering, and perhaps even a touch of inspiration to design a grinder game that facilitates flow. But I assure you it is worth it. Game software has not only the potential to maximize the productivity of countless "workers," but can instill the greatest gift of all—happiness.

—Excerpt from "Introductory Instructive Archive for Grinder Developers of House Tesla," by Darwin Scazaan

---

Todget grudgingly awakened. How could he sleep with that female thrashing and moaning next to him? He asked himself again why he slept in the same bed with that creature. Their humble apartment consisted of only a single room with an attached bathroom, but he could always sleep on the floor. That would be easy for him. Years ago when he was playing the running game in the Land of the Stag, Todget slept wherever he needed to. Crushed ferns placed beneath him provided more than adequate comfort, and with a blanket of heavy evergreen branches and some debris from a rotten log to provide camouflage and to mask his scent, he had himself an honest night's sleep.

Sleeping in a bed for the last two years had made him soft, but Todget felt compelled to keep Lily as close as possible. Todget, like all of his tribe, was strong, fast, and cunning. He would protect her. *We only have each other*, he often reminded himself. As fugitives, they were pitted against the entire world. Perhaps it was only a matter of time before they were caught and killed—or worse yet, taken back. Nevertheless, he would keep her close and safe until his last breath.

Todget lay quietly, scanning the numbingly familiar room. The living fiber that enclosed his chamber changed color depending on the season, and the walls even allowed some sunlight to filter in through its strange, waxy membrane. This was helpful because their dwelling was not furnished with any artificial lights. Lily had told him that humans did not need lights in their lairs because they could see in the dark. Todget, however, had no such skill, so he had purchased a small, inexpensive hand lamp. Lily insisted that he only use the lamp on its lowest power since bright lights could attract attention.

Generally speaking, Todget did not mind bare walls. Since he knew they might have to flee at any moment, decorating seemed pointless. Lily, however, had been adamant on making changes. One day she brought back some slimy seeds and smeared them in dark patches on the walls. Within a day or two, flowers began sprouting from the patches. At first Todget had been very annoyed at this, having to duck his tall, muscular body underneath the flower stalks lest he be chided for his oafishness, but he soon grew fond of the red and gold spotted flowers. Sweet honey juice (Lily said the humans called it nectar) collected in the bulbs, and every morning Todget would drink from these bulbs like a newborn fawn suckling its mother.

Todget's eyes wandered to the luminescent ceiling. Today the color of their dwelling was red with subtle bluish swirls. He hoped that he would live to see them turn bright green again when the air was at its warmest.

Todget and Lily always slept during the day, while the shiny-eyed humans played their pretend games outside. The frazzled players would storm up and down the steps, shouting childishly. Once the moon rose and the night was at its blackest, all but a few would retire indoors. That is when Todget and Lily would awaken. Although not completely dark yet, Lily seemed to be suffering during this day's sleep, whimpering and gently flailing as though drowning in slow motion, so Todget decided to wake her early.

"Lily, wake. It is only a dark vision." Todget shook her as softly as he knew how.

Lily's blond hair was splashed about her pillow and partially covered the soft curves of her face. Her lips, thick and pink, were slightly parted as she gasped, and her forehead, normally smooth and without blemish, was furrowed. He shook her again, this time with more force. Her blue eyes suddenly shot open, and her breath stopped. A moment later a slight smile came over her, but then it disappeared as her eyes closed again. She then whispered in halting breaths, "I saw a man. He was tall and cruel. He had no eyes, no mouth, and no nose, just skin stretched tightly over where his face should have been. He wanted us."

Todget did not understand dark visions. He never had such visions when he went into dark time. Lily did not used to have them either. It was only after she started working for that human—that professor, the one who implanted the machine in her head—that she had begun to experience these visions. At first the visions had been pleasant, but not recently. Todget had warned her to not work for the human, but she was stubborn.

"Was it like the one...the one before?"

Lily's eyes opened up again as though fully recovered from her recent terror, and she said, "Todget, do not worry yourself. It is *not* a bad omen." She smiled sweetly and mussed his hair.

The young female swung out of bed and stood up quickly to reach for her gown. Lily slept in light undergarments but kept her robe nearby. Todget watched her carefully. As a Star Sister, Lily was supremely toned and shapely, although her muscles were smaller than Todget's mate back home. Since the Sisters were, athletically, a near match to the females of Todget's race, by appearance alone Lily should be a suitable breeding partner—suitable enough, at least, since Todget had been having intense breeding urges lately—but Lily's scent reminded him that she was not of his species, at which point he always felt ashamed and told himself to not think about her that way. But he still noticed how the human males watched her. Everywhere they went, men—and many women—followed Lily with their eyes.

"Humans have dark visions all the time and they mean nothing," Lily commented while donning her robe. She turned to face him. Her face glowed with health, tan but not weathered.

"How do you know that?" Todget asked.

"I asked one," Lily returned to bait him.

Todget felt his heart speeding up. "What? Who?"

Todget didn't understand Lily's social interest it humans. It was bad enough that she chose to work with them. Granted, they could use the money, despite the handsome sums Todget himself brought in from the tournaments. Still, living discreetly in this human land, even modestly, was very expensive. Privacy and protection had their costs.

Lily put up her hand reassuringly. "Don't worry, I'm not out talking to random humans. It was just Professor SlippE. He said that almost all humans have these visions. Humans call them 'dreams,' except that when they dream, they hear things. Some even feel things or smell them."

Todget looked at her with a blank expression.

It was times like these that Lily spoke as though to herself, assuming that Todget was not listening. "Thank Stag I only *see* visions. I would hate to know what the vile things in my visions smell or feel like." Lily's face contorted in revulsion.

"What kind of things? What are these words you come home with?" questioned Todget with irritation.

Lily raised an eyebrow, surprised that Todget was listening. It brought her out of her short-lived reflection. "Vile. It means terrible. As in, you don't want to be around it." Lily gave a little smirk and then asked, "So what are you and I up to tonight?"

"I have to fight tonight." He looked up at the clock. Its numbers glowed dimly. It was the only human construct that decorated the wall.

Lily frowned. "Is it high stakes?"

"Yes, the money will be good."

She walked slowly to him, leaned over, and tenderly kissed his wide forehead. "I wish I had not asked."

"And you?" Todget grunted.

"I'm not working today." Lily's voice was flat as she walked toward the bathroom for her first shower of the night.

A strange creature she is, Todget thought. She always took two showers a day. Todget would not shower at all if it were not for Lily pestering him to do it before she would get into bed with him. It was for the best. He did not need to draw human attention to himself on account of his smell—a smell that Lily teasingly assured him was "most foul."

Normally, Todget started off the night by working out his muscles and stretching. He would spend over an hour contorting and lifting his body. For extra weight he would get Lily to lie on top of him. Lily would also work out, but later, right before her second shower and bed. Tonight, however, Todget had a fight and needed to save his strength, so he spent the entire hour stretching and clearing his mind in preparation. Although he didn't tell Lily, only one of the fighters would leave the ring alive.

CHAPTER 7

MetaGame, also known as a "Divine Quest" or a "House Crusade," is a high-stakes real game typically played by nobility. Each month, one major house is selected to play the MetaGame...

MetaGames are comprised of a series of quests. These quests can be of any kind, the only stipulation being that it must be real—real meaning that the game is not illusionary, as is typical of spanker games. Examples include classic mazes furnished with traps and hostile products, off-world scavenger hunts, and authentic murder mysteries complete with real killers and victims. Other examples...

Teams score points based on the difficulty of quests and the time they take to complete them. At the end of the year, the twelve MetaGames are compared and the winning house is crowned House Champion. In addition to the honor and points collected by the House Champion, it is widely believed that the victorious house receives divine favor from the OverSoul...

MetaGames are extremely costly to run since they do not rely on software for special effects and storyline, which is one of the reasons these games are only played by the nobility of major houses. While wealthy commoners might be able to afford such games, they usually view them as pointless and therefore do not initiate them. MetaGames, then, may be viewed as a cultural phenomenon. Indeed, they are firmly entrenched in aristocratic culture. The stakes are extremely high, and the games are taken very seriously, so much so that a winning team becomes a source of pride to its family and the envy of others. Said Grandmother Sillia of the House of Tesla, "Let the plebs play in their dreams. We, the free, have always required light."

Participating houses ante in the points used to run the MetaGames and reward the victorious. Depending on the quests undertaken, the Divine Authority may also contribute points to the pool, which is perhaps why some call it a "Divine Quest..."

Due to the stipulation that the game use only real components and the fact that there has been a gradual but notable escalation of game intensity over the years, injury and even death are relatively common in MetaGames. Serious injury 15%, death 4.43%. Statistics are per game, per person.

—Excerpts from "MetaGame Summary," gathered by familiar #409083094839 (alias Smorgeous) and presented to D_Light Ravi (#39309283271938)

———

D_Light clasped his hands together and smiled as he peered down on the spanker ghetto below. *This could be the beginning of something HUGE!* D_Light thought to himself. *I'm definitely on the nobility track now! I just have to play this right...*

In response to his thoughts, Smorgeous overlaid in his mind a dance composition including choral singing and a fast, low bass beat. D_Light silently reveled for a few seconds before ending the song.

The apartment mounds spanned out in front of the team as far as they could see. It had taken nearly two hours for the team to arrive in this part of the world, and so the sun hung low in the sky. The rounded hills were covered with harvester flowers laid out in clusters of reds, pinks, purples, and every other hue imaginable. D_Light knew from sky images that these low-rent residential areas resembled oriental rugs from high above. The slow, dull buzz of countless harvester insects surrounded them as they gathered precious nectar in their tiny mouths. The players were scattered throughout the twisting, crystal white pathways that snaked their way to and between the gently rolling apartment mounds. There were hundreds of them, and by the looks of them, they were mostly spankers. Spankers were easy to spot. Their eyes were always glazed over, and they'd swing their arms at unseen foes, ducking and weaving to avoid invisible dangers. D_Light was only accustomed to being around spankers when he was plugged into a spanker game himself, so he never realized how insane they looked to an outsider— how ridiculous *he* must look when playing them.

The ghetto was vast and densely populated, and somewhere in these hills or underneath them stalked a demon. It was the team's task to hunt it down and report it to the Divine Authority. Mother Lyra ran her fingers absently through her long, dark hair as she peered out over the landscape. "How in Soul's name are we going to find a demon in all of this?"

"The proverbial needle in a haystack," Djoser said dryly.

Having decided to speak only when it mattered, D_Light said nothing. From the dark looks he got from Djoser, D_Light surmised that the noble, who still questioned the software engineer's worth, was barely tolerating him. He would reserve his comments for when he was clearly being helpful. Worse than Djoser, however, was Lyra's bodyguard. In what must have been a cruel joke, Lyra had brought with her Brian, the hulk of a guard who, just the night before, had been threatening him with a mace called "Tiffany." And based on the glares and obscene gestures Brian gave him when his mistress was not looking (his favorite being the cupping of his crotch), D_Light concluded that the warrior's opinion of him had not yet softened.

The group's other bodyguard was also an interesting choice. Since MetaGame rules allowed for one bodyguard per noble, Djoser brought with him a female product who looked to be as much a concubine as a soldier. *Why not bring a concubine along for a MetaGame? Mix play with more play,* D_Light thought.

The bodyguard's name was Amanda, and there were several telltale features of this product that placed her in the concubine category. To begin with, there was the way she was dressed, if you could even call it dressing. She wore only the legal bare minimum of clothing, consisting of two strips of fabric, held in place by devil knew what. Her face was classically beautiful, classically concubine, boringly so in D_Light's opinion. Her hair was contemporary, striped with jet black, blond, and reds, all of which sprang out in tails over her head like the whips off a willow tree. She had large blue eyes, exaggerated as though she had just stepped out of an old-time anime visual feed. So typical.

However, it was her body that hinted that she was along for more than mere amusement. A standard concubine product was typically designed to be a little softer around the edges. Amanda's curves, on the other hand, were just a little too suppressed, and her muscles were a hair too pronounced. Her body was built for speed, and she appeared to have just enough strength for when she needed to put down versus put out. And then there were the less subtle hints of her formidable abilities: two samurai swords—one short and the other long, a wakizashi and a katana—were tucked into the strap around her waist. Last but not least, Amanda possessed a nice set of vampiric fangs that D_Light had gotten a glimpse of on the rare occasions that she spoke. Of course, the fangs were not for sucking blood, but just another weapon that could be used in a pinch. D_Light had seen archives on the Cloud about products designed with poison-injecting fangs, poison to which the product itself was immune. D_Light wondered if Amanda had that capability, but he knew better than to ask.

Of course, the undisputable sign of a product was tats on their cheeks, and Amanda had none. Apparently, Djoser had paid a little extra to have a servant without the tats. Customers often did this to enhance the illusion that the product was actually human and that the affection they gave their owner was genuine, rather than from the chemical coercion known as "imprinting." She had even been given a classic human name, Amanda, to aid in this fantasy. Nevertheless, her methodical, mirthless attitude—a constant dearth of emotion so complete that it could only belong to a being designed in a lab for a narrow band of behavior—gave her true identity and purpose away. The dolling up of this toy to try to pass it off as human irritated D_Light, although he had to admit to himself that his annoyance was perhaps just envy, envy because he could not afford one of his own.

"Flip, it could be any of these fools, right?" Djoser's question was rhetorical, for they all knew that demons did not sport cloven hoofs, horns, or any other fiendish feature to announce themselves.

In this way, the word "demon" was a misnomer. Demons were not *born*, as were the demons of mythology, but rather *made*—made by the Divine Authority when the subject transgressed divine law, at which point they were "demonized." Historically, these types were called "criminals" or "fugitives." Therefore, the demon could be *anyone* in this ghetto, or *anything*, as in the case of a product.

Lyra's ferret-styled familiar, PeePee (the initials for Pretty Princess), stood beside her mistress, grokking everyone in sight. *Who knows, maybe we'll get spectacularly lucky? Maybe the demon is strolling by right now,* Lyra thought. Lyra frowned down at the ferret. She was not at all fond of PeePee, but since MetaGame rules prohibited the use of high-powered familiars, she was forced to leave her much preferred lynx at home. Because the ferret was the House Tesla mascot, only this style of familiar was available for loan from their house. Normally, she would have spent the time and points to rent something more fashionable, but the MetaGame invitation had sprung up suddenly, and there had been far more important preperations to attend to. Having to rely on a more primitive familiar did, however, add to her sense of adventure and excitement.

This is going to be fun, she thought. The first quest of the game— to find a demon in a densely populated spanker ghetto—was interesting, challenging, and even held a hint of danger.

Djoser raised his eyebrows and cocked his head slightly while accessing his own house-loaned ferret. "There are four gates to Anywhere," he announced.

"Where?" Lyra asked, irritation seeping into her voice.

Djoser chuckled. "*Anywhere* is the name of this ghetto. Apparently, the plebs who named it thought they had a sense of humor."

"They'd be wrong," interjected Brian. As though realizing his mistake, the bodyguard turned away from the conversation and resumed standing at attention near Lyra like a watchdog waiting for an intruder.

Lyra licked her lips impatiently and then spoke quickly. "Okay, so there aren't enough of us to cover all the gates and effectively search this ghetto, right?"

"Not by my reckoning," Djoser answered. "I mean, look at this place!" Djoser waved his arm as though to encompass all the spankers, apartment mounds, trees, and flowers before him. "There are 2,834 citizens registered to this ghetto—2,834!" he exclaimed.

This is it, D_Light thought. This was his first challenge of the most important game he had yet played. He remembered Minister A_Dude's words from the MetaGame blessing earlier that morning. The minister had taken each member of the team aside to impart a few words before they set off on their crusade. "Deeeelight," he chuckled with his large, toothy grin. "You've been *called!*" D_Light had flinched as the word boomed against the stone arches and walls of the cathedral. "This ain't your usual grind, boy. This…this is a game close to the Heavenly Soul. No rules, understand? You gotta set that mind free and make your family proud."

It puzzled D_Light that the game presumably knew the location of a demon, or at least the general area to look. After all, demons were wanted by the Divine Authority, and therefore it was a sin to know the whereabouts of one and not report it. But as the minister said, "No rules, understand?" *Anything goes now*, he reminded himself.

The two noble-borns stared blankly at one another for what seemed an eternity. Finally, Djoser took a deep breath and let out all the air with a big whooshing sound. "Standing here is wasting time and hemorrhaging points. We need a plan, and it better not suck!"

CHAPTER 8

It is wrongheaded to think of medicine in terms of "fixing" or "repair." Treating our bodies like old-time automobiles whose parts wear out is a primitive paradigm. Cloning organs as though they were spare parts or injecting nanobots to fix tissue were stopgap measures for previous generations, but in the long run, that's an uphill battle. Rather than growing old and trying to piece us back together as we fall apart, is it not more desirable to simply remain young? Using the divine wisdom of the OverSoul to instill youth at the cellular level, we now "heal thyself." Aging is a disease, no more, no less, and once you cure it, everything else falls in line.

—Excerpt from Dr. Arrest_Ya_Hart in her "Kickass Address" to players of Medical Game

---

"Well, there's always the brute force method," Djoser said with a certain resignation in his voice. "We split up, canvass the area, grok everyone in sight, and hope we get lucky."

The team had wandered away from the gate of the spanker ghetto. They were debating how to find the demon—the quest objective—but had not yet settled on a plan. The air was beginning to cool as the blurry orange glow of the summer sun faded. Despite the coming of nightfall, the harvester insects did not slacken their humming activity; their bulbous bodies bobbed under their bloated masses, and the bee-derived products resembled small balls of yarn as they went about their business.

Lyra shook her head skeptically. "I don't think there are enough of us to do it the brute force way, Djoser. According to the maps, it's a good-sized area. Besides, it's getting dark. Is it likely that the demon will just be roaming around? For what purpose?"

"Why do demons do anything?" asked Djoser with a shrug. "We don't have any idea who or what we're dealing with here, so I'd rather take a long shot than just stand around while our time bleeds out. Soul, if anyone's got a better idea, let's hear it."

Djoser had given D_Light as much of an opener as he could hope for, so D_Light cleared his throat and swallowed hard in preparation to speak. Thanks to a cocktail of focusers and a mild sedative delivered with precision by Smorgeous, D_Light did not even feel the slightest twinge of nervousness when he finally spoke up. "If I may," he interjected, "the two of you are nobility, so you may not know as much as I do about how we plebs live in these spanker zones."

Djoser's eyebrows lifted as he regarded D_Light with a slightly mocking expression. He gave Lyra a quick smirk and then returned his attention back to D_Light. "By all means, *avatar artist*," he said. "Earn your keep as our advisor."

D_Light gave a humble smile and nodded. "Spanker ghettos attract a specific type of person, and so we ought to be able to take advantage of that fact."

D_Light paused for a moment. He had everyone's attention, even Brian's, who did not try to mask the look of contempt on his face. D_Light did his best to ignore the mixed reception. "Perhaps we can think in terms of process of elimination. Let me run it down for you. A ghetto like this is zoned for spankers and spanker games. That means that anyone living in this area is assumed to be hardcore—that is, into the most intense and addictive entertainment games out there."

Lyra nodded affirmatively. "Indeed, and I think it's safe to assume our little demon isn't a spanker. I mean, how would he or she even get an account to jack in?"

D_Light became excited as he realized his idea might get traction. "Right! Spankers have their own culture. Soul, they even have their own way of speaking—and we can use that, starting with the word 'him.' I can tell you right off the bat that most spank games are aimed at men. We're talking about violence and sex. All those guys you see around us swinging imaginary swords, cradling invisible guns, and dry humping the lawn—they're playing those sorts of games." In a grand gesture, D_Light swung his arms about, urging everyone to take a look around them in order to fortify his point.

Concerned that he may have offended the nobles with his coarse talk and flamboyant body language, D_Light looked at his present company for signs of disapproval. To his delight, there were none.

Lyra clapped her hands once and spoke with authority. "Okay, so for the kind of games played in this ghetto, any woman we see is worth taking a second look at."

"Consider it done," replied Djoser with an impish grin. He put his hand on Lyra's shoulder in mock tenderness.

D_Light stammered out, "Begging your pardon, sires, what I mean is since demons are as likely to be male as female, and few spankers are female, then the probability of a female we see—"

"Yes, we get it!" Lyra rolled her eyes at D_Light. "We might be nobility, but we're not inbred."

D_Light took a generous breath and bowed. "Begging your pardon, Mother." He bowed again. "At your leave, I have another suggestion."

"For Soul's sake, D_Light, if you don't stop bowing and begging my pardon and otherwise wasting our time with your pleb-speak, I'm going to have Brian here beat the shit out of you," exclaimed Lyra, who was smiling in a way that D_Light had never seen before—a nasty smile that made him wonder in earnest if she would, indeed, unleash that oaf on him. D_Light took note of an overly eager Brian, who stood proudly behind Lyra, grinning from ear to ear.

Her smile disappeared in an instant, and her voice adopted a certain icy edginess. "You will address me without formality during this game. Formality only slows the communication process, and speed is of the utmost importance. I chose you as my advisor, so I expect you to participate effectively. Is that clear?"

D_Light was about to bow to signify acknowledgment, but then he nodded instead. Regaining his momentum, he continued. "Another thing about ghettos like this is that most private apartments are open to other spankers. When you lease an apartment here, you have a choice of whether you will allow the common rooms of your apartment to be open to spank games—that is, open to other spankers."

Djoser interrupted abruptly. "You mean, someone would allow spanked-out plebs to bumble about in their own private living space? Why would anyone opt for that?"

"Because you earn reduced rent if you allow public access," D_Light answered. "And believe me, if you're spending all your time spanking, you need to keep your expenses down."

Lyra snapped her fingers. "Right, but a demon would not elect for that. A demon would want privacy."

"That's my expectation," confirmed D_Light, "but that brings up a good question. How is a demon able to pay for anything at all? Their status is illegal, so they can't play the Game of Life, earn points, or spend them."

Lyra brought in a sharp breath. "Oh, I researched that. Demons typically use what are called 'proxies.' A proxy is a player with an account who conducts transactions on the part of the demon. Demons usually pay the proxy with hard currency—you know, side-liner money."

"Sounds like a dangerous profession," Amanda purred, her long canines flashing as the words slipped out. It was disquieting to hear Djoser's bodyguard speak, mainly because D_Light had only heard her speak once or twice thus far. Indeed, he had nearly forgotten she was there.

"But lucrative, no doubt," added Djoser, who wrapped his arm around Amanda's waist; she arched her back subtly to accommodate him. The nobleman then looked over at D_Light and spoke to him directly. "Okay, so if we find a female living in a private flat, there's a good chance she's a demon. Or maybe we should be looking in the bushes. Why would a demon want to pay rent anyway?"

Just then, a bleary-eyed man in a grass-stained skinsuit jogged up the hill toward Lyra.

"Yo, Amber, you here for the PartyMiiix?" he asked.

In a flash, Brian, with a snarl on his face, was between Lyra and the man.

"Um, yeah, I guess not," the spanker muttered and then trotted back down.

D_Light took another look around. Like most residential areas, this ghetto appeared to have perfectly manicured landscaping with little in the way of underbrush. "I doubt there is enough natural cover here to hide for very long," he answered. "Most everyone's living in these mounds." He pointed at one of the towering grassy hills. "You can bet all that real estate under there is inhabited."

"Who says the demon *lives* here?" asked Lyra. "Maybe it's just passing through. Don't make any assumptions unless you have good reason for it."

D_Light nodded thoughtfully. "Could just be passing through. That would be easier yet. Check this. Since a demon doesn't have an account, it's not going to be plugged into a game. Look around you. Pretty much everyone's jacked in. If we see someone walking around normally—"

"Especially a woman," Djoser interjected.

"Yes, especially a woman," D_Light said. "But I'd bet the demon *is* living here. Soul, this would be a clever place to hide! Everyone's jacked in, so who would notice you? Who would even see you? You could hide right out in the open. To someone who wants to get lost, someone who's *not* a spanker, living here is like living in the middle of nowhere."

"Nowhere, officially known as Anywhere," Lyra quipped. "What did I tell you all? MetaGames are the best!"

Djoser sighed. "Nevertheless, *if* the demon is just passing through, then we had better get looking real fast."

Djoser tugged on one of the numerous tails of hair sprouting from Amanda's head. "You, my dear, are the fastest of us all. Why don't you have a quick look around?"

Amanda gave a curt nod and then sprinted off without uttering a word. The product did not have a familiar and so would have to rely on her mind interface chip to grok those she saw. The additional processing power of a familiar would be more efficient, but since Amanda now knew the profile of the prime suspects, she could focus her processing power on just those who were of particular interest.

Watching the genetically engineered product running off, Lyra asked, "Should we worry that she might tip off the demon?" The noblewoman looked noticeably vexed.

Djoser shrugged. "Look around—lots of people are running toward or away from Soul knows what. It's like everyone is narced out in a wrong way. Nah, she'll fit right in."

"Everyone is running for their virtual lives, eh?" Lyra stared at D_Light for a moment until he realized that she was talking to him, at which point he smiled awkwardly and nodded.

Wanting to cover as much territory as possible in the least amount of time, Lyra then ordered Brian to take leave of her and assist Amanda in the search for possible suspects. Brian was quick to protest, insisting it was unsafe to leave the two nobles completely unprotected, but Lyra assured him that they would be fine in his absence. Hesitantly, the dutiful bodyguard set out to the streets, holding his trusted mace, Tiffany, firmly at his side.

"So, with the hired help doing their little ad hoc search, what does that leave for us to do?" asked Djoser, his voice sounding bored.

"I'll show you," D_Light called back over his shoulder as he jogged down the hill. The others followed, somewhat reluctantly, into the entrance of the nearest apartment mound.

"My bet is that the demon is holed up somewhere in these mounds," D_Light said.

"What do you propose we do, advisor?" Djoser asked. "Knock on the doors and give a sales pitch? There must be a thousand apartments in this ghetto!"

"More apartments than we could know," Lyra said as she pressed her hand against the soft, fuzzy dro-vine wall. "These mounds are living things. The walls, the floors—everything's alive."

"Yeah, *D*, this whole ghetto is constantly shifting its halls and chambers around. My guess is the whole complex has gone feral, so forget about a rational floor plan," Djoser said.

"And I can't even call up a nanosite map! What kind of backwater is this?" Lyra asked as she stared down at her familiar.

"Anywhere's like anywhere else—there's nanosites covering everything and everyone, but spankers usually opt out of allowing their community maps to go public. Remember, this isn't just a place to live, it's one big gaming labyrinth. Having a real-time map would spoil the fun."

"Sounds great so far," Djoser said sarcastically as he bounced a few times on the spongy floor. "So let's cut to the master plan here."

"You mentioned going door to door with a fake sales pitch? Yeah, that might work, except I don't mean to knock on every door. Remember what I said about a demon opting for a private apartment? I recommend we just check the doors that are off-limits to the spank games. That'll narrow it down a whole lot...and as far as mapping goes, we're just going to have to explore manually and let our familiars keep track of where we've been."

Lyra looked unconvinced. "Well, why don't you enlighten us n00bs on how we are to ID the apartments that are off-limits. Do they have a sign on the door, or do we have to jack into a spank game or something?"

"Exactly!" D_Light said. "Yeah, when you're in a spank game you don't even see the private doors, but of course those outside the game can see them." D_Light walked over to a nearby silver plexi apartment door. "So obviously this door exists, right? But let's say this is the door to a private apartment and I'm jacked into a spank game."

"You won't see it. It'll be skinned as like a wall or something," Lyra said with a smile.

D_Light touched his finger to his nose to indicate "spot on."

Master, that gesture is obsolete and 83.6% likely to incite negative feedback from your peers. Would you like me to demonstrate a more fashionable—

Not now, Smorgeous.

"If you say so," Djoser said skeptically. "So what? You have to be jacked in and jacked out at the same time to see the real door that doesn't exist in make-believe?"

"Yes," D_Light affirmed. "I'll jack into a spank game, and Smorgeous, my familiar, will ping the locations of those doors that appear in the real world, but do not exist in the game. Those will be the private doors."

Lyra nodded. "And that's when I knock on the door and ask them if they're interested in a once-in-a-lifetime offer for reducing their rent, and all they have to do is open their apartment up to the games."

"You two are beautiful together," Djoser said dryly.

D_Light laughed. "Nice. We then grok whoever is at the door." D_Light took a moment to access Smorgeous and then said, "The family that manages this zone is called Gallant Guild. We'll just say that we're representatives of G&G."

"You want me to do door-to-door sales?" Djoser clutched at his chest.

"I'm afraid I can't do it because I'll be jacked into the spank game," D_Light replied apologetically. "It'll be more efficient if I don't have to jack in and out."

Lyra frowned. "That sounds like fun, D, but Djoser and I are not exactly dressed as salespeople."

D_Light took note that Lyra had just addressed him by his nickname. He liked that. "I'm not exactly sure how salespeople dress, but I think you should at least consider hiding your royal seals. And

I recommend you do the talking, Lyra. Once they see you, they'll believe anything you say. Remember, spankers are mostly men." He gave Lyra a flirtatious wink.

"Well, well, look at you, D!" exclaimed Lyra, smiling wryly. "Feeling pretty comfortable now, I see." D_Light smiled bashfully.

"And I will do what?" asked Djoser, who was clearly irritated by the back-and-forth banter between D_Light and Lyra. "Oh, I know, maybe I can do the sales pitch to the *gay* spankers," Djoser said sarcastically.

Lyra smiled sweetly. "No, Djoser my dear, as much as I'd enjoy watching you work your charm with the gentlemen of this ghetto, we need you on security detail. Remember, it's not the spankers we care about, it's the demon, and if the demon thinks there's something up, there might be trouble." Lyra's expression became serious. "You need to stay alert and keep your hand near your hilt."

"True, and I'll be jacked in, so I won't accurately see what's going on," D_Light added.

Djoser glared at D_Light, a slow smile spreading across his face as though he was thinking, *Like you would be of any use anyway.* "Funny, I thought we brought bodyguards for that very purpose," he said.

Lyra rolled her eyes. "Look, we've all lived under Rule Seven for decades, right? I would hope the three of us could handle one demon."

D_Light thought about his throwing discs, Djoser's short curved sword, and Lyra's unmatched skill with open-hand martial arts fighting styles. Yes, his mother was correct that they had all become resourceful in combat in their own individual ways. From the day they joined House Tesla, this had been a priority.

Djoser looked skeptical. "Yeah, well, demons are not constrained by divine law, so we're likely to be up against modern weapons. We'd better not get confrontational. Let's just ID the bastard and call it in."

CHAPTER 9

Dro-vine is the wood and steel of the present day. Why waste resources and labor to build a house when you can grow one from seed? If you want to get fancy about it, build some synthetic stairs and some basic skeletal framing. The dro-vine will happily grow over your scaffolding; however, don't expect this plant to do exactly what you planned! Because of its variability, dro-vine is not for the control freak, but rather for those who want a cheap yet comfortable place to live. To grow a house, just find some land and plant one—that is, if this ubiquitous organism hasn't already colonized the area on its own.

Thanks to hyper-photosynthesis during the growing season, dro-vine goes from seed to a small cocoon large enough to sleep in within two weeks. Within a month, you'll have yourself a small home, complete with several chambers. What makes dro-vine brilliant is how it naturally forms cavities in itself, which tend to connect with one another.

To make a door from one cavity to another, you simply cut out a rectangular hole in the wall and place a hinged door in the opening. The dro-vine, in an attempt to fill the hole, will grow over the hinges, but it won't grow over the door itself since such doors are coated with chemi suppression enzymes suspended in a tough polymer. However, if you really want to be lazy, don't even bother with a door. Just cut an upside down "T" *slit (like an old camping tent) and treat the edges of the wound with the suppression enzyme to keep the wound from healing.*

Cutting windows is even easier than doors, but why bother? In our minds, SkinWare can adorn the chamber walls, ceiling, and floor with any vista we desire—from faraway canyons, to the ocean, to a rainforest, to the Martian landscape—all in real time (with a little over a three-minute delay in the case of the Mars scenery)...

In summary, I'm afraid that for those of us who enjoy the building games, we had better forget about the mass market and focus our play on the distinctive but often unpredictable tastes of the rich.

—Excerpt from "The New Builder's Game," presented by Might_E1

D_Light heard the familiar whistling noise as he jacked into NeverWorld. The hallway that connected the apartments of this floor was brightly lit in real life, with subdued shades of green and brown Van Gogh swirls for walls and a bright green mossy floor, but as his nervous system plunged into the game, the light dimmed and the hallway turned to rough-hewn stone. Torches spaced at regular intervals materialized to light the way. In the distance he heard someone screaming. A woman, he thought, being tortured. Or perhaps it was just a lure set by some clever fiend, patiently waiting for a hero to fall for the ruse.

There were the sounds of other creatures too—faint groaning, the occasional snarl, the familiar distant clang of metal against metal signaling combat underway. And there were more ordinary sounds, like the subtle cacophony of dripping water from a thousand sources. This labyrinth, its hallways and chambers filled to the brim with terrors and treasures, was leaky, dank, and in great need of repair.

The smell of rotting flesh—faint, but unpleasant just the same—permeated everything. Olfactory input in NeverWorld was not as sophisticated as auditory or visual, being less important for game play, but the game did have a few scents in its inventory. Unfortunately, most of them were foul. Rotting was particularly popular. The rotten stench of death left by carcasses in the battlefield, the pungent aroma of moldy food abandoned by the long since ambushed caravan, and the ogre's breath (who lived on an assortment of Soul knew what).

D_Light had barely acclimated to his surroundings when the sound of heavy footsteps caught his attention. They were close by and growing louder. Without hesitation, he summoned an invisibility spell. Waving one hand while tracing a symbol in the air with the other, he murmured an arcane phrase. As his spell completed, D_Light was relieved to discover that he could no longer see his own hand. That was a good thing, as he sometimes made mistakes, especially when rushed.

The spell took effect none too soon, for only a few seconds later, a lumbering beast of a creature turned the corner and headed in his direction. A maltoc, as the creature was called, resembled a man only in its general shape, having two arms, two legs, a torso, and a head. This was fitting, given that maltocs were human before their corruption by Salem, the son of Pheobah, the Dark Queen. But the maltoc's general shape and size was the end of the similarities between these nasties and men. Bristling, greasy hair covered mounds of muscles and other more irregular and freakish lumps. Through the amorphous face peered beady, pink eyes, which glistened slightly in the torchlight of the hall. Around the eyes were crimson red sockets that excreted thin trickles of blood down its wrinkly face—a face that most closely resembled raw hamburger. The creature did not breathe as it stalked, for it had no nose or mouth; only its footfalls betrayed its passing. Maltocs, incidentally, were only lesser devils, but nonetheless, they were not something to be trifled with.

Having played NeverWorld for countless hours in the past, D_ Light's gaming habits were nearly hardwired. He had to fight the urge to blast this nasty in the back as it passed by him. "Nasties" was the term spankers used for computer-generated enemies in the game, and destroying them was one way to get points in Never-World and build up the power of the character one played. He had to remind himself of his purpose here—he was not here for treasure or glory in battle, but to look for doors or the absence thereof. For D_Light, this was a sort of agony, akin to sending a gambler into a casino just to count men with brown hair. It was a numbingly mundane task in an exciting world.

Two ghosts stood nearby, one to his left and another just behind. They looked like human-shaped jellyfish with only the very edges of their bodies highlighted by thin, translucent lines, while the fill of the form was nearly transparent. D_Light supposed the ghosts to be Lyra and Djoser, but he could not ascertain which was which because NeverWorld rarely skinned objects or people as they looked in the real world. In fact, one could never predict how the game's artificial intelligence would skin non-game objects and creatures. From the game's perspective, it was only important to make clear who was a spanker and who was not. Skinning non-spankers as benign ghosts enabled those submerged in the game to identify the non-players without losing the continuity of the game.

Both ghosts had the appearance of being men. One was an old man with an unrelenting crooked smile, wearing only wisps of rags.

The other was younger, although D_Light could barely tell because the man's face—his entire head, actually—was split down the middle to the root of the nose, much like a log of wood cleaved on the edge by an ax. This ghost was naked, and one of his arms twitched.

No sooner had D_Light focused in on the ghosts than a pop-up sign appeared over each one declaring, "Not in play. Do not interact with this agent." It really was an incredible use of space, when D_Light thought about it. All of these alternate dimensions occupying the same physical area, dimensions facilitated by software. Consequently, NeverWorld was not the only game available in this ghetto. There was Mission Flipp'n Ridiculous (a spy game), Samurai on Top (a samurai death match), Golden Age (a twenty-first-century war game), Grokstania (a social networking game), and several other less popular options. One would think that with so many people playing so many different games it would be chaos, but unless two spankers were in the same game, they were skinned as a "sideliner prop" to one another—just like the two ghosts appeared to D_Light.

Although spankers avoided running into sideliner props, they otherwise ignored them because the props typically had no real importance to the game they were in. D_Light now found himself in the unique position of caring about the props, at least the ones that represented Lyra and Djoser. How else would he coordinate with them on finding the demon? In response to this, Smorgeous verified that the old man was, in fact, Lyra, and the lumberjack accident was Djoser.

Returning his attention back to NeverWorld, D_Light breathed a sigh of regret as he watched the thicket-dense hairy back of the maltoc continue down the hall. It was uncommon to find one of these devils by itself, and D_Light had the advantage of full surprise. He felt a twinge of frustration as his opportunity for easy experience points disappeared around the corner, but he reminded himself that he was playing a much bigger and more important game this evening.

"Smorgeous, watch for doors that appear in the material world but not in the game. When you see one, go sit next to it," D_Light stated out loud so that Lyra and Djoser could hear. Because D_Light was now playing a fantasy game in a quasi-medieval setting, he was supposed to role-play using fantaspeech, which included words like *thee*, *thou*, *nay*, and so on. However, he was not going to embarrass himself by speaking this way to the nobles. His score flashed red as NeverWorld exacted a minor penalty.

His familiar pinged confirmation of his master's verbal command.

Although Smorgeous was not as intelligent as most humans or human-based products, he did have the advantage of being able to process multiple inputs at once. Smorgeous could monitor the game D_Light was jacked into while seeing the real world. However, D_Light had to be personally spanking in order to give Smorgeous access to the game. Spank games like NeverWorld did not allow familiars or other software to access it without a human sponsor being jacked in. Otherwise, spankers could use software to scout out the game before jacking in, which was cheating.

It was a while before they found a private door. D_Light watched the Lyra ghost knock on it. Just as D_Light had expected, the door upon which she was knocking appeared to him as a solid wall. There was some muffled talking, but D_Light could scarcely make out any of it, for real sounds were always somewhat muted while jacked in. Unable to hear much, he did manage to catch Lyra saying the phrases "interested in" and "thank you." Her voice, husky but silky feminine, sounded surreal as it emanated from the old man's ghostly mouth.

Additional doors were discovered as the night wore on, and the team soon dropped into an efficient routine. Fortunately, it was getting late and most residents had retired to their apartments. Unbeknownst to the residents, Lyra was having her familiar take images of them as they came to the door and then compare them to images in the demon database. After doing this for a while, Lyra even dropped the ruse of being a salesperson and simply told the often groggy-eyed occupant that she had the wrong apartment. Such a terse exchange was adequate, as it only took a second or two for PeePee to grok the suspect.

Meanwhile, D_Light spent most of his energy on avoiding being seen by the nasties. As his invisibility spell began to wear off, he had to renew it, and his spell manna was dwindling. Worse yet, some of the creatures lurking about could see him, despite the invisibility. He tried especially hard to avoid these, often doubling back down the hall, which confused Djoser and Lyra as they tried to stick with him.

Where the flip are you going? Lyra asked over a blink.

Uh, can't talk. There's a goo coming. D_Light sent his mental reply as he ran. The gelatinous mass of undulating slime that slithered after him was not fooled by D_Light's invisibility, having no eyes anyway.

A what? Lyra's thought signature was irritated. *For Soul's sake, this is stupid! I can't believe I agreed to this...this...whatever it is we're doing.*

D_Light streamed as he ran. *Look, I don't want to get fragged. If I die, I get tossed out, and it'll be a half hour before I can re-spawn.*

What? returned Lyra. *We didn't take you along to do any spawning, okay? You want to do that, get a concubine and a room!*

D_Light sprinted down a flight of stairs and out onto a grassy courtyard. He had lost the goo, but maltocs were now chasing him. Numbering at least four—more than a match for D_Light—they too could see through his invisibility. Perhaps something, maybe the goo, had cast a spell on the maltocs which enabled them to pierce through his invisibility illusion. Whatever the case, he could hear them storming down the stairs, and he had only a moment to hide. With one forceful leap, he hurled himself onto the ground and took cover behind some virtual rubble.

D_Light could have chosen a peaceful game like Grockstania where virtual death was not a problem; however, D_Light was not adept at social networking games. Other players would expect him to mingle with them. He would either have to waste his time chatting and flirting with these ghetto residents, or blow them off. Being antisocial in a social networking game would get you voted out quick, which would be no better than death in NeverWorld. Worse yet, bad manners tended to attract attention. Even if the demon wasn't a player, he or she might have friends who were. The last thing D_Light wanted was for his plan to actually tip the demon off. He would never be invited to a MetaGame again.

Lyra followed, Djoser trailing behind her. She looked around furtively to confirm no one was watching and then glowered down at D_Light, who was lying motionless, all curled up like a possum playing dead. Lyra blinked D_Light, knowing he could not properly hear her audible voice. *Are you insane? Why are you lying on the ground?*

I'm hiding. I'm behind some rocks and stuff, D_Light blinked back. *You'd understand if you were jacked in.* D_Light's blink was faint, as though he was trying to whisper with his mind.

Well, I understand you need to spank, but we feel like idiots following you around like this—not to mention it might look conspicuous to the demon if it were to observe us. From now on, Djoser and I will just chill somewhere while you ping us on the map where the private doors are, and we'll follow up.

Djoser trotted up alongside Lyra. He was slightly winded. *Yeah, why don't you take care of the legwork? You know, you be the brawn and we'll be the brains.*

Sounds reasonable, D_Light pinged back. He wondered why they hadn't done it that way from the start, them being the brains and all, but he was careful not to send the thought.

Having been left to his own devices, D_Light continued seeking out private doors. As soon as he and Smorgeous identified a door, Smorgeous forwarded the coordinates to Djoser and Lyra. And then, without waiting to see the results, D_Light moved on. So far he had not found many private doors, even fewer than he had expected—only thirty-six private doors, compared to over a thousand residences open to the public.

The small number of private doors made Djoser and Lyra's job easy, but it did nothing for D_Light as he struggled to keep his bearings in the massive apartment mounds. The mounds went several stories above the ground, and the tunnels that connected them were like fat, mossy dikes with narrow paved roads on top. And worse than the scope of mounds was the unpredictability of the layout.

Because dro-vine dwellings had no real floor plans, no reliable maps existed. Indeed, even if they did, they would not remain accurate for long as existing walls and chambers shifted and new ones formed. Consequently, D_Light found it extremely challenging to find all the hidden hallways and chambers, many of which presented themselves awkwardly. Trapdoors in the floor, knotted rope ladders going upward, hidden crawl holes connecting adjoining chambers—it was anarchy. Spankers were usually too busy to put much energy into sweating the details of elegant interior design. Indeed, D_Light imagined they fancied their ad hoc architecture, believing it added variety and a tinge of surprise to the games played here.

Several hours passed before D_Light finally got fragged. He had wandered into an arch devil's lair. Gold coins, jewelry, fine armor and weapons, books of lore, and magic items of various sorts gaudily adorned the walls and tables in the resplendent room. The devil prince was not in his lair, but his dog was. And it was not just a run-of-the-mill canine—it was a hellhound, and worse yet, it had been super buffed-up by some dark magic. D_Light barely got a look at the treasure before the hound came out of nowhere and ripped out his throat.

CHAPTER 10

Photosynthesis, perhaps THE most important chemical pathway on our planet. And yet from an engineering perspective, it is a failure. You heard what I said—an absolute and complete FAILURE! Four percent efficiency? Hell, Mother Nature worked on this grand creation for four billion years and this is her feeble offering? Surely we can do better.

—Edward Crumble, PhD (Monsa Corporation), 2018

Todget's right eye was nearly swollen shut, and the gash on his neck was deep. Still, he did not stop to properly tend to it. Like always, the moment the fight was over, he took just enough time to get his money and then he got out. For tonight's fight in the pits, Todget was paid more than five hundred thousand dollars. His opponent had paid with his life. Todget clutched the bag of filthy, crumpled thousand-dollar bills tightly. *The money may be good, but my ritual is even better*, he thought while walking home to his apartment.

It was his well-deserved unwinding time, and he could hardly wait for it to commence. First, he would remove the little white box from under his bed, take out the appropriate medical supplies, and then carefully and methodically rub his body with pungent healing ointment and wrap his wounds with antiseptic white gauze. The gauze was magic in its ability to seethe and slither its way into the wounds, bringing welcome relief to the localized pains. Next, he would take a shower to wash away the filth of both the human's and his own rage. The shower would be extra hot, and while standing in the stream of scalding water, he might even smile. Finally, naked and sitting cross-legged at the foot of the bed, surrounded by darkness, he would let his muscles and mind relax.

Todget let himself dwell on such things, which is probably why he did not notice the female human standing suspiciously close to his door, looking like a stranger to these parts. Glowering out from under his heavy hood, he recognized the woman. She was the one who had knocked on his door hours ago, before he had left for the pits. He had not answered the door. *By Stag, what is she about?* he wondered. It was too late to turn back, for if he did so it would appear odd and he would draw attention to himself. Instead, he decided to walk right past her and his apartment and return later when she was not lurking about.

"Greetings," the woman exclaimed as he passed by. She bowed her head slightly while turning her face upward so that her emerald green eyes could remain fixed on him. She showed him a big, gleaming smile. *Such white teeth, so straight,* Todget thought. Teeth always reminded him of what these humans really were—just a skull with a little softness around it. That's how he thought of humans every time he went into the pits with one to punch, kick, and tear at it.

A hairy muskrat of a thing slinked about the mysterious woman's calf. Its eyes turned up at him in an unblinking stare. *It is a machine,* Todget thought. He did not like these constructs, for it was difficult enough to trust the living, who at least had some common ground with one another. What would compel any living creature to want to make such monsters?

The woman's lips parted slightly as though about to utter something, but she did not. She simply smiled again and then began walking down the hall past him. Todget did not return her smile. Rather, he hung his face down, watching only the floor as he walked unhurriedly away down the corridor in the opposite direction.

She's not in the pretend place. She actually looked at me. He had felt naked under that stare. Although she was merely a feeble human female, there was something confident, even powerful about how she carried herself.

A good fifteen minutes passed before Todget felt it safe enough to return to his door. Looking around, he did not notice the tiny points of eyes belonging to the ferret peering at him from around the bend of another hall as he waved his card past the key panel. Todget was one of the few in the mounds to have a lock that could be opened with an actual key card. It cost extra for a lock of this type; instead, most residents preferred to have a microchip embedded in them that proved their identity when approaching their dwelling. Todget would not abide anyone injecting machines into him. To him, the key card lock was well worth the money.

Having been slain by a hellhound and forcefully ejected from NeverWorld, his entire gaming account had been locked down. It would be nearly a half hour before D_Light could re-spawn and continue his search for private doors in the spanker ghetto. And so, after notifying the rest of the team of this setback, he sighed deeply and mouthed a silent prayer, asking that they find the demon fast. The sooner they found it, the more bonus points they got. That is, if they found it at all.

He then leaned against a poplar tree, its paper-thin leaves rustling enthusiastically under the moderate night breeze. There was no light, save the moon, which cast soft shadows upon the scene below. He was standing on the top of an apartment mound. Thick, dewy grass blanketed the dro-vine beneath him. Stationing himself at the top of this taller-than-average mound enabled him to get a better look around. From this vantage point, he hoped to get an idea of how much was left to search.

Smorgeous informed him that it was nearly dawn. Any minute the eastern sky would begin to glow as the rising sun began her ascent. D_Light's view of the surrounding land was hindered by other tall mounds in the distance and by tall, woody-stalked flowers that surrounded him. D_Light pushed aside a few of the more ambitious flower stalks that had managed to grow up to his eye level. The stems bent gently, but they did not break—breaking them would actually take some effort. They had been engineered to be pliant but tough, a good design for wafer-thin plants in a place where people held little regard for designated trails. Soon, when the sun broke, these beautiful and patient marvels of industry would get to work converting the sun's rays into energy—energy to be used by the mound beneath. The strong, fibrous texture of the dro-vine mound contained just enough elasticity to give him the sensation of walking on an exceptionally tight trampoline.

It was quiet at this time of the morning. A few hard-core spankers sprinkled the streets here and there, but for the most part, the place had cleared out. However, as soon as the sun came up there would be more of them to be sure—the morning players, the responsible ones who tried to get in a little spank before they reluctantly grinded for an hour or two to get a bare ration of points. They would then take the rest of the day, as well as night, to spank some more. D_Light knew the drill, intimately.

Years ago, D_Light himself had been hard-core, the hardest of the hard-core, in fact. He used to engage in a lifestyle called "ramboing," a term that meant he lived entirely off the land. Not that ramboing was that big of a deal, as many spankers did it at one time or another. Finding free lodging was easy. There were tons of wild dro-vine burrows in between the official housing tracts. The stuff grew anywhere, and it spread tenaciously. If you could find a bit of abandoned land, chances were you had somewhere to stay. And dro-vine did more than just shield you from rain and the morning dew. It actually regulated its own internal temperature and humidity, which made for quite a cozy dwelling. Nevertheless, living in abandoned dro-vine burrows meant that you had to go without a few things. For one thing, you had no electricity, no lights, no wiring of any kind. However, this was of little concern. You could just jack into Skin-Ware to be able to see, and your familiar or onboard computer could provide trivial entertainment, like music and video. D_Light rarely used electricity at home, except to recharge Smorgeous.

What was more of a hassle than lack of electricity was no running water. Luckily, bathing was not a high priority to most ramboes. And when it came time to relieve yourself, you could do that outside, or if you were lucky and had an extra dro-vine chamber in your hovel, you could just do it there; after all, although dro-vine was efficient at extracting nitrogen from the air, it did not mind the extra fertilizer.

For a rambo, the acquisition of food in the wild was even easier than the acquisition of shelter. Everywhere you went there were trees and flowers engineered for the sole purpose of creating nectar, the most ubiquitous source of energy on earth. People, products, most machines, and many plants, including dro-vine, could eat the sticky, honey-viscous liquid. And nectar came in many flavors, all of them tasty enough to impress even a distinguishing palate, at least for a while.

Indeed, ramboes did not have to sweat the basics, and they did not have to beg anyone for anything either. The real downer of living off the land was the loss of drugs, and not just the performance enhancers that helped you sicken your game. Worse than that was the eventual revocation of your health contract. The health contract was one of the main costs any player—spankers and grinders alike—had to bear. You could always tell which gamers had been ramboing for a while because they were the ones who were starting to show their age, having gone off contract. Not much at first, maybe just some bags under the eyes and a few laugh lines. But little lines would soon become deep ones, laugh lines would become permanent creases, and the next thing you knew, you just started to look like shit in general. D_Light remembered how one guy he used to rambo with had even developed a few specks of gray in his hair. That served as a wake-up call for D_Light, who knew he was headed down the same destructive path. It was then that he knew it was time to turn back to the OverSoul, back on the road to salvation, an undertaking that was both a great relief and a painful loss.

D_Light peered down on the soft rolling hills, trees, and trails below. He imagined what it would be like to have to depend on artificial light to see in the dark, as was the case generations ago. He had played spank games set in post-industrial era times. These games strove for authenticity, so he felt he knew the old-time night city well enough—the countless eyes of car headlights snaking along the freeway, the R-shaped streetlights, the illuminated curtains of countless windows of synthetic shelled apartment buildings and the distant light patterns of partially lit skyscrapers and high-rises. Most of these unsightly artifacts of the past had since been removed or overgrown by dro-vine.

D_Light was grateful to be living in a day and age when artificial lights were unnecessary, when you could just patch into a skin to navigate in the dark without spraying photons everywhere—wasting them. He was grateful to be living in the age of nanosites, the technology that made this possible.

Indeed, nanosites were the only thing more ubiquitous on earth than dro-vine. They were far too small to be seen with the naked eye, but they were everywhere. Although these simple bots had limited capabilities, what they could do they did extremely well. Nanosites coated everything on the planet—every plant, every rock, every wall, every surface of everything. They climbed onto animals and people and then embedded themselves in the living tissue. As they travelled, looking for a place to plant themselves, they would listen to the tiny, short-range signals that emanated from brethren. Once they found a spot that was neither too close nor too far from others of their kind, they would plop down and stick to the surface on whatever object they had chosen. Once they had found a permanent home, they would send out their own "I am here" signal over and over until their energy source finally exhausted itself.

Nanosites spontaneously formed a regular pattern whereby every nanosite was exactly 0.694 millimeters apart from one another. Although this spacing might seem miniscule to a person, it is like an ocean of distance to a nanosite, which consists of a mere few thousand molecules itself. Together, their intensive global coverage and their talent for announcing their existence created a three-dimensional map of the world that software could easily understand. And they did this with greater precision than any satellite. More importantly, they marked moving objects in real time, whether outdoors or inside.

Hence, there was no need for artificial light at night in this contemporary world. The tiny, invisible chips implanted in D_Light's eyes when he had his mind interface kit installed could "see" the nanosites and rendered for D_Light a perfectly accurate representation of his world in total darkness.

And it wasn't just the ability to *see*, but also the ability to *hear*. By focusing his attention on a location covered with nanosites, it was likely that there would be some audio output there along with the visual. Even now, as D_Light scanned the vista below him, he heard a male's voice calling, "Fighter needed. Join the Orc Slayers. Preferably a tank." There was an icon next to the message hot spot indicating to inquire within. As D_Light's eyes roved to the right of that message, a video of an armor-clad party of heroes battling a small army of nasties popped up, which arrested his eyes for a moment. This pause encouraged the pop-up to zoom in so that D_Light had the opportunity to see the action up close. This message was just a brag, a spanker willing to spend a few paltry points to display his proudest moments over his doorstep.

Messages like this, ones aimed at other spankers, had been barraging him whenever he was skinning, and since he was not there to spank, it was getting more than mildly irritating. It fact, it had become downright overwhelming, and he felt a slight headache coming on. Jacking out of the SkinWare, he let the world go dark again, save the meager glow of the moon and surrounding stars. He then picked up Smorgeous and held the cat up above the flowers so he could get a good look around. Smorgeous had better sensory hardware onboard than D_Light, and the familiar would not only be able to see everyone in sight, but he would also be able to get a good image of them for the purpose of grokking.

No longer using SkinWare, D_Light was now "realing," meaning that now he saw only what his natural eyes could see, a meager vista of shadow and silver provided by the moon and stars. This was a little unsettling, but he fought his urge to immediately jack back in. *Is this how the demon sees this place?* he wondered. Demons typically did not have mind interface chips and therefore would not be able to jack into SkinWare. Maybe seeing the world like the demon did would yield a clue.

After a minute of staring down the mound at the gloomy landscape below, he shook his head and sighed. *How depressing,* he thought. He wondered how people years ago could stand such bland and colorless monotony. *Just plants, rocks, and dirt. Can't even see those things clearly at night. What did they have to think about?*

Master, I have detected the emotion you've in the past labeled "sad and pointless dwelling." Would you like me to take countermeasures?

No, D_Light answered as he jacked back into the base skin. The view sprang to life again, and he felt the pit that had been forming in his stomach ease.

D_Light was tired. He had been grinding hard through the night, and the peps he had been taking were beginning to wear off. The very moment this thought occurred to him, Smorgeous offered to give him another bump, but D_Light declined. He had an overwhelming urge to sleep. *Just a tiny nap*, he told himself. It was as good a time as any to go unconscious since he had time to kill before he could re-spawn into NeverWorld. He ordered Smorgeous to awaken him in twenty minutes, just long enough to feel refreshed, but not so long as to fall into a deeper slumber. Leaning with his back to the poplar tree, he slumped down in a heavy heap. His eyes closed before he even hit the ground.

Master, awaken. You have slept exactly twenty minutes. The voice was soothing, and it was as though it was coming from his own mouth. A sharp but not quite painful ping echoed in his mind, bringing him to a fully awakened state. There was soft pink in his vision, and so he opened his eyes as slits. The sun had just begun creeping up from behind the mountains on the horizon, a sliver of fire that straddled the distant precipices as though it wished to consume them. The glow warmed his face ever so slightly.

He had been dreaming, as he always did, of sailing on *Terralova* on a brilliantly sunny day, the wind just perfect. D_Light always looked forward to sleep because his dreams were always relaxing— a welcome respite from the intensity of the Game. He very much wanted to just close his eyes again and let the sun's warmth ease him back to that place. Maybe just for a few more minutes.

Master, you still have a quest to finish. Do not let your teammates down. As his familiar relayed these words in D_Light's mind, he hated the machine and its ability to read his thoughts. However, the hatred began to subside and give way to mere irritation as the pep Smorgeous had just given him began to work its chemi magic. D_Light had not asked for the drug. It was the sort of thing that made Smorgeous worth all the points D_Light had spent buying and maintaining his on-sale, higher-end familiar. Smorgeous knew what his master needed, as opposed to what he wanted.

D_Light stood up slowly but did not take a step, instead allowing himself a minute for the fog and heaviness of sleep to lift. The shadows cast by the multitude of flowers around him were long and getting deeper as the sun continued its ascension. A few more spankers had filtered out while D_Light had slept. It was rare for D_Light to be around spankers while not jacked in himself. Watching the drones as they careened about, intent only on their game, reminded him of a horror spank game he once played, a game that featured zombies. The similarity was eerie and a bit unsettling. He found himself breathing as shallowly as possible so as not to attract their attention. Reminding himself that they were not, in fact, zombies, he took in a series of deep breaths and let them out slowly. His uneasiness, however, did not leave him, and so he pushed himself off of the tree he had been leaning against and turned around in a circle, surveying the area with a heavy dose of paranoia.

He spotted a woman only one tree away. Her face was tilted up toward the sunrise, and her eyes were shut—not pressed shut in concentration as one communing with her familiar, but merely to avert gazing directly into the sun. D_Light realized that he had not seen her earlier because the trunk of the tree on which he had been leaning obscured his view. He assumed that she could not see him behind her closed lids, so he did not hesitate to stare. She was beautiful, fair, and there was an innocence about her that D_Light found alluring. Her long, blond locks, illuminated by the sun's early light, shimmered like corn silk, and they commenced to slow-dance with the flowers and poplar branches stirring in the morning's gentle breezes. Entranced, D_Light could not take his eyes off the creature.

Master, as you have pointed out, a female in this male-dominated region is uncommon, and so I took the liberty of attempting to match her to an individual in the demon database. Result: no match found.

Still studying the mysterious woman, D_Light was about to ask Smorgeous to expand his search when the dutiful familiar informed him that he had already performed the task and had found no matches for anyone in the Cloud.

D_Light was perplexed. It was rare to come across a "nobody," someone who had managed to remain completely anonymous to even the Cloud. Indeed, even a run-of-the-mill sideliner could usually be found somewhere in the Cloud. He scrutinized the woman again and quickly determined that she was no sideliner, as her face was entirely too perfect to be a descendant of a "native" bloodline. She must have had engineering in a recent ancestor—perhaps the last generation before human genetic engineering was banned.

He immediately thought that perhaps she was a concubine. That would explain why she was not found in the Cloud. In most cases, the owners of high-end concubines would spare no expense to scrub their property out of the Cloud or to give them fake identities. It added to their mystique. But something in his gut told him that that theory was incorrect, so he quickly discarded it. D_Light had rented his fair share of concubines, and this woman simply did not fit. First, the lines that framed her face were just a tad softer than they should be. For example, the Thesies line (a well-established concubine family that D_Light favored patronizing), although absolutely stunning, had defined, almost cruel lines which projected a nearly predatory look that declared, "I'm going to rock your world, little boy." Of course, there was a variety of concubines to keep even the most jaded client interested, and this included more innocent-looking choices like this girl. However, D_Light had spent many hours over the years scouring catalogs and had never encountered one quite like this one. *She must be custom built*, he thought. She bore no visible product tats, but that was to be expected. Only the most ghetto rent-a-body products wore tats.

D_Light tilted his head and leaned further to one side in hopes of catching some clue as to the girl's identity. He determined that while her looks did not completely rule out concubine, her body language certainly did. A high-end rent-a-body would not be caught dead carrying herself like this girl. Her back was arched like a bow, her arms hung loose and downward as though pulled by gravity with more force than the rest, and her face was turned upward into the light. In contrast, concubines always had a stock posture, which they vigilantly maintained—a tall and straight stance, chest lifted slightly, face tilted only a few degrees upward, and vacant eyes that were always fixed straight ahead. This was not so much a matter of training as it was instinct. Training cost resources and could be botched or unlearned, while DNA offered far better quality control.

She could be a human concubine, D_Light thought. They were much less common than their engineered counterparts, but they offered a uniqueness and spirit that their cloned competition could not. *But what the hell is she wearing?* She wore a long, black cloak that opened in the front to expose a cheap synthetic blouse with far too many flower imprints on it to be considered tasteful. *No concubine, whether human or product, would wear that atrocity. Period.* Still gawking at the hideous blouse/cloak combination, D_Light could make out a slender but athletic torso with somewhat larger than proportionate breasts. Clothes aside, this woman was striking—so striking that it had taken him far too long to notice the blouse.

A member of the Bergstrom family? Although typically not concubines, they were uniformly attractive, and most—for family branding reasons—had remained Northern European in their ancestry. They also happened to have a large house not fifteen miles from this location. D_Light furrowed his brow. The Bergstroms seemed unlikely. Again, that clothing! The Bergstroms were very socially conscious, and any family member who dressed like that would have been disowned without hesitation. *Unless it's some sort of hazing ritual*, D_Light thought. Every family had its own entrance requirements for new player draftees. An interesting thought, but still not likely. The Bergstroms were devout and thus rarely idle; this woman was just standing there. Also, D_Light had never seen a Bergstrom without a familiar nearby.

It was all very mysterious, and D_Light felt frustration at the realization that despite all of his scrutinizing and hypothesizing, he was still no closer to an identity for this girl than when he first set eyes on her.

D_Light decided it was time to take a different approach. He thought it would be useful to initiate a conversation in order to gain some additional clues. He was then about to spout off some inane remark about the weather when he stopped himself. He had a better idea. *Smorgeous, publish a new game challenge to my usual contacts. The challenge is to correctly guess this girl's family. If no one gets it before she tells me, I win. Ante-in is a thousand points. Give 'em a real-time feed from me, but limit it to audio and visual only.*

Smorgeous pinged confirmation, and D_Light leaned back against the tree and waited quietly. The girl remained still.

Yo, Dee, count me in! D_Light heard a familiar voice in his mind.

The generic game mediator followed this with, *K_Slice has joined the game.*

Easy points, Dee, K_Slice chimed in with a Taunticon™. *I say there is no family. She's a sideliner for sure. I mean, what the hell is she wearing?*

I'm on this bitch, relayed another familiar voice.

TermaMix has joined the game, intoned the artificial game mediator.

Come on, K, you got no judge of character, declared a cocky Terma Mix. *Sideliner? That bitch is way too raw to be one of those crack hippies! She's gotta be sellin' all that lushness to the spankies. That cloak she's wearing, whew! That'd turn them on for sure.* TermaMix sent the blink and followed it up with a micro-archive of him doing a stupid, taunting dance that resembled running backward in the air.

The debate continued over the next few minutes as D_Light peeked around the tree at the woman in question. Additional players joined—C, Flava_God, Boo_Girl, Blitz, and Sugar_Papa. Players anted in and additional bets were made. When D_Light thought enough interest had accumulated and the pot was sweet enough, he decided it was time to break the ice. He pushed off from his tree and came out into the open.

"Is there something I can help you with?" she asked. The girl did not move, nor did she so much as open her eyes.

D_Light was caught off guard, completely shocked and speechless. Soul knew for how long she had been aware of his surveillance of her. She must have a familiar nearby. Maybe she was a Bergstrom after all. If so, D_Light decided it was best to be direct, logical, and honest.

"Um, because you are beautiful, I prefer to look at you more than anything else currently available. I apologize for staring. I meant no disrespect. I, um, I didn't think you would notice." D_Light scrunched up his face and smacked himself lightly on the forehead for stammering and sounding like an idiot.

As he finished speaking, the girl's eyes shot open and she turned her head to look at him, hard. Only her head moved. Her body remained slumped as though so content with its current position that it refused to obey its mistress. She seemed surprised, puzzled even.

Wow, creepy and stalker-like, Dee. Way to work it, K_Slice said over the game chat, finishing off the remark with a n00bicon™. D_Light put the chat on mute.

There was an awkward silence. Then, all at once, the wrinkle in her brow dissolved and her lips relaxed, although she did not smile. Her body straightened, and she took a slow step toward D_Light. The dawn's light colored her face pinkish, and her skin glowed. Now that she was fully facing him and a touch closer, he could see her with greater clarity. Yes, her features were indeed soft. Soft, but not weak, like a torch's flame that gently flickered to entrance an onlooker—just before burning him.

"So I'm about the best thing around here, huh?" The woman casually stretched out her languid arms and swept them about, looking back at him pointedly with large, unflinching blue eyes.

D_Light felt stupid now. *That's what I get for gawking,* he thought. *Oh well, everyone comes off as a fool from time to time.* Since he did not live here, chances were he would never see this woman again anyway. So why not play the idiot? He had nothing to lose and everything to gain, especially all those points floating around in the guessing game he was hosting. He noticed more bets were being placed. Apparently, the players were excited by this first exchange.

D_Light took a breath and nearly shouted, "Yeah, you are! I mean, don't get me wrong, these are great!" He waved to one of the vacant-eyed zombies who stood several meters down the mound. The spanker to which he motioned was a man who was crouching down, apparently spying intently on an unseen menace.

A silken laugh suddenly erupted from the amused girl. "Fine then, you don't look so bad either, I suppose, for a—" Her voice had been confident and smooth, but then she stopped suddenly like a sprinter at his finest hour rushing full into a stone wall. Just then her smile, a byproduct of laughter, vanished, and her nose crinkled. Her eyes flashed.

A moment passed, and then it was D_Light who was puzzled. "For a what?" D_Light leaned in inquisitively. He saw what could be a look of disgust on her face. He repeated the question. "Don't leave me hanging. Not bad for a what?"

"Well, for a male, I meant to say. Your kind is not exactly what anyone would call beautiful." She shook her head as if in mock sadness.

D_Light smiled. "Yes, we men are all angles and boxiness with little to interest the eye." He gestured over the length of his body as though to say, "Have a good look."

The girl nodded and puckered her lips with mock admiration. "Aesthetics aside, might I ask what you are doing out here? I saw you leaning against that tree and it inspired me. I thought, why not just stand here and take in the new sun?"

"Oh, I'm just waiting for some friends," he replied.

"I'm here as much for the sounds as the view," the girl said, looking into the horizon. "There was a storm a few mornings back. There's nothing like the wind in your face and the rush of the leaves and the branches and the grass." The poplar tree leaves rustled with a hiss as though in agreement.

Damn, D_Light thought. *K_Slice was right. She's gotta be a hippie sideliner.*

Although not happy with the prospect of giving K_Slice the pot, it thrilled him to think that he was speaking to a sideliner. He had only met a few in his life.

"Yes, it's nice—for a *ghetto*," returned D_Light. *Oh Soul, I'm being stupid again. She might live here,* D_Light thought at the very moment the words left his mouth.

The girl seemed oblivious to his faux pas. "The flowers are especially appealing," she said. "I hate it when those clods go off the paths, stomping about without a thought in their heads, crushing them underfoot like they're nothing."

D_Light nodded with feigned sympathy. "*Those* clods, huh? So I take it you don't play spank games?" D_Light grinned at her. He decided it was time to start fishing for clues regarding this girl's identity. There was a game on, and he needed to keep up the players' interest.

She shook her head.

"Um, you *do* know when those clods are jacked in they can't actually see the flowers, right?"

She nodded, but D_Light detected a note of surprise crossing her face. "These guys can't see you, me, or anything the way it actually is," D_Light said offhandedly so as not to sound like a know-it-all.

The woman seemed to hesitate as she toed the dirt. "No, I don't...um, I don't do them. What are they like?"

Although muted, D_Light could see in the periphery a text from K_Slice. It read, *She doesn't "do" them? Is that some kind of throwback hipster-speak?*

D_Light cleared his throat. "Well, a spank game works basically like any SkinWare app works. The game software keeps track of what is in the game and how everything behaves and, just as importantly, where everything is. So, like if I was jacked in, that tree would look different. Maybe it'd be a pillar from an ancient ruin or, I don't know, a big ol' lamppost. The tree's still there, it'd just have a different skin."

"And the flowers?" she asked. "What do they see those as?"

Since D_Light had been playing in NeverWorld among these very mounds for the last eight hours, he actually knew the answer. "Oh, they don't see the flowers at all. The game is only obligated to show you stuff that can hurt you if you run into it."

"So the flowers don't make the cut," she remarked with disappointment. "They don't make the cut, so they don't even exist."

"You have the idea, yeah," replied D_Light with a tone of encouragement. "Spankers can feel them a little bit, maybe even be tripped up when they're running hard, but in general, they don't pay them any mind. Spankers really are oblivious to this world."

Enough lecturing the n00b. When you gonna ask her how much? Terma Mix texted.

The girl crossed her arms, drawing her cloak around her. She adopted a pensive look, as though seeing spankers with a whole new level of understanding.

"Allow me to demonstrate," D_Light said. He enthusiastically started down the mound while waving for her to follow. She crinkled her brow suspiciously, but smiled faintly as she tentatively trailed behind.

D_Light got on his haunches not two feet from the crouching spanker he had pointed out earlier. He then spoke loudly at the crouching man, using a strange, unidentifiable accent. "I say, dear sir, do you have a fresh bowl of porridge?" The spanker did not move, but continued staring straight ahead. His body, however, tensed up.

D_Light stood up. "You see? They can barely hear you. That probably sounded to him like a faint echo."

The girl chuckled softly. "Interesting," she said quietly. She then walked over to D_Light and the crouching man, somewhat hesitantly as though approaching a beast caught in a trap. She waved her hands in front of his face. The man followed the movement and scowled, but he did not get out of his crouching position. Her eyes widened with surprise. "I thought they were blind to the outside world."

"Not exactly blind," D_Light whispered. "They see you as something, probably a ghost, um, but not a nasty or dangerous sort of ghost. If the game could cut you out completely it would, but—" D_Light interrupted himself with a chuckle. "I mean, just because you and he are in different audio and visual worlds does not change the hard fact that you share the same physical world. The game has to take that into account."

The girl seemed intrigued, having the curiosity of a young child. "What about touch?" she asked.

"Oh, certainly. I don't recommend—" D_Light was going to discourage any physical contact, but it was too late. The woman stuck her index finger into the ribs of the spanker. The man let out a grunt, and then his lips curled into a snarl as he swung his arm around hard. The young woman leaned back just outside of his swing. *Nice reflexes,* D_Light thought.

The man boomed, "Don't make me come out there and beat you senseless, you bloody clod!" His eyes were fixed on the woman, and he crouched low, as though to pounce. The girl had already assumed a position, D_Light supposed a defensive one. Her knees were bent slightly, and her body was turned askew so that she did not face him head-on. Instead, her left flank was turned half toward him while her left arm bent up like a shield. He stepped forward and threw a punch hard and straight. She moved swiftly to one side while her left arm swept away his blow. He hit nothing. Although his punch left him wide open, she did not counterstrike; rather, she stepped back a pace and resumed her defensive position. She did not appear afraid or angry, merely curious.

The spanker looked like he was about to yell at her again when he stopped cold. He looked over his shoulder for an instant and then ran off—sprinted, as though the devil himself was chasing him.

D_Light's eyes met those of the confused girl, and he grinned while biting his lip. "As I was trying to tell you, yes, they can feel just the same when in the spanker game as when outside of it. Oh, and as I imagine you now know, they don't much like being messed with. It's considered very impolite."

The woman relaxed her posture as she watched the spanker go. "Crazy, all this!" She let out a short, nervous laugh. She paused, her bottom lip transforming into a pout. "I feel bad for him. I am sorry I bothered him. Still, how interesting, how sad."

"Sad? How do you mean?" D_Light inquired.

"I mean, why would someone choose to blind himself to this world? To move around like someone—I don't know, like someone who is..."

"Perfectly insane?" D_Light interrupted with a laugh. "Don't pity them. Spanker games are designed to be fantastic! I play them myself. However, unlike the plebs who haunt this place, I try to control my appetite."

She looked over at him. D_Light hoped that it would be a look of affection, trust, warmth, or some other positive sentiment, but her expression did not contain any of those things. Rather, she appeared as she had while observing the spanker. She looked like an adult who was discovering something with new, childlike eyes, or perhaps like a young scientist who was hot on the trail of a new and exciting discovery.

D_Light lowered his gaze and kicked at a rock near his shoe. "Well," he muttered self-consciously, "if you're going to hang out among spankers, you might consider trying one anyway."

"Hmm, yes, I expect the experience would be worthwhile, but I don't know… Going around trusting this, this software? I wouldn't want anyone messing with me." She giggled uncomfortably.

"Yeah, unfortunately, spanklets—er, spanklets being the name for girls, I mean women—they get groped all the time. The guys usually get away with it 'cause the spanklets can't ID the guy unless they jack out of the game, and by then the guy is gone."

"Groped?" The woman looked at him with an amused smile.

"Forget it," replied D_Light. "Okay then, so you're obviously not a spanker. So how does a lovely creature like you spend your time?"

A text from player Blitz came into D_Light's periphery. *'Bout time. Need more info on this girl to get a lock.* This was followed by a text from K_Slice that read, *Yeah, Dee, you're bleeding this out. Wrap it up, n00b!*

The girl adopted a soft, warm smile and answered, "Most nights I work at the university, but not tonight. I'm just taking a walk."

D_Light was about to ask what "taking a walk" was when a priority-one blink from Mother Lyra barged into his mind. *We have confirmation on his apartment!*

Djoser chimed in. *Got it. That's it then. I'll call it in!*

No need, I called it in a few minutes back, Lyra replied.

A little late saying so, don't you think? Djoser inquired. *Holding out on us?*

Thought it prudent, Lyra returned. *I didn't want you all jumping up and down for joy, tipping off our friend. As they say, it ain't over 'til it's over.*

As the two nobles volleyed back and forth, D_Light thought, *The demon located? Nailed the first quest!*

Lyra had sent the coordinates of the demon's apartment, which indicated that it was located in the mound directly across from D_Light, less than one hundred meters away. It would not be long now. An angel would have been dispatched quickly. He had never seen an angel in action. Of course, he would want to keep his distance nonetheless.

Due to all the blinks going off in his head, D_Light had been quiet for a while and had momentarily forgotten about the girl, who appeared to take the silence as a hint. She sighed. "Well, it's late. I think I ought to get going."

Presently, D_Light returned his attention back to the girl and said, "Oh, you're going to want to stick around. You're about to see something you don't see every day."

She looked at him quizzically.

"Ever seen an angel?" he asked.

"Uh, no. I...I don't understand what you mean. Is this about the game thing? I don't believe—"

D_Light interrupted. "No, not a game. Angels are the highest agents of the Divine Authority."

The woman smiled and nodded and took a few shuffling steps backward. She appeared slightly uneasy. "That sounds interesting, but I'm, well, I'm late."

D_Light persisted. "You know, the Divine Authority, the Over-Soul?" *Where did this woman come from?* D_Light wondered. Having to explain spanker games was odd enough, but the OverSoul? It was like being ignorant of gravity.

Indeed, the girl did not explicitly say that she didn't understand what he was talking about, but D_Light could tell when someone was trying to fake it—someone trying to pass as knowledgeable, but not having a clue. A faker always had a dismissive look mixed with a little fear that screamed out, "Sure, sure, let's just move on to another subject." He saw that look a lot in his profession (who didn't?)—people trying to wing it. *Doesn't know the OverSoul? Was she from one of the outer colonies?*

"Look, there is a demon in that building there," D_Light announced bluntly, pointing down at the mound below.

The girl's eyes widened and the color in her face drained instantly. Judging by her reaction, D_Light surmised that she *did* know the definition of a demon.

D_Light quickly added, "Don't worry. The angels are on their way. They will take care of him."

The girl looked away from D_Light, her body tense. "Todget! Todget! Run!" she screamed.

CHAPTER 11

"Out, out, brief candle! Life's but a walking shadow, a poor player that struts and frets his hour upon the stage and is then heard no more: It is a tale told by an idiot, full of sound and fury, signifying nothing."

So wrote Shakespeare on the subject of the human condition. Depressing, eh? Countless past generations of people all over the earth armed themselves against such unthinkable sentiment with faith—faith that life actually did have a purpose. But faith—the act of lying to oneself because it is convenient—the foundation of past religions, is no more than a historical footnote today.

We no longer need to ritualistically console each other in temples or churches chock-full of symbols and idols. God is no longer a ghost. God is no longer reduced to an imaginary guide through the inscrutable and indifferent jungle of our lives. Who can question the divinity of the OverSoul in a world where no one is hungry? In a world where sickness is a choice rather than a hand dealt by fate? In a world where immortals walk among us?

—Minister A_Dude, archives, "From the Pulpit"

The angel approached slowly and quietly. There was at least a 94% chance the demon was in its residence, so there was no need to hurry. For the current mission the angel was a "he," and if it ever came up, he had chosen to give himself the name "Jacob." Of course, human labels like "gender" did not apply to an entity like Jacob. His name and gender were more a reflection of how he chose to appear to others at the present time rather than based on any physiological or psychological characteristics.

Having landed near his target, Jacob proceeded at a brisk walk toward the apartment mound. He had a disheveled mat of black hair and serious eyebrows. His large brown eyes scanned about casually, taking in the world around him. But Jacob did not use those eyes, as they were only for show. Jacob's true eyes could see so much more, and not just in front of him, but also all around. Jacob's senses radiated out like a great bulb of light, illuminating even the darkest of shadows.

The angel passively scanned everything, alive or not, that came within the reach of his scanners. Humans, products, vegetation, inanimate matter—all were inspected and categorized. Most of this data was filed away and not processed further. It was not important, at least not at present.

Jacob walked up the flight of steps that cut up into the bowels of the building. He had to decide whether to fly up the stairs or climb them manually. Low-speed flying was 434% faster than manually climbing and cost only 115.45% more energy; however, his "stealth protocol" did not call for flight, so he decided to climb the stairs manually.

"Todget! Todget! Run!" a voice called from a distance. Based on the wave pattern of the voice, it was 93.6% likely to belong to a female human or human-based product. In addition, the pattern suggested (86.45%) that the caller was emotionally distressed.

Jacob instantly deduced that this was a warning to his target, given that "Todget" was the social name of the target.

It was now highly likely (approximately 78%) that the target had just been warned of impending danger. The protocol Jacob had been using up to this point was based on the assumption that the target would be caught by surprise. The scenario had changed, justifying a change in protocol. In other words, more extreme measures were now worth examining.

The first protocol he considered was to use the direct approach. As Jacob knew from his constant scanning, the walls of the mound in which his target resided were a common dro-vine derivative, and so he knew its tensile strength. He could rip through such walls like paper, but this was not optimal. Although the walls would grow back, it was unnecessary to damage them. It was wasteful under the current circumstances, and openly using his powers around unsuspecting humans was suboptimal to their productivity, and could even cause (although rarely) long-term emotional disruption.

Not that Jacob was capable of empathizing directly with any of the various agents around him. He simply acted in accordance with the math. That is to say, he used the most logical protocol available based on risk/reward analysis. For example, the risk of "emotional disruption" had an estimated negative score. The added advantage for apprehending the target using "disruptive measures," such as smashing through walls, had an estimated positive score. These scores and many others were factored in with the relative value of apprehending the target. For instance, was the target likely to be dangerous to other people, products, or property? If the target somehow avoided capture on this occasion, what was the likelihood of apprehending him later? For a being like Jacob, any decision could be boiled down to the return value of a mathematical formula.

Given the data available, the "direct approach" protocol was given a value of "false." He went through a series of other protocols, and within a billionth of a second he settled on simply flying to the target's apartment, but taking the time to use the existing hallways to get there.

Before proceeding to the target's apartment, Jacob briefly considered apprehending the woman who was warning the target. It was a sin to knowingly aid a demon, giving Jacob the authority to arrest her. She was not far away. Judging by the direction and intensity of her call, coupled with the obstacle layout of the area, Jacob estimated her position at around one hundred meters. However, subduing the subject would take some time, and now that the alarm had been sounded, time was of greater importance. Furthermore, she was not his target. Worse yet, she could just be a distraction. Perhaps the warning did not emanate from a human at all, just a voice simulation. This had been used on Jacob before, and he was not about to make the same mistake twice. No, Jacob would continue on to the primary target and deal with her afterward.

Jacob took flight with a thunderous boom as he broke the sound barrier. His flight applied pressure to the surrounding walls, but they did not tear. Almost instantly, his sensors detected a humanoid around the corner ahead, right in his path. This forced the angel to land before the corner and run. Jacob was heavy, and the impact points of his feet were relatively small, which increased the risk of generating great amounts of noise and damaging the floor. This was not optimal. However, Jacob could not fly past the citizen. The pressure emanating from an angel passing a human in these tight quarters would likely cause injury.

Passing the human, Jacob scanned the citizen to confirm that he was not the target. He was not. Passing the startled man as a blur,

Jacob then returned to flight, causing another sonic boom. He had to immediately slow down to negotiate the corners of the hallway, after which he accelerated again, creating another sonic shockwave. By the time he got to the door he had made four separate shockwaves, although they were so close together that to a human ear it would only sound like a single deafening blast.

Jacob was now within scanning range of the target's dwelling. His scanners penetrated through the walls, indicating there was nothing inside that matched mammalian tissue density. He did a quick calculation based on his pursuit algorithm. The woman who screamed out the warning did so only 0.8 seconds ago. Assuming that the target was in the reported dwelling at that time, he could not have gone far.

———————

Although alone in his home, his sanctuary, Todget did not feel safe. It was that female human he had seen in the hall as he was about to enter his apartment. There was something about the way she looked at him, something about how she walked away from him that made him uneasy. The only reason he had returned to his apartment at all and lingered there now was because he expected Lily to return. *She knows not to wander after the sun rises,* Todget thought. He had chastised her about her carelessness before. "Travel only when the humans sleep" is what they had agreed on. Yet, where was she? Todget did not allow himself to entertain his most awful fears about her absence. He assured himself that Star Sisters were, by their very nature, capricious and independent to a flaw. She had done this before.

Nevertheless, he would not have escaped the reserve or survived as long as he had in the outside world if he had not learned to trust his instincts. Since returning to his apartment, he had prepared himself for the worst.

Quickly, he drew his knife from his pant leg and slit the mattress open. This abuse of furniture was of no consequence, for the living fabric would mend itself in a week or so. He thrust his hand deep into the foot of the mattress and extracted the weapon. It was in the shape of a long rifle, nearly a meter long. It had a set of three canisters mounted side by side under the weapon, just in front of the trigger guard, running up to the front of the barrel. The weapon had no stock; it did not need one. Its recoil was minimal and it was only effective at short range, so bracing it for careful aiming was of little use. At over forty kilograms, the weapon was heavy—even without a stock—but this was of little consequence to Todget, who was stronger than any human male.

The weight of the weapon was mainly due to its ammunition. In the middle cylinder there was a composite metallic mixture that had a boiling point of over thirteen thousand degrees Celsius. In the two flanking cylinders there were potent chemicals that, when combined, created so much heat that the resultant mix would melt any material known to man. When the weapon was fired, contents from all three chambers were injected into the ignition chamber. Although relatively stable apart, the combination of the two ignition chemicals would cause a tremendous exothermic reaction. This mass of rapidly heating liquid would fuse with the metallic slurry from the central cylinder, and long before the chemical reaction could reach its zenith, the contents of the ignition chamber would be expelled out of the barrel. Then, over the next few nanoseconds, after the superalloy slurry had burst out of the muzzle, its temperature would rise to its full potential. The superheated goo would stick to anything it hit, melting and boiling via its own unearthly heat.

The weapon was called a BB gun. The "BB" stood for "bombardier beetle," which was the inspiration for its design. Millions of years ago, the bombardier beetle had evolved a unique and ingenious defense mechanism. The beetles stored two separate chemicals, hydroquinone and hydrogen peroxide. When the creatures perceived a threat, the two chemicals squirted out through two tubes. They mixed, along with some catalytic enzymes, and then underwent an extremely powerful exothermic chemical reaction. The boiling, malodorous liquid underwent flash evaporation, and when the gas was expelled, it created a loud pop.

The BB gun had cost Todget a small fortune. Since it was a sin to buy, sell, or possess modern weapons of any kind, the excessive price was appropriate. However, its status as an illegal modern weapon was only part of the story, for the BB gun was in a class of blasphemy all its own. Aside from being a modern weapon, it was specifically designed to combat agents of the Divine Authority. It was well known that Divine Authority enforcers were only vulnerable to nuclear weapons, and even then, only if the source of the blast was nearby.

But all solid matter, regardless of its "divine" properties, had its melting point, and so the BB gun was meant to exceed the melting point of all known things, thereby obliterating *anything* it hit. Even the nanotech crystallized metal that was used for the ammunition of the weapon could not withstand its own heat for long before it also vaporized. Because of this last point, a BB gun was only effective at short range—fifty meters maximum—and although the weapon would still kill an armored human at a much longer range, it would do little to one of the Divine Authority's enforcers. Todget knew he needed to get near his enemy to be effective; however, Todget also knew that if an angel was that close, chances were that he would already be dead.

His finger caressed the trigger. The weapon rested on one leg, hidden under his heavy cloak as he stood facing his bedroom wall.

As was typical of apartments in this neighborhood, the apartments were connected directly together, and although Todget and Lily always kept the doors locked, Todget now left the door open to his neighbor's living room in preparation for flight. He wasn't exactly sure how the open door would assist him; perhaps it would serve as an exit or as a decoy. All that he knew for certain was that he didn't feel comfortable being penned in.

The man next door peered curiously through the open doorway. He and his neighbors had never met, and Todget briefly speculated that the hollow-eyed spanker probably wondered why his reclusive neighbor had left their adjoining door open. But the truth was that the neighbor had little interest in Todget himself or his unprecedented exhibitionism; instead, he was trying to catch a glimpse of Todget's beautiful roommate—the girl that every guy in the mound talked about but rarely saw and never spoke to.

His neighbor would have been taken aback if he had actually been able to see Todget's face, for it was caked in a gel that was both fire retardant and heat insulating. Upon returning to the apartment, he had quickly caked his entire naked body with this gel and then shimmied into his fire-retardant clothing, making a sticky mess underneath. Such discomfort was trivial to him, however. If he did need to use the BB gun, most likely he would need some protection from its awful power. If he did not need it, well, then it was easy enough to clean up later.

Todget waited nervously, but his wait was short-lived. Presently, he heard Lily shriek out his name, her voice radiating with such fear and intensity that he knew there was no time to think. He didn't need to think anyway, having rehearsed this escape in his mind many times before. He expected they would surround him and come at him from all sides, so he needed an alternative exit. He pulled the trigger. The BB gun was set to spray a razor-thin fan of molten fire, which instantly vaporized a sizable fiery hole in his floor. Then, as casually as a swimmer jumping into the deep end of a pool, he leaped down through what looked like a shaft into hell. He fell feet-first through his downstairs neighbor's apartment and prepared to bend his knees as he landed, so as to absorb the shock. He already knew where he would run from there. He and Lily had mapped out their entire apartment mound weeks ago, and with any luck, the layout of the living mound had not shifted much since then.

Unfortunately, when Todget hit the apartment level beneath him, he ripped through the floor as if it were a thick, rotten web laid by some massive, long-dead spider. As it turned out, the dense, molten-hot alloy did not stop once it burned through his apartment's floor, but continued to fall ahead of him, instantly burning everything it touched. The substance fell further and further downward, continuously burning everything in its path. Clearly, Todget had not fully appreciated the power of this devastating weapon. Indeed, it would later be discovered that some of the larger droplets of metal had ended up burning through six stories of apartments, killing two people and injuring six, burning all the way down until it embedded itself deep in the soil beneath the mound.

Todget continued to fall floor after floor, through the blazing shaft created by the BB gun blast, until at last one of the Swiss-cheese floors grudgingly bore his broad-shouldered frame. Fortunately, dro-vine was surprisingly elastic, especially under intense pressure. Nevertheless, Todget nearly lost consciousness as he slammed into the final floor and bounced off it again.

He was in agony. Not so much from the fall, for his frame was built for punishment, but from the burns. The burns were intense and had eaten away his flesh, despite the fire retardant gel and clothing. And unfortunately, it was in the places he had been burned the least that he felt the most pain. His third-degree burns—the worst kind—did not hurt because where the skin had been completely incinerated, there were no nerves—nothing to tell him he was in pain. He rose from the floor, ripped off his burning cloak, and then, bloodied and smoldering, ran.

It took Jacob a long time to find Todget, nearly six seconds. By that time, Todget had almost made it to the end of the hallway where, just as he reached for the door, he felt his legs go numb and his eyes darkened for a moment. When he came to, only a moment later, he was on the ground, unable to move, his eyes frozen open and his bladder emptying.

Although there were several dro-vine tissue walls between Jacob and Todget, Jacob's short-range sensors confirmed the creature moving rapidly down the hall was, with a probability of over 98.6%, his target. Jacob could not confirm this with a visual ID, but the speed of the suspect (which was more rapid than any human), along with the massive body type and the shape of the object he carried (probably a modern weapon), gave Jacob probable cause to fire the stun pulse. The pulse, strong enough to temporarily paralyze but not kill, penetrated through the intervening walls, knocking the suspect flat. Jacob wanted to be absolutely certain that he could interrogate this one. The weapon he carried and his unusual method of escape was worth further study.

When apprehending a dangerous suspect, the usual protocol for an angel was to first paralyze the suspect, monitor from a distance for some time, and then move in slowly. Jacob did not follow this protocol, however, having too much to do. First, he needed to secure the demon. Next, he needed to extinguish the series of devastating fires that threatened to consume the mound. Finally, there was the task of apprehending the woman who had called out a warning to this demon.

Jacob assumed the first task of securing the prisoner was nearly complete as he rapidly sliced through the walls toward the paralyzed suspect. What the angel did not know was that the BB gun was waiting for him. The gun, a new design, had sensors of its own, sensors that detected other sensors, specifically the shortest of the electromagnetic pulses used by angels to see their world. And as the weapon "saw" its enemy close in, it injected all the contents of all three of its canisters into the firing chamber. For a millisecond, it sucked oxygen into the firing chamber to fuel the reaction and then clamped down on all the valves, allowing the pressure to increase until—in a terrific explosion of fiery, superheated shards—it obliterated itself, Todget, and everything else around it. The angel, had he been capable of fear and surprise, would have been full of both.

CHAPTER 12

Why are products not allowed to exceed a DNA similarity with humans above 96.3%? Because anything above that threshold is no longer judged a product; rather, it is human. The percentage of 96.3 is not arbitrary. It is the approximate similarity between nature's closest relative of humans—chimpanzees. I suppose the reasoning is that, historically, if chimpanzees were not considered human, then neither would a product having a DNA signature deviating at least as much as a chimp. Keep this number in mind. Personally, I shoot for no closer than 95% similarity in the products I design. You know, to give yourself some breathing room.

—Excerpt from "Musings of an Immortal," by Dr. Stoleff Monsa

Having shouted her warning to Todget, there was nothing more Lily could do but run. As she and Todget had discussed before, their hunters were numerous and formidable. To fight them was a fool's errand, a last resort. Just as she began her sprint, there was a loud boom followed by a low rumbling roar as though lightning had struck dangerously close.

The human she had just met—the one who talked about spankers, angels, and demons—was yelling at her. "Stop! Stop!" he shouted. "Where are you going?"

She glanced back over her shoulder and was alarmed to see the human and his cat-machine running after her. It was no matter. Like every human, he was slow and she would soon lose him. Still, she did not like the attention. He might call upon other, more effective pursuers.

"Stop! Let me help!" she heard him cry beseechingly.

At first she planned on pacing herself somewhat. She knew she would need to be on foot for a while and so did not wish to push her long, powerful legs to their limits. However, this human had to be lost immediately, prompting her to open up into a full sprint. It was shortly after she had turned up the speed when the human's cat became a problem. The furry, black quadruped machine was far faster than its master and quickly closed in on her, at which point the cursed thing began running underneath her legs as though to trip her.

Lily soon realized she could not effectively escape with this automaton dogging her, so she slowed down and waited for her opportunity. The machine was fast, but not smart enough to anticipate Lily's well-placed kick. Despite the fear of breaking her foot, Lily put all her formidable strength behind the blow. She was relieved to find the impact soft, as though striking spongy flesh, as her foot connected with the machine's side. The force of her kick sent the cat through the air, but Lily did not look to see where it landed. Instead, she kept running. But certainly, the cat would recover and be on her again in a flash, or the man would call for aid. She decided that she needed to take the offensive. And so as she rounded a small mound which, although small, was thickly festooned with flowers and bulbous shrubbery, she hid and waited for a few long seconds for the man's arrival.

_____

Flip, this girl is fast! D_Light thought. He fancied himself fast. He had trained hard and had his share of engineering in his ancestry that gave him an edge in a foot race. Swiftness, after all, was more likely to save one's life during Rule Seven than fighting ability. But this girl was off-the-charts fast! Clods of grass and soft soil ripped up and were flung behind her with every stride.

As D_Light rounded the mound, he was surprised to see that the girl was nowhere in sight since the path ahead was straight and stretched on for quite a distance. He'd barely had time to contemplate the girl's whereabouts when he heard a sudden rush behind him, but it was too late. He felt a hard kick and one of his legs was swept back underneath him, sending him face down on the ground. The girl was on his back and he felt a cold, pointed object pressing into the flesh of his neck. His head was turned, his cheek pressed firmly into the grass. In his peripheral vision he could just make out the glint of the blade.

Ownage^{TM}*! D's getting spanked by the hippie!* TermaMix texted.

With a thought, D_Light turned off the feed entirely. It would piss them off, but he wasn't going to let his family watch this in real time. He could resolve the bet later...that is, if he survived.

He spat out his words as fast as he could. "Don't! You won't make it! I'll help you! Listen to me!" Gasping for breath, he sucked in a mouthful of lush grass.

Smorgeous, who had since recovered from the kick, trotted up to them, his stride uncertain. Lily's face was flushed and her eyes were wide. She shot an upward glance at the machine, at which point he stopped advancing and sat back on his haunches as though entering feline meditation. She straddled D_Light and bent down over him, close, her legs gripping him tightly—more tightly than seemed possible by her toned but feminine legs.

From D_Light's vantage point, he could not tell if anyone could see them. Even if one of the spankers in the vicinity was not jacked in, he or she would probably just assume that the two of them were actively engaged in a spanker game—perhaps a social networking game with a sadomasochistic bent.

He could call for his companions, Lyra, Djoser, Amanda, perhaps even Brian, but they would certainly not reach him in time. He cursed himself for being so easily duped by this girl who, only moments before, had seemed so clueless. He relaxed as best he could to show her he meant no harm. She was a demon—he was sure of it—and as such, she probably had nothing to lose by plunging that blade down into his throat. He had to convince her otherwise, and he needed to do it fast.

"I will help you, I swear it." His voice was softer now and muffled, distorted by the fact that his cheek was being crushed into the soft dro-vine grass.

Lily tightened her grip with her legs, pressed her lips violently against D_Light's ear, and growled, "You did not help Todget." The girl was breathing hard, perhaps on the verge of panic, D_Light thought. But there was a steeliness in her tone that told him to speak plainly and as truthfully as possible.

"I was sent here to find him. I had no choice," he stammered. "But not you. I know how to get you out of here, if you'll let me help you."

"Help me? You must really think I'm a fool. Now you're the one who needs help." She bit her lip hard and pushed the tip of her blade harder against his neck. Her hands trembled.

"Wait!" D_Light begged. "You've got to trust me."

"Trust you? I have no reason to trust you!" she shouted. D_Light felt her cutting him.

D_Light collected himself as best he could and spit out his words into the grass like a stream of water. "I don't want to die! Let's make a deal. I help you escape, and you let me go. Without me, they *will* catch you!"

There was a long silence that D_Light could not interpret, an eerie quiet that he felt compelled to fill with additional rushed pleadings. "Listen, you have to blend in. You can't get away by running. They'll be looking for runners, and you can't outrun an angel. They have satellites. They could be watching you now! I know how they do things. I swear, I can help you!"

Suddenly, D_Light felt her weight lift from him and the girl was on her feet. "Don't bother me with your machine or I'll kill you," she said flatly as she pointed to his familiar. D_Light quickly sat up and instinctively clutched his neck where the blade had been only a moment before. He felt the wet of his blood, but the wound did not seem deep.

The woman took a quick look around, including in the air, and then turned as though to resume running. D_Light got to his feet quickly and said loudly but calmly, "Don't, you need to follow me."

With this, she suddenly stopped and faced him. Her eyes locked on his as though measuring him. "Stag, I let you go and yet you still persist?"

"I never lie to a pretty girl," D_Light said with the best smile he could muster. "I said I'd help you if you let me live, and I am."

He thought about his throwing discs. She was only about five meters away, easily within range. She had no armor on, so he knew he could have two discs in her before she could get to him with that knife. He knew this, but he did not move. *There is a much better opportunity here—to match wits with the Divine Authority itself! This would be a contest to remember...* It was madness of course, but in the past it had always been his craziest ideas that led to the biggest payoffs.

Lily stared into the eyes of the strange human. She was confused. Seconds before, she had been a motion away from killing him, and yet he wanted to *prolong* their engagement, indeed, even help her escape? And for what? Because of a pledge he had just made under duress? She was not aware of humans being particularly duty-bound. And if he had honor, was he not bound to his own kind?

On the other hand, she knew about the technologies of the ones who hunted her, or at least Todget had whispered of these things many times. He spoke of their speed, their invulnerability, and their cunning. And he spoke of their eyes—eyes everywhere, even in the darkness of space above. She would be a fool to trust any human, and yet this was their world. This man was most likely lying, but what were her chances alone?

"The angel certainly heard you yell out for your friend. It will come for you. Follow me now!"

She ran at him with sudden ferocity. His eyes widened in surprise, and he took a step back, putting his palm up as though to calm her, as though suggesting peace.

Her knife still drawn, Lily stopped less than a meter from him. *He is either very brave or an imbecile,* she thought. But she supposed that if he wanted her caught he would have just let her run and then called upon one of those "angels" to take care of her. None of this made sense. She sheathed her knife in the fold of her cloak.

D_Light smiled genuinely and bowed. "Let's get inside fast! They can see you when you're outside." He then jogged off and waved for her to follow.

He led her to the first mound entrance he could find. As usual, he could not get a map of the mound area he was in. Nanosites coated every surface area within the mound, so technically a map could be drawn using software. However, this was not an option here thanks to local spanker-imposed mapping restrictions.

Once inside a hall tube, D_Light asked, "Okay, do you have a chip?"

She looked at him quizzically.

"An MIC—you know, a mind interface chip? Back here?" D_Light tapped the back of his head.

Lily nodded slowly.

A demon with a chip? Interesting, D_Light thought. This was a stroke of luck. D_Light wanted to log her into a spanker game, but without an MIC he would have had to make Smorgeous attempt to beam sensory input directly into her eyes and ears, essentially turning the familiar into primitive virtual reality hardware. It was much better for a computer like Smorgeous to work though an MIC, a chip that was properly hooked up to the subject's nervous system.

"Great, open a blink channel to me now," he said.

Master, subject Cave_Girl_123432 has opened a port, Smorgeous informed him.

Connect to her, D_Light commanded.

D_Light heard a ping as he connected to her profile. He skipped her introduction. Maybe he would have time to watch it later.

"Okay, Cave Girl," he said, suppressing a smile. "I'm going to log us both into a spank game. Just follow me and try to stay alive." D_Light would have preferred to communicate telepathically, but he was uncertain of her chip's capabilities.

"Please, call me Lily," she said. It was not her real name anyway, and although she thought "Cave Girl" was amusing at the time she filled out her profile, she did not want this human calling her by that name.

"I'm *Deelight,*" he said with a roguish grin. Lily gave him a strange look but said nothing in return.

Another prolonged ring echoed in D_Light's mind as he began to slide gently into NeverWorld. As usual, his sight momentarily went dark. Then the darkness was replaced by blurs of objects that quickly came into focus. The ringing sound faded, giving way to the game's audio.

Now inside the game, the hall tube was transformed. The walls were no longer covered with the swirl-patterned exoskeleton of drovine. Instead, it was now a wet rock passageway. It would have been pitch-black here if it were not for the fact that Ascara—the name of the witch character D_Light chose to play—carried a wand with a magical light emanating from the tip. The only sounds were those of water dripping on rock.

Lily stood a few meters away. She wore brightly polished armor, fitted perfectly to her body's curves. As was typical in these games, her breasts were exaggerated in size, made even more pronounced by the armor. It was an unspoken rule in visual game design to make women look the way men wanted to see them.

The warrior that Lily was playing was a randomly generated guest character named Boobooma of Sanadas, which, for whatever reason, was the first thing that jumped into D_Light's head as he initiated the guest account. D_Light created a guest account for Lily because she did not have a game account of her own. Trial-basis guest accounts were allowed in NeverWorld because it was a good way to introduce new customers to the game and, from the perspective of the Seriah family that ran NeverWorld, lure new subscribers.

Lily blinked at the bright light emanating from D_Light's wand. He whispered a curt command to the wand to dim the light. He did not want to attract any unwanted attention just yet. As the light dimmed, allowing her to see clearly, she focused on D_Light's face, and her eyes widened.

"Who?" She looked at him with a start and then turned all around like one desperately searching.

If D_Light had not been in such a hurry, he would have relished this moment with the NeverWorld n00b, perhaps messed with her mind, or at least teased her a bit. Unfortunately, there was no time. *Soul, she's such an adorable n00blet, though*, he couldn't help thinking with a chuckle.

"My lady, it is I, the man you made a fool of earlier. Thou art a damsel in distress, but fear not, for I..."

It was evident from Lily's stare that telling her not be afraid in fantaspeech was having the opposite effect. D_Light decided to drop that part of NeverWorld role-playing for now. He would just have to endure the point penalties.

"Look, it's me, okay? I'm D_Light, the guy who's helping you," D_Light whispered urgently.

"You look like a woman...and you sound like one." She looked at him hard as her jaw clenched.

D_Light would have picked his male wizard character, Hyge-lac, to make things simpler, but that character had gotten his throat ripped out by a hellhound earlier.

"You're in the game, remember?" D_Light asked. "Everything looks different. Everything is going to sound different too. Soul, you might even smell things that aren't there. Look, I'm the guy who ran after you and then you stuck a knife halfway into my throat." He pointed at his now long, sexy neck. "I'm not really a woman; it's only an illusion."

Lily was breathing hard, almost panting. Her head shot around in all directions. She looked like she was going to bolt.

D_Light put out his hand, now a smaller, more feminine version of his own, in a gesture that he hoped would calm her. *Damn, I should have warned her that I would look different.* D_Light rarely considered what he looked like in the game, as it usually made little difference in typical play. He tried to reassure her. "Everything is fine. You're doing great. Just take a moment to look around." Sounding even more effeminate than he'd like, D_Light felt self-conscious of his voice. He remembered how it had taken him hours to choose that voice when he first created this witch. He usually played women characters because he tended to get more aid and cooperation from other players who, at least in NeverWorld, tended to be men. As an added bonus, whenever he chanced to look in the mirror or into a reflective pool, the scenery was nice.

Lily watched him as he spoke. Her face was rendered just like her real face. This was the default. She closed her eyes for a moment and then opened them again. She grinned weakly and said, "I think you look better here."

D_Light smiled back, relieved that she was now adjusting. "Yeah, people tend to. Okay, I'm going to have to cast some spells now. They're not real, just part of the game. These will help protect us."

"Protect us from what?" Lily peered back over her shoulder.

"Just from the stuff in the game. You know, monsters and such. They can't hurt you in real life, but if you die in the game, you get kicked out for a while, and we don't want that. We want to blend in, remember? And the best way to do that is to stay in the game."

He wondered if, perhaps, he should have jacked her into a game with less violence and horror elements than NeverWorld. Maybe a social networking game like Grokstania would have been a better introduction to spanker games. In such a game they could walk around bowing, complimenting, flirting, or otherwise trying to make friends and influence people in a palace, garden, or some other visually rich and romantic setting. But D_Light was sure Grokstania was not popular in this spanker ghetto, and they needed to follow the crowd. Plus, in order to escape, he planned to do a lot of running. Grockstania was a game of subtlety and witty banter, not a game of hell-bent sprinting.

D_Light spent about a third of his manna on protection spells. He could have gone invisible like he had done earlier, but he decided against it. To blend in, they needed to appear to be like any other spanker, and most spankers fought monsters—they didn't try to avoid them. You got more points and treasure that way. Besides, they couldn't sneak around very well with this n00b clanking about in that armor.

D_Light began making his incantations. Lily remained quiet as a mouse. He was grateful that the girl seemed to know when to shut up. She did, however, look at him oddly during his spell castings, but he could hardly blame her for that.

Done with his spells, D_Light turned to Lily to give instructions. "Okay, try to stay behind me as much as you can, but don't run unless I run. Stay close. Oh, and if you have to, go ahead and swing that." D_Light pointed at the long sword in the sheath hanging from her belt. Lily took the sword out and gave it a good swing.

D_Light flinched. "Uh, yeah, like that. But don't swing so close to me, right?" Lily responded by turning her back to him and swinging some more.

"Um, sure, you can cover my back, okay?" D_Light was mildly surprised she took to the virtual sword so quickly since the touch sensory input for spank games was not very advanced. No doubt she could feel only the slightest weight and pressure on her hand as she gripped the weapon.

"You can practice as we go," D_Light said. He then took a deep breath and trotted off down the dark, dank hallway.

CHAPTER 13

Jacob's sensors picked up the unusual heat signature right before the BB gun exploded. This warning, despite being only a fraction of a second before the event, gave Jacob enough time to evade much of the blast. Nevertheless, he was engulfed in superheated flames and sprayed with a fine sheet of molten metal that fused into his nanofiber-constructed shell.

Many of his systems were knocked out. Of course, his most important ones were redundant, particularly his sensory and communication systems. Jacob reallocated his available power to his scanners to take a good "look" at the scene and, upon taking this final snapshot, uploaded the data to a secure location in the Cloud.

After completing these momentary tasks, he shut down. Somewhere hardwired on a chip at the center of his body, sheathed in layers of additional armor, was his most primitive programming. It was here that his emergency shutoff routine was housed. An angel that had withstood massive injury but was still operational was a potential liability, an unknown quantity. Such a complex machine was difficult enough to test when it was fully operational, much less when it was damaged. A compromised angel that incorrectly processed input could be a lethal instrument, and so its designers had enough foresight to give their creation less than a second of life, enough time to "phone home," before it went to sleep.

Bitch, we would be so made, stompin' into Rudy's with matching Moon Booties™! Katria sent the blink with as much enthusiasm as she could summon.

I dunno, I think we might look like a couple of n00blet showoffs. Example, I watched this archive of one fool wearing those booties that thought he was the meow, but ended up pinging his brother in the head as he jumped over 'im, OffDaLeash responded.

Katria did not bother to assimilate the archive. She was well aware of the dangers of using the gravity-defying boots. In her own experience of using them, she had sprained her ankle several times already and nearly brained herself when she nicked the ceiling in her apartment. All of that was beside the point. If she could convince OffDaLeash, her sister and longtime friend, to buy a pair, she would get herself a handsome shot of points from OwnYoAss™.

Katria decided to drop it. She knew OffDaLeash hated it when she tried to milk her. She was old-fashioned that way. Any scene player knew that a conversation could be more than just fun; it could be profitable. *Yeah, I guess Moon Booties™ can freak some players,* she replied. *Next time you're at my pad you can try 'em on though. Speaking of, it's been a while since we hung. What are you playing tonight?*

Oh, I have to patch up some hard feelings between a few locals, but then I was thinking of taking a real break, said OffDaLeash.

Who? asked Katria.

Who what?

Who all needs to kiss up? Anyone interesting? Katria asked.

You know I'm not at liberty to say. OffDaLeash's thought signature was amused, but Katria knew her sister was not kidding.

OffDaLeash practically specialized in mediator games, which was a good choice in a family as competitive and yet interdependent as theirs. Pretty much any family, even the hippie ones, always generated a good supply of emotional flare-ups and long-held grudges.

Issues like that were often not handled well by computer agents; rather, they required a human touch. OffDaLeash had that down since she could be as practical and objective as AI, but she also brought the empathy and social graces needed for a good long-term outcome. And the points! When it came to rev time, her clients showered her with them. Even when they remained pissed off at each other, which was most of the time, they did not take it out on her.

As such, Katria did not blame her longtime friend for refusing to spill on her clients. After all, her reputation was part and parcel of her livelihood. Still, she was no fun when Katria was in the mood for some good smack talk.

You need to play something that we can at least gab about, Katria said, followed with a Whinicon™ featuring a bawling baby in an old-fashioned diaper.

You should talk, Sis! OffDaLeash flashed back. *You with your high-security shenanigans. When's the last time you talked about your grind?*

True, Katria admitted. *I guess neither of us is much in a conversation. Ya know, since we can't talk about what we do, maybe we should just make stuff up.*

Sure, why don't you start by telling me if you and Jerkle are fast-tracking, or what? OffDaLeash sent this with a howling, humping puppy emoticon.

His name is Dirk! And as far as our intimacy status, I'll say— Katria dropped the blink with her friend, midsentence. There was some serious shit going down in her game.

The angel she had been monitoring, the one she simply referred to as "the Tool," had a live one. Some crazy demon was burning down an apartment mound with some kind of flamethrower! And no sooner had she realized this than the demon blew himself up, taking down the angel with him. *It's a shit storm!* she thought. The impact of the blast was nothing special, but the heat signatures that streamed in before the angel shut down were way higher than typical demon weaponry.

Rhemus sent her a blink. *Flip! The Tool just got melted!* Rhemus was a game ally of Katria's. They both were into law enforcement games and typically played closely together.

Katria could barely respond. Despite what the data was feeding her, she could not believe it. It was inconceivable. No angel she had ever monitored had gone down. It was time for the two of them to get to work.

Looks like the demon's completely gone, Katria sent.

No way there's anything left of him. Not enough brain to get any intel, Rhemus replied.

The girl—the one screaming to warn him—she's our intel! Katria sent the message along with a two-second clip from a dance song to emphasize her point.

Right, the Tool was going to apprehend her, but he sure as hell isn't going to now. I'll scramble a sky eye on the area, Rhemus said.

It was standard protocol when hunting someone outdoors to immediately get a satellite on the area.

Katria cursed herself for not being more vigilant in her monitoring. It had seemed like a routine mission. The target was pretty low level, and there was a positive ID on him when entering his apartment. An angel was overkill for such a job, but since one was available nearby, it was deployed.

Missions like that never really required human help. The onboard AI of an angel was top-tier and therefore far faster and more reliable than a human when it came to rote work like this. Humans were occasionally useful for adding an assist here or there, but for the most part, they just watched the show. Even for more complex missions it was hard to be of much help to a fully decked-out angel. Nevertheless, when Katria was on top of her game, she could get in a contribution or two. And working with premium Authority agents like angels was high-stakes grinding. Any help you gave was big points, which kept her logging in. Besides, it had taken her a long time to get the security clearances required to play these types of games, so she felt invested.

But this had seemed like a cakewalk, so she had felt free to shoot the breeze with OffDaLeash while she casually monitored. Even when that bitch started raising the alarm with her "Todget, run!" routine, Katria didn't bother to end the blink with her friend. A couple of ghetto demons could not stand a chance against an angel, or so she had thought six seconds ago.

Now the unthinkable had happened, and Katria was elated— one demon out and one little bitch still on the run, but no angel to catch her. That left Katria, Rhemus, and anyone else who was willing and able to log into the game and finish the job—something they never got to do. DNA samples that the Tool found in the apartment shortly before he got fried confirmed the runner's identity. As was protocol, Katria sent a request to the Authority, asking to upgrade the priority of the demon girl. Within a second the Authority sent back confirmation upgrading her from low priority to medium; the status change was only because, in light of recent events, the girl might know something useful, not because she was estimated to be dangerous.

This rating was good for Katria. It meant that the stakes of the game just went up, and with it, potentially the reward. However, the priority was not so high that another angel would step in and relegate her back to the sidelines. Fortunately for Katria, the Authority was very reticent about spreading their top resources too thin.

Okay, Rhemus, you handle the air surveillance. I'll see if there are any nearby sniffers I can snag, Katria ordered.

Katria's familiar, a black Labrador puppy she called Snazz, was scanning for the closest sniffer bots available. Sniffers were Frisbee-sized robots used to ID suspects and, if necessary, detain them. Snazz found two bots within a fifty-mile radius and six more within two hundred miles.

Katria decided to rent all the available bots. It would be expensive at ten thousand points each per hour, but she figured she would need them. This demon had a head start, and it was running in a highly populated field. There were bound to be a ton of suspects to filter through.

Nothing ventured, nothing gained, she told herself.

It would be a few minutes before her sniffers got to the scene, so she decided to take some time to do analysis. She thought about leasing some hard-core AI for the job, but she decided that would be too expensive. Every player had an expense cap (which depended on the game) to keep a single rich player from dominating every time. Having caps in place encouraged more thoughtful use of resources versus brute-force methods for solving problems, which tended to strain infrastructure. Katria had already burned well into her cap by renting eight sniffers.

She messaged her familiar. *It's going to be just you and me, Snazz.* The dog cocked his head adoringly and got to work analyzing the data the Tool had uploaded before shutting down.

Rhemus sent another blink. *I got an eye on the area. No surprise our girl is no longer in her last estimated location. By the way, there's some heavy cloud cover. Grokking suspects is going to be a little slow.*

Satellites could still be used in heavy cloud cover, but their effective sight radius decreased due to the need of focusing in more for greater penetration.

Get another satellite then, Katria responded.

Soul, that's gonna tax, Rhemus whined over the blink.

We'll get paid. We underestimated the first demon. Let's not make the same mistake on this bitch, Katria shot back.

Okay, I'll work it out. Rhemus had learned by now to trust Katria's instincts, which was the main reason Katria continued to play with him over the years.

Snazz returned with an analysis of the data. Katria skimmed it and highlighted a few points she found interesting:

- Spanker ghetto (from Cloud statistics)
- The two demons were living together (DNA traces found on the scene)
- Voice of demon was likely female and in distress (voice analysis done by the angel)

Despite the fact that satellites and sniffers would arrive soon, there were thousands of potential suspects in the search radius, so Katria knew she needed to narrow down her suspect list. Of course, she would start with the most obvious, a direct match. That would be what the satellites would look for first, but it was difficult to get a positive ID from overhead. If that did not work, then they would look for female runners in the radial zone in which the demon could theoretically be. The demon already had over a minute head start and, according to her profile, was a very swift runner. This would make for a rather large search area.

I have another sat online, Rhemus reported. *How about those sniffers?*

The first one will be here in 'bout twenty secs, Katria replied. *Your sats catch any candidates?*

A couple of running girls, but nothing definite. Body type on all of 'em seem a little off.

Probably just spankers, Katria responded. *But we should check them anyway. Our girl might have customized.*

The term "customized" referred to the common practice of demons changing their appearance using various illegal means, such as gene therapy or old-fashioned plastic surgery.

It took less than a minute for the first sniffer that arrived to check the candidates, which all came back negative. Katria scowled and blinked a message to Rhemus. *Have sats feed my sniffers all the women in the area, starting with the ones farthest out in the search zone. She might not be running; she might be smarter than that.*

Rhemus pinged confirmation.

As the first sniffer widened its search to include all women, the next sniffer arrived, to which she assigned the task of picking up the girl's trail from her estimated last location.

You can either run or you can hide, Katria thought. *If you run, we'll see you run and get you faster. If you hide, we'll sniff you out and find you later.*

But there was a third option, one employed by the more clever demons she had hunted. The demon could be trying to blend in. *Perhaps this one thinks she can simply walk away,* Katria mused.

Only minutes later Katria started having doubts, discovering that all the women came back negative.

Damn, maybe our demon isn't a woman. Maybe it's a man who used a voice disrupter. Katria felt her stomach wrench as the thought came to her. *No, the DNA in the apartment could not lie. The demon is female. But maybe she's disguised, using an illusionary veil or something.*

Yeah, I already thought of that, Rhemus chimed in. Katria was startled, as she had not realized she was broadcasting her thoughts through the blink. *The sats aren't just watching for chicks. I'm tagging anyone hauling ass out of the area.*

What if she's disguised and just walks out? Katria countered.

Yeah, that would suck, Rhemus replied. *We need to sniff everyone who leaves. Do you have the bots for that?*

Katria inspected the foot traffic patterns. Most people were leaving the area using designated paths, but some went off trail.

Looks like I've got enough to handle it, Katria sent. *You just have the sats mark 'em, and the sniffers will check 'em.*

There was a brief pause and then Katria continued. *Anyway, my bet is the bitch isn't on the surface. She's probably holed up in one of those mounds—that's what rats do.*

Rats have tunnels, Rhemus sent. *You see on the map?*

Rhemus displayed the subterranean map of the ghetto. This particular map was not public for some reason, but law enforcement spankers like Rhemus and Katria had access. Wherever there were nanosites, software could map surfaces. All SkinWare maps were accessible to law enforcement with a permit, an electronic permit that took Rhemus only a few seconds to request and obtain.

Katria said, *I'm seeing three subterranean tunnels out of the ghetto. Since we don't have sats to help out under there, I'm going to have to assign a bot to guard each tunnel. Damn!*

Yeah, it's going to cost you some resources, but securing the perimeter is priority one. Rhemus stated the obvious.

Just then, Katria got a ping that the scent trail had been found. *Finally, some good news,* she thought.

Now that the trail was picked up and the exits secured, Katria knew the noose was tightening. In less than a minute, she learned that the demon had indeed gone into one of the mounds. That explained why the satellites had not found her. *No problem,* she thought. *The underground exits are covered.*

Still, Katria was not comfortable just sitting back and watching events unfold. Because it was still early in the morning, there was not a lot of traffic on the surface, and so only three bots were busy up top. Three more bots were covering the underground exits, which left two more with nothing to do. All this hardware was costing her points by the second, and there was no benefit in sending the idle ones home since she had already paid for the minimum rental and still had over fifteen minutes left on them. She needed to find the demon sooner rather than later if she was going to come out ahead in this game.

Katria asked herself, *How do I find the demon quickly if she's hiding?*

A demon inside a mound could not be observed as easily as one outside. Privacy rules prohibited nanosites—the invisibly small chips used by SkinWare—to be equipped with observation instruments such as cameras; rather, they were designed to simply announce themselves, to be observed, but not to observe back. Outside one's home was public domain, so satellites could be used on evildoers, but indoor areas were a different matter.

Katria had obtained a search permit for the mounds and therefore could have her extra sniffers check everyone systematically, but that was woefully inefficient, even for machines as fast as these. The tunnels and chambers of the apartment mounds of Anywhere were extensive, to say the least. Worse yet, many of the chambers and tunnels were sealed by doors, hatches, or more exotic impediments, slowing down the sniffers considerably. When a flying Frisbee-shaped sniffer encountered such a portal, usually the most expedient way past was to slice a small slit in the surrounding dro-vine and slip through. If this was not feasible (for example, in classic buildings that did not use dro-vine), the sniffer would extend a set of mechanical arms and picks out from its smooth, shiny hull, but sniffers were not adept at manipulating knobs, handles, and locks designed for human use.

All these factors added up to the fact that the simpleminded tactic of systematically sniffing every resident in Anywhere would be disastrously slow and therefore expensive. Katria decided she needed to filter candidates somehow.

She knew the apartment mound complex was primarily populated with gamers. Certainly the demon was not a gamer since Katria had never heard of such a thing. That single fact separated their demon from just about everyone else in the area.

Rhemus had already obtained a permit to tap into SkinWare, so Katria decided to run a query on all the active games in Anywhere, looking for anyone who was a ghost to all games—that is, a person not logged into any game. *Certainly our demon will fall into this category,* thought Katria.

Her familiar connected to the games MyLife, Grokstania, Samurai on Top, Lust Bunnies, NeverWorld, Golden Age, Treasure Island, Mission Flipp'n Ridiculous, and Covert Ops V. Only 23.6% of the population were hits, but that was still 668 people! However, when she narrowed it down to the region to which the sniffer had tracked the demon, it was less than two hundred. Katria immediately dispatched her two idle sniffers to check them.

CHAPTER 14

An optimized economy relies on proper incentives—incentives for innovation, incentives against corruption, incentives to share knowledge rather than hoard it, incentives for hard work, incentives to find what you love and to do it every day! The Game, the divinely inspired fabric under which players live and the bounty of the universe is being realized, bequeaths these incentives to us.

—Excerpt from "Introducing the Game," as it appears in the Game help documentation

---

Deep under the rotting trees of Meredith Forest, within the slime-covered tunnels of the Nardar catacombs, D_Light moved quickly while Lily trailed behind him like a kitten chasing a string. D_Light was multitasking as best he could. It wasn't easy getting directions in the catacombs while simultaneously keeping the nasties at bay. He had already spent more manna than he wanted by frying a couple of corrupted elves they had come across in play.

A hustler opened a blink with D_Light. *The Nardar catacombs, yeah, I've been there before…eh, a while back.*

D_Light was not impressed with the thought tone of the hustler. Given the generous amount of points D_Light was auctioning off for a guide to the apartment mounds, he expected top quality. He replied unceremoniously, *Okay, well I want out of here fast, so there'll be a bonus in it if you can keep sharp.*

The hustler, who went simply by "Bone," asked, *Right, so where you at?*

I don't know. That's why I need you, replied an irritated D_Light.

D_Light stopped suddenly in his tracks, trying to get his bearings. Lily, who had thus far proven to be an excellent shadow, nearly bumped into him and then looked at him with dagger eyes. She wasn't privy to the conversation taking place in his head, perhaps making her unsympathetic to his thoughtless movements.

This reminded D_Light to throw a word or two of praise and encouragement at his guest, which he thought was appropriate; then again, he wasn't sure. "Hey, nice job, by the way," he whispered over his shoulder. "I know this is kind of crazy and uh…" D_Light thought about patting her on the arm as a comforting gesture; he raised his hand to do so, but then decided against it. His arm fell back to his side. He did not really know what to expect from a towheaded demon. He did remember her knife though, so instead of attempting any physical affection, he smiled stupidly while nodding and then promptly turned forward again.

The witch and the warrior woman were standing in a large hall lined on both sides by statues. The pale limestone skin of the statues was blotched with dark stains. D_Light panned his eyes slowly over them and had Smorgeous upload the video to the hustler. He took his time. He chose to send the video in high definition even though it would take a little longer to upload. He wanted Bone to get a really good look.

Oh yeah, I know where you're at, I think, blinked Bone. *Hey, pan back to your left a bit. Check that chick on the end o' the hall. Yeah, that chick, the one with the big ol' titties. Yeah, I know that one.*

The hustler appeared to be referring to the statue of a mythical female creature. She had deer legs bent as though ready to spring. Her upper body was that of a nude human female. Vestiges of what were once long bird wings extended out only as jagged stone stubs from her back.

There was a moment of silence followed by another blink from Bone. *All right, I'm on it. Just let me bring up some of my old maps.*

Bone sounded a bit more confident now, but D_Light was not convinced. Unfortunately, he didn't have much choice but to give this guide a shot. None of these catacombs were auto-mapped; that would defeat the allure of the game. D_Light had been wandering these apartment mounds for hours and had a pretty impressive map of his own, but since he had not yet mapped out this quadrant of the ghetto, he was already lost. He didn't dare go back outside to get back to familiar territory, either. There they would be fully exposed to the satellites.

"Keep an eye out," D_Light whispered over to Lily.

He could see that his remark was completely unnecessary. She looked like a frightened little rabbit. Of course, that was no surprise. The catacombs were skinned to look absolutely frightful. The corrupted living walls quivered and excreted a thick, slow moving, bloody slime. Even the statues were bleeding. The woman statue before him had tears of blood running down her blotched and stained cheeks, progressing downward from her nipples to her groin. These were common thematic tricks designed to hammer home a sense that you were indeed in a place of evil and in imminent danger. D_Light wished he could log them both out for a short while—just long enough to put the n00b at ease—but that would be a poor choice. For one thing, it would waste precious time. For another, her genuine fear was bound to make her react more realistically. If she was going to blend in, she could not just casually saunter about like a non-player.

Bone blinked again. *Okay, now I know where you're at. I'm gonna upload a map that'll help.*

Presently, a map showing a way out appeared in D_Light's mind. It displayed exactly one route that started in the statue hallway where he was currently located and led to one of the tunnels that exited this spanker ghetto. Because of the hive-like interconnectedness of the apartment mounds, there were obviously many other routes to the exit. However, spankers jealously guarded their maps and rarely gave more information than was required.

Using the map and Smorgeous's onboard compass, D_Light was able to follow the directions fairly well. He darted down this hallway and that. He mostly tried to avoid trouble, but would occasionally attack a nasty if it seemed like easy pickings. After all, it would help keep up the appearance that he was truly gaming. At one point they passed a large party of fellow spankers, maybe ten or so—several fighters, a few priests, even two wizards. They eyed D_Light and Lily carefully until D_Light put up the hand signal for his guild. It was a good-aligned guild, which apparently satisfied them. They looked like they were heading into the thick of the catacombs, which was a pity since D_Light would have liked to hitch a ride with them.

Master, you have a call from Mother Lyra, Smorgeous messaged to D_Light.

D_Light, caught off guard, cursed. He had forgotten all about Lyra and the others, being so focused on the task at hand.

Hey, D, where you at? Lyra's mental signature sounded more curious than annoyed.

Down in the catacombs, er, I mean, down in one of the apartment mounds. D_Light was sending his thoughts with little buffering.

This made for faster communication, but it often resulted in tripping over his words.

Lyra replied, *Why are you down there? Making new friends?*

D_Light was startled by this, and he wondered if Lyra knew the truth. He quickly dismissed the thought. He had to be careful when blinking, as he might send something he didn't intend to reveal to others. He decided to send a response that was close to the truth. *I saw another demon, or I think it's one. I'm looking into it.*

Forget that, replied Lyra. *The angel nabbed the one we targeted up here. We only need one to satisfy the quest, you know. You need to get up here before we get the next quest. We all need to be ready to move out fast.*

Respectfully, Mother, please allow me to tag this demon, D_Light returned. *It's bound to be worth a generous bounty, and of course, I would be sharing that with my game-mates.*

There was a pause. No doubt Lyra was conferring with Djoser.

The mental silence was broken when Lyra messaged her reply. *Well, the next quest isn't in yet. Anything we can do to help?*

I could use a lot of help, D_Light thought, but he didn't send it. The others could not know that he was actually helping the demon escape. He couldn't take the chance of them tipping off the Authority.

Naw, but thanks, answered D_Light. *You showing up might spook her. Just let me handle it.*

All right, we'll just chill here, but if the next quest comes in before you wrap it up, you need to drop it. We don't have time for any side games.

With that, Lyra ended the blink. D_Light was glad she could take a hint. It was more than he could handle to synchronously keep track of the map, the conversation, his thoughts, and the nasties.

His previous research had revealed that there was always a pause between MetaGame quests. Usually, the next one came the following morning, but sometimes it was much sooner. He needed to stay on task.

D_Light resumed his blink with Bone. *Hey, Bone, you sure this map is legit? I'm running into a wall here—like, literally.* D_Light slid his hand against a smooth dro-vine wall, a sensation that belied the slimy, bleeding wall that NeverWorld skinned it as.

There was no response from Bone. *Damn n00b,* D_Light thought. *He must be sweating something in his own spank. Multithreading with me? He's definitely not getting extra props when it's time to do an eval.*

D_Light was about to close the blink and flame his so-called "guide" when Bone blinked in. *That map was solid when I made it. Dunno, according to the OwnYoAss Cloud Service, that ghetto you're in is high-morphing. If that's true, you might have to find a local to help you out. Or play it old-school.* Bone sent over an animated shrugging zebra to emphasize his bewilderment.

Indeed, Smorgeous had already warned D_Light that the dro-vine that made up these apartment mounds was a high-morphing variety, one that grew quickly. For this reason, he had already feared that any map more than a few weeks old would be obsolete. Discouraged, D_Light replied, *Yeah, okay, I'll improvise. Thanks.* D_Light terminated the blink with Bone and sent him a few complimentary points, a kind of "thanks anyway" tip. D_Light almost always did this, even for fairly poor service. You didn't want gamers thrashing your profile or, worse yet, to find yourself on a blacklist just because you were too stingy to throw a hustler a little something for his time.

Having no reliable map, D_Light decided it was time to go where the action was and snag himself a local guide. The first sign of said action was the high-pitched sound of metal clanging against metal, a sound that travelled far, serving as a signpost pointing out the nearest spankers. As they ran closer, he started making out the yells of the spankers and the snarling of the nasties. The anticipation always raised D_Light's pulse. He looked back at Lily, and despite the sounds of the brawl ahead, she appeared a bit more at ease now. She returned a look that hinted she was unimpressed with his escape plan so far, although she did not complain out loud. Just then, a particularly blood-curdling scream jolted out from ahead of them, and her apprehensive look returned.

D_Light slowed his pace. Although in a hurry, he did not want to find himself in some gory mess that resulted in his death and ejection from the game. There was a flickering light from around the corner ahead, probably from the lanterns the spankers were carrying. From what he understood, the nasties in this catacomb, known as "Salem's Corrupted," did not need light, as they could see in total darkness.

D_Light motioned to Lily to stay put. He then crouched down low, crept up to the corner, and peered around. This was definitely where the action was.

Before him was a large chamber with a dais that swept up to a long altar. Atop the altar was a statue of a tall, proud woman who wore a dress that swept out in all directions like an explosion, the skirt part interwoven with stone leaves and flowers. She cradled a delicately carved baby who, with wide eyes, stared up adoringly at his mother. The statue and altar below were rusty in color and bore dark smudges that, D_Light assumed, were the marks of years of sacrificial blood. The eyes of both mother and child were inlaid with large emeralds, bringing realism and beauty to an otherwise perverted depiction of motherhood.

All around the statue the corrupted and the spankers battled. There were over a dozen nasties and four players. Several of the corrupted had already fallen, but it was evident to D_Light that the good guys were hard-pressed.

There was a lot of virtual blood. The nasties flailed about dramatically as they got sliced by the warriors' blades or blasted by the sorcerers' lightning bolts. The spankers were having a devil of a time since the alarm had been sounded; nasties were making their way in from the various tunnels that intersected the large room.

D_Light feared that it would only be a matter of time before a set of nasties, attracted by the commotion of battle, came upon him from behind. Time to work fast. He slunk back completely out of sight from those inside the room and began his incantation. He spoke the words of the spell as quietly as he could, although he doubted very much that the combatants would hear him over the din anyway. He waved his arms in an intricate pattern, and as he finished, he cupped his hands together to create a small, hollow sphere. He shifted a thumb to allow himself to see inside his cupped hands. A tiny icicle had appeared.

D_Light blew into the improvised womb. With a few more arcane words and several additional breaths, the icicle grew and transformed into a cube, which melted into the shape of a mouse nearly too tiny to recognize. He continued to breathe life into the creature, and with every breath he knew his manna—his spell casting power—was diminishing. It was worth it. In fact, he was willing to pour a good deal of his strength into this spell. *One shot. This needs to work,* he thought.

Gradually, he opened his fingers to give the mouse room to grow as he peered around the corner again. One of the spankers, the wizard, had died since D_Light had last checked. The corpse was on the ground, and the player's ghost was standing over the body, throwing a silent tantrum. The rest of the party, now numbering three (a hulking barbarian-looking fellow, a stout battleaxe-wielding dwarf, and a mace-swinging cleric), stood back to back in a triangle, hacking, bashing, and stabbing for their lives.

D_Light decided this was about as good a time as any. He let the mouse go. Its tiny translucent body glowed with shimmering blue flame, and its portly belly dragged along the ground, leaving a thin trail of ice behind as it scurried toward the combatants. D_Light whispered arcane commands to the mouse under his breath, urging it to the left and the right until it had made its way under the nasties and right up to the foot of the gnarly bearded dwarf. D_Light did not dare to wait any longer. If the mouse were stepped on, the spell would end. He shouted out the final command word, and not a moment too soon. The dwarf looked down at the mouse, and his eyes widened with surprise. His thick lips curled into what was certainly going to be a curse, and he raised his foot up to squash the rodent. But before his foot came down, the mouse exploded with a terrific *crack!* Countless shards of ice eviscerated those nearby, and cold blue flames washed over them like a boulder crashing into a pond. Everyone, spankers and nasties alike, was struck down.

D_Light called for Lily, who was at his side so quickly he wondered if NeverWorld was playing tricks on his perception of time. The blue wave and the ice shards strewn about like shattered glass suddenly vanished in a torrent of steam. The sliced and stiff dead were lain out roughly in a circle around ground zero. All the nasties had fallen, as had the barbarian and the cleric. Only the dwarf moved. Now, two additional ghosts joined the first one, their heads swiveling around wildly as their mouths opened wide in quiet rage. D_Light was not surprised to see the dwarf still alive. Dwarf warriors were the definition of hardiness.

Reflexively, D_Light stepped out of the hallway and prepared to finish off the dwarf with a nicely placed lightning bolt, but then he remembered that the dwarf needed to live at least for a little while longer. The dwarf raised his ax slightly while crouching, preparing to charge.

"Don't move, good dwarf, or surely I will finish you!" D_Light rallied his most commanding voice. The dwarf raised his ax higher but did not move his feet.

D_Light motioned for Lily to step out. "You are outnumbered, and we are fresh. You cannot possibly triumph against us. However, I do not ask for your surrender; nay, I ask for your aid!"

D_Light always felt a bit embarrassed using words like "nay," but the game system rewarded good role-playing with extra points. He was not particularly good at fantaspeech, the quasi-medieval form of speaking used when playing in this fantasy world, but he at least tried to use enough to avoid a point penalty.

"We need a good guide to lead us from this foul place," D_Light said. "I suspect you are our man. In return, you will keep your life and a third share of the treasure taken. What say you? Let us plunder and move on fast before more of Salem's fallen hinder us!"

"Why should I trust a bitch-ass pisser like you?"

The term "pisser" was game slang for "player-slayer," which was not at all in character, nor was his use of the term "bitch-ass." D_Light realized this spanker must either be truly angry or a n00b.

"No choice!" boomed D_Light. "You are either useful alive as our guide, or you are useful dead, less your valuables. Quickly now!"

The dwarf reluctantly agreed. Apparently, he had enough sense to not end up a ghost like his friends, who were then shouting thinly heard obscenities at D_Light and Lily. However, the logged-out spankers did not dare physically interfere with them. Such activity was a clear violation of NeverWorld rules and would likely result in a stiff point penalty. Instead, they just hovered nearby, waving their arms around in an attempt to distract D_Light and Lily. Lily stared at them, but D_Light was used to this. It wasn't the first time he had slain other players' virtual characters for loot, but on those occasions the players he smoked were evil in alignment. According to the coat of arms adorning the armor of one of the nearby fallen, these characters belonged to a good-aligned guild, and so his misdeed would surely come back to haunt him, perhaps the next time his witch character visited a village or city of civilized lands.

As the ghosts made obscene hand gestures at D_Light and made pelvic thrusts in the air near Lily, D_Light instructed Lily to start rummaging through the virtual bodies on the floor and grab anything that looked valuable. The dwarf was already at work on the statue, attempting to pry the large gems from the eye sockets. D_Light enjoyed searching for treasure after a fight and typically took a great deal of care in making sure he did not miss anything, particularly any small magical items like rings, potions, and the like. But this time he took only what was obvious without looking for any secret caches in the room or hidden pockets in the burnt remains covering the fallen. His haste was, in part, due to the fact that he knew more nasties were bound to show up soon, but mostly he just wanted to get moving. Still, getting treasure was what one did in this situation, and D_Light wanted to keep up appearances. All actions in NeverWorld were recorded.

Soon D_Light had a sizable sack of gold, a powerful magical sword, and an assortment of magical potions and scrolls. Because he was a witch, he could not use the sword effectively. Worse yet, the gold was very heavy, and it was going to slow him down. It did not have any real weight, but the game system warned him that he was now "heavily encumbered" and so would not be allowed to run, only jog. The game could not directly force a spanker to behave appropriately when something bad happened—for example, if a spanker was paralyzed by poison or the victim of a spell that caused a thorny wall to spring up in front of him. Instead, the game would notify the player that an effect was upon the spanker, and the spanker would then have to role-play the situation.

In this case, although D_Light was still physically capable of sprinting at his full speed, to do so while carrying this much virtual weight would be cheating. A spanker only got a few warnings for poor role-playing before they were point-penalized or, if the infraction was serious enough, their character was instantly killed. Spankers called this "getting wrathed" because such a death in Never-World was attributed to inciting the wrath of the gods.

D_Light decided to hand the sword and gold over to Lily. Since she was playing a warrior and was therefore strong, she was allowed to carry much more weight without being affected.

The dwarf had finished prying loose the stones, and D_Light demanded one, which the dwarf handed over silently, but with a fierce look.

"Okay, guide, take us out the swiftest way you know. Keep indoors, though. I don't want to go outside just yet," D_Light ordered.

"Outside is the fastest," the dwarf said emphatically. "There's an exit from the catacombs nearby, and then there is a gate out of this ghe—" The spanker caught himself before saying the word "ghetto" and corrected himself. "Out of the Corrupted Lands."

"There is danger in the open air that you know not of," D_Light warned. "Nay, we must travel inside. Surely there is an underground cavern that will take us out of the Corrupted Lands."

By "underground cavern" D_Light meant a spunnel, although he did not use this term because it was not fantaspeech. Spunnels, or spanker tunnels, ran underground, usually between nearby spanker ghettos. These avenues were constructed so that spankers, who were always jacked in and distracted by the various games they were playing, did not make themselves a nuisance to other travelers. This segregation facilitated more orderly traffic in the common avenues. Spankers could use the common avenues too, but most games encouraged spankers to use the spunnels by placing more interesting objects and scenarios in the spunnels than in the common avenues.

The dwarf seemed to know what the witch meant, and after a moment of thought, he pointed to a passage out of the room.

"Before we away, I must heal a few of my egregious wounds," the dwarf said, extracting a pink-colored potion from his belt.

"Don't!" D_Light commanded. His feminine, bejeweled hand glowed green with a half-finished spell. He extended his other hand for the potion. "Sorry, my fine dwarf, but I'll take that. I need you at less than full strength, for I cannot have you feeling stupidly brave and swinging that ax of yours in our direction." The witch's voice was smooth and alluring.

The dwarf truly looked furious now, but he regarded the witch's glowing hand carefully, and after a moment, he threw the bottle down, shattering it.

D_Light frowned. "Now there you go, wasting a perfectly good healing potion. Not a good way to make friends. Go on then, we must away! You lead."

D_Light and Lily followed behind. D_Light hoped the dwarf was not foolish enough to try to give him the slip. Besides, the dwarf was short and stocky, so unless he was willing to cheat or was wearing some magical enhancement, he would not be allowed to run very swiftly.

———

Although Lily had ceased some time ago deliberating about whether or not to escape from the human, she wondered, as she trailed behind the other two, what alien madness she had agreed to. It was like a dark vision that kept going and going. She decided that just as soon as she was out of this place, far away, she would leave them. How could she not? She knew that humans rarely acted outside of their own self-interest, and Lily did not see how it was in this human's interest to help her. *Unless he wishes to mate me,* she thought. Todget had warned her that humans would want her for that. If that was the case, Lily did not reciprocate the interest. He was pleasing to the eye, as were many human males, but he did not smell quite right.

CHAPTER 15

Techlepathy, that is, using technology to enable human telepathy, is one of the great technological achievements of our time. However, with this power comes danger. Early developers of techlepathy feared "mind hacking." After all, early malicious hackers only attacked your computer, a violating experience to be sure, but nothing compared to someone forcing their way into your consiousness!

To combat the "mind hack," software/hardware firewalls were created. Protecting a person unobtrusively against such varied and complex attacks takes a ton of computer processing power. The primary purpose of a familiar is to shield its owner from unauthorized access. Even with computers as powerful as they are today, familiars are rather large, which is why it is convenient to have the firewall carried by a companion robot rather than carrying the machine on your person.

As expected, mind hacking has occurred and even now still happens on occasion...

—Excerpt from "A Brief History of Technology," by NoiceBooty

All the non-players, the suspects Katria had instructed the sniffers to check, came back negative. Most of these suspects turned out to be men who were asleep, but she had them checked anyway. It was beyond her reckoning how the demon had escaped this search filter. *Had the rat escaped? But how? All exits are covered,* she assured herself. *There is no escape.*

She had to admit that it was possible that the demons had created a secret escape route of some kind. This had been done before—once, to be exact. But it was an extremely difficult task. Nanosites crawled relentlessly over all surfaces, penetrating the smallest cracks, and they were even present in the air. The one time it had been done, the demons created a tunnel that was virtually a vacuum. However, such a thing could not be constructed from drovine. It was hard for Katria to imagine these demons constructing an escape vacuum tube right in the middle of a spanker ghetto.

It has to be something else, she thought. *Maybe a personal transport? Something fast enough to get her out of there before we got the satellite in place?* She ran the possible scenario through her mind.

Rhemus, who was monitoring her shared thoughts, broke in. *I doubt it. I had the satellites check for emissions. There's nothing in the area.*

What about a closed system? Katria asked. *A simple electric bike or something?*

I just don't see it, Rhemus replied. *It's hard enough for a player to get personal transportation, especially something souped-up enough to escape the perimeter I'm monitoring. Sloth is a sin, remember?*

Demons don't care about sinning, Katria shot back testily.

Soul, I know, I'm just telling you I don't see it, Rhemus defended. *When was the last time a demon got hold of a lift car?*

When was the last time a demon fried an angel? Katria countered.

Katria suddenly dropped the conversation, having received a report from the sniffer assigned to dogging the demon's faint scent trail. Had the trail been stronger or the path straighter, the sniffer might have been able to use its nearly supersonic speed to catch her in a matter of seconds, but as it was, it was barely able to follow the trail at all. The bot finally had something to say besides "status unchanged." The scent was stronger, consistent with the demon having lingered in an area for longer than usual.

Katria patched herself though the video feed of the sniffer. There were four spankers standing rigid, submitting their full cooperation to the bot. All four of them were logged out of the game, which made them viable suspects; the sniffer had already checked them. Katria felt a thrill up her spine. The DNA trace was relatively new, probably only a few minutes old. *Surely the demon has not escaped the mounds yet,* she thought. Quickly, Katria grabbed the ID of one of the spankers from the sniffer's log and opened a blink to him.

WootWood sat on the soft dro-vine seat in the chamber where he had just died. His longtime teammate, CootThis, paced back and forth, nearly frothing in his agitation. GoodLookin, also known as "new guy," leaned against a dro-vine wall, frowning.

"That mother-fraggin' pisser," shouted CootThis, throwing his arms up in anguish. "He detonated an AOE spell right in the middle of us! Just waited for us, waited for us to do the heavy lifting on the nasties, and then he smoked us all!" He was breathing heavily, his rants pounding out like a jackhammer.

"Yeah, and CT, did you see how that blond bitch just stood around looking like a n00b? Oh, until it was time for her to yank our stuff. Then she got to it!" WootWood was more sulking than angry now.

"How long 'til we re-spawn?" WootWood asked the question to avoid silence in their commiseration rather than out of need for an actual answer. His onboard clock was only a thought away.

"Twelve minutes and twenty-three seconds; then we're gonna track them down and put the hurt on!" CootThis pointed down one of the tunnels. "You heard them—they're going for the spunnel."

"When we catch up, Spookle will turn on 'em, and then we'll have 'em outnumbered!" WootWood punched into the soft living sponge of his seat. "He better turn! I can't believe he went with those pissers. We oughta kick his ass real-time for pulling that!" WootWood stood up, his fists and jaw clenched.

"And what's with that pisser playing cross-gender like a deviant? I wouldn't 'ave half minded getting fragged by a hot witch bitch, but then I come up and see that guy? Damn!"

"Yeah, I was like, 'Hey, I'd pump that,' and then *pow!* The chick's got a scrote! That's some serious misrepresentation bullshit!" WootWood exclaimed.

"It's the deviants you need to watch out for," chimed in Good-Lookin. "Don't know what they'll do. Bottom line is he took us down easy. If we're gonna bring the hurt, we can't go in rough-rider. We need a strategy, eh?"

"Let's start with defense then," CootThis said. "What are we gonna do about that witch, wizard, or whatever it is—and that ice spell? I don't have my potion of cold resistance; they pinched it."

"I say we—" WootWood's voice suddenly broke off, and his eyes widened. "Oh flip! Oh flip! I've got a ping from the Divine Authority!"

"The wha'?" CootThis looked distracted.

"The flippin' Divine Authority! They're pinging me." Woot-Wood was pale in the light of CootThis's UV torch.

"Wha'?"

"Are you stupid? What did I say?" WootWood was breathing fast now. The heat drained from his face, and he felt like he had just swallowed a glass of acid.

"N00b, don't leave them waiting!" CootThis wrung his hands.

WootWood closed his eyes to concentrate on the blink. After a pause he said, "Shit, they want to know about the girl. Gotta be that doe-eyed blond bitch."

"What about her?" GoodLookin asked.

"Look at me! Do I look like I know? Shit, maybe this is about—" WootWood paused as his eyes darted about as though his optic nerves had been cut.

"What? What did you do?" CootThis asked, fear in his voice.

"I dunno, I might've touched her ass. You know, just brushed it." WootWood's jaw was slack.

"N00b, shut up! You cupped her ass? Don't even think that shit! They can scan your brain. I think they can scan your brain. You gotta calm the flip down and get back to 'em before they think something's up." CootThis shoved WootWood's shoulder.

WootWood took a deep breath and was quiet while CootThis sped up his pace, keeping his eyes on his friend who looked like he was going to fall off his seat.

"I don't blame him," GoodLookin chuckled. "That ass was shapely." This remark earned him a hard look from CootThis.

WootWood's eyes opened, and he looked up at the others. "Shit, I gave 'em the archive of everything with the girl."

"All of it? Even the ass cup?" GoodLookin was smiling.

"Yeah, what was I gonna do? I don't want an angel coming down here and reformatting *my* ass."

———

The interview had been profitable. Katria had always found it amusing to remotely interview subjects. When playing law enforcement grinder games, she came through blinks as an "official agent" of the Divine Authority. She commanded the bot to continue to track the demon, but she had it deploy a set of cameras before continuing on its way. The cameras were too small to be seen with the naked eye. Unfortunately, the nanocomponents that made up the cameras were complex and inherently unstable, and would therefore break down within minutes. However, this gave Katria enough time to watch the subjects as they squirmed. Of course, she did not need to watch them to detect deception. No, the unfiltered memories from the subject's mind could not lie, and it was more than an interrogator from earlier times could have extracted after days of intensive grilling. It was seeing the panic on their faces that made watching them in real time worthwhile. She knew it was silly, the sort of human vice—among other reasons—that made angels the first-string enforcers while humans were relegated to mere backup or support. Still, she had to have fun once in a while.

Besides confirming where the demon was headed, the interview had revealed another interesting data point. The demon had actually been playing a spanker game, which is why she was not caught in the initial sweep. And just as surprising, she was playing on the guest account of another player, common alias D_Light, a member of House Tesla, which was based over twelve hundred kilometers from there.

According to WootWood's recent memories, there was now another player in their party, common alias Spookle, who was leading D_Light and the demon. Dialogue spoken near the interviewees before the demon and her friends left suggested that the runners were trying to leave via a nearby exit tunnel—a tunnel currently covered by one of Katria's sniffer bots.

Nice work, Katria, said Rhemus, who had been monitoring her work in his periphery. *Now, let's query the spanker game for their location and end this.*

Am I a n00b? I already did that, snapped an irritated Katria. *They're no longer logged into NeverWorld—they're not logged into any spank game.*

According to the log from NeverWorld, her target had been kicked out of the game due to game death. They were now "ghosted" from that game's perspective, and the game was not programmed to keep track of the identity of ghosts. For some reason, there was also a ton of other ghosts in the area, making it impossible to tell who was who.

My Soul, there's a slaughter underway! Spankers gettin' ghosted en mass! What the Soul is going on? Rhemus asked, vexation filtering in with the blink.

Shit, whatever, responded Katria. *They got ghosted less than a minute ago, so they can't be far from where they got licked. I'm sending all available bots to their last known location. They're done like dinner.*

CHAPTER 16

To be divine one must be true, and so it is, even for the OverSoul herself. She demonstrates her grace by being the first to admit imperfection. Even intelligence far out-stripping our own—divine consciousness—is limited to the physical world, limited to the tools of the physical universe. And so it is that the Game, the software-based framework that organizes progressive humanity—the shepherd's staff of the True One—is not perfect. And so it is our responsibility—no, I say our privilege—to aid the OverSoul by fixing the Game when we find flaws and by making improvements where we see opportunity.

I expect that most of you feel elated by this challenge, to serve the Eternal Purpose, which is good. There are others who are elated too, but for a different reason. You think you can fix what is not broken or improve what requires no development, not for the glory of all, but to benefit yourself. Be warned! No player can approach God's work with an impure heart. She knows you better than you know yourself.

—Minister A_Dude, archives, "From the Pulpit"

As he walked, D_Light rummaged through his virtual backpack of magical items. There were various potions, a wand for control-ling animals, an amulet he used to speak with the dead, and several spellbooks. It wasn't like the old-school RPG games when you had all your inventory in a virtualized, easy-to-navigate list. In Never-World you had to actually find items as though you were in real life.

What a pain, he thought.

At last he found the ebony case he had been looking for, but it took him a minute longer of fiddling with the box before he remembered how to open it without setting off the trap. He peered inside at his most prized magical item. It did not look like much, just a rolled up piece of parchment, yet this scroll contained a very powerful spell. He had been saving it for an emergency, something to save his ass when all else failed.

He took the scroll out of the box and gently slid it into his pocket for quick access.

Master, a sniffer bot is ahead. With a ping, Smorgeous loaded a visual of the bot.

D_Light had instructed Smorgeous to stay well in front, to scout the "real world" with explicit instructions to watch out for bots. Through the visual feed, D_Light watched the disc hovering just inside a wider tunnel.

"Stop, dwarf," D_Light commanded.

The dwarf let out an exasperated sigh. "Mistress, your beloved escape tunnel is just around this corner."

"There's a heavy hitter there. We stop here for now." D_Light had been so distracted by the appearance of the bot that he used the term "heavy hitter," modern slang for a powerful nasty. D_Light saw his score pulse red as fifty points were deducted for not using fantaspeech. Smirking at D_Light, the dwarf must have noticed the slip.

The dwarf's smirk persisted. "Verily I say unto you, mistress, you appear a fine specimen of your race. Perchance when this is all over, you and I—"

"Quiet, I'm trying to think," D_Light interrupted. "Besides, dwarf, I should think your taste runs more to the short and portly."

Through Smorgeous's visual, D_Light watched the bot long enough to decide it was not going to move. *Covering the exits,* D_Light thought. *Not particularly creative, but a good move nevertheless.*

After a long pause, D_Light asked, "This is the Corrupted Lands, correct?"

The dwarf gave him an exasperated look as though he were the biggest n00b in NeverWorld. "Uh, yes mistress."

"And it is the domain of Queen Pheobah and her abomination of a son, Salem?"

The dwarf winced and ducked down as though cowering. "We don't say… We don't say those names out loud! You could draw their attention," the dwarf hissed. He then threw up his hands and whispered, "My gods, just let me go before you get me killed! I took you to the tunnel."

"Soon, just have to get past this last nasty. Then, by gods, I'll give you the gold my shieldmaiden carries. A user of magic such as myself far prefers magic over gold anyway."

The dwarf did not look entirely convinced, but he held his tongue.

"Queen Pheobah…she is a demigod, then? Or merely a powerful devil?"

The dwarf took a step closer and whispered, "She is the undisputed ruler of the entire Corrupted Lands! Her son, the spawn of fear and hate, is even more sadistic than she."

"Powerful then? You have met the pair?"

"Met them? Of course not! No mortal adventurer has set eyes on them and lived to tell the tale!" The dwarf ran his finger across his throat. "Please, mistress, can we move on?"

D_Light sighed to himself as he lifted out of his pocket the scroll of the powerful gateway spell. He looked over at Lily, who stood expressionless next to him, and muttered under his breath, "You owe me one."

To release the spell, he unrolled the parchment and spoke the arcane word scrawled at the top. He then named the being to which he wished to open a gate. "Queen Pheobah of the Corrupted Lands," he bellowed. The parchment was consumed in a fiery flash. A deep boom echoed and the ground shook while an enormous, blue, semi-transparent oval gate spread out before them.

"What have you done?" the frantic dwarf shouted in disbelief.

Although Queen Pheobah, Mistress of the Corrupted and Demigoddess of Evil, was merely a software agent running in the larger NeverWorld software program, she did not know this.

Now, she lay perfectly still, staring straight up through the vastness of her high-domed ceiling. It was pure darkness in the queen's lair, but nothing could be hidden from her ancient eyes. The only true darkness for the queen was in her own mind, dark corners she strove to forget. Memories of happier days. Fair memories tortured her far more than the parasites that had long ago infested her body, although such worms showed no evidence of their intrusion as her terrible beauty grew with every passing season.

Her son, Salem, was nearby, spinning out his eternity of time with ever-decaying pleasures. Prolific torture and feasting on the innocent had long since grown old for him. The closest thing to pleasant distraction he could muster now was to corrupt. He smirked and whispered to himself as he watched his prey through his great mirror. A little boy, a human one no older than seven, cried himself to sleep. A week ago, Salem had visited this little boy and had given him a present, a great red ruby. He told the boy to give it to someone. The unlucky recipient of the gem was then devoured by Salem that very night, and the gem was returned to the boy, who was to give it to another the very next day. If the boy ever failed to give the gem away, Salem would devour his parents. It was a self-perpetuating plan of torture that was designed to be fail-proof.

The queen, on the other hand, wished she could feel and see nothing, to cease to exist, but that was not possible for a goddess such as herself. She desperately wanted to shut off all her senses, but when she scratched out her eyes, she could still see. And her eyes grew back anyway, more luminous and haunting than ever.

To be alone in her lair was the closest thing to relief that she could find. Alone, except for that cursed son of hers of whom she could not rid herself. She fed off his wickedness, a kind of power that sickened her even as she partook of it. But if she did not partake, she would receive instead a great hunger, a hunger of such heightened torment that even a god with an eternal will such as hers would do anything to sate it.

Imagine then what Pheobah, Queen of the Corrupted and Mother of Abomination, thought when a portal opened in her lair, right on the ground next to her outstretched porcelain feet. And on the other side of that portal was a mortal woman, clad in witch's garb, peering in with an idiotic grin on her face.

The queen pondered what could be going on. Some rival deity laying a trap? No, she could not sense any other presence of any significance; only the stench of the human and her kind wafted through the portal.

Never mind, she thought. *If this insect went to the trouble of barging in on me uninvited, she must have something foolish to say. I will receive her, and by the time she has finished blathering and begging for some favor, I will have had time to think up a proper place in hell to send her.*

The queen's son was already standing beside her and also looking very unhappy about the intrusion. Pheobah saw in his eyes that he was about to obliterate the mortal, but she put up her hand to stop him. She then walked through the portal.

D_Light was impressed with how NeverWorld rendered Queen Pheobah. His optic nerves were nearly overloaded with input as the radiant goddess stepped into the chamber. The text of his heads-up display said, *You are overwhelmed with the queen's splendor!* but he scarcely needed the warning to role-play appropriately. He averted his eyes.

The dwarf was on his knees, blubbering, "Please don't—I've worked for years on this character."

D_Light looked over at Lily, who had fallen on her back. She was staring slack-jawed, and she seemed unable to breathe. D_Light decided he had better get this over with before she had an aneurysm. Although it hurt, D_Light forced himself to look directly at the unearthly face of the queen. He then took a deep breath, and with the most haughty and casual tone he could muster, he said, "You don't look like much."

It was at that moment that the three of them—the witch, the dwarf, and Lily's character—were eviscerated by a blender of long, blue blades that appeared from nowhere. D_Light saw this view as his ghost left behind the explosion of blood, bone, and chunks of flesh that had been, only moments before, his female virtual body.

The queen had never felt such rage. She had been insulted, violated by a worm! Oh, how she regretted killing them so quickly, which only enraged her more. Now, out of her remote lair, the stench of mortals filled her nostrils.

"This place is crawling with vermin," she seethed to her son, who was now smiling broadly over her statuesque shoulder. Although he loved his mother in his own way, Salem enjoyed seeing her suffer just the same.

"Truly, Mother, let us burn them," Salem hissed lovingly in her ear.

"Take your time. Make it slow," his mother commanded. "I want to hear the music of their screams."

The instant after D_Light uttered his last words as the witch Ascara, he was forcefully logged out of NeverWorld. Only a second later he heard cries of panic echoing through the halls.

"Holy Soul, it's her!" he heard someone shouting from down the hall.

Soon there was a second voice screeching, "Run, run, run like hell!"

"Mercy, no!" pleaded a third.

Individual voices rose into a cacophony as the alarm spread, quickly becoming a chorus of pandemonium. D_Light smiled to himself, but the smile was quickly wiped from his face as he stumbled forward from a rear blow that nearly knocked the wind out him.

"Flippin' pisser, you cost me two years of play!"

D_Light turned and blocked the next punch from the man. No longer as short as the dwarf he had been skinned as, Spookle was still plenty stocky and did not seem worried about getting charged with assault.

"No sweat, you'll get paid!" D_Light yelled as he blocked another punch. But Spookle was not listening. He was crying with anguish as he rained down blows on D_Light.

Lily, still rubbing her eyes in an attempt to recover from the bizarre world from which she had emerged, looked over at the two men who had now been reduced to rolling around on the ground. She yelled, "Stop! Stop that or...or I will hurt you!"

"Hurt him," D_Light panted. "He's hurting me!"

Lily walked around the combatants for a moment, looked for her opening, and then gave a soft kick—at least it was a soft kick for her since her legs were stronger than most men's, but what the kick lacked in force it made up for in accuracy, making perfect contact with Spookle's scrotum.

Like a spring toy, the man immediately disengaged and rolled up in a ball, groaning. D_Light rolled away on the spongy floor and stood up. He laughed while rubbing the side of his head. "Thanks, but I could've taken him. I was just afraid I'd hurt him too bad and I'd have to pay restitution."

Lily shrugged and chuckled. "I don't even know what in Stag's name that was about. You—you males are stark raving mad!"

It was the first time D_Light had seen Lily smile. Her teeth were unreasonably straight and white. Something told him that it was her nature to smile, or maybe it was just that he hoped to see her do it again.

As Spookle continued to writhe on the floor, the other two looked up as some distant commotion suddenly got nearer. Down the hall, running as though chased by the devil himself, mobs of spankers thundered toward them. D_Light and Lily barely had time to flatten themselves against the wall before they flew by, eyes wide, some of them shouting, although most seemed to be saving their breath for the mad dash.

Spookle's groans of lament for his scrotum soon turned into cries of terror as he was partially stampeded by the mob. More spankers poured through the tunnel. Many more. It was like a rats' nest set on fire. Spookle finally had the good sense to roll over next to the wall.

D_Light laughed. "My Soul, would you look at that!" He aimed his LED torch down the long tunnel behind them. Spankers were streaming into the main tunnel from countless arterials, all of them with the same agenda—to get the hell out, now!

Lily did not look amused. "What's wrong with them? What's going on?"

In this moment of triumph, D_Light wanted to say something clever and memorable, but there was too much noise, too many legs and arms flailing and pumping. He settled for shouting, "Let's go!"

With that, he grabbed Lily's hand firmly, and the pair ran into a gap in the mob, joining them. D_Light ran as fast as he could, and that was just fast enough not to get trampled because spankers were, as a rule, very fast runners. After all, NeverWorld was a physically demanding game.

The sniffer bot was guarding the nearest exit of the ghetto, so naturally, all the spankers who did not want to be fragged by the rampaging Queen Pheobah and her devil child ran straight at the bot. The bot was not designed for processing samples this quickly. Worse yet, the AI onboard was not very advanced and so was not adept at improvisation; it did not prioritize the samples taken from the people rushing past it. Having been instructed to sniff everyone who came by, that was what it did, processing the samples in order of appearance. The spankers were completely heedless of the bot's authority, and they would have knocked it out of the air and trampled it underfoot had it not been for its sophisticated maneuvering system.

Nearly an hour passed before the bot finally found a DNA trace of the target. Being a heavily utilized tunnel—especially recently—the target would be difficult to track. Better equipment was required.

During that hour head start, D_Light held the hand of his prize and ran. Due to Rule Seven and a wish to keep his health contract dues to a minimum, D_Light had trained hard for years and was in excellent shape, but after an hour of scampering through every random side tunnel and chamber he could find in a sincere attempt to get lost, he was exhausted. Of course, he couldn't really get lost; Smorgeous's GPS kept him apprised of his location, and he was gratified to see that they had made some excellent progress. Presently, they were several communities away.

The two fugitives and the cat familiar were no longer running. Lily looked somewhat flushed, but her breathing appeared steady. D_Light struggled to stop panting so loudly. Next to her, it was embarrassing.

Lily twisted her hand, and D_Light reluctantly let it go. He spoke to her in bursts between great gasps of air. "You can swing a sword…kick a crotch…and run all day… Will you marry me?"

She rolled her eyes and did not answer, but the corners of her mouth turned up ever so slightly.

D_Light decided that this girl might ditch him at any moment, so while wanting nothing more than to just curl up on the spongy ground in the middle of this thoroughfare, he decided he better cash in on his prize.

He allowed himself to indulge in a moment of exhilaration. *What a long shot, but I beat them! I beat the Divine Authority! Damn, I'm good, and now I'm soooo going to get paid! Smorgeous, open a line to the Divine Authority.*

The blink went through. A voice on the other end, conspicuously absent of gender, greeted him. *You have reached the Divine Authority Triage Center. You are citizen #AZ324082394829, common alias D_Light. Please be advised that your legal status has recently changed. Your status of "citizen, level eighty-three" has been updated to "suspected demon." All correspondence between entities of your status and the Divine Authority will be monitored. D_Light, please state your business.*

Although not surprised, D_Light felt a rock thud down in his stomach when the disembodied voice referred to him as a "suspected demon." He figured it would not take long for the Authority to link him to the girl; nevertheless, he did not like to hear his expectation confirmed.

I wish to provide valuable data to your enforcement division, restore my previous status, and apply for a merit award.

The voice replied, *This appeal will require a legal hearing. Would you like to schedule a hearing now?*

Yes, I would like my hearing immediately.

Very well, if you have a legal representative, you may add him or her at any time.

The blink cut out for a moment, and then the voice returned. D_Light appreciated that the Authority did not even try to pretend that he was blinking with a living thing. *You, the defendant, D_Light, are charged with aiding and abetting a convicted demon. This charge is a sin under Article #35631 and may result in a status demotion to "demon." Do you plead guilty or not guilty?*

Not guilty. D_Light could not help but send some emphasis with his words even though he knew the court would not be swayed by sincerity of tone—real or feigned.

Your plea has been noted. Do you have an opening argument? As a reminder, legal representation is recommended at this time.

Yes, D_Light answered. *I wish to submit my full archive of the time in question, between the time of 05:12 this morning and the present.*

Very well, please upload your archive now.

D_Light took a deep breath as he gave Smorgeous the order to upload. The archive being sent was a deep archive, which meant that it included all brain activity, including thought content. It would prove conclusively that although D_Light did help the demon escape immediate capture, this was only to test the Authority's search algorithms. By beating the system and then telling how he did it, they could improve their protocols. This sort of out-of-the-box opportunistic thinking was what got D_Light to level eighty-three at only age fifty-four. How may sermons had he attended where the theme was "Calculated Risks Are Divine"?

Of course, now that he had achieved this objective, he needed to turn the girl in. That would be necessary; otherwise, there would indeed be a case against him. This fact settled uneasily on him. After all, he had nothing against the girl, and to betray her trust was not something he relished. However, she was a demon, and although he did not know her sin, she must deserve her fate. *Besides, she would have been caught with or without me,* he thought.

It would take a while to get his verdict. The archive included a huge amount of data, so the upload time alone would take several minutes. D_Light would have had Smorgeous hook into a nearby data socket to speed up the process, but he did not want to raise any suspicion with the girl.

"You know what? You smell great," D_Light said to Lily nonchalantly. He wanted to start up a conversation, and this was the first thing to pop into his head. He hadn't really noticed her scent before, at least not consciously. Maybe because there was too much else on his mind until now. But since they had been running so long, the enticing aroma was now excreted in her sweat. Perhaps her sweat was enhanced by a chemi skin product, or maybe her blood contained nanobots or a virus that excreted the perfume through her pores. Whatever the case, it was absolutely intoxicating.

Rather than react the way he expected—laughter, a smile, or even one of those eyeball rolls he had seen her do earlier—Lily started to cry. She cradled her face in her cupped hands, her shoulders shuddering gently with each sob.

"Er...what I just said? That's a compliment, you know." D_Light spoke feebly. He was not sure how to react. He was not even sure if he should react. He had scarcely seen any grown man or woman cry. Members of his family and of any other house he knew of would never show such a sign of weakness.

He looked around to see if anyone was watching. Fortunately, there were only a few people in sight, and they appeared to be in their own remote worlds; their eyes scanned their surroundings as though blinded in a fog. *This has to stop,* D_Light thought. *If someone sees her acting this way, they will surely investigate. She would probably get scanned, and then...* He was not sure what would happen.

Perhaps coaxed by a video feed he had once seen, D_Light placed a hand on her shoulder. She did not remove it, but the action seemed to only intensify her weeping. D_Light then slid an arm around her and tried to steer her toward a deserted arterial tunnel, but she pushed him away with surprising strength.

"Why did you help me?" she demanded. Her voice was nearly normal, only a bit throaty. Her eyes were bloodshot and her face wet with tears, but she was no longer crying, as though she had simply turned the faucet off.

D_Light did not answer. Instead, he motioned for her to follow him to the side tunnel, but she did not move. "You let him be taken, but not me. Why?" she demanded.

"I'll explain, but not here. Please, this way." D_Light mechanically repeated his coaxing motion to follow.

Lily shook her head in refusal. "Why?" She breathed out the word with such ferocity that D_Light felt compelled to answer, lest she escalate into shouting and make a scene.

D_Light tried to mix just enough truth with his lie to sound convincing. "I already told you, my friends and I did not come for *you*. We were sent to get *him*. We didn't need you. You seem nice, like...like a good person. I feel bad about your friend, but I had no choice. Now I want to help you."

She stood silently for a moment, regarding him with a long, penetrating look as though trying to peer into his heart. "Forgive me if I don't thank you," she finally said. She then straightened up and started to walk away.

"Where are you going?" D_Light asked quietly. He followed behind her, took a quick glance over his shoulder, and whispered, "They are still looking for you."

"*They?*" She turned and faced him. Her vulnerable countenance had been replaced by something that looked slightly dangerous. "From what I can tell, you're one of *them*."

She turned again and resumed walking, only with greater determination. She then hissed over her shoulder, "Go back to your spank game—or whatever the hell that was."

"You can't find him, if that's what you're thinking," D_Light stated without emotion. "They killed him. They'll kill you too."

D_Light knew nothing of the other demon's fate, nor did he know what they would do to her, but he was desperate.

Lily shot an intense look back at him over her shoulder, lightning flashing across her vivid blue eyes. D_Light tensed up, ready to dodge a blow, but she did not strike. Her lips curled upward with obvious disgust, she took one hard look into D_Light's eyes—a look that made him feel exposed—and then turned her head forward again and continued walking.

D_Light hesitated, but then he followed, lacking any better ideas. At first he tried obvious questions like, "Do you know where you are?" and "Do you know where you're going?" but she did not answer. D_Light finally resigned himself to silently walking a few paces behind her. He figured he would just keep following her until she bolted or did something else. He had to keep an eye on her, at least until he got everything squared away with the Authority. He wondered what Lyra and Djoser were up to, but he did not dare to blink them for fear that they would demand his immediate return.

Lily did know where she was, for she too had a GPS in her chip, but she did not know where she could go that would be safe. For now, she felt she needed to just keep walking. Walking with purpose was something she had been taught to do, and she could sort things out as she went.

The fact of the matter was that Lily knew better than to trust this human. As she reflected on recent events, she had to admit to herself that her trust was based only on a hunch, a mysterious and surprising feeling about this human that had been creeping in the back of her mind since the moment she first caught him staring at her from under the tree. It was like she had met him before, perhaps in a dark vision or in another life. Todget had always cautioned her against her hunches, although her instincts had never failed her before. But this human, with his insipid name and stupid comments, had stood by as an eager spectator while her dear Todget was killed. Instincts or not, how could she abide him?

On the other hand, as far as she could tell, the human had lived up to his promise. She was still free. She remembered Todget speaking of the many technologies possessed by those who hunted them. He said that their powers were so great and destructive that if the two of them were ever found, they would not escape. Yet escape she had, at least for the moment.

———

D_Light, are you prepared to receive your verdict? The androgynous voice in D_Light's mind startled him, having been wrapped up in his own internal dialogue.

Yes, D_Light replied.

The Divine Authority has found you guilty of the crime with which you are charged. Your status is hereby updated from "suspected demon" to "demon."

"Impossible!" D_Light sputtered the word out loud involuntarily. He suddenly felt dizzy, his chest tightened, and a high-pitched ringing sounded in his ears. Lily, upon hearing the unexpected exclamation, peered back at him, but D_Light did not return her gaze to read her expression. Suddenly, she no longer mattered to him. He was alone with his fear.

There has been a mistake! Review the evidence again! he commanded to the voice in his head.

It is inadvisable for you to dispute this verdict unless you have additional evidence. Please stand by for important information that will help you improve your service to the Divine Authority.

The voice took an infinitesimal pause before continuing. *Please be advised that under Rule #3398439 the Divine Authority is unable to use information contained within an archive that is voluntarily submitted from a defendant for purposes other than those expressly stated by the defendant.*

D_Light knew about this rule. It was in place to encourage defendants to submit their archives—a most convenient form of evidence—to the Authority. Before this rule went into effect, defendants were afraid to submit archives because, in addition to ascertaining the guilt or innocence of the charged crime, the archive could also be used to detect additional crimes or locate the defendant. Now archives were off-limits for all uses except those explicitly given by the defendant.

D_Light's mind raced. *Further evidence?* He'd given them a deep copy of his archive. There could be no better evidence of his intentions! No harm had been done. The archive of him outwitting them had to be very valuable, and he was ready to hand over the archive *and* the demon. What had he done? *I am a loyal citizen, a model player! How could they not see this?* he thought feverishly.

It's a bug, thought D_Light. *A bug in their legal protocols. That must be it! Outrageous!*

Smorgeous, sensing his master's distress, gently asked if he would like a downer. D_Light, agitated, declined. He needed all of his wits about him right now.

D_Light had a sudden revelation. *There is one way to fix it,* he thought. D_Light had fixed system bugs in the Divine Authority's software before, although never software related to divine law. It was not something one did every day; indeed, few programmers ever did it once. However, being such an obvious bug, certainly he would get access and change his status back.

He sent an order to his familiar. *Smorgeous, patch me into the Divine Authority Protocol Association. And give me both visual and audio.*

Smorgeous opened a blink. A user interface for the DAPA appeared in his mind, semitransparent and superimposed over his vision such that he could still see where he was going, more or less. He was still trailing behind Lily.

A chrome number eight, fallen on its side, the mathematical symbol for infinity and the official banner of the Divine Authority, showed momentarily while D_Light's credentials were approved.

D_Light, player #49937593, status "demon," how can the Divine Authority be of service?

I wish to correct an error, D_Light responded.

The Divine Authority appreciates your time in remedying the matter; however, due to the possible security ramifications of your request, you are required to submit to a deep scan to confirm your intention is in the best interest of the OverSoul. Would you like to learn more about deep scanning?

No, D_Light responded. He had undergone deep scanning before. He knew what to expect.

Very well, if you are not familiar with the terms and conditions of deep scanning, please review them now. At this, D_Light was given the option of a textual or visual blink of the terms and conditions. As he always did, D_Light agreed to the terms without reviewing them.

In response, the neutral voice continued. *Thank you. Do you agree to a deep scan at this time?*

Yes.

D_Light saw a graphical progress bar constantly apprising him of how much time he could expect the scan to continue. As the scan commenced, he felt tingling that came and went in various parts of his body—in his hands, his lower back, his neck, the calves of his legs. He heard sounds, soft but distinct, humming that was replaced with a high-pitched whine. He heard voices whispering and muttering: "For the neospore we give thanks...why is your flavor...what is not what it cannot be..." The voices merged together. Some of them sounded like they came from him, some from people he knew, most from people he did not recognize, but this did not matter, as it all was nonsense anyway. He knew enough about brain scans to know that you could never predict what you would feel and perceive as your brain was being probed.

What precisely the scan was looking for was unknown. Information from the Cloud was hazy at best, with only general guidance from the Divine Authority itself such as, "Only a pure heart may access the Inner Divinity," or "Let pure love guide you."

Of course, the Cloud forums were chock-full of speculation about what these cryptic hymns meant. There were even a few players who, upon successfully passing through the deep scan, later attempted to upload a deep archive of their deed such that they and others could analyze the successful brain patterns. However, according to the terms of use, which no one ever read, you gave the Authority permission to intercept your live streaming archive before it could be written to memory or streamed up to the Cloud. It was like temporary digital amnesia, where the only recollections were what the unaided organic brain could retain, which, like all native brain memories, were vague and of little analytical value.

Finally, after a few more muscle spasms and minor hallucinations, an error box appeared in D_Light's consciousness and a voice stated, *You are unworthy of access at this time.*

Having taken advanced security training, D_Light knew better. He replied, *Being a demon does not bar me from accessing the code base.*

The voice responded as another box opened. *Correct. Under Rule #8939543, no one will be denied access to the code base or protocol databases due to profile status, past or present.*

D_Light was dumbfounded. *Then why in the hell don't you give me access?* he shouted in his mind.

You are unworthy of access at this time.

Unworthy! It was as though the monotone was taunting him.

Is it because I am upset? Is that why I don't get permission?

You are unworthy of access at this time, the voice repeated.

D_Light tried several more questions in an attempt to understand what the problem was, but the voice merely answered him with the same "unworthy" statement.

While frustrated and furious, D_Light at least understood the Authority's repeated, opaque answer. It was all about hackers. For someone trying to maliciously hack into a system, it was best to give him or her as little information as possible. If a hacker knew why they were being blocked, they would be better able to work around the issue.

After a second failed attempt to pass the deep scan, the DAPA forcibly terminated the blink and D_Light could not log back in. Again, this was a security measure to inconvenience hackers. He knew that he would not be allowed to log back in for twenty-four hours. It was at this point that a cold realization came to him. *Soul, I'm a demon and I can't fix it! What the hell do I do now?*

D_Light was so exhausted from the physical and mental demands he had recently endured that he found himself unable to truly panic, or even to despair. For as long as he could remember, he had worked every waking moment to be the best player he could be so that one day he would become one of the chosen ones, one of the immortals. He worked hard to escape the endless darkness that waited at the end of every loser's life. Now the dream he had held all this time was in peril, perhaps gone.

He let out a low wail. His eyes swelled, and he felt the formation of involuntary tears. A lump formed in his throat that made him swallow hard, as though he was stifling the uprising of a terrible internal monster. It was all so terrifying, sensations not experienced since he was a child. Sensations he had hoped to forget.

D_Light stopped dead in his tracks. There were people around, but he didn't care. Lily may have been staring at him, but he wasn't sure and it didn't matter. He did not look directly at her. Warm, runny snot started dripping from his nose. "Aghhh!" he cried out and quickly sniffed it back up. Then, without a thought to where he was going, he started running down the nearest side tunnel. He ran as fast as his already exhausted muscles would allow.

Smorgeous assured him that everything was going to be fine. The familiar reminded D_Light of difficult times in his past when he had managed to pull through. The mistake would be fixed.

Sensing, perhaps, that his counseling was not helping, Smorgeous repeated an offer for sedatives. D_Light ignored this and, upon finding an exit from the mounds, found himself in the morning sun. He immediately beelined for a nearby grove of trees, which was just dense enough to conceal him. Finally able to lie down, D_Light agreed to the sedative. As exhausted as his body was, his mind was overly active, spinning in a whirlwind of activity. He needed to calm his thoughts, and none of his trance mantras were working. Besides, D_Light had no reason to use drugs sparingly anymore because, as a demon, his health contract was null and void anyway. In fact, as a demon, he was no longer in the Game at all.

An electromagnetic pulse beamed out of the embedded chip at the base of D_Light's skull, focused downward through his carotid artery. Some of the nanobots suspended in the area where the blood had been irradiated were then activated, releasing their payload of drug molecules into his bloodstream. D_Light felt the effects immediately and lay face down on the ground; a twig pressed uncomfortably into his cheek. He did not even bother to make himself more comfortable before he lapsed into unconsciousness.

CHAPTER 17

A tight feedback loop—that is one of the primary components of facilitating flow in any grinder game you design. Even as I speak, your feedback on my performance is trickling in, affecting the points I receive. Ah, I see many of you liked that example. Another twenty-three points for me! Thankfully, you did not have to send this feedback explicitly, as was necessary in the past. Instead, your brain patterns, your BPs, offer the feedback, requiring no effort from you. Otherwise, how could you concentrate on what I'm saying?

Now, this constant appraisal of my work puts me into a state of flow. I'm not off thinking about what I'm going to do with my newly won points. I'm not planning what I will be doing in the next hour or the next week, or thinking about the funny story my brother told me less than an hour ago. There is only the here and now. In such a state of mind, is it any wonder that grinder games yield such high productivity from their players?

—Darwin Scazaan, from "Introductory Instructive Archive for Grinder Developers of House Tesla"

Takin', whose name was short for "taking care of business," was playing well tonight. He had a fleet of twenty-five cleaning bots under his command, and thus far his team was ahead of every other cleaning team in his zone. Of course, this was no surprise to Takin', who constantly strove to live up to his name. He had studied his route carefully. He knew the high-traffic tunnels and chambers with the greatest likelihood of filth. He knew how to deploy his bots in just the right ratio so that the high-traffic areas were cleaned properly, but not with too many bots which might be better utilized elsewhere. This was important because quality cleaning was not enough to bring in the big points; you had to be fast at it, too.

Takin' only owned five of the bots he was using. The rest were rented, so the faster he finished the more points he would net. Besides, the house that ran these mounds and was sponsoring this cleaning game factored speed into the bonus system. They wanted their clients to have to contend with cleaning gamers as little as possible. The best cleaning crew came through like a gust of wind—gone by the time you knew it was there.

Which brings up the third qualification for a high score—no customer complaints. Since logging a complaint was only a thought away, pissing anyone off, even just a little, meant your house would hear about it right away. Nailing all these goals was tough, but Takin' enjoyed the challenge. And it sure helped that the game kept him constantly apprised of his progress. He had mental threads on all his bots that turned colors—red, yellow, and green—in accordance with the amount of grime they were picking up. Red meant that almost no cleaning was occurring, while green indicated it was keeping very busy with its work.

Takin's goal was to keep at least a quarter of his bots in the green and the remainder in the yellow. If he kept up that level of performance, he would constantly get reassurances from his game genie, a smooth, young female voice. She said things like, "I *liked* that move," or "Oh, yeah, you do that so well." His favorite one that was reserved for when he was really cleaning up was, "Takin'! Oh yes! Takin'!" which the disembodied voice cried orgasmically. She had tons of prompts, and the AI improvised well.

Takin' had a hunch to play at the Anywhere apartment mounds today. He wasn't sure why he should play there, as it was a little out of his way, but he had learned to trust his hunches—the subtle promptings of the OverSoul. And this time his hunch had really paid off. A massive stampede of unprecedented magnitude had just gone through Anywhere like a spanker cattle drive, and Takin's bots were cleaning in the green across the board. It was going to be a good game.

———

Katria was on the other side of the planet, walking along a well-worn trail through a multicolored but orderly orchard of nectar trees. This was one of her favorite paths to stroll while grinding. The scenery of this route was beautiful, but due to the regularly spaced rows of trees and monotonously brilliant green grass carpeting the ground, it was not distracting, which was perfect for thought-intensive grinding.

Against all odds (as she understood them), she and Rhemus had lost the demon girl. Or at least for the moment. A sudden and disorderly exodus of the spanker ghetto had overwhelmed the sniffer bots that were stationed at the ghetto exits. The bots were very good at what they did, but they were not designed to process so many so fast.

Do you suppose this player, D_Light, as he's called, knows that she's a demon? blinked Rhemus. *Is he actually helping her?*

Hard to say for sure, replied Katria. *The things he did, like logging her into the game and then starting that riot... Well, if he wasn't trying to help her, I couldn't imagine a more effective way to accidentally escape.*

Yeah, and his beacon is off, Rhemus added. *Few players run cloaked. I'd say he knows what he's doing. We need to factor him in. It's not often a mainstream player works with a demon. Might make this hunt pretty interesting.*

Katria did not want an interesting hunt; she wanted it to be over. She had already spent far too many points on the sniffer bot rental fees. Having escaped the ghetto now, the two could have gone in any direction with nearly an hour head start. It had taken that long for the pandemonium to die down enough for a sniffer to find the scent trail again. Worse yet, shortly after finding the scent trial, they lost it—or more precisely, the trail had been demolished. Katria cursed her absurdly bad luck. A cleaning crew had gone through and scoured the area through which the fugitives had escaped. Now the few sniffer bots Katria kept on retainer hovered about where the trail had gone dead, impotently sifting the air.

I think it might be time to bring some heavy artillery into this game, Katria said.

A seeker, eh? That'll be expensive, Rhemus replied with an attached Whinicon™.

It's the right move though, Katria assured him. *Now that the demon's out of the bag, the bots are just too stupid to deal. It's time to step it up.* Katria sighed as she focused on a nearby purple and pink nectar blossom.

Rhemus paused for a few seconds and then said, *I concur. I'm in for half of the fee.*

That was why Katria always played with Rhemus. He did what needed to be done. They thought enough alike to work together easily, but diverged enough to not be redundant.

Thanks, Rhemus. I'm calling the bots off. The seeker will be in play within fifteen.

After making the appropriate arrangements, Katria opened a blink to her friend, OffDaLeash, to shake down what was what for the night. Katria figured she deserved a little break. The seeker would take it from here.

CHAPTER 18

I'm growing tired of this question: Is the OverSoul God? In answer to this I say, "To do is to be." Does the OverSoul not bring out the best in every one of us? Does the Over-Soul not answer our prayers? Does she not see all, even into the darkest corners of our soul? Can she not bestow everlasting life? Let me tell it to you straight—the Over-Soul meets every condition of the gods of the ancient world, so who are we to add more qualifications?

—Minister A_Dude, archives, "From the Pulpit"

D_Light was awakened from his chemi-induced slumber by a nightmare. Nightmares never happened. The dream started the way it always did. He was on his sailboat with a strong, steady wind, a wind that shifted to keep him on a reach, the best point of sail. But then there was a beautiful witch who flew across the sea toward him. As she approached, he saw it was Ascara, the character he played in NeverWorld. "I'm coming for you," the witch said in a menacing whisper that carried over the cresting waves and the whipping wind. "The others cannot find you, but I can. I have magic."

Suddenly, a great storm rose up, and his boat soon capsized. He was drowning, and as his ears went under the water, he heard his own screaming.

Having woken from the nightmare, relief washed over D_Light. He did not, however, open his eyes.

Smorgeous, what the hell was that?

Master, please specify your request.

My nightmare! What the hell? With the witch? I was dying. Play it back to me.

I have no reference to any irregular dream patterns, master. Would you like me to play back your most recent dream?

Yes, D_Light answered. He spent a few minutes fast-forwarding and rewinding through the archive of his dreams. There was nothing. Had he imagined it? But if so, wasn't that what dreaming was—a hallucination? Hallucination or not, it should be in the archive, as all conscious experience was recorded.

Smorgeous, check again. Check for something like what I'm remembering now back while I was sleeping.

I'm sorry, master, but there is no archive of anything similar to the distressful events you are imagining now. To summarize, your most recent dream cycle was 16.4 minutes long and consisted of you and I aboard Terralova *sailing to an unspecified location. Aside from adjusting the sails and a few minor steering corrections, the dream was uneventful.*

But I was dying!

Evidently, you were not. There are some research findings that correlate stress load with false memories. Given recent events, we might hypothesize—

Piss off!

Smorgeous pinged confirmation.

Soul have mercy, am I being punished? Is the Authority haunting me even as I sleep? he wondered.

D_Light lifted his head from the hard ground. His skinsuit was not designed to insulate, and lying outside in the shade had chilled him. He shivered. There was laughter close by, a lilting little chortle. Although the laugh was unfamiliar, the scent that accompanied it—the one he had thought wonderful in the recesses of his uneasy dreams—now filled him with dread. It was painful verification that recent events had not been part of his nightmare.

"Do you always nap like that?" Lily was smiling nearby. She made brushing motions with her hand over her face. D_Light mimicked her, small twigs and bark falling from where they had been embedded in his skin. Indeed, the sedative had done its job. He made a note to Smorgeous to lower the dose next time.

D_Light looked around. Nope, it had not been a dream at all, and therefore his situation was incredibly depressing. He really *was* a demon hiding in a thicket. Yes, he had been divorced from his family and his point account frozen. And until he sorted this out, assuming he could, he had no chance at immortality. *Just another loser crawling toward death*, he thought wretchedly.

How is this possible? Decades of kicking ass, and I lose it all? How could the OverSoul do this to me? His present reality seemed surreal, which gave him hope that he might actually be back at the castle having a nightmare right now. He smacked the back of his head on the ground. It hurt.

Having completed this painful test followed by a few others, he reluctantly resigned himself to the fact that he really was awake. "You followed me?" he asked Lily at last.

"Yes," she answered simply as she gently threw a pinecone at him. It bounced off his chin and she smiled, but it was a sad smile.

D_Light let himself fall back into the needles and twigs. He stared up through the branches above. Rays of sunshine filtered down in a shimmering tapestry of light.

"In ancient times people believed that there were demons that lurked in the forests," D_Light said. "Well, here we are, a couple of demons in the woods."

"Not much of a forest," Lily returned. "And funny, you don't look much like a demon. Me either, I like to think." She stood up and walked to the edge of the thicket to peer out.

D_Light maneuvered his body underneath a patch of sunlight, and as he lay there wondering what to do next, Smorgeous's soft voice pressed into his consciousness. *Master, there is a blink summons from Mother Lyra. It is being sent as a high-priority message.*

D_Light sighed. *Now, on top of everything else, I have her fury to bear,* he thought. But what else could he expect? His mother invited him into her exclusive high-stakes game and he promptly abandoned the team without a word and got demonized. She was going to freak out. His only comfort was that he was kilometers from Anywhere now, and so Brian and Amanda couldn't be ordered to cut his limbs off just yet. It pained him to think that he could have merely done what was simple, what was safe, rather than leap off onto this misadventure of his own design. He could have done the obvious thing and turned in the demon as soon as he realized her status. That would have furnished him with a nice bounty without fuss. But instead, he got greedy. *Or maybe it wasn't about the points—maybe I just wanted to beat the Divine Authority and show everyone how smart I am,* he speculated gloomily.

Stop whining, he scolded himself. *What's done is done.* Although D_Light did not explicitly give permission to Smorgeous to open the blink, the AI onboard the familiar was good enough to infer the permission.

Mother Lyra's face materialized before his eyes. The blink did not make her semitransparent or a mere window in the corner of his visual perception; instead, Smorgeous correctly guessed that D_Light wished to focus on the blink, causing the here and now of the forest canopy to blur and be completely replaced by the noblewoman.

I don't know how you did it, but congratulations! Lyra was beaming with a dazzling smile. *I was so right about you! You're proving to be a FANTASTIC advisor.*

Such sincerity in her voice, as if being demonized and hunted down like an animal was not enough. Now she had to kick him with this theatrical sarcasm? Tesla royalty were not known for their compassion, so he could expect no better.

D_Light said nothing, just shrugged and bowed his head. The shrug was not a very respectful gesture to a superior, especially under these circumstances, but D_Light didn't care. He respected Lyra, but he would not grovel. This was not entirely because he had nothing to lose. On the contrary, there were many degrees of severity for the rehabilitation of a demon. Sure, on one end of the spectrum a demon could be destroyed, but this seemed unlikely for D_Light's offense. He assured himself there would only be a stiff penalty coupled with some mandatory community gaming, maybe even some counseling.

Lyra did not seem to notice the slight at her son's shrug. Instead, she laughed—not a cold laugh, but a happy one. *This has to be a record,* Lyra exclaimed. *You accomplished a quest before the rest of us even knew what it was! How did you learn of the next quest so fast?*

I...I beg your pardon, Mother. I do not understand. D_Light fell over the words he sent telepathically.

Lyra threw up her arms. *You're a demon, right? The next quest was for one of our party to become a demon. You know, 'the hunter becomes the hunted,' the theme of the quest? Imagine our surprise when the quest came up and it said we had already accomplished it!* She laughed and pointed off to the side, out of D_Light's view. *My Soul, even Djoser is impressed.*

D_Light was dumbfounded. Were they making fun of him? Were they ensuring his trust so they could spring a trap on him to get a bounty? This seemed like too farfetched of a story for that, and he could easily check its validity.

D_Light commanded Smorgeous, *Show me the updated MetaGame log.*

Immediately, Smorgeous brought up the newest entry. D_Light selected the text version of the entry to keep his audio inputs free for the blink.

> *The Hunter Becomes the Hunted*
>
> *After aiding in the capture of a demon, one or more of your party is to become a demon themselves. Be careful! If you are apprehended, you will face the consequences and will likely be out of the game. Tip: Keep your sin as minor as possible. Your participation in this MetaGame will not excuse you from a deadly sin.*

The text flashed green, and underneath the quest entry appeared the text "Quest Accomplished."

Lyra's voice cut in. *By the way, you need to answer your BRs. I was trying to reach you all morning. You were busy, I presume?*

Yes, escaping the authorities and all, he answered.

She winked at him. *So tell me now, how did you do it?*

D_Light hesitated, still in shock. *Huh, well, there must have been a glitch or something. I must have received the quest before the rest of you. Better to be lucky than good, they say.*

Better to be lucky AND good, I say. Lyra winked again. *Why in Soul's name didn't you tell us what you were up to?*

Like I said, I was doing a lot of running and such.

Lyra chuckled to herself and shook her head. *So where are you, handsome? We've been trying to locate you, but your beacon is turned off. Now I know why. We need to hook up and prepare for the next quest.*

D_Light gave his coordinates. Upon receiving them Lyra exclaimed, *Damn, you did do some running! I think we'll grab a transport. See you soon.* The blink cut out.

"Yes!" D_Light exclaimed as he made a fist and pumped his arm. He was about to start whooping ecstatically when he remembered the warning in the quest log about being caught; he was still a real demon.

Instead, he ran straight at Lily with the intent of embracing her, whirling her around, and maybe planting a few kisses on her exquisitely chiseled face, but she dodged to the side and, with one arm, swept him along over her outstretched leg. He tripped completely over her leg and crashed violently into the brush, his face narrowly missing the trunk of a tree. A bit befuddled and even more embarrassed, D_Light sat up. "Hey, I wasn't trying to hurt you. I was going to give you a kiss!" D_Light was sure he looked idiotic, but he didn't care.

Her eyes were wide, and she stood in a defensive stance, similar to how she looked when the spanker had attacked her earlier that same morning. "I do not wish to mate with you," she stated matter-of-factly.

Upon hearing this, D_Light laughed with abandon and pounded the dirt with his fists, sending up a cloud of dust and pine needles. "I think you're cute, but I don't just run up to women and start mating with them. That's never panned out for me." He laughed some more.

Lily did not seem to get the joke entirely, but she laughed anyway. It was contagious. "You are—" she squished up her face and shrugged her shoulders. "You are a rather unusual male, I think."

CHAPTER 19

Treva, the seeker, sniffed the floor of the spanker ghetto hallway on her hands and knees like a dog. This was fitting since her olfactory system was actually inspired by dogs—inspired by, but then improved upon, one thousand times over.

With a sense of smell so much more powerful than her human-like eyesight, she saw the world much more with her nose than her eyes, and Treva did not like the view. The tasty male and female she had been imprinted with had vanished to be replaced by the scouring chemical residue of the cleaning bots.

Nearly as unsavory as the smell of the detergents was the leftover metallic, greasy stench of the sniffers. These pathetic machines had originally been tasked with finding the meat-puppets, but thankfully they had been sent away so Treva could work alone and undisturbed—as a seeker must.

Treva inhaled again. Nothing, not a trace! She stood and stretched her long, sinuous muscles. Although her olfactory system was modeled after a dog's, her musculature was more or less derived from the feline family—an irony completely lost on Treva. The cat in her enabled lightning reflexes and speed. Unfortunately, these fast-twitch muscles now burned with pent-up energy. She wanted to resume the hunt so bad!

A couple smiled and nodded to Treva as they passed. Treva nodded back, but she was careful not to return the smile. She always kept her short, razor-sharp fangs hidden from those who were not prey.

Seekers were trained to keep a low profile and genetically engineered to blend into the populace. She appeared to be a mundanely attractive woman. Too beautiful and she would be noticed, but too ugly (or even average by old-world standards) and she would likewise stand out. She had a typical pandectic appearance—dark hair that fell down her back in two thick braids, pretty brown eyes, and moderately dark skin.

Anyone who grokked her would find her name and a terse biography in the Cloud, which spoke of her introverted personality and love for long runs. Professionally, she was a level sixty-six player who preferred grinder games related to chemi product testing, mostly lotions and perfumes. All this was a fabrication created by the house that owned her, in cooperation with the Divine Authority, to which she was often of service.

For those few who spoke to her, they did not find her eloquent, witty, or a good listener. Nevertheless, she still passed as human—albeit awkwardly at times. Few, upon meeting her, would feel compelled to invite her to a party or on a date, but that was of no concern to Treva, who only desired the hunt.

And now she had a terrible hunger, a hunger only to be satisfied by those she was imprinted with.

She took a step, leaned back down, and inhaled another slow breath. She concentrated harder this time. Her brain processed the millions of scent threads, ignoring the irrelevant, sifting for just the two. Even clones—genetically identical—could be distinguished from one another through scent. The scent threads of her prey were unique.

Tracking clones was one of the training techniques her masters used. In her early training days, they would not let her feed on what she hunted—cloned products were expensive to raise to adulthood, and it would be a sin to waste them.

But her masters were not here now, and occasionally her nature got the best of her. A few months ago she had tracked a runner to a mall where, it being a public place, he'd assumed he was safe from immediate execution. But this runner did not appreciate the intensity of Treva's hunger. The runner had been elusive, so by the time she caught up with him, she could no longer contain herself; the poor soul was very publicly torn apart.

Because there were many witnesses, her image was suddenly everywhere in the Cloud. Subsequently, Treva had to undergo some plastic surgery and gene therapy to change her biological signature and restore her anonymity—but only after she was severely punished.

She took another step and inhaled deeply again. The cleaner that had sanitized the area had done the job well, but she had picked up a faint trace. She could not identify the direction yet. *Ah yes, tender ones, I'll have you soon,* she thought.

CHAPTER 20

Lily watched the humans as they performed their peculiar ritual. Three of them, D_Light included, were arranged in a circle. They did not speak, but instead made hand gestures and occasionally laughed, winked, nodded, or tapped their feet. Lily knew all the real communication was telepathic. Nevertheless, she thought they looked silly in their silent speech. They reminded her of children playing a strange game of their own invention, rather than the masters of the universe that humans fancied themselves to be.

There were two others near the circle, but facing outward, ever so watchful. The pair was bristling with weapons. The male one looked at Lily only intermittently while scanning the rest of the surroundings, but the female allowed her gaze to linger on her as though probing.

Lily reminded herself that she had to be insane to remain with this pack of eccentric "players," as they called themselves. If he were alive, Todget would be horrified and perhaps profoundly disappointed to know she was putting such trust in the enemy—perhaps the very ones who were responsible for his death. It was then that Lily had to admit to herself that her trust was not founded in a genuine hope for safety, as D_Light would have her believe, but out of simple curiosity...and something else. Intuition?

It was customary to have an intermission between each quest in a MetaGame. This allowed players to rest and regroup between challenges. Also, it was thought that this pause gave time for the next quest to be chosen for them by the artificial intelligence software or whatever was running the MetaGame. D_Light had been a little afraid that the others would turn him in during the intermission. After all, the quest did not say that those of the party who became "demonized" had to *remain* in the party. However, he hoped that this was inferred. Besides, had he not proven himself a valuable asset? Still, moving forward with a demon in the party was bound to be problematic. The others might be demonized as well for aiding and abetting him. They were taking a big chance, and so it came as no surprise to D_Light that when the party reunited, the topic of who stayed and who went immediately came up. D_Light, Lyra, and Djoser opened a conference blink.

Djoser began. *It's one thing to bring you back into the party, but her? I mean no offense, D_Light, in case you've taken a liking to that girl, but she's an additional risk. Besides, you cannot add a member to the party. It is against the rules.* Djoser crossed his arms to signal that the conversation was over.

Lyra smiled smugly. *Actually, read the rule again.* Lyra then shared a text visual of the rule to which she was referring.

MetaGame Rule #11: You may lose a member of your party at any time for any reason, including death or incapacitation, without being dropped from the game. You may not replace or add another member to the party unless doing so directly accomplishes a quest.

Well? Lyra threw up her arms. *D_Light became a demon because he helped this girl, Lily, right? Because he took Lily with him—because she joined him—he became a demon, and becoming a demon was the quest. Her addition to the party was a natural byproduct of the game.*

D_Light added, *A rather ingenious way to add a member to the party, if I may say so myself.* D_Light patted himself on the shoulder and grinned. He preferred to let the rest of them think he had planned it all out this way. Djoser looked mildly amused, but his smile seemed to suggest, "Don't push it."

Fine, and what does this girl bring to the table? Djoser asked while raising his eyebrows.

D_Light anticipated this question and answered without hesitation. *She's in good shape. She can run like hell. She seems to be able to defend herself pretty well. She adapted to the spanker world really fast, so I think she's got a good head on her shoulders. Most importantly, she's been a demon for a while and never got caught. She's bound to know a few tricks to keep us free and clear.*

Lyra frowned. *I thought you helped her escape.* D_Light had briefed the others on the events earlier that morning while they journeyed to their rendezvous location.

Yeah, I don't think she knows much about the Game, D_Light said. *She needed someone like me who could log her into a spank game so she could blend in. But she knows how to live outside the Game, and that's something none of us really know, right?*

What is her deal anyway? Djoser asked. *Is she a sideliner or something? Maybe a product? There's something off about her.*

D_Light knew what Djoser meant. *She doesn't have the markings of a product. So, yeah, my best guess is she's a sideliner, but she hasn't said anything.*

Have you asked her? Djoser asked.

Of course, replied D_Light, *but I think she's been a demon for a while, so she's learned to not blather.*

Lyra nodded and took a deep breath. *We don't have time to explore her life history right now. We need to get going before the Authority catches up. We can learn more about her on the road. If something doesn't jive, we ditch her, no problem. Besides, if at the end of this game we can't fix her demon status, you know...*

We can turn her in for the bounty, Djoser said with a satisfied smirk on his face.

Lyra shrugged. *For the record, you said it, not me.*

"Okay, enough of this," Lyra said out loud. She walked quickly up to Lily. "So, little demon, would you like to join us?" She extended a hand as though she expected Lily to kiss it.

Lily did not. Instead, she inspected Lyra's hand as though measuring the character of the stranger based on her finger length. "I don't see why—"

Lyra cut her off. "Thanks to our association with *you*, we are all demons and now share the bond of being pursued. If we work together, we have the best chance of eluding our hunters. You have been a demon for a while, right? Surely you can help us."

Lily returned an uncertain look.

Lyra laughed. "Look, let me start off by helping you. I have a present." Lyra fumbled about in her travel pack for a moment and pulled out a shimmering one-piece skinsuit.

"This was supposed to be a spare, but you look like you're about my size." Lyra's voice betrayed a hint of disappointment at this observation. "Put it on. I already have a pattern for you to wear that will disguise your face and hair, and best of all, you'll look fabulous!"

Lily smiled and graciously accepted the garment. She quickly found the hidden zipper in the back, looked inside the suit as though expecting to find it lined with scorpions, and then smiled and curtsied to Lyra. "Excuse me while I change," she said, running off to conceal herself behind a solid clump of foliage.

Djoser leaned over to Amanda and quietly said, "Looks like she has seen a skinsuit before. Maybe she's not such a primitive after all."

Amanda did not smile at her master's joke, but that was not surprising to D_Light, who doubted the product had any sense of humor at all.

Lyra sighed as she watched Lily retreat. She then tugged at something on the back of her collar. With this, Lyra's head and face briefly shimmered and then transformed. Her long hair shortened into a jet-black bob, her face rounded, the corners of her eyes narrowed, and her lips thinned. She now appeared to be from the Japanese bloodline. The device that disguised her head and face was called a veil, which consisted of countless nanotubes of fiber optic wires so thin as to be individually invisible; however, collectively they created an ever so subtle shimmering appearance when not activated. The glass tubes were highly flexible, but they held the shape of petals curving up from the collar of her skinsuit, encasing her head like a closed tulip. With a veil on, one could project an illusion of just about any face and head imaginable—or at least whatever an illusionist could program.

Lyra's clothing changed also. She now wore a loose-fitting silken blouse and pants. The microspeakers embedded in her skinsuit did an excellent job of simulating the sound of swishing fabric as she walked. Lyra smiled, showing fangs similar to Amanda's, and then she twisted and crouched down into a traditional kung fu fighting stance. "Who wants some?" she asked.

Djoser applauded and called out, "I think I just pissed myself!"

Amanda watched Lyra intently and ran her real fangs over her lower lip.

A pretty woman appearing to be of Middle Eastern descent emerged from behind the trees. She wore a shawl that would have been a traditional Muslim shawl had it not been streaked with a seemingly infinite number of colors that pulsed and shifted. The shawl was semitransparent, making visible a hint of her well-fitting skinsuit beneath it.

Lyra smiled at her. "You look perfect, Lily. PeePee, show her how she looks." Lyra's ferret familiar dutifully opened its jaws and projected a hologram of Lily so she could see herself.

D_Light had forgotten that Lily had no familiar of her own and therefore had no way of seeing what she looked like to other people. He took it for granted that he could see how he looked anytime by having Smorgeous view him from the familiar's perspective and send him the video feed. This was so routine, in fact, that D_Light never even had to tell his familiar to do it. D_Light would just have to wonder how he looked, and there he was.

Lily looked pleased with her appearance as she hopped about in a circle while watching herself. The motion did not cause any distortion in her image. The veil did a good job of compensating for gravity and movement. High-quality veils never distorted, except with the most violent motion.

D_Light looked over to see that Djoser had engaged his suit now. He resembled an ancient Victorian era gentleman, complete with a tall top hat. His face had changed from a man of roughly Indian descent to one of a darker African ancestry.

"You guys want to blend in, right? Why not choose a more common look?" D_Light was referring to the pandectic racial features of most contemporaries—skin that was a very dark tan, almost black, with relatively angular facial features close to that of a Caucasian.

"What's the use of playing a game if you can't have some fun?" Lyra shrugged. "Oh, we did some shopping on the way here and got you a veil too."

D_Light laughed. "Let me guess, a greased-up albino in a G-string." Not that it mattered. D_Light knew he could just select a design of his own choosing from his virtual closet.

Lyra walked around and up behind D_Light, whispering near his ear, "Close." She unsnapped his collar and replaced it with the one embedded with a veil.

D_Light almost thought he could hear a low whistle as the nanothreads overhead scanned his face. With the momentary scanning complete, D_Light became a little girl. More precisely, he was a six foot one inch girl with the infantile facial features of a child no older than three. He wore a pink leotard, a large bow in his long blond hair, and frilly pink dancing shoes. D_Light chuckled as Djoser nearly busted a gut laughing.

Lyra frowned. "Oh, not funny! Not funny at all! Okay, I'll change you fast before this is imprinted upon my psyche."

Presently, D_Light's body and face blurred and focused back in, displaying a Victorian like Djoser.

"I say, spot on!" D_Light did his best to mimic a British accent to accompany his new look. The country of England, like most countries, no longer had any real identity, but the accent still belonged to a few and, more importantly, remained part of entertainment culture.

"So now that we all look fabulous, where shall we go?" Lyra asked with enthusiasm. "We don't have a quest yet, but our handsome couple here," she said, pointing one index finger at Lily and the other at D_Light, "is surely being chased down by Soul knows what."

D_Light nodded and added, "They'll be using sniffer bots to find us. That's what was chasing us at the spanker ghetto."

"Righty-o! No one will be able to ID us with an image grok, but we're still vulnerable to sniffers," Djoser said with his own poor imitation of a British accent.

"Actually, not all scanners scan visual appearances, you know, not all scan light," Lyra said. "Some use seismographic scanning, which draws our physical features and contours. The light illusion created by the suits we're wearing will not fool these types of scanners." Lyra smiled and added, "I did my research on my way here."

"Sure, but these disguises will still fool people just using famscans," D_Light said.

Lily furrowed her eyebrows slightly and said, "I must confess that I do not follow all of this discourse, but might I make a suggestion?"

Everyone turned to regard Lily; even the familiars fixed their cold eyes on her.

Upon gaining their attention, she said, "I would often go for walks at night, but as a precaution I would go for a swim before returning home. A scent cannot easily be followed through the water. The lake I swim in is only a few miles from here."

No one answered her. Rather, they opened a conference blink with one another, again leaving Lily out. Despite some hesitation by members of the party regarding swimming in a cold and possibly dangerous lake, it was finally decided that going anywhere was better than staying put to be hunted down.

At last, Lyra said out loud, "Thank you, Lily. Let's have a look at your lake."

They followed a path covered by gold-colored fungi that offered excellent traction; it yielded enough to make walking comfortable, but not so much as to be extra work. Brian, skinned as a retro wrestler complete with evil leather mask, strutted ahead of the others, vigilantly grokking everything in sight. Djoser and Amanda lagged in the back, Amanda deftly massaging Djoser's shoulder as they walked. Lyra was in the middle, apparently lost in thought. D_Light walked beside Lily, mesmerized by the undulating colors of her shawl. "You said you didn't understand what we were saying earlier?" D_Light asked her quietly.

"Very little," she nearly whispered. "What is a famscan?"

"Do you know anything—"

D_Light was startled by a nectar bat, the size of an eagle, flapping by on its leathery wings. *I'm a jumpy newbie demon,* he thought. *Gotta get used to it.*

Lily raised her eyebrows at him, and he quickly tried again. "Do you know anything about familiars?" He nodded toward his cat as it prowled just ahead of them.

"Some. I have used one before," Lily answered.

"A famscan is an optical scanner familiars use to see light similar to a human, which can then be fed into its master's mind. The reason these are bad for us is because of grokking."

Quizzically, Lily looked over at him again. D_Light smiled and said, "Right. So, grokking is something strangers do to each other all the time. Let's say you see someone you think is interesting." D_Light winked at her. "The first thing most people do is discreetly have their familiar take a visual of the person with its famscan. Then they search the social registries to find the person's profile. From there you can find out all kinds of stuff about the person."

"How intrusive!" Lily recoiled. "But, well, maybe not," she said thoughtfully. "Those profiles are voluntary, right?"

"Yes, and people love to blab on and on about themselves, so most players don't mind being grokked," he replied. "And why should they? No one's finding out anything you're not volunteering, and chances are that info is going to be pretty idealized." He chuckled. "There's always stuff on people in the Cloud besides their profile—stuff that might not be so flattering."

Lily grinned. "Hmm, it still sounds a little creepy."

"Not at all, once you get used to it," D_Light assured her. "In fact, most players love it. For example, there are a lot of public places with the sole purpose of being seen and seeing what there is to see.

These places are called grokstas. A groksta could be in an outdoor setting, like a traditional park, or indoors, like at a club. Of course, to most players the entire world is a groksta."

They had passed by dozens of people on the trail. Most of them had familiars. Lily wondered if any of them had grokked her.

"Actually," D_Light said, hesitating for a moment, "I have to confess that the first thing I did when I saw you was give you a grok."

Lily rolled her eyes up at him. "I was wearing my cloak, was I not? You couldn't 'get a visual.'"

"No, no, your hood was off. You were under that tree just staring up into the branches." D_Light hoped he was not blushing. Meanwhile, Brian had slowed down ahead and was cocking his head sideways as though attempting to listen in. D_Light slowed his own pace to widen the gap.

They were quiet for a moment. Then D_Light said, "But you weren't in the register. In fact, there was nothing at all on you in the Cloud. You're a demon—I know that now—but you didn't come up as one when I grokked you."

Lily was not eager to talk about why this would be, or anything else about herself, so she employed the strategy of harvesting information from D_Light at a furious rate. She had an endless array of questions that she fired off in rapid succession, and each answer prompted additional questions. As they spoke they watched the birds and bats gliding on the air currents high above. The two were so absorbed in this interview that when they finally reached the lake, they nearly tripped headlong into it.

CHAPTER 21

The beady eyes of fish #4332, which resembled the head of a push-pin, stared out into the murk unblinkingly. Its vision was poor, but a fish like this did not need to see. In fact, it had few needs at all. Like most animals throughout the eons, only two essentials existed for it—feeding and reproduction. Fish #4332 had no predators in the lake to worry about, which was a fortunate thing since it was a predator's dream. It had no teeth for defense—it did not need them. The algae it fed upon (algae #12543) was high in nutrition, easy to swallow, and easy to digest. The fish could not swim swiftly, for it had no tail. Its tiny pectoral fins, which fluttered furiously when they were engaged, afforded the animal just enough locomotion to slowly approach its food, and not even that if there were any currents to contend with.

The water-dwelling animal was merely a streamlined oval hunk of meat that grew larger as it lazily grazed on the algae that greased the surface of the lake with streaks of brown and green. The highlight of its life was releasing its eggs, which were pre-fertilized since this product was gene-clamped and could not benefit from sexual reproduction. It was rumored that one of the wetgineers who designed #4332 added a primitive pleasure feedback loop so that at some level the creature could enjoy this climactic moment. It was also rumored that this resulted in a stiff point penalty for the smart-ass wetgineer; brain matter, nerves, and the like cost energy—energy that could be better used creating meat and fat.

One additional feature that was added to the creature was an instinctual attraction to light. At night, robotic trawlers would shine lights on the water and wait for the fish to collect in large, slowly rippling mobs near the surface. When adequate numbers gathered, the automated nets would scoop them up. Fishing had never been easier or more efficient.

Floating motionlessly in the lake, slowly gulping the murky waters that passed over its gills, the fish now saw something, albeit dimly. It was a disturbance in the surface above. In addition to light, such fish were also attracted to any oddity on the surface. It often meant that fish flakes, a welcome supplement to their regular algae fare, had been poured in from the bright sky, zigzagging downward as they sank. The fish, and many others of its kind, began whirring its tiny pectoral fins to slowly make its journey toward the splashing above.

Other than Lily and Brian, everyone was having a devil of a time swimming. Brian's armor provided floatation thanks to the tiny nanofiber-lined air pockets designed to provide padding to protect against blunt force trauma. Lily, to her credit, was simply an excellent swimmer. The others paddled feebly over the surface of Lake Washington, desperately clinging onto their respective buoyant familiars to keep themselves afloat. Amanda, who did not have a familiar, was weighted down by her swords and panted and spat as she struggled along.

No one spoke except Brian, who was saying something to Lily up ahead, but D_Light could not make out the conversation over the sound of his own splashing and gasping. He was about to yell at them to wait up when he felt something bump him from beneath the water. He suspected he had brushed against some tall-growing aquatic plants, but then he felt another soft bump. Then another. Next he felt a gentle pinch. He was about to look down for the source of this molestation when he heard a blood-curdling scream coming from Lyra, followed by shouts from Djoser.

My soul, they're under attack! I'm under attack! He then began shouting and flailing too.

Amanda said nothing, but her eyes were wide and her fangs were bared. She appeared to be trying to paddle closer to Djoser, but his panicked kicking was making that a difficult endeavor.

"Mother!" Brian shouted and commenced a frenzied swim back toward his mistress.

"Oh, the fish have come!" Lily exclaimed joyfully.

Looking down, D_Light vaguely recognized what appeared to be a writhing mass of dark shapes in the water.

"The fish are schooling around us. They might think we're food," Lily said with a lilt in her voice.

"We're food!" someone shouted, and the general panic continued.

Lily began laughing so hard she nearly sank. She then took a deep breath and shouted, "They can't hurt you! No teeth!" And with that she gently plucked a fish from the water. The gray oval creature was nearly too large to be held effectively by Lily's small hands, but it flexed back and forth so feebly that she was able to hold it effortlessly. Its scales glistened dully in the sun, and its tiny mouth opened and closed rhythmically and idiotically, like the mouth of a puppet.

Panting and still splashing some, the others stared at her.

"See? They are sweet and cannot hurt you," she called, giving the fish a kiss right on its mouth.

Lying behind a boathouse to dry off in the afternoon sun while mocking each other for their theatrical performances in the lake, the party enjoyed a hearty laugh-fest. Their familiars collected archives from each person and patched together a 360-degree rotating video of the event and dubbed it "The Feeding." Djoser nearly published the video into the Cloud, thinking that an entertainment grinder might use the content and kick some points his way. However, he quickly caught himself as he remembered that they were supposed to be fugitives. They were in disguise, of course, his own monocle and stupid top hat playing a major comical part in the video, but he decided that it would be prudent to publish later—after the MetaGame was over.

Since their skinsuits naturally repelled water, the party dried rapidly. The next quest had not yet come in, and thanks to their little swim, Lily assured them that they had thrown off any would-be pursuers—or at least delayed them. If there was a good time to get some sleep as a demon, this seemed like it was it. Djoser could not remember the last time he slept. His last boost had not worn off yet, so he had his ferret-styled familiar, Moocher, give him a downer. He tugged at one of Amanda's long hair tails. Dutifully, she crawled around him and began massaging his shoulders.

As he felt himself entering deeper levels of relaxation, his eyes becoming heavy, Djoser considered the bit of brown scum from the lake that had hitched a ride on Lily's naked ankle; the heat of the midday sun was baking it into a flaky crust. Groggily, he could smell her wet skin, and it made him wish that she was the one massaging him. But he decided not to request this just now. He could work on Lily later.

Djoser, you're a pig, Lyra's voice chided him over a blink. Djoser was startled back awake. *Did I broadcast that last thought?* he wondered.

Always thinking of yourself. Has not our advisor, the one you thought so inadequate, proven himself instrumental in our success thus far? Djoser caught the wink from Lyra, who was lying nearby on her back, her veil down so he could see her real face. Her wet hair was crumpled around her head.

Djoser let out a low groan of frustration. *If it will shut you up,* he sent back to her. Djoser then tugged on Amanda's hair again, beckoning her down to his lips. He whispered in her ear.

Amanda crept up behind D_Light, who was lying on his side. "Your father asked me to thank you," Amanda purred softly.

D_Light, who was in limbo between slumber and wakefulness, initially thought he was dreaming. The product's long nails—lethal in other contexts—scratched softly and expertly over his scalp, her warm breath doing something wonderful to his ear that caused a shudder of pleasure up his spine. He wanted to ask her what Djoser was thanking him for, but her hands were moving over him now, going to all the right places. D_Light did nothing but groan quietly. His hands clenched into fists in the lawn. His eyes opened into slits. Lyra was smirking at him. She spoke softly, almost in a whisper. "You deserve this."

D_Light felt conflicted. This was rather unexpected. Did he respectfully decline? Perhaps ask to delay his reward for a later time, a time when he was not out on a lawn surrounded by his teammates? But this indecisiveness lasted only a moment, for Amanda's limbs began intensifying their play as her fangs gently raked his neck and her hot breath washed over him. *I cannot risk insulting them,* he thought. *I do deserve this.* He smiled back at his mother.

Lyra opened a conference blink with both D_Light and Djoser, which Smorgeous accepted instantly. *Stick with us, D_Light,* she sent. *We'll take good care of you.* Her eyes sparkled as they flickered down suggestively to where Amanda had reached into the opening of his skinsuit.

We're good friends to have. Djoser's thought signature was faint, indicative of one drifting off to sleep.

I know. And— D_Light did not finish sending his thought before he whispered out loud, "Oh Soul!" D_Light decided it would be best if he expressed himself naturally. Certainly Djoser would like to know his gift was appreciated.

Lily turned over on her side and propped her head up with her arm to see better. Her brow was furrowed slightly, and her lips parted as though she were forming a question. Brian tapped her on her foot, and when she looked at him he rolled his eyes at D_Light. She gave him a faint smile as though the two of them were sharing a joke, and then she nodded her head in agreement.

It was a strain on Lily to force a smile. What she wanted to do was scream. Only hours ago, she had never engaged with any human besides the professor, and even that was purely in a clinical and professional manner. Now she was lying in a pool of them. They seemed friendly enough, they listened to her, and they even followed her into the lake. She sensed that some of them cared about her well-being. Nevertheless, they were insane—every last one of them—with their games, their thought speech, their peculiar facial expressions, and now this. *What is she doing to him?*

Lily understood what humans did to reproduce, and it was supposedly a normal and necessary thing, but this did not appear to be what was taking place. The mechanics were all wrong. She looked like she was eating him rather than mating with him. Perhaps it was a sort of courtship that would culminate in a proper union. Or perhaps she was witnessing how humans died. Despite her research at the lab, it was evident that these creatures still held many secrets. She turned away from D_Light and the fanged woman to stare out at the lake. She wondered if she should leave this group, or if ultimately these humans were inexplicably linked to her fate. Perhaps they could provide her a path into their world; therein, she could find what she was looking for, whatever that was.

———————

The seeker let out a low growl as she stood at the water's edge. Her prey had gone straight in. They had left their clothes on. Perhaps they swam off, or maybe a boat had picked them up.

No...not a boat, she realized after a moment. She no longer had their scent, but she had been tracking them long enough to know them. She was certain there was no boat because the trail they'd left was not that of a party with a good escape plan. Their scent and tracks spoke of anxiety and lack of resolve. Ironically for a killer, a seeker had an extraordinary sense of empathy. Such was needed to imagine themselves in the place of their prey. Now Treva imagined the party swimming in the frigid water, their fingers going numb while their clothes dragged. She imagined their disgust at the dark water and fear of what was beneath the surface.

Finally, there was the fact gleaned from the Cloud that most of those in the party were not strong swimmers. *They will stay together. They did not swim far.*

She stood still and concentrated on the scent threads that came to her. There were thousands of them—threads from the water itself, threads from the algae scum on its surface, threads from the thick aquatic plants that grew up from the heavy mud below. But there was no trace of her prey, not yet. Although irritating because it distracted from her work, she would now have to send word to the Divine Authority of this recent development.

Katria swore out loud, catching the attention of the waiter product that was busily wiping down a nearby table. The waiter bowed and asked if he could be of further service. She waved him off without looking at him.

So the little shitters ran straight to the water, Rhemus blinked in. *Well, two points to them for doing the obvious.*

Katria chuckled despite herself. *Good thing I contracted the seeker for the job rather than by the hour,* she returned.

Yeah, just think, if it doesn't catch them, we don't pay a point. He paused. *You made the right call. Don't sweat it. Once a seeker gets imprinted, they don't give up. It's just a matter of time.*

What Rhemus said was more or less true; however, there was an eventual timeout clause in the contract. House Xando knew better than to sign a contract that took one of their precious seekers indefinitely out of operation.

Forget it, Rhemus said. *Kick back and let it do its job. What's that you're eating?*

I'm not sure, Katria replied. *I never like to know. I just want it to taste good.*

And here I thought you didn't like surprises, Rhemus teased.

Only pleasant ones, Katria answered with a grin.

Earlier, Katria did have a pleasant surprise, a gift from the OverSoul. Having offered the necessary prayers and point sacrifice, the OverSoul dispensed the divine inspiration she needed through her familiar. It was so simple. Like a judo master, she would use the demons' own weight against them, and they were bound to fall hard. No matter about the stymied seeker. Perhaps it was a blessing, for now she would have the opportunity to see this divinely inspired plan come to fruition.

CHAPTER 22

Human genetic engineering started in the United States. This was a surprise at the time to those who speculate on such things. The expectation was that China would fire the first shot. China, a newly minted superpower, had both the means and a seemingly unhindered view on ethically problematic issues. Nevertheless, many historians believe that the catalyst for America's plunge into "accelerated human evolution" was in response to Asia's economic rise to power. The West did not want to give up their hegemony. As the American middle and upper classes' grip over exclusive and high-paying employment continued to erode in the global economy, so did their qualms about tampering with nature. Parents had always wanted to give their children an edge, but then on the competitive international stage, "want" became "need."

But let's not be too harsh on these U.S. parents and their suppliers. Pandora's box was destined to open eventually, and when it did, it did not even take a generation before nearly everyone in the world was saving their dollars, their yen, or their euros to level the playing field for their own child.

Improving the long-term health and attractiveness of their children was easy enough, but the real demand was for boosting intelligence. Historically, parents had always secretly hoped for a "gifted" child, and now this gift could be purchased.

Thanks to such market forces, it was only a few generations before much of the world was genetically homog-
enized. Now was the opportune time for a virus to strike.
When the TerriLove virus exploited a weakness in our
shared proteomic signature (one related to the nervous
system, incidentally), it raged with abandon. We were
like identical shafts of wheat, standing straight and im-
mobile, awaiting the scythe.

Is it any wonder the OverSoul banned engineering on humans? Only through the seemingly random drunken walk
of sexual reproduction do we gain the diversity needed
to meet an unpredictable future.

—Excerpt from "Musings of an Immortal," by Dr. Stoleff
Monsa

---

*I will find you. It is impossible to hide from me. You think you are clever, but
your vanity is your undoing,* Ascara the witch cooed as D_Light sank
below the frothing waves.

It was then that D_Light woke, not because of the nightmare,
but from the numbingly recognizable voice of his familiar. *Master,
your quest log has been updated.*

*Another nightmare? How is that possible? Smorgeous, analyze the
dream...somehow. What's that about my vanity?*

*Master, you have not experienced a dream state in the 23.4 minutes you
have been asleep.*

Not that again! What the hell is going on?

*Master, you have another quest. You have made it clear that the Me-
taGame is your highest priority.*

D_Light groaned. His head swimming, he cursed at his computer. He was sticky. He remembered where he was—remembered the lake—and wondered if he should go take another swim to wash off. Without waiting for permission, Smorgeous saturated his master's optical senses with the quest log.

Quest: Seek out Dr. Monsa, great-grandfather of the House of Monsa. Dr. Monsa is the head patriarch of the House of Monsa. The House of Monsa is located at the following coordinates...

That is nearby, only thirteen kilometers from here, Lyra's thought broke in. D_Light did not realize that Smorgeous had joined him into a blink with the nobles. Now the three of them were sharing thoughts as they reviewed the quest. It was more than a little disconcerting when his familiar shared his mind without explicit permission. Now he had to be careful to shield his thoughts in case something embarrassing cropped up in his head.

Finally, we get a softball, Djoser said. *Go find a local immortal. What then? Say hello?*

The doctor is by all accounts an elusive and unpredictable man, Lyra replied. *Might not be so straightforward.*

D_Light opened his eyes. Lyra stood over him, arching her back in a grandiose, catlike stretch. She spoke out loud, groggily and to no one in particular. "Let's move out. We can work out the details on the way."

After creeping out from behind the boathouse and through a yard overlooked by the large bay windows of an old-fashioned brick and mortar dwelling, they found their way onto one of the public trails. They walked quickly, trying to make good time. As they travelled they discussed how best to tackle the quest. According to what they could gather from the Cloud, the doctor would be very difficult to contact by remote means.

"Dr. Monsa is all about the biogames," Djoser said. "He's not going to talk to anyone that isn't either a crack-shot wetgineer or otherwise on his short list."

Lyra asked, "We will need to visit him in person then?"

Djoser nodded. "Yes, for outsiders like us, that would probably be the only shot at meeting him." He frowned. "I blinked my mother about it. She won't even try to arrange a meeting."

"Same here," Lyra said. "I tried to pull a few strings, call in a few favors, but nada." Grinning, she added, "I think everyone who's in the know is afraid of this guy. Afraid to piss him off or something."

"No doubt," D_Light joined in. "He's holed up in his main house, the one not far from here. And by holed up I mean he's in deep, in a part of the house called the inner sanctum." He chuckled. "Sounds a little intimidating, eh? That's where he does his research. Apparently, it's some sort of Darwinian freak show in there and only the truly determined would want to enter—enter the sanctum." D_Light did a mock shiver to feign fear.

"Well, I'm determined," said Djoser with confidence. "Have you seen the action on this MetaGame lately? A whole lot of people want to get a piece. The point spread is looking good, and the sweet pot is up to thirty large." Djoser patted Amanda on her rump to add emphasis.

Thirty large! D_Light thought. The term "large" was not a denomination of one thousand as it was in the old days; it now meant million. If they won, even his tenth share of the pot would be worth more than what he'd made off fragging Fael. *My Soul, this could be my week!*

"Hey, by the way, when I contacted my people, I didn't have to explain our fugitive situation to anyone," Lyra said. "It looks like none of us is in the public demon database."

"Yeah, but did you check your own private status?" D_Light asked.

Lyra replied, "That's just it. I come up as a 'suspected demon.'"

"At least you're only suspected," D_Light muttered.

"Curious though, don't you think?" Lyra asked. "If the DA really wanted to catch us, why wouldn't they make our status public?"

"I'd hate to think they were *not* chasing us," Djoser grumbled. "That would mean I took a swim in that slime lake for no reason." He gave Lily a hard look meant to be teasing, but she seemed to misunderstand it, at which point he patted her on the shoulder. Lily merely arched her eyebrows at him.

"Well, I for one have never been hunted by the Divine Authority before, so I'm not exactly sure what to expect," Lyra said. "I say we proceed as though we *are* on the hot list. Better safe than stunned and reformatted."

————

Night had fallen by the time the team neared House Monsa. Presently, they were crossing an immense suspension bridge, the railings and lines of which were overgrown by light-emitting vines that merged into a shimmering glow, a glow that stretched out over the kilometers of bridge ahead and behind.

Lily had hustled several bicycles from players using her paper hard currency bills, which were still wet and crumpled from the lake. Now all had bicycles, except for the bodyguards, who had to share one. With excellent balance, Amanda sat on the handlebars. Brian didn't appear to mind the view.

The only automated transportation on the road was the commercial bots, heavily laden with goods. The team had entertained the idea of trying to hitch a ride on one of these, but the AI-controlled vehicles could not be bribed and moved too fast to hop on the way a drifter might catch a boxcar. Other House Monsa commuters either strolled on the pedestrian lane of the bridge, lost in their own virtual worlds, or hissed rapidly by overhead in liftcars. Renting a liftcar was out, so the team did a great deal of furious pedaling and eventually approached House Monsa, which loomed ahead like a mountain at the terminus of the great suspension bridge.

Using the enhanced vision of the familiars, which rode in saddlebags on the bikes, the party members could see the great house as though it were daytime. It was unlike anything any of them had ever seen. They stopped and silently regarded the sight before them.

The house itself was constructed of an unusual variety of dro-vine that was unfamiliar to the curious onlookers. Unlike the soft, green, spongy dro-vine of the spanker ghetto, this species was colored silver and its exoskeleton was hard with sharp edges. The splendid quality of this dro-vine, coupled with an inordinate number of sparkling windows, made the castle's sheer, jagged walls resemble an inverted cluster of icicles that jutted from the lake into a high-altitude display of splendor, the turrets and towers being the icicle tips. However, unlike the austere and barren ice found in high mountaintops, these soaring spires were sprinkled along the ridges with rich greens, luminous blues, blood reds, and every other color imaginable. The effect was as though a god, quite haphazardly, had thrown confetti across this mysterious structure. This confetti, however, actually represented private and public gardens, some of which clung precariously to their perches, hundreds of meters, if not a thousand, into the air. The garden lights were the product of a billion photo-emitting flowers.

Besides the photoflower gardens, there were lights lower down on the lake, artificial ones, used by the house marina to guide boats in and out. The marina was situated inside a sea wall where a few thousand boats were lashed to a network of dimly lit floating docks.

Large commercial barges, lit with their own reds and greens, floated by soundlessly.

D_Light realized this was likely a romantic setting. Remembering the events of a few hours before, he smiled at Amanda, who rode arm's length from him. "Hi there," he said.

The ever-vigilant bodyguard detected his gesture, but she rested her eyes on him only momentarily and then moved them away without acknowledgment. He might as well have been one of the bridge railing posts.

That must be insects, Lily said in D_Light's mind. Because they were sharing Smorgeous's visual at the moment, Lily was able to blink D_Light without permission. It wasn't polite to blink without first sending a request; nevertheless, D_Light let it go.

To show what she was talking about, she pinged on the vid feed a subtle, smoky mist that collected here and there about the spires.

Smorgeous magnified the view. *Not insects,* D_Light declared. *Those are bats! Big ones!*

D_Light had never seen so many creatures being used to fuel a single dro-vine structure. He supposed it made sense. The living structure was incredibly thick and therefore did not have adequate surface area to survive on hyper-photosynthesis alone. The bats were needed to ferry nectar from the nectar trees of the mainland to the island, the distance being too great to use insects for the task. Indeed, larger animals were required, ones that could efficiently make the crossing. These bats fit the bill, being genetically engineered animals. By imprinting them with the location of their roosts throughout the dro-vine castle, they tirelessly gathered their payloads and brought them back home. There they dispensed the nectar into receptacles that fed straight into the building's circulatory system. The bats took for themselves only enough of the energy and nutrient-optimized nectar to continue their work and, when energy reserves were sufficient, reproduce.

Lily went on. *They are so breathtakingly busy! Collecting, collecting, depositing, depositing...*

And to think that many of them are probably asleep! You see, for harvesters, when it's time for a nap, half their brain shuts down while the other half controls flight. Some migratory birds have done this for millions of years. We have since borrowed that nifty innovation.

Fascinating, Lily replied. When asked, Smorgeous did not detect any sarcasm pattern in her thought signature.

D_Light relaxed and allowed himself a moment to take in the silver and black cloud of harvesters rapidly swirling around, in, and out of the glowing icy crags. *My Soul, what is this place I'm going to?* he thought.

Just look at it, Lily. This...this ecosystem is an example of God's work. Efficient, elegant, beautiful.

God's work? I thought this was all designed by people?

The OverSoul is in everything.

It's beautiful; however, those bats just seem lost to me, lost in their single-mindedness. A little sad, I think, Lily said.

We are all just thralls of biochemistry, D_Light replied. *Besides, it would be wasteful to make them any other way. Have you heard the old saying "The world is a jawbreaker"?*

No, she answered.

There was a time, a time before the OverSoul, when the world was like a jawbreaker, a hard, round candy, that we sucked and gnawed on over the centuries, slowly consuming it. We didn't do this because we were evil, we were just animals doing what animals do—eating.

What a silly saying. So are you—I mean, we—no longer animals?

Of course we are! However, we now have a shepherd.

Perfect! So we're not even handsome animals? We're the livestock, chewing our cud and grinding our lives away?

Yeah, I suppose. Just like that, only less nihilistic.

Too late, I think I'm going to drive my bike off the bridge, just like a big dumb cow, Lily said with a laugh. *So on the bright side, the world's no longer a jawbreaker?*

No, it's this. In a grand gesture, D_Light had Smorgeous pan out for the optimum view of the House of Monsa. He then turned to look over at Lily to see her reaction. He was startled to find her gazing right back at him. She was obviously not watching Smorgeous's feed.

"Umm," D_Light said out loud as he stumbled over his words. "Your, your veil is off." D_Light's front tire wobbled, and he struggled for a moment to keep from colliding with the railing.

"When you plugged me into your cat's eyes, I saw myself as another person. It was...unsettling. I'd rather keep track of who's who," Lily said.

He could see the silhouette of her exquisite face in the glow of the marina. *Fine for now. No one's around. Put it up again before we arrive,* he said through the blink.

She nodded as she returned facing forward. He glanced back over his shoulder at the seemingly endless bridge behind. From time to time, he continued to look back while he pedaled as though making sure the shadowy bridge was still there...and to keep an eye out for rogue bot trucks.

Meanwhile, Lyra and Djoser were just ahead, riding side by side. The two nobles chatted aloud. "I've arranged to meet a friend of mine," Lyra mentioned. "She's not of very high rank, but she is a mother of this house and has promised to get us in. Actually, Djoser, you know her. Sweet_Ting?"

"Sweet_Ting?" Djoser shrugged. "Uhhh! I'd look her up, but—"

"No! Don't even consider pinging the Cloud. We don't know how we might get traced. Only peer-to-peer blinks," Lyra warned. "Look, you met Sweet_Ting when I did, at that mixer last year, remember?"

"Hmmm, drawing a blank here."

"For Soul's sake, Djoser, you perved the woman!"

There was a pause. "Oh, right! That skinny, bug-eyed girl!" he exclaimed. "Hmmm, she wasn't the brightest, was she?" Djoser chuckled.

"That didn't stop you from going in on an intimacy permit with her," Lyra jibbed.

"Actually, that bitch made me pay for the whole thing. Said it would 'soooo be worth it.'" Djoser turned his head and spat over the side of the bridge rail, down into the blackness below.

"Maybe not so stupid after all," Lyra said, "although seducing you is about as difficult as pedaling this bike." She then looked back over at D_Light. "Not that I would know from firsthand experience," she added with a wink.

Lyra leaned back on her seat. "Aside from convincing you to foot the bill for an IP, I believe your estimation of her intellect is correct. She can't even get a breeding permit. She told me she was turned down just last week."

"Ouch," Djoser said. "But she's a mother of an important house."

"True, but she was born with her title. Apparently, the DNA fairy chose to withhold the brains. I guess even parentage like hers is no guarantee," Lyra replied.

Djoser let out a low whistle. "Her parents must be peeved. Imagine spending the points for a breeding permit and then having a dud like that? I bet her parents wished they could have engineered her like in the old days. Makes you wonder why the OverSoul changed the rules."

"*Everyone* knows why the rules were changed. Even Sweet_Ting knows that," Lyra spat.

Djoser looked back at Lyra. "I know, but if I ever decide to have one, I'd like to make sure. I mean, I want to get some kind of return on my investment!"

Lyra switched to a blink, effectively shutting D_Light out of the conversation. *Genetically engineering humans is a deadly sin,* she said with emphasis. *Would you want to risk being demonized? You need to have your familiar erase your archive of this conversation.*

We're demons now and it's not so bad, Djoser responded.

Suspected demons, Lyra corrected. She looked over toward D_Light. *Only Dee and the new girl are demons. Besides, our sins were necessary to win the MetaGame and will be purged upon completion.*

Lyra's thought pattern was a little ragged, and Djoser thought it sounded like she was trying to convince herself. He would have preferred more resolution in her tone. After all, he was taking a big gamble with this whole game. He had half a mind to turn D_Light and Lily in to the Divine Authority and be done with it. He did not want to lose the MetaGame, but he did not want to get on the wrong side of the OverSoul either. The last thing he was curious about was what, exactly, "demon atonement" entailed.

"Anyway," Lyra continued out loud, "even D_Light didn't commit a deadly sin." She looked pointedly at Djoser. "You watch it or I'll turn you in for heresy. Erase your archive or not, I've got mine and D_Light has his."

"Oh, I'd prefer you left me out of it," D_Light said flatly.

"Look, thinking outside the box is divine. I'm not serious. It's not a sin to think about sin, right?" Djoser's voice was pitched an octave or two higher than usual.

"Well, at any rate," Djoser continued in a tone that seemed to suggest that the conversation may as well end, "lucky for you and me that we both have good parentage *and* the brain genetics came through."

Lyra was quiet for a moment and then said in an offhanded tone, "By the way, if Sweet_Ting brings it up, you know, about the breeding permit? Be sure to console her properly."

Djoser rolled his eyes.

The stairway leading up to the main entrance of House Monsa was long, and it towered over them. Snaking down the staircase was a line of tightly packed people waiting to get into the lounge, the house groksta. Some were there simply to enjoy the groksta, while others hoped to find a way into the house itself and perhaps—if they possessed the right traits—even apply for family membership.

Following closely behind Lyra, the party ignored the line and withstood the weight of many hateful glares as they ascended to two enormous doors that stood wide open. Half a dozen armed guards flanked the doors, and while a few of them nodded to people as they passed through, most of the square-jawed men just stood stoically.

Lyra walked straight up to the first guard and said, "We are here to see—" Her sentence was cut off by a screech from just inside the immense doors. A slender pandectic woman with a beautiful face but distinctively bulging eyes rushed out and embraced Lyra, nearly sending them both backward down the vast stairway below.

The woman's assault was so fierce that D_Light half expected an edgy Amanda to sink a blade into the stranger's side. Amanda, however, did not react at all except to watch the newcomer carefully. Products like Amanda were designed to read body language very well, much better than most humans, which was no small feat given that human evolution had dedicated a great deal of effort to learning how to perceive subtle signs from one another.

"Lyra, it's you!" Sweet_Ting exclaimed as she carefully parted Lyra's nanofiber veil. "At last you visit me!" Sweet_Ting let the veil fall back into place to hold Lyra by the sides of her head as though gazing into a crystal ball. Lyra smiled and looked like she was about to say something when the whirlwind of a woman let her head go and moved to Djoser. She parted his veil. "Djoser!" she squealed and kissed him squarely on the lips before he could even speak. "Oh, what a perfectly stupid top hat! My, it's a dream to see you again."

The greeting confused D_Light. In his experience, nobles of different houses exchanged formal greetings when they met. For example, when a noblewoman like Sweet_Ting greeted another noblewoman, they would each bow and say something ingratiating like, "The face of a princess, only younger!" A noblewoman's greeting to a guest nobleman might sound something like, "I avert my eyes, for your virility makes me blush." This process tended to take some time since it was expected that each party would try to one-up the other's compliment, resulting in a tedious arms race of flattery.

Sweet_Ting, in contrast, made immediate physical contact and was saying things that were not scripted. It amused D_Light to watch Lyra and Djoser squirm under the ambiguity of such a reception. He also found himself taking an instant liking to the woman, unsure if it was due to her unexpectedly casual nature or her remarkable ability to make her uptight friends uncomfortable. Whatever the case, he appreciated the brevity with which Sweet_ Ting immediately beckoned them to follow her into the lounge. The gesture was made specifically to Lyra and Djoser, but the others were apparently welcome also.

Just inside the doors was a small secondary line. Smorgeous strode ahead to have a better look.

Master, it's a blood scanner, Smorgeous said as he beamed the visual back. Under the watchful eyes of a guard, visitors were taking their turn placing their palm down on a small, veiny, gelatinous slab.

Mother, they are going to take a blood sample! We will be exposed!

Relax, D. None of us are in the public demon database, and there are no flags on any of us, remember? Lyra was using her soothing tone.

And the guest list is supposed to be discreet. House Monsa won't send it to the Authority without a special request. There's no reason for the DA to suspect us to be here...and don't look so frightened! That actually might raise suspicion, Djoser said. Further up in line, he was peering back at D_Light with his monocle.

Anyway, House Monsa requires blood of all visitors. Just a chance we have to take, Lyra said.

CHAPTER 23

Sweet_Ting strutted through the lounge of House Monsa as though it belonged to her, which, in a sense, it did. Although she was not an exceptional player by any measure, she was still the daughter of nobility, and one of the many benefits of being a noble—aside from immortality—was a traditional minimal status given to your offspring, a base status that noble children could rise above but could not fall below. There were houses that waived these nepotistic house rules, favoring a purer meritocratic flavor, but the House of Monsa was not one of these. And so the waifish Sweet_Ting strode forward with her light and luxurious gown flowing behind, confident that the crowd would part for her. She seemed genuinely surprised as, time and time again, she had to pause for some poor pleb in the crowded hall who did not see her coming and stood dumbly in her way. Each time this happened, Sweet_Ting had to dislodge the oaf with insults and threats, her eyes bulging as she did so. She might have even resorted to violence if it were not for the fact that she was not built for such exertion. She knew that any kick or punch she dished out would harm her more than the receiver.

Right behind Sweet_Ting strode Lyra and Djoser, who, upon again finding themselves among society with norms they benefited from, had also adopted a certain confident, if not regal, gait. Amanda guarded Djoser's side and swiveled her head about, one hand resting on a sword hilt, watching for dangers. At the very least she would protect Djoser from undesirables, such as stupid plebs who lacked the sense to give them a wide berth. Unlike Sweet_Ting, Amanda was designed for dishing out pain and was not at all averse to shoving those whose offense was only mild and delivering debilitating hand jabs to those less fortunate. Brian also cleared groksters from their path, but he relied primarily on his broad shoulders, which mowed through the crowd like a plow through snowdrifts. He enjoyed this activity and secretly hoped for a small altercation that might require a brief demonstration of his other, more impressive skills.

Bringing up the rear were D_Light and Lily, who would have been left behind in the shifting throng of guests had they not determinedly shoved and stumbled behind as quickly as they could. More accurately, D_Light did the shoving while Lily slinked her way through the crowd like a mongoose, which was no easy feat given how distracted she was by the lounge scene. She had never seen anything like it.

The groksta-goers alone were a sight to see. Swarms of people were on the floor all around them. People were lined up on winding stairs that twirled their way high into the air, up toward the massive vaulted ceilings above. There were people on transparent-floored verandas, people who seemed to float on nothing, people on stages, people lying near an elaborate fountain, people everywhere doing everything. And how these people dressed! It was obvious that veils were allowed in this groksta, as many of the hairstyles and hats defied natural laws of physics. The clothing, both real and illusory, was outlandish in both volume and color. Accessories were random and odd, such as children's toys or ancient building tools. Taken together, the scene reminded Lily of a dark vision she'd had one night when she was ill with a particularly bad strain of a hallucivirus.

And then there were the products. There was a giant rabbit so massive that a fully-grown woman was perched in a saddle on its back. The rabbit, however, did not move much. Thankfully, it was trained to not smother the people who were stroking it under its huge, furry rump. The woman did not seem to mind the rabbit's docility. Perhaps it was enough for her to know that she was riding a rabbit, however slowly.

Lily caught glimpses of mermaids and mermen breaching a nearby stone-lined pond. Great gouts of water flew here and there, drenching onlookers who screamed and laughed. Genderless human-shaped figures without faces stumbled around with outstretched arms, stalking giggling groksters in a sort of perverse game of tag. Furry little snakelike creatures gently made their way through slumbering groksters, occasionally stopping to groom someone's hair with their long, forked tongues.

All of this madness was contained in a chamber so terrifically immense it felt as though they were outdoors in the hot, moist evening of an alien world. Giant video screens adorned every wall. Some screens displayed performers in real time on stages sprinkled over the vast floor, while other screens assaulted the viewer with images and video of all kinds—some beautiful, some grotesque, and many more that Lily had no idea what to think of.

A woman was walking pointedly toward Lily. Aside from her face, she was skinned entirely as a leopard. Lily turned to press forward through the crowd, trying to catch up with the others, but she ran into a man in front of her. She made a motion to pass, but he quickly moved sideways and blocked her path. His hand came up toward her face, but she blocked it. Another hand reached out, and she slapped it aside. There was laughing from those who pressed around her and then more reaching and clawing. Finally, her veil was forced aside by someone. A man whose eyes shone like hot coals pressed in for a momentary peek. Upon seeing her, he gasped and took a step back. "My lady," he said and bowed. The leopard woman curtsied. Others near her began bowing and murmuring. Lily hurried on her way.

Stag preserve me, they're insane! she thought.

Eighty meters above the swarming floor, a small girl was perched atop a dro-vine throne. This was Love_Monkey, who was on watch duty for her father, Dr. Monsa. She enjoyed presiding over the lounge, the family groksta. It gave her an unobstructed opportunity to observe intelligent beings as they played out their dramas and comedies on the floor. Often, usually at least once a day, someone worth noting would grace the lounge. Tonight, it was the Middle Eastern woman trailing behind Sweet_Ting like a water-skier towed by a speedboat.

Love_Monkey was not interested in this woman because she was a celebrity. Being a celebrity, even a newly minted one, did not by itself earn one interest from a groksta hostess like Love_Monkey, who by now had even grown tired of A-listers. No, it was not *who* the woman was, but *what* she was that fascinated the daughter of Dr. Monsa, the most revered wetgineer on earth.

Love_Monkey opened a blink to her eleven cloned sisters. *OMG, you will never guess who just walked through the big doors.* Love_Monkey did not wait for them to guess. *A camper!*

There was a general chorus of chatter back and forth between the sisters, who, although engrossed by their various assignments, were very interested in the news.

Love_Monkey deduced that the camper was disguised because her appearance did not match her expected genotype of blond, blue-eyed bombshell. The rest of her party was disguised too, but such optical veils were of no use to anyone entering House Monsa. Unlike most houses that at most used DNA sniffers to sift through visitors, House Monsa required blood, a miniscule amount collected painlessly as patrons passed their hands over the detector.

What would a camper be doing here? the hostess wondered. She shivered with excitement, looking forward to finding out.

Shortly after the appearance of the camper, another interesting specimen stalked through the door. *A seeker,* the hostess thought. She frowned. Seekers were rare, but wherever they went, trouble soon followed.

Led by Sweet_Ting, the party ascended a stairway up to a private pillbox that was anchored on the side of the crystalline dro-vine wall. Bright green vines intertwined the pillbox banister, making it look like an elegant tree house. A table resembling black obsidian sat in the middle with several CumfiMoss™ chairs surrounding it.

One of the seats was occupied by a smooth-skinned man with a face that reminded D_Light of a hawk. This bird of prey eyed the party intently, as though appraising how good they might taste. A limestone-faced man in a dark suit and crimson red tie stood at attention and, as the party approached, scooted seats out for Sweet_Ting, Lyra, and Djoser. The nobles took their seats gracefully, their respective bodyguards standing attentively behind their charges. The marbled servant made no motion to seat D_Light or Lily. Sweet_Ting glanced up at them, frowned, and shook her head dismissively.

Lyra smiled apologetically to D_Light and Lily. "I believe the remaining seats are taken," she said. Her voice was less apologetic than her smile and far more formal than it had sounded during their adventure up to this point. She then added, "Maybe the two of you could find a seat down on the floor or at the bar."

D_Light turned away and looked down over the expansive floor below. He would have descended the stairs, but the way was blocked by an ascending crowd, so instead he stood at the side of the stairs and waited for his turn. He noticed there was a throng of people on the floor below who appeared to be gawking at him. One of the throng was pointing. He didn't like that. *Perhaps we should go up the stairs instead,* he thought.

As she waited for D_Light to move, Lily faced away from him and the stairs and looked toward the table. Lily did not gawk at anyone in particular. She was familiar enough with human culture to know that staring was generally considered rude. Instead, she merely scanned over the guests sitting at the table, taking note of their posture, how they held their drinks, how they held their utensils as they daintily stabbed at colorful morsels of food that she could not identify. She had never been in a groksta before, and there was much to see, so much to learn. As her former employer, Professor SlippE, would say, "Watch and learn, for the most expedient way to anonymity is through imitation."

Sweet_Ting, however, did not appreciate seeing Lily's veiled brown eyes sweeping over her party as though she had a right to do such a thing. "Pleb, I asked you to leave," she snarled. "If you think there is a place for you at this table, then you truly must be a n00b," she added with a pretentious chuckle. She then gave a curt nod to her servant, who, without changing his stone expression, set his dark eyes on Lily and withdrew a short-barreled pistol—and then he promptly shot her.

The impact gave Lily a jolt, and she fell back a step. Her illusionary dress and headscarf sputtered and then blanked out, leaving her shimmering skinsuit exposed. A fluorescent pink spatter marked where she had been hit. Lily might have retaliated against her attacker—Todget had taught her several effective defensive moves—but by the time she recovered from the surprise of the assault, the servant had tucked the pistol back into the fold of his suit and had stepped back to his post, arms folded, presumably no longer a threat.

Sweet_Ting turned to Lyra and Djoser and demanded, "My Soul, where did you get that one?" She then looked back at Lily, who was still mulling over what had happened. "Yeah, dimmy, you're a n00b and now everyone knows it! You should learn to be where you're not wanted." She then let out an exasperated sigh and added, "I mean *not* to be where you're not wanted. Like not wanted here in *my* house."

D_Light, startled to discover how quickly things had gone downhill while he was not paying attention, put a hand on Lily's shoulder and whispered near her ear, "You're fine, you're not hurt. Just follow me." He motioned for her to go down the stairs. D_Light then bowed deeply to the annoyed noblewoman and announced, "My lady, my apologies. The pleb does not find herself in civilized society often and—" D_Light's sentence was cut off abruptly as Lily, her eyes narrowed and her face flushed with rage, grabbed an unattended glass on the table near her and flung the contents onto Sweet_Ting. The noblewoman let out a ragged gasp, her bulging eyes swiveled, and her jaw dropped as though she was witnessing the end of the world. Her hands were rigid and splayed out in front of her.

D_Light stood in shock. "Oh Soul! Lily, what have you done?" Lily did not have time to answer, as she and D_Light suddenly found themselves surrounded by two men and two women with a variety of hipster hairstyles, all wearing identical tight-fitting yellow organic body suits. D_Light reflexively grasped the hilt of his dagger. He would have preferred his throwing discs, but these goons were too close. Somewhat disconcertingly, the new arrivals did not have goon expressions on their faces. Rather, they were smiling—not the kind of smile that said, "We're going to enjoy beating the living devil out of you," but regular smiles, the kind friends give each other. D_Light didn't know what to make of it.

One of the men, an unusually tall and gaunt specimen, beamed at D_Light and Lily and then bowed low. Presently, he spoke. "Begging your pardon, but do I have the honor of addressing Ascara of Hexos and Boobooma of Sanadas?"

Over the prostrating man's head, D_Light could see that Sweet_Ting had stood up with what force her frail body could muster, nearly knocking over her chair. She pointed at them while speaking, but D_Light could not make out her rage-garbled words. Her servant stood at her side, and his eyes roved over D_Light, Lily, and the four strangers. He seemed uncertain about what to do.

Of course, D_Light instantly recognized the names Ascara and Boobooma. After all, they were the names of the NeverWorld characters he and Lily had used that very morning. *Yesterday morning,* Smorgeous corrected as the familiar flashed the time of one seventeen in the morning.

"Ah yes, that is us," D_Light responded to the gracious stranger. "You know of our work?" D_Light could not help but grin as he said, "However, as I recall, those two fine heroes were vaporized by Pheobah the Dark Queen and her abomination of a son, Salem."

As the tall, smiling man returned to his upright position, D_Light could not see Sweet_Ting's bodyguard (dubbed "Mr. Personality" by D_Light) or the rest of his party, but Smorgeous, who was near the ground and was able to peer between the legs of the throng, assured D_Light that while Sweet_Ting displayed distraught facial expressions and body language, neither she nor her muscle-bound servant were making any obvious hostile overtures. D_Light was tempted to pipe his familiar's visual feed into his own, but he decided that he preferred being ignorant behind his screen of bodies. The scene couldn't be pleasant.

A splay of peacock feathers suddenly erupted from the smiling man's head, a veil trick D_Light had seen before. It was a gesture that some people, usually of the more flamboyant variety, used to show respect to another. However, under these circumstances, D_Light was more startled than honored.

"Heroes indeed!" The smiling man clearly intended the words to erupt as a majestic boom, but instead they ended up escaping as a grating screech. "Verily, you were smitten by the wretched queen, but you were not lost! Do you not know?"

The man looked at D_Light incredulously. D_Light ratcheted his full grin down to a half grin, raising his eyebrows expectantly. He could hear squeals of excitement from his other new "friends." The smiling man blushed, managed the impossible feat of widening his smile even more, and then broke the news. "You are celebrities! Celebrities the world over! Everyone in NeverWorld has heard of your deeds!" He bowed again. "You honor this groksta by coming here."

Another yellow-jumpsuited man could contain himself no longer. "Please, please allow us to escort you to a VIP table," he exclaimed while clapping his hands in rapid, dainty succession.

Lily felt completely disoriented, and her face was flushed with blood. One moment she was being shot by order of an enraged noblewoman, and the next thing she knew she was being bowed to and informed of her celebrity status. D_Light looked over at her and could see her anxiety and feel her apprehension. D_Light couldn't blame her for not trusting these strangers; however, he felt they were in no position to refuse. He wanted to get away from Sweet_ Ting's icy stare, and this seemed like a good exit.

It was unlikely that this mother, as stupid as she was purported to be, would directly harm D_Light. After all, he was a human and even had life insurance. Injuring him—much less killing him— would come at a dear price. Even if Sweet_Ting were willing to pay the cost required to harm him, she would most likely be breaking divine law. D_Light's complicity in insulting Sweet_Ting was circumstantial at best. Nevertheless, Mr. Personality was most certainly a combat-ready product, and if his mistress lost her cool, D_Light and Lily may find themselves getting hit with something far worse than a n00b pellet.

Having weighed all factors, D_Light now bowed to the stranger and replied, "We thank you and would be delighted to take you up on your offer."

D_Light grasped Lily's hand firmly as the strangers led them up a few open flights of stairs. As they ascended, the smiling man's entourage packed around them closely, particularly around Lily. D_Light was not sure if this was for their protection, to threaten them, or simply a poor understanding of personal space etiquette. There was nowhere to run to anyway. If this was a trap, they were as good as caught.

CHAPTER 24

Dr. Monsa: As you know, I never decree a house rule without explaining my reasoning. Rules with a poorly understood purpose breed contempt and are therefore destined to be broken. Rule number eight states, "All that enter the House of Monsa must submit a blood sample." Why?

Love_Monkey: The answer is obvious. A family has a right to know who enters their house.

Dr. Monsa: That is one correct answer.

Curious_Scourge: Father, a sniffer could positively identify entrants. Why do you require blood?

Dr. Monsa: Sniffers can be deceived! But there is a more important reason. More than just DNA can be gleaned from blood. Indeed, even the power over life and death.

Curious_Scourge: Spare us the melodrama, Father!

Dr Monsa: Allow me to explain. Circulating in the blood of most citizens are deployment bots called D-bots.

Curious_Scourge: D-bots?

Dr Monsa: They are nanobots, a little larger than a red blood cell. They are merely boxes that contain useful chemis. When they are given the right signal, they empty their contents into your bloodstream. Most commonly, they contain pharmas. Say you want to relax. Send a signal to release some DownTime™ into your system. Instant relaxation without a pill, without an injection, merely a thought. The reason none of you have heard of D-bots is because none of my children have been inoculated with them...for reasons that I will explain.

Love_Monkey: Okay, so you know what drugs the person prefers. So what? Power over life, you say?

Dr. Monsa: I mentioned that the deployment bots require a signal to activate, right? Well, every strain of D-bots has a unique activation code or key, if you prefer. To activate the key, you must fire a sequence of radio waves using the correct frequency and timing.

Love_Monkey: So when you get your booster, what? You're given a key to unlock them?

Dr. Monsa: Exactly. Your familiar is given the encryption key so that when you want the chemi deployed, the familiar can fire off the sequence and activate the bots.

Curious_Scourge: So if you could hack the familiar, you could activate the key?

Dr Monsa: That is an impractical strategy. As you know, familiars are designed with security as the top priority. Indeed, the bulk of their computing power is dedicated to being an effective firewall. They are not easily hacked.

Love_Monkey: Aha! This goes back to the blood. You analyze the bots in the blood. You can unlock the sequence.

Dr Monsa: Well done, yes. There are micropanels on the surface of the bots. It's the precise orientation of these panels that specify the sequence. You see, as each electromagnetic pulse hits the bot, a different panel is unlocked, and once they are all unlocked, the bot deploys its contents. By analyzing the surface of the bot, we can deduce the sequence.

Curious_Scourge: And using a radio emitter keyed into that sequence, one can exercise control over a subject's biochemistry.

Dr Monsa: Yes. So, you see? As so often happens, one man's convenience is another man's weapon.

—Excerpt from private archive of Dr. Monsa's "Dinner Discussions"

Upon ascending several stories, D_Light and Lily were led into an opaque plexi-encased pillbox. As they entered, D_Light realized that the plexi was transparent from the inside, so they could see out but groksters outside could not see in.

"Before showing you to your table, let us first attend to the lady." The smiling man nodded at Lily. One of the entourage handed him a smooth silver wand. "This," he said, "will deactivate the tagging dye you were shot with." He passed it back and forth over Lily's torso without touching her. "I deeply apologize for Sweet_Ting's behavior," he said in earnest. "She has a tendency to tag people without provocation."

D_Light now realized that the human wall their fans had formed around them on the way up the stairs was a way to shield Lily from onlookers. Tagging someone with a n00b dye pellet was a common means of publicly humiliating a player. The tagging dye did this in several ways. First, it interfered with the signals used by one's skinsuit so that he or she could not cover up the stain with illusion. The lenses in the suit simply did not work, leaving the victim with a bare suit marked with a large florescent stain on it. The stain made one's "n00bness" apparent to anyone "realing," anyone not jacked into a skin.

This, however, was a subtle effect compared to what people who *were* jacked into the skin saw. In nearly all cases that D_Light had seen, the victim had large, three-dimensional text hovering over his or her head that said "n00b." In addition, the victim's body was rendered in some humiliating way. For example, virtual excrement continuously falling out of their buttocks, clown clothing might appear, or they may find themselves nude with large tattoos like "Being a slut is divine" or "I dun't understand smart stuff." Sometimes these outfits would scroll from one to the next to keep it interesting. Of course, the face was never covered up. That would defeat the purpose; in fact, it was usually magnified like the gigantic head of an old-time cartoon character. D_Light had seen one n00b cover his face with his hands and try to run, but since he could not see well he bumbled into groksters, which only led to more kicks and having food and drinks thrown at him. Finally, if these effects were not getting enough attention, a spotlight would appear and follow the n00b around.

Thankfully, Lily had been protected. No one could see her behind the bodies of their newly found entourage, and only the most determinedly sadistic jeerer would try to force their way through that phalanx.

Having finished deactivating the dye on Lily, the smiling man asked if it would be all right if he and a few friends joined them after the two had taken some time to relax. D_Light quickly consented. The smiling man's smile consumed his whole face now, and he bowed several times on his way out the door of the VIP box, coined the "veepox."

Although not asked to do so, Smorgeous had grokked the entourage that had taken them up to the box. As expected, the smiling man, whose name was WholeLottaLuscious, or just plain "Will," was a midlevel noble. He was 103 years old and in the fifty-fifty queue for salvation. *Not a bad guy to impress,* D_Light thought. The others were just regular players, but of pretty decent level, except for one who was a product. Judging by her product line and manufacturer, she was probably being used as a general assistant.

Inside the veepox was a large crystal table, suffused from within by a soft blue glow. Several large, elevated chairs invited the guests to sit. Once perched upon their seats, D_Light and Lily commanded a perfect view of the fray several stories below. A handsome, muscular product immediately swept in to present them with drinks from a plexi platter. "Our house special, just to start. Please feel free to browse the menu." He then bowed and made a swift but graceful exodus.

Smorgeous notified D_Light that he had been given command of the veepox controls, which meant that D_Light could now control the temperature, lighting, sound filters, and various other properties of the chamber with no more than a thought to his familiar. *I could definitely get used to this lifestyle,* he thought. He took a deep, satisfying breath and slumped back in his chair, allowing his legs to fall gently apart. *Yeah, this is the life.* He took a sip of his complimentary beverage and enjoyed a moment of silence while the warmth of the potent libation worked its magic.

Having appreciated his brief moment of relaxation, D_Light began to think about how they should be acting in this situation. He had spent plenty of time in grokstas before and knew that it was customary to lift the one-way opacity of the plexi windows once your party was seated so that others could see you, and so that is what he did, except for the plexi that covered the floor. He assumed Lily would not appreciate people looking up her virtual dress at her virtual lingerie or whatever her restored skinsuit styled under there.

They had an excellent view of the main floor below, and they could also see the pillbox they had just left. D_Light caught Lyra and Djoser stealing glances. Sweet_Ting did not even try to hide her contempt as she glared up at them. This veepox definitely seemed swankier than the pillbox that the rest of the group still occupied. To be in a superior position to his superiors, so to speak, should have been a moment of glory for D_Light, but he could not relax enough to enjoy it. He couldn't help but wonder if this was an elaborate trap laid out by Sweet_Ting. What a cruel joke it would be to be treated as celebrities and then, just as the two had been convinced they were stars, find that the whole hall was laughing at them. Fortunately, the bubble-headed noblewoman did not seem capable of such an elaborate ruse.

Smorgeous, give me a summary of what all this NeverWorld celebrity talk is about. It sounds a little too good to be true.

Master, you gave explicit instructions not to access the Cloud.

I know. Try to be discreet while you search.

Smorgeous pinged confirmation.

D_Light took another sip of his tangy drink and sank back in his chair again. He felt like he could sink to the bottom of the sea in this thing. In a place as rich with sensory stimulation as this grocksta, most patrons preferred to real; however, D_Light wanted to ensure the dye-deactivating wand had done its job, and so he decided to jack into a skin to look at Lily. He jacked in and was given a menu of skins from which to choose. He chose the theme "Ancient Rome" and saw Lily's clothes transform into a loose-fitting dress. Her hair was curled up into coils, and she was suddenly wearing dark, heavy makeup. Apparently, the illusionist who designed (or fantasized about) this one thought that this was how the women of ancient Rome looked. No n00b sign hovered above her head. The wand had indeed done its job. D_Light then noticed that the table before him was no longer blue-glowing crystal, but white marble. Everywhere he looked, everything and everyone was gilded with the same Roman motif.

Just to amuse himself, D_Light flipped through the menu again and selected "Victorian High Society." Lily was now in a voluptuous dress that spread out like a mushroom. Her waist was cinched by a painful-looking corset. Piano music drifted in from an unseen source. He flipped through several other selections, but in the end decided that even "Almost Real" wasn't real enough; he jacked out. There was enough to see here without a skin.

He turned his gaze to Lily again. "So are we having fun, or what?"

Lily's laugh was short and soft. "I don't know what I'm having. It reminds me of...what do you call it? A dream."

D_Light was trying to think of a clever reply when he saw the mime coming toward them. "Mimes," as they were called, typically looked nothing like mimes from previous eras. Essentially, they were the groksta mascots, and like the mascot of a sporting event, could be dressed as Soul knew what. This one wore a huge, multicolored, shimmering cloak and a mask with an outrageous birdlike beak, something that might have stepped out of a Brothers Grimm fairy tale written while under a hallucinogen. In one hand he held a long leash, on which he walked a large brown bear that was ambulating on its hind legs. Presently, the bear snuck up on a man sitting at the bar and gave him an enormous hug from behind. D_Light could not see the man's face, but he imagined the poor slob was terrified.

That was the other thing about mimes that made them like mascots—it was their job to keep the party going, often at the patrons' expense. Indeed, the friends of the man receiving the bear's affection were laughing hysterically. The mime appeared to be cradling a rifle of some sort in his other arm. Although his bear was occupied with the man sitting at the bar, the mime's snout was pointing directly at their veepox as though watching them. D_Light quickly turned away, hoping the mime either did not notice him or would soon lose interest. As D_Light looked around at the other groksters, he noticed many others peering back at them as well. D_Light found this unsettling. *A dream indeed,* he thought. *The old dream where I'm naked in front of everyone who matters.*

D_Light suddenly noticed the reason for the public interest in Lily and him. There, on a hundred-meter video display that appeared on multiple walls, were Ascara and Boobooma, the duo's NeverWorld characters. Pheobah and her son Salem were standing before the two heroes. The groksta was playing clips from this morning's NeverWorld game. The current clip was of the moments just before he and Lily—or Ascara and Boobooma, respectively—got obliterated. Although filters dampened sound from outside the veepox, D_Light heard the words, "You don't look like much," being chanted from the groksta crowd in sync with Ascara as the beautiful witch mouthed the same words on the video display.

Lily appeared mesmerized by the far-off video display. "So we're famous for that?" She looked over at D_Light, puzzled. "But that was just a game, right?"

"Yup, but it's a game that *a lot* of people play. I mean, over a billion!" D_Light spread his arms wide for emphasis. "When you have that many people playing a game, it's kind of like a parallel world. You get fame in one world and you'll get fame in the other."

Lily leaned slightly toward him. "Okay, but we didn't win the game, right? That Queen Fooba, or whatever her name is, blew us up. It seems to me that *anyone* could get themselves killed like we did."

D_Light chuckled and replied, "Yeah, that's where the old expression 'better to be lucky than good' comes in." D_Light swiveled in his chair to face Lily. "I don't expect you to understand this since you're a n00b when it comes to spank games. Like I said, Never-World is just about as complex as any real world." D_Light took a gulp of his drink before elaborating. "Okay, so we, er...I used a powerful spell to open a portal to one of the most evil and powerful creatures in NeverWorld. That would be Queen Pheobah. Few, if any, spankers in NeverWorld are powerful enough to take on the queen, much less her *and* her son, Salem, at the same time. But we didn't open the portal to fight her or to steal from her unfathomable treasure hoard; no, we did it just to insult her." D_Light put up a finger as though he was making an important point.

Lily nodded. "Right, and that infuriated the queen, who isn't really a queen at all, but just part of a software program."

"Right," confirmed D_Light, "and then she goes on a killing spree, causing a massive panic among the spankers, which—"

Lily put her finger up to D_Light's lips to shush him so she could finish the sentence. "Which allowed us to escape the sniffer bot because it couldn't find us in all of that chaos."

D_Light gently batted Lily's finger from his face and pointed his hand like a gun and fired at her. "Bingo," he said with a wink. "OverSoul gave with both hands to you, Lily, both brains and beauty."

She shrugged in response while her veil covered her blush.

"Right, so that should have been the end of the story," D_Light said. "I sacrificed my character to create a diversion for our escape.

Period. But that wasn't the end. From what Smorgeous has gathered from the NeverWorld forums, Loki, the NeverWorld god of mischief—well, one of the trickster gods at any rate—saw our little confrontation and thought it was hilarious. Loki loves to watch the humiliation of other deities. And so Loki used his immense magic to resurrect Ascara and Boobooma just to vex Pheobah!" D_Light grinned and shook his head.

"So your software characters are alive again? I suppose that makes you happy," Lily speculated.

"It does," confirmed D_Light. "I whiled away countless hours playing Ascara, and I hated to lose her. But all's well that ends well 'cause now we're celebrities of NeverWorld. It is a great honor for a mortal to get the attention of any deity, even one as dodgy as Loki!"

D_Light pounded on the table in excitement. "My Soul, I can't wait to see what plans Loki has for me—or us. That is, if you're interested."

D_Light was interrupted when Lily's hand shot out and gripped his arm. Physical contact from her, with the exception of when she'd knocked him down and put a knife to his throat, was unprecedented, and so his attention was now hers. Lily looked into his eyes steadily. "You look very pleased, and so I hate to bring this up. So we're famous, right?"

D_Light smiled, nodded, and winked all at the same time.

Lily took a deep breath. "And all these people are staring at us, right?"

D_Light looked around him. Indeed, many of the groksters were unashamedly staring, some waving, which meant Soul knew how many others were being more covert. "Yes," he answered.

Lily then put her hands up in the air exasperatedly and hissed, "Demons, remember? I don't know about you, but I could do without all the attention!"

D_Light's smile faded. After a few long seconds of consideration of Lily's words, the truth of her observation suddenly dawned on him. It was so obvious that he felt like smacking his forehead down on the table as punishment for his own stupidity.

D_Light looked around the groksta again, only this time he was not looking for admirers, but for hunters. D_Light knew that agents of the Authority were not obvious. Any one of these people could be an angel, or worse. His thoughts were interrupted by a knock from behind him. It was the mime. He was smacking the snout of his mask against the door like a woodpecker. D_Light assumed it was the mime's way of asking for entry. The dancing bear was standing beside its master, its paws flat against the plexi. Its beady eyes stared vacantly inside, and its breath fogged the transparent wall.

We got those little bitches. Katria sent the message to Rhemus, her longtime playmate. Along with her mental message she sent a video feed of a crowded groksta, but the feed followed two individuals in particular. *They're disguised, but it's definitely them,* she added. *Confirmed by several sources.*

Rhemus replied, *Wow, a popular feed. Looks like a lot of players are hot for them.*

Sure, they're newly minted celebrities, Katria sent in response. *Ah yes, demons. You can always count on them to fall for everyone's favorite sin—vanity.*

Actually, I think lust is everyone's favorite, Rhemus sent back playfully.

Katria sent a n00bicon™ to Rhemus. *Don't be such a bore! You're probably right, but I sound cleverer when I tie together a well laid out plan with a timely idiom.*

Sorry, accuracy is a bitch, Rhemus quipped back.

Katria offered a silent prayer of thanks to the OverSoul. It was in a flash of divine inspiration like a voice in her head that she had thought to set this trap. It was sheer brilliance. Rather than making the conventional move of adding these demons to the demon database and hence put her prey on high alert, she instead made them stand out in a less threatening way.

All she did was use her law enforcement security clearance to nudge the NeverWorld game in the right direction.

Just a little cheat, a little unearned divine favor from a pretend god, she thought. *And then I let the spanker forums and media outlets do the rest. Enjoy your freedom and fame while you have it, fools.*

The sweet scent of the meat puppets was nearly overwhelming to the seeker. It was always a challenge for Treva to focus her attention on her intended prey in such tempting surroundings. This groksta was laid out like a banquet. Warm, sweet meat was everywhere—up on the walls, up on the catwalks and platforms above, undulating and crying on the multiple entertainment stages as though taunting her. She nearly snarled at one fool who stupidly brushed up against her, his neck moist with sweat, so close she could literally taste the tangy high notes of his essence. Her blood sugar was low, and she was feeling very edgy.

It had been with a great deal of relief that Treva got the call notifying her of the location of her prey. She had been searching the lake shoreline attempting to pick up their scent trail again, but the search had been frustratingly unsuccessful. The moment the coordinates were sent to her, she rented an airlift (an expense to be passed on to her client) which dropped her onto this island smothered by the immense edifice of House Monsa. Using her security permits, she skipped the line of sycophantic wannabe groksters. She was, like everyone else, required to give a blood sample before entrance. The guards, designed to be ever suspicious, were not happy about letting a seeker in, but they had no choice.

It took her no time at all to spot her targets. They were the center of attention, appearing to be gift-wrapped for Treva in their pretty glass box. Of course, she would not take them now. Such a public display of violence, especially against these apparent guests of honor, would not bode well for her eval. Instead, she intimidated a patron out of his seat and ordered a drink—a clean one since she was on duty, but sweet enough to take the edge off.

D_Light did not want to give entrance to the mime and his side-kick of a bear. However, he did not want to get on the wrong side of a mime. They were masters of monkey business, and if you snubbed one, they would get you back. Besides, everyone was watching, and the only thing that tended to attract more attention than a celebrity was a rude celebrity.

The mime spread his arms wide as he entered while the bear got on all fours to clear the doorway. "Ah, Deeeelight," the mime began, and then he pointed his snout at Lily. "And his lovely accomplice,

the mystery girl! The floor is abuzz with speculation about you."
The mime sprang over to Lily, snatched her hand, and kissed it. At
least D_Light presumed it was a kiss, as the mime's lips were not
visible under his beak. In any other context one might think a great
bird had taken to gnawing on the woman's hand.

Lily's face went blank. "You can call me Lily," she managed.

"A classic name for a classic beauty!" declared the mime. "Not
your real name, I'm sure, but fine, fine. I can appreciate a mystery
better than most."

D_Light might have had some sympathy for Lily and the awk-
wardness of the mime's greeting had it not been for the fact that he
was having to contend with the unwelcome advances of the bear,
who took him into his great furry arms and squeezed him heart-
ily. The beast, which must have weighed as much as seven men,
knocked D_Light out of his chair. D_Light found his face enveloped
in musky fur, and he could hear the animal's heartbeat. Luckily,
after a brief squeeze, the bear let go. Now free of the humiliating
embrace, he heard the mime say, "Your friend has a sense of humor, although he doesn't look like much." The mime then jabbed
D_Light in the stomach with the muzzle of his rifle and laughed
with a high-pitched bark.

"Never mind all that though," the unrelenting mime continued. "Here's what I came for." The mime then took a long step back
and swung his rifle up to point at D_Light. D_Light felt a jolt of
adrenaline, and his mind raced. *My soul, an agent! Is he going to just
frag us right here?* D_Light clutched at one of his discs but did not
throw it. There was no point in fighting here. He would never make
it out alive.

The gun popped loudly, and a puff of bright pink smoke
emerged from the barrel. Blinded in the pink fog surrounding him,
D_Light heard yet another pop. He expected it was one for Lily. He

then realized that he had felt no impact from the shot and panicked. *My Soul, poison gas!* Instinctively, he fumbled around for Lily and, upon feeling her body, pulled her to the ground with him.

"Compliments of the house," the mime said with a squeak. "Heroes, may your legend grow with every passing day."

D_Light huddled over Lily in a desperate act of protection. By the time the fog had dissipated enough to see, both the mime and his bear were gone. And it was at about the same time that D_Light recognized the familiar scent of the gas that surrounded them. *Not poisonous gas, but LoveGas™.*

D_Light let out a good laugh, allowing his tense body to go limp and fall to the ground in relief. He enthusiastically grabbed Lily by the sides of her head and declared, "Lily, I'm afraid we've been drugged against our will!" Still laughing, he gave her head a couple more little squeezes and then turned to scratch the head of his familiar. "If I want a drug, I'll ask my cat for one." He chuckled at his own joke and then looked to Lily for affirmation that he was indeed funny.

Lily, her expression light and carefree, had what might be the goofiest smile on her face that D_Light had ever seen. Goofy, but beautiful. D_Light had never seen her smile with such abandon. *Ah, the drug works fast, as should anything that comes out of the barrel of a gun.* The words floated through his mind like cumulus clouds on a warm summer day.

"Your cat is beautiful," Lily purred. "I want one."

D_Light nodded with exaggerated vigor. "His name is Smorgeous. He's Smorgeous because he's both small and gorgeous. Get it?"

Lily rolled onto her stomach, crossed her ankles, and kicked back her legs. "I never met a male who liked cats," she mused. Lily reached over to Smorgeous and stroked the indifferent robot's fur.

"You know, where I come from men aren't called 'males,' but hey, I won't fault you on precision." D_Light watched intently as Lily began to nuzzle his familiar, nose to nose. "I'm afraid I hate cats too—real ones anyway," D_Light said. "Every real cat I've met didn't care for me one bit either. Stick their tails up and walk off or, worse yet, hiss at ya. Useless, as far as I can tell. I only bought Smorgeous 'cause he was on sale."

Lily grabbed the robot's head and covered its ears. "Don't listen to him, Smorgeous!" Lily scratched under the cat's chin. "Do you want to come live with me? Do you?" Lily's question was met with blank, staring eyes.

Master, I have failed to identify an effective LoveGas™ countermeasure cocktail available from your onboard stores. The nearest booster station is—

Shut it, D_Light replied.

D_Light chuckled. "You want him to live with you, huh? Well, if he had any taste at all, he would take the trade. Fortunately for me, he's just a stupid computer."

D_Light rested his head against the cool plexi floor and watched Lily's delicate hand caress the cat's faux fur for what seemed like an eternity. The LoveGas™, true to its color and name, was having a wondrous effect. Lying there beside the magnificent creature, D_Light was suddenly consumed by an overwhelming awareness that Smorgeous *was* beautiful. And not beautiful because of his advanced engineering or elegant design, but from the mere fact that he was Smorgeous and Smorgeous was intrinsically beautiful. Or maybe it was the graceful, supple fingers that meandered through his fur that made this picture so exquisite, or the dainty, welcoming hand to which the fingers belonged. The arm, perhaps? Muscular, yet soft and curvaceous. Certainly, that was beautiful. Countless millions of years of evolution culminating in the finest intersect of form and function. *My Soul, the shoulder and the face... No, that is not her face,* D_Light realized.

D_Light moved in closer to Lily and whispered, "Take down your veil."

"Hmm?" Lily asked absently, still absorbed by the task of stroking the robot as though, with enough concentration and a refined technique, she could magically bring pleasure to the machine.

Smorgeous pressed into D_Light's mind, his voice warping slightly like an audiotape losing integrity. *Master, the female is displaying unprecedented behavior. There is a high probability that she is under the influence of—*

Shhhh, D_Light sent back absently. *One hundred and eighty thousand points for that cat and all its upgrades, and it tells me this?* he thought.

D_Light leaned in even closer to Lily and lowered his voice. "Your veil—take it off. I want to see your real face, your real hair." He gently stroked her hair, winding a silky lock around his finger. His lips slowly wandered toward her ear, and he whispered, "Pleeeease."

Lily turned her head to face him, their faces only inches apart. "What about my disguise? I'm a demon, remember?"

"Yes, you are a demon," D_Light said slowly, using his best seductive voice, "a wonderful demon. I want to see the demon, the real demon. The one I saw under the tree this morning." He ran a finger across her cheek, down her neck, and along one shoulder.

Yesterday morning, Smorgeous corrected.

"Lower yours and I'll lower mine," Lily answered coyly.

D_Light lowered his veil before she had even finished her sentence. His dark, wavy hair was disheveled and sticking up in tufts. His chiseled olive-toned face appeared relaxed and free of worry. His dark eyes, fully dilated, resembled large glass marbles.

Presently, Lily lowered her veil. Her long, blond locks suddenly seemed to free-fall from a net as the illusion lifted. Her big cobalt blue eyes resembled crystal gazing balls of old, and D_Light could not break free from their stare. They were dazzling, mesmerizing, and suddenly appeared much closer. His breath stopped. Neither of them moved, but Lily finally spoke. "They're coming for us. We should run." The words emerged softly, but with certainty.

"Don't care," D_Light replied nonchalantly. He did not want to talk. He did not want to think. He did not want to run. The only thing he wanted to do at this very moment was indulge in this all-encompassing feeling of being pulled toward her, into her. He fell closer still, their lips nearly touching. He could feel the warmth of her sweet breath pass by his lips. His hand ascended to the crown of her head, and he gently ran his fingers through the beautiful locks that flowed down her side.

Lily closed her eyes and stroked D_Light's cheek with the tips of her fingers, leaving behind trails of a subtle but intoxicating scent. Now free from the enchantment of her eyes, D_Light was ensnared by her tranquil smile that highlighted her plump, luscious lips. "I think we should run now," she repeated.

Lily rose to her feet, pulling D_Light by the wrist. D_Light followed her lead and would have done so even without being physically coaxed. All he wanted right now was to be near her, and he would do whatever it took to keep her at his side.

The couple floated toward the door as though carried along by the few remaining wisps of LoveGas™ that hovered low near the floor. Outside, people immediately gathered near them. Some of them murmured while others shouted, but D_Light could barely hear their congratulations. Such beautiful people. *My Soul, the humanity!* That thought echoed in his brain again and again, and while under normal circumstances he would have chastised himself for thinking such drivel, tonight he would congratulate himself for thinking it. Right now, in this very moment, he wanted to revel in the noise, the warmth, the sweat of his fellow man…and woman, yes, particularly the women. And although loveliness was spread out in all directions, it was the loveliness of Lily that he continued to follow. She was his siren.

Meandering through the madness, Lily briefly let go of D_Light's wrist to fend off the unwelcome advances of an intoxicated grokster, and in doing so she was suddenly enveloped by the crowd. D_Light shouted something unintelligible and, like a madman, scratched at his arm in anguish. He then launched himself at the human wall, ripped it apart at its seams, and shouted her name. There was laughter, shouts, and screams from those groksters he pushed aside. He found her almost immediately and grabbed at her wildly. She twisted out of his grip easily, caught his wrist again, and twirled him around. His back was now against her soft but strong frame. He could feel her moist lips, so full and so soft, slide across his ear. Whispering, she asked, "Do you remember this? Do you remember when I had you just this way? Should I have killed you then?" She gently bit the lobe of his ear.

He heard an intoxicated shout from the wall of groksters around them. "Hey, me too! I want a biting!"

D_Light's mind was humming now that the effects of the Love-Gas™ were nearing their peak. "You can kill me now if you want," he said. He turned his head so that his cheek was against her lips. D_Light felt pathetic, but he did not care. The only thing he cared about at this moment was making Lily happy. Bodies forming the sea of groksters pressed into the couple from all sides.

"Oh, never mind." Lily's eyes shimmered with tears as she laughed and pushed him away. "What were we doing?"

"We were about to kiss, I think," D_Light answered.

"Oh, we were about to have some fun!" She grasped a handful of hair on the back of his head and pulled, forcing his face to tilt upward. Apparently, they had made their way to the front of one of the stages. Several performers were present, but the spotlight's attention was on the two of them. Lily, as though it were perfectly natural, lifted herself up onto the stage.

CHAPTER 25

"OMG, that n00b slut is on stage," said Sweet_Ting, her voice metallic with irritation.

Djoser sank back into his CumfiMoss™ chair as he slid his pelvis beneath the table. "What an entertaining surprise," he declared.

Lyra frowned and looked about nervously. "What the frag is she doing? Her veil is down! Is she trying to get caught?"

Being that there were many stages in the groksta, the nobles instructed their familiars to zoom in on the one stage in question. Two performers, a man and a woman, had been singing a duet, but having seen that the celebrity was asserting control, they quickly retreated back into the shadows.

Lily took her place on stage, swaying slightly, and adopted a serious, perhaps pensive look. "I want to dedicate this performance to the feeder fish of this lake," she announced, her voice amplified by some unseen device. "You know the fish I'm talking about," she teased. At this she puckered her lips and put her hands up against her chest and flapped them, simulating the feeble pectoral fins of the feeder fish.

Unsolicited music emerged from nowhere, a rhythmic, deep bass vibrating the floor. Lily's eyes opened wide as she heard this cue, and she belted out in a clear melodic voice, "Because the fish..." The bass cut out and then a slow, heartfelt strum of an electric guitar played as Lily paused for a long moment and then belted out, "...ARE SPLENDID!"

The simulated guitar went wild, and the bass picked up again, ascending to a torrent of deep beating. It was at this point that Lily launched herself into the air. Jumping high, seemingly suspended in flight, she wiggled her body in the air like a great salmon jumping out of the water to make the next watery ledge. She leaped again and again, undulating in the air as the music continued at a frenetic pace.

Perched upon a catwalk that overlooked the stage and the crowd, the generous mime fired his gas gun liberally upon them, causing a pink mist to settle over the entire area. The now Love-Gased™ groksters nearest the stage, arms waving high in the air, crushed in tightly and screamed with pleasure.

Lyra was speechless—almost. "Is this embarrassing to you?" She nodded toward the stage.

"No, I'm good," Djoser replied in a tight voice. Amanda was sitting beside him, and judging by the rhythmic movements of her shoulder, she was up to something under the table.

Lyra sighed deeply and cringed at the sight of Lily. "This performance is bizarre, even by groksta standards." She squinted her eyes a bit, unable to tear herself away from the odd performance, but also unwilling to commit her full vision to the spectacle. She then let out a terse chuckle despite herself, a chuckle that turned into a sudden gasp. "Oh frag, now D_Light's getting up there! Someone tell me this isn't happening!"

Lyra turned her attention to Brian, who stood at attention at her side, his eyes glued to the performance below. "Brian, they're making fools of themselves! This is not desirable. Go down there and... well, see what you can do."

Brian nodded in confirmation without removing his eyes from the stage. Then, like a menacing wind, he began deliberately dodging and pushing his way down the catwalk stairs toward the stage.

Brian had no plan. None. In fact, he wasn't even clear on the expectations of his mistress, but he did have an inexplicably strong urge to get closer to Lily. The style of her dance was not sexy, to say the least, but there was something about the way she moved that was alluringly innocent. Not innocent in a naïve way, but in a way that assured the spectator that she was both good and uninhibitedly true to her goodness. Indeed, that seemed to be the effect on the crowd that gathered to watch. Some were laughing, which was obviously the intended effect, but many more were just staring slack-jawed or smiling unselfconsciously as though finally realizing something they had long been trying to work out.

Like pink cotton candy, the LoveGas™ emanating from the mime and his bear on the catwalk above fell down over Treva and the rest of the crowd. If Treva had been a pharma grinder, she might have appreciated the significance of this. Not only was she being drugged, but the effects of LoveGas™ were not necessarily the same for humans as for products—products like her.

All she knew was that she had a hunger, but not the typical hunger she felt on the hunt; rather, it was more intense and…strangely euphoric. She wondered if it was like sexual desire. Treva knew she had no interest in sex. In fact, her designers had not bothered to provide her with a vagina, only a narrow urethra for the purpose of urination. She had no clitoris, of course, as there was no point. Even the hypothalamus, the peach-pit-sized lump of brain tissue that was the key to sexual libido, had been altered to free her of any sex drive. And so this feeling that was growing in her, this titillation, this aggressive sensuality, was all the more bewildering.

She wanted more.

Treva followed her prey toward the stage, pushing her way to the front. Not wanting to attract attention, she did not use her formidable strength for this task, but instead she slowly wove through the frenzied groksters. She was drawn along toward the stage as inevitably as a leaf floats down a river, toward her destiny. And with each and every step, the seed within her grew. Her eyes locked on the girl, the one making the singing noise and the silly, exaggerated movements—movements that attracted Treva to her like a kitten drawn to a dancing string.

Treva was a seeker, and as such she was trained for restraint above all else. Since seekers were born with the innate desire to hunt, they had to be trained in the discipline of self-control. Indeed, without restraint such products would be a dangerous liability. A world where products ran around chasing people and consuming them out in the open would be terrifying and would sow the seeds of fear and discontent, none of which were optimal to productivity among the populace.

Treva knew what she *should* do, just like she always had. She would simply continue to watch her prey and wait for her opening. It was best to take the target when they were alone, where there was less likelihood of witnesses. Although dispensing with demons was perfectly legal, the Authority did not wish to see a slew of seeker-attack videos being published on the Cloud for their shock and horror value. A seeker who did not show proper restraint was punished appropriately, the punishment being simple yet effective. They were suspended from duty for a time commensurate with the infraction, a truly arduous punishment for one engineered for hunting. They were allowed their typical rations of intravenous food, but nothing more—not even feeder products used for training purposes.

It was because of this conditioning in restraint that Treva now felt fear mixed with the thrill. As the traces of LoveGas™ continued to work upon her nervous system, her desire heightened, her inhibitions began to shut down, and all the layers that covered up her true nature were stripped away. Somewhere in the back of her mind she knew she would be punished, but when that girl—that meat puppet—sprang up, flipping in the air as though teasing, it was more than Treva could stand. It was then that the dam that held back her appetites shattered wide open and the floods came rushing in.

Treva's lips parted like they were attached to springs and she snarled, baring her long, deadly canines. She vaulted up onto the shoulders of a stocky grokster and launched off him onto the stage before he even realized he had been used as a springboard. With two leaps Treva closed the gap between herself and her prey; she pounced, but Treva was too confident and Lily too fast. Lily twisted in midair, and Treva clawed at her as she sailed through the air. The seeker scratched the meat with her steel-hard nails but was unable to get a grip on her prey, and Lily crumbled to the stage floor with a crash. Using the momentum from the tumble, she rolled back up on her feet just as Treva, now snorting with excitement, came back at her. Like a bull and a bullfighter, Lily dodged and swept aside the claws as her attacker flew past again.

The crowd roared in a chorus of startled shrieks, gasps, and cheers.

Judging by the fangs and the creature's movements, D_Light immediately identified it as a product, which meant that it could legally be dispensed with. However, that was beside the point. The lovely Lily, the mistress of his soul, was under attack, and that thing wished to rend her flesh and sink its filthy teeth into her flawless bronze skin. The very moment that the creature was clear of Lily, D_Light threw a disc at it. The throw was hard and true, but the creature somehow ducked it and the disc sliced on through the air out into the groksta, perhaps to an innocent's detriment. Never mind the discs anyway. The thing moved too fast, and he might inadvertently strike Lily. D_Light shouted as he unsheathed his dagger and charged at the seeker with the intent to kill.

Treva saw D_Light coming. Normally, Treva would have swiped the throat of an attacker and let him bleed out in a whimpering pile, but she did not wish to take the time for that. Instead, charging at Lily for another pass, she leaped up and sent down a mighty kick that struck D_Light in the thigh and swept him off his feet. The impact spun Treva around, but she landed well and continued the charge. Rather than dodging to one side or the other as Treva expected, Lily ran straight at the seeker and, at the last moment, dove into a somersault, tucking herself into a compact ball that smacked Treva in the leg and knocked her off balance. As Treva struggled to keep her footing, she shrieked with rage. Several people from the audience taunted and threw food at her, but her instinctual hyperreflexes denied the jeerers any hits.

D_Light was on the ground. The kick had been like a sledgehammer, and unbearable pain streamed up his leg. It was not broken, but there was something out of place that prevented him from standing up. D_Light looked desperately over at Lily and her attacker as they danced around the stage. Lily was not running, but she was not fighting either, merely evading. Perhaps she knew that if she retreated into the throng around her, the product would be on top of her. At least here on the stage there was room to maneuver. D_Light might have thought this to be true except that he suddenly realized that Lily was laughing. Laughing! And not the half-crazed kind of laughter belonging to someone whose stress response had overloaded. It was genuine, unabated amusement. She was amazing! Someone pelted D_Light in the back of the head with something soft and watery, but he did not care. He needed to save that wonderful girl!

Treva's prey was proving to be more of a challenge than expected. The hungry seeker had come on the stage to rip this human limb from limb with her bare hands and fangs, but the little girl was staying out of reach. Treva pulled out her stun baton, and the corrugated shaft extended with a rapid series of clicks. Appearing to be a simple rod, there was nothing remarkable about the weapon, but with one hit Treva could bring down a man far larger and stronger than this little fawn of a girl. All seekers had permits for modern weapons, specifically a "low-efficacy modern weapon permit." That meant that Treva could legally use any weapon that fit the requirements of not being deadly, having limited range, and having a limited area of effect. Her baton fit the bill, but Treva soon wished she had a more potent weapon as the taunting little meat puppet continued to duck and weave, avoiding the seeker's wild swings.

With Lily in danger, Brian intensified his push to the front of the stage. It was his time. His time to do what he had trained all his life to do, and he was not about to miss this opportunity. He used the butt of Tiffany, his mace, to prod people aside and, upon reaching the stage, leaped up like a man clearing a high jump. The guard landed on his side and rolled up onto his feet in one graceful move. He heard cheering behind him. *They think this is a theatrical performance,* he sneered. A blink came in from Lyra, but he ignored it so that he could keep his focus on the task at hand. Although the woman swinging the baton at Lily had no product tats on her cheeks, Brian immediately recognized her as a combat-ready product, having fought so many in his training sessions. He knew how they moved, inhuman in the physics of their actions, although this one lacked the precision of most of her kind. Then a thought hit him: *My Soul, Lily is a product too!*

Seeing Lily in action left no doubt. No human could move that fast. Nothing else could have evaded such an intense onslaught for even a second, much less for the duration that Lily had already survived. But there was no time to lose. Lily was now driven into a corner, and the one who meant her harm was slowing her approach, making sure not to overextend herself and allow Lily to escape. This lovely creature only had a second or two left to live.

Brian charged and leaped at the product like a lion ambushing an unsuspecting gazelle. However, when he landed he set his feet and bent his knees to absorb the impact so that he could stop dead in his tracks. His ploy had worked. The product had heard him, as he knew she would. As he landed, she turned and swung her long baton back at him, the tip of the weapon whistling just millimeters away from his chest. She had expected him to be a little closer, but he had anticipated the swing. It was a trick that hypersensitive products liked to play on humans—act as though they don't know you are coming, lull you into thinking you have the element of surprise, and then *bam!*, hit you like they have eyes in the back of their head. It was a move that Brian was all too familiar with.

Having swung her baton with the confidence that she would deliver a decisive blow but then missing, Treva was now open. Brian knew his opportunity would last only for the briefest of moments, which is why he was already swinging good ol' Tiffany. Only a moment ago he had been swinging at empty space, but now—right on cue—the baton was there in the path of his swing. Brian's preference would have been the product's arm or, better yet, its torso, but the savvy guard settled with slamming the heavy, bulbous tip of his mace into the stun baton with a mighty crack.

Treva, not expecting the blow, lost her grip on the rod, which smacked against the hard stage and clattered off into the roaring crowd. She was enraged. She had been watching this new meat puppet in her periphery, the one with the club. Relative to a being like herself, the human guard seemed to attack slowly and recklessly. She had expected to neutralize him with a single strike with her baton, but the seeker had underestimated this one. Now she had lost her weapon. Normally, she would have enjoyed the challenge of a worthy opponent, but now all she desperately wanted was her prey. And this guard was interfering!

Treva turned toward the man as he aimed another blow at her head, but this time she was watching and dodged it easily, and as the club sailed past her, she launched herself on him.

Love_Monkey, the watcher of the lounge, gazed down at the stage from her throne high above. *This will not do,* she thought. Due to the nature of their work, seekers were never a welcome sight, but Love_Monkey had never witnessed one unleashing itself in public. Sanctioned by the Divine Authority or not, Love_Monkey would not abide such violence on her watch. Without hesitation she leaped off of her balcony into empty space, eighty meters above the groksta floor. She fell rapidly at first, but the nanothreads gradually slowed her descent. It was at times like these that Love_Monkey was grateful for the groksta's safety matrix, the web of threads so thin that they were invisible to the human eye.

Groksters were not allowed to use the safety matrix for fun (although they were often tempted); rather, it was there to avoid the stiff point penalties imposed for wrongful death. However, Love_ Monkey was not just a grokster, she was the watcher, and as such she would do what she pleased. This was a true emergency. Falling toward the groksta floor, billions of nanothreads crisscrossed across her small body, stretched, and then, unable to withstand her weight, snapped. Although the threads broke, each one absorbed a tiny amount of her kinetic energy, the collective influence causing her to decelerate as she neared the floor. The damage to the safety matrix was of no concern to the hostess, who knew the threads would self-assemble again.

During her fall, Love_Monkey had withdrawn an emitter from a QuickPocket™ in her dress. Her familiar had called up the blood profile of the seeker, but Love_Monkey was too far from her target for the emitter to work properly. As the floor zoomed in, she readied the kill switch.

The human male was adept with his weapon, and so Treva endured some solid blows, one of which nearly broke her arm. But seekers were built to take a beating and Treva had no time to play, so she took her licks and then proceeded to rip into Brian. She tore at his flesh indiscriminately with her sharp fangs and steely nails, and his body quickly became slick with blood. Astoundingly, the girl—the one Treva had hunted all this way—jumped on the seeker's back, grappling with Treva and screaming. Treva felt the dull sting of a blade as Lily stabbed into her shoulder and neck. Lucky for the seeker, her prey was less adept at attack than it was at evasion, and Treva estimated her wounds to be nonthreatening.

Treva bit down into the throat of the troublesome man and then snapped her head backward, effectively severing Brian's carotid artery. He crumpled to the floor in a dead heap, blood spurting from his neck. With the nuisance now disposed of, Treva turned her attention to the little girl on her back, the one Treva had been imprinted with. The scent of her prey pressed up against her was overpowering. Soon she would feed. And when she had satisfied the worst of her hunger, she would then feed on the other one, the man limping toward her with his pathetic little knife.

The bloodthirsty seeker snatched a handful of Lily's hair, and just as her brain was sending the signal to her muscles to pull the prey off her back, Treva felt the most wonderful feeling of her life. She threw back her head, moaning in ecstasy. She then fell to the ground. Her back bowed and she started to pant. Lily was still on Treva's back, cutting into her wildly, but the hunter did not feel the knife; rather, the seeker writhed on the ground sensuously. The quiet from the audience was deafening. Then, all at once, Treva's body convulsed in an explosion of haphazard movements and then went limp. The whites of her eyes turned pink as the blood vessels ruptured under pressure. Lily was still on top of the seeker, hacking away like there was no tomorrow. Blood spatter now covered Lily's body, but no one could see it behind the illusion of her skinsuit. Treva's limbs started twitching violently.

D_Light, dragging his injured leg and clutching his knife, then fell on top of the seeker and joined Lily in the grisly task of butchering the downed hunter.

Love_Monkey bent her knees slightly to absorb the shock as she landed on the stage. She looked down at the emitter's clearly lit readout display. It was targeting the D-bots in Treva that carried the pharma MaxiDrive™. This drug was often used as a well-being pharma, but it was also a very effective pep. No doubt the seeker carried MaxiDrive™ in her bloodstream for those times when she needed an extra kick of adrenaline. Love_Monkey had set the emitter to an infinite loop, which meant that it sent the release signal over and over very rapidly. This emptied all of the MaxiDrive™ available into the seeker's bloodstream over a fraction of a second. Her pulmonary and circulatory systems were overloaded, or at least that was what it was supposed to do. Love_Monkey was unsure if her emitter had killed the seeker, or if it had merely incapacitated her while the other two stabbed her to death. Either way, her objective had been met.

"My Soul, it's like the murder of Julius Caesar down there," Djoser said as their party watched the show from their pillbox. Lyra's mouth hung agape, and speaking to no one in particular, she muttered, "We are all going to be reformatted for this." Sweet_Ting said nothing, her lips pursed tightly and her eyes bulging more than usual.

Lily and D_Light, as though waking from a trance, ceased their butchery. The great hall was nearly silent. With expressionless stares, they looked up at each other and then out into the audience. Suddenly, the hall erupted in deafening cheers. The point reader above the stage shot up as the audience ratings began streaming in. By now, several guards had taken positions along a railing overlooking the scene, their crossbows leveled down, uncertain where to point as hundreds of rabid groksters rushed the stage to embrace the talented "performers."

CHAPTER 26

"My father does not take appointments and rarely keeps the ones he makes," Love_Monkey stated coldly to Lyra. If the child-framed daughter of Dr. Monsa was intimidated by Mother Lyra, the tall and beautiful noblewoman, she did not show it.

Lyra smiled pleasantly down at the girl. "It is imperative that we speak to him. Certainly you can grant us an audience with your bio-father."

Love_Monkey smiled sweetly. "Perhaps I should do this as payment for the live entertainment members of your party gave us—you know, the performance that left two unrecognizable corpses up on stage in the middle of *my* groksta?"

Lyra's lips turned into a thin line.

"No matter," the girl continued. "I'm not even going to ask why there was a rabid seeker chasing after your friends or how you might have run afoul of the Authority."

"The seeker was a rogue product," chimed in Djoser smugly. "They are no more than predators. Surely one is bound to snap. It is we who should be upset. Mother Lyra just lost a good man, an exceptionally talented and dedicated guard. It will be expensive to commission and train a new one. Perhaps we should upload a formal complaint." Djoser made the threat in a casual tone, but his smirk was instantly wiped away when he saw the expression on Love_Monkey's face.

The girl glared back at him with her small, pale hands clamped into fists. Her watery blue eyes then darted over to one of her guards who stood at attention nearby, loaded crossbow at the ready. "I suggest that you not speak again," she snarled, malice dripping from every word.

D_Light sat on the soft dro-vine floor, paying no attention to the conversation. He had stripped off his skinsuit, wearing only his undershorts. A medic with product tats knelt down on one side of him, rubbing some chemi into D_Light's leg while a medical bot scurried around, instruments extending in and out of its metal body as it ran its routine diagnostic protocol.

D_Light's mind was still reeling. Having left the groksta and its overwhelming sensory overload, he now felt numb, deaf, and mute. Fortunately, the LoveGas™ had not yet begun to wear off, so he felt fine despite the pain in his leg.

Lily stood nearby, leaning back against a wall. She too appeared to have stepped out of a chainsaw massacre. D_Light lay back, flat on the floor, and reached up to stroke the back of her calf. The snakeskin texture of the microlenses hissed softly with his strokes. Her large blue eyes shot open at his touch. She watched him. Her expression was neutral, an unreadable mask, and she did not move her body. D_Light just stared back and smiled for what felt like a pleasant eternity.

Katria watched over and over in shock as her rented seeker was butchered on stage in front of thousands. It was as though she could hear her god laughing at her. First, against all expectations, the demons escaped the spanker ghetto. Next, their path was wiped clean by a cleaning crew. Then their trail was obliterated again in the lake, and now this? This grisly public spectacle? Could it be that the OverSoul was conspiring against her? *My Soul, are you testing me?* she wondered.

That seeker flew off the leash! Rhemus pinged.

It's not supposed...it's just not supposed to do that, was all Katria could send back. She felt as though her life had drained from her.

Yeah, where the hell is the subtlety? I mean, damn! The... Rhemus tripped over his thoughts. *I mean, first the Tool gets knocked out, and now our seeker gets fragged? Are we insured for this?* Rhemus's blink thread was somewhat garbled.

Katria did not respond.

Rhemus broke the silence. *What now? I can get another seeker— that is, if anyone is willing to lease one to us. Actually, I think we should go with a human seeker this time.*

No, Katria said at last. *I'm not risking any more points chasing them. They're in the inner sanctum. If they come out we'll know it, and we can deal with it then.*

Yeah, Rhemus replied, *the key word here is "if." Maybe the doctor's little infamous Darwinian gauntlet will solve the problem for us.*

Eventually, the MetaGame team was ushered through the multiple airtight portals that guarded the entrance to the inner sanctum and were left there. Love_Monkey, the watcher and high hostess of the lounge, had given them permission to enter the inner sanctum, but only because she wanted them out of her sight, or so she said.

This arrangement was not what Lyra and Djoser had hoped for. From what they could tell, Dr. Monsa was not expecting them. "So we're just going to what? Tell him we were in the neighborhood and thought we would drop by?" Djoser spoke, but his voice seemed to get swallowed up by the alien vegetation around them. It was extremely dark, which was no surprise to the party since the elevator they had used to get there seemed to travel downward for ages. According to their familiars, they were now under the bottom of the lake.

All was quiet, except for the sniffles and soft crying emanating from D_Light and Lily. Still bloodied, they hung onto one another, belatedly mourning the loss of Brian.

"He rescued us!" Lily sobbed. "He was a rescuer. And that thing..."

"He was like a lion, fierce and with no thought for his own life," D_Light blubbered. "Oh, the horror! He was my brother!"

Lyra looked back at the two mourners, contempt clouding her face. "My Soul, when will that damned drug wear off?"

Djoser said nothing, only smiled. Moocher, his familiar, was facing back toward D_Light and Lily, its oversized eyes fixed on them. *Ah yes, record it all,* Djoser thought. *This will be worth a good laugh later.*

"Notice, Lyra, that whenever one of your entourage dies, your new friend D_Light is somehow involved?"

Lyra rolled her eyes as Djoser continued. "Certainly he has proven himself useful, and I expect that with his help we may very well win this game, but I fear none of your employees will survive."

Lyra laughed. "Lucky for me I'm out of henchmen. Maybe he'll move on to yours!" She smirked at Amanda who, heedless of the conversation, was carefully surveying their surroundings.

"Oh, I wouldn't underestimate him," Djoser said. "I suspect he can kill your people remotely. Maybe you should check in with your servants back home."

Lyra smiled as she was teased, but she had to fight the urge to open a blink with her house. The team had agreed not to communicate with anyone unless absolutely necessary since no one was sure what the Authority could trace. They were probably being paranoid. Although it was true that the Authority used to eavesdrop on blinks and data-mine the minds of players via their mind interface chips, the Authority later imposed a series of privacy rules—collectively called "Free Agency Rules" (FARs)—on itself. Apparently, these rules were in response to a study the Authority sponsored which concluded that players who knew they could be listened in on showed a decrease of "free and innovative thought" and that this led to "suboptimal productivity."

Nevertheless, Lyra did not feel like testing the validity of the FARs just now. The stakes were too high.

Lyra turned her attention to the black foliage ahead of them. It was a dark zone, a place void of nanosites, so no one could jack into a skin to see. The dull, greenish light that filtered in from the plexi portal seals behind them was their only source of illumination. It was eerie and unsettling. Djoser and Lyra piped their familiars' night vision into their own minds in order to get a better look.

The vegetation that surrounded them was dense and much of it unfamiliar. There was no discernable pattern to the plant life, just a wild hodgepodge of alien flora. The only thing that the trees and plants seemed to have in common was the size of their leaves, all of which were enormous. Lyra supposed that the purpose of these gigantic offshoots was to maximize photosynthetic potential, yet there was no sunlight.

"Is that a breeze I feel?" Djoser asked into the darkness. The nobleman confirmed through Moocher's night vision that they were indeed indoors. A smooth ceiling loomed about two hundred meters above.

PeePee, Lyra's familiar, swiveled her head about, surveying the area while Lyra faced forward with her eyes shut so as to better concentrate on what she was seeing. "I presume the good doctor is trying to simulate the outside world," Lyra proposed. "If so, then I expect the sun to come up at some point, an artificial one...although, the inner sanctum is obviously not synced to local time. It's dawn in the outside world right now."

"I don't know. Seems warmer in here too. Probably an optimized climate for parasites to infect us," Djoser said sarcastically. "Anyway, we're not going to find the doctor just standing here. Looks like a path over there." Djoser pointed to a stone paved path and stumbled toward it.

"Our familiars have a different vantage point, so we're going to fall off a cliff or something if we try to walk around using them as our eyes," Djoser said gruffly.

"Stick Moocher up on your shoulder or hold his head in front of you," Lyra suggested, holding back a smile.

"Screw it, let's do it the old-fashioned way," Djoser exclaimed. He then pulled out a tiny glow stick from his pocket and turned it on.

Lyra frowned. "Might that attract unwanted attention? I suspect there's more than experimental plants in this place."

"Well, I'm not walking around holding a flippin' ferret in front of my face," Djoser snapped while continuing his journey toward the rough stone path ahead.

D_Light and Lily giggled as D_Light mocked Djoser. "Flippin' ferret in front of my face! Flippin' ferret in front of my face! Try saying that three—"

"Shhh, listen!" Lyra whispered.

"What?" Djoser hissed back.

Lyra was straining her eyes into the darkness ahead. The light from the glow stick cast long shadows into the forest. "I thought

I heard a cry or a shout, but not like a person. I dunno, something freakish."

Djoser's eyes narrowed. "How the blazes can you hear anything over those two?" He pointed toward Lily and D_Light, who had reverted from giggling back to their inconsolable sobbing.

As though an afterthought, Djoser dispatched Amanda to shut them up. Amanda was not practiced at this particular task, and so she simply pulled them apart. When they continued to sniffle and whine, she hissed threats and slapped them both—once for Lily and three times for D_Light—after which they finally quieted down.

The nobles concentrated on the sounds around them. After straining their ears for a minute, it was apparent that the forest was packed tight with bizarre noises. There was screeching, singing, and something that sounded akin to burping. One unsettling call from the forest sounded like a voice, but it was too guttural to have come from any man unless that man's vocal cords had been violated. Upon hearing this last sound, there was some discussion about waiting for the faux sun to come up—assuming there was one—but Lyra insisted that they did not have the luxury of time. She reminded them that they were on an urgent quest and that the stakes were high.

Finally in agreement, Djoser gave Amanda his glow stick and sent her out in front to lead them down the narrow stone path. The party walked in single file with D_Light and Lily—still consoling each other, albeit quietly—bringing up the rear. The path was uneven and not particularly well maintained, boasting large rocks, roots, and a constant encroachment of plants. This made for a clumsy march for D_Light and Lily since those ahead of them blocked the light from the glow stick, casting dark shadows down over the path. D_Light multithreaded his vision so that he could see from his own perspective, limited as it was, and from Smorgeous's perspective, who at least had night vision, although at a different angle. Lily held onto D_Light's hand for guidance.

After many minutes of this quiet and clumsy march, Lyra began feeling more comfortable with using artificial light and so turned on a glow stick of her own. She held it high so that D_Light and Lily could see as well. Lily let go of D_Light's hand, no longer needing him to guide her; he, however, did not let go of hers. He felt the need to keep her close. *To protect her,* he thought, although he knew this was not his true motivation. From what he had observed so far, she was handier in a fight than he was. D_Light did not look back to see her face. The LoveGas™ had finally worn off, for the most part, and he no longer felt that bold. Presently, her hand returned his grip.

Lyra eventually stopped and looked around intently as though to penetrate the wall of alien plant life. She scowled. "What? That kid couldn't give us a map? We have no idea where we're going," she said plaintively.

"If you're referring to the girl who goes by Love_Monkey, I don't think she's actually a child, at least not in terms of her age," Djoser said.

D_Light agreed. Love_Monkey was obviously much older than suggested by her appearance. It was uncommon for someone to go into age stasis before attaining physical adulthood, as it was typically disadvantageous to remain weaker and smaller than one's full potential. D_Light knew of only one example of a "stunted" being, a concubine product girl whom his brother C recommended as a "unique flavor." However, D_Light never rented her. To him there was something unsettling about the prospect, although he could not identify specifically what it was.

"Smells like a trap," Lyra muttered. "This whole 'walking around in the woods' thing is really suspect."

"Hmm, what was your first clue?" Djoser asked sarcastically. "Was it the angry woman-child whose guards shoved us into her dad's wild laboratory and locked us in? We're probably already infected with some incurable flesh-eating bacteria."

With a feeling of impending doom creeping over them, the team moved faster and they no longer took the time to stop and listen. They stormed along the path for what seemed like hours before the trail suddenly plunged into a long, steep stairway. Down below they saw what looked like an immense garden that stretched out as far as they could see, which was quite far because the garden was festooned with light-emitting plants providing patches of light in a variety of different colors, highlighting all manner of flowers, trees, fountains, sculpted rocks, and statues. Tall and short hedges were carved like soft stone into arcs and swirls. Paths threaded though the garden, bending this way and that, fading in and out of shadow. *Perhaps the game involves a maze. That would be classic,* D_ Light thought.

Since the garden was below a sheer cliff that bent around it, the only visible way down was the stairs ahead of them, which was also where their trail ended. With no better idea, the team began their descent into the unknown. As they walked, the only audible sounds were from fountains and streams of varying sizes, most of which were in the shadows or hidden behind something. Cool colors from the photoflowers glowed invitingly, soft blues, reds, greens, and every other color imaginable; each color dominated a small area containing a centerpiece, like a flowering nectar tree, a stone sculpture, or the falling water from a fountain. Having only slept for a combined hour or two, D_Light was exhausted. Peering into the private nooks and crannies of the garden, he longed to lie down in one of those dark shadows and let the soft, spongy grass cradle him and the gurgling waterfalls lull him to sleep.

D_Light left the path and inspected a long-stemmed blue-petaled flower that glowed. Looking into the bulb, he could not see any obvious light source. It appeared that the light was emitted from the tissue of the plant itself. *Remarkable,* he thought as he ripped one of the succulent petals. It tore easily enough and excreted a thick, glowing liquid that ran down between his fingers. It was viscous and sticky.

"D_Light!" Lyra whispered from the path. "Don't mess around with these things. You don't know what they are."

Lily was at his shoulder peering down intently at the torn flower. She dabbed a finger into the palm of his hand where a few drops of softly glowing juice had run down and collected. She then brought her finger under her nose and inhaled deeply. Just as D_Light was about to bring his sap-soaked hand up to his own nose, Djoser opened a blink to the team. *There is someone behind us.*

Instantly, D_Light was given a visual. It was a large humanoid shape that moved quickly, visible only for an instant before disappearing behind a tall flowerbed. *It's gone. What is it?* Djoser asked. Without waiting for an answer, he played the visual clip back slowly. D_Light could not make the figure out clearly, as it had been largely concealed behind beds of flowers and the trunk of a tree before disappearing behind thicker cover. Even so, D_Light thought he could make out a large humanoid head like that of a large man.

Djoser immediately sent over a version of the video feed that had just been enhanced by his familiar. The creature was shaped like human, a man, more or less. It was naked and had no hair, save at its groin, which had only a tuft of hair and no visible testes. His skin was striated with what D_Light supposed were bulging veins over well-defined muscles. The eyes were oversized and showed up well in the image. They were pink as though thoroughly bloodshot. The nose was enormous, and it glistened as though wet. The mouth was shut, but it also looked several times too big. A large flap of skin hung underneath the jaw, such that no neck was visible from that angle.

Master, no organism in the public taxonomy fits the characteristics of that image. Smorgeous's calm voice in D_Light's head contrasted with the feelings of panic beginning to wash over the robot's master.

The others shared D_Light's feelings of anxiety as the blink went rapid-fire. It was standard for members of House Tesla to be trained in psychological strategies for times that required quick action. Extraneous thought patterns were shut down to focus on the problem at hand while still keeping the senses keen.

Options? Djoser pinged.

Hide, Lyra responded.

Hiding good, D_Light sent as though he had a vote.

Stay together, Lyra commanded.

Because Lily had no familiar, she could not handle the security processing required by an unfiltered blink without a long delay and was therefore completely unaware of the discovery and discussion that had occurred over the last few seconds. Without even realizing it, D_Light grabbed Lily's hand to guide her. She did not resist. He then had Smorgeous create a summary of the situation and send it to her as a standard, low-security message.

The team's familiars watched their backs for any pursuer. Through the blink the team discussed other tactics. It was decided that if evasion failed, the party was certainly capable of defending itself. All of them carried weapons, and based on the image, the creature did not appear to be armed. They decided on a "bear trap" configuration if the enemy attacked alone. This consisted of a simple line with Amanda, the strongest, out a meter in front of the others. This would ensure that Amanda would meet the attacker first and that the others could then surround and snap shut around the attacker. If, however, there were multiple enemies, they would instead use a "flesh fortress" configuration, which simply meant they would all stand back to back, Amanda facing the most likely direction of attack.

But fighting was plan B. Plan A was still to hide, and to do this they sprinted with the intention of getting some distance from the thing and then hiding once out of sight. The plan seemed reasonable to D_Light, but he was also afraid of dashing headlong into another one of these things. Or something worse.

My familiar is scouting ahead, D_Light informed the others. The familiar's quadruped robotic legs afforded it much greater speed than its master or any of the other bipeds in the party.

Lyra's thoughts came fast. *Good, Djoser, Moocher watches our back. Princess watches our flanks.*

Djoser was beginning to breathe hard from the run, but unlike audible speech, this had no effect on his blink communication. *Moocher can't see it back there anymore. That thing probably knows the garden though. Knows where we're heading.*

Fine, see that large stone ahead? To the left is cover. At the hedge, we'll leave the path and hide. Lyra pinged the location in the team's minds. *Princess will maintain along the path. She can mimic my voice. She can mimic us all! With any luck, the thing will follow her.*

Momentarily, the four arrived at the stone, at which point they moved quietly off the path while Lyra's familiar continued on. They crawled and slithered in among the thick stalks of a patch of large, broad-leafed plants.

D_Light tried to suppress his panting from the run, but it was a few long seconds before he had quieted himself enough to faintly hear Djoser's voice off in the distance saying, "Run! Don't stop!" to which his own voice answered, "But I'm tired...and scared." D_Light could see Lyra smirking at him. When he cracked a smile back, she winked.

I want to get a look around, Djoser sent telepathically.

Stay hidden! Lyra seized Djoser's wrist. *If you can see it, then it can see you.*

That freak show might be creeping up on us right now. Djoser splayed his free hand out in frustration. *We don't know its capabilities.*

Exactly, Lyra sent back. *We don't know anything about it. In fact, we don't know anything about this place at all, so I say better to play it cool.*

Djoser's eyebrows shot up. *I'm not suggesting I peek out myself. I'll send out Moocher. He's small, so he'll be hard to spot. And he can see better than any of us anyway.*

Lyra nodded. Moocher, with his tube-shaped body, then began a low, slinking crawl around the plant stalks out toward the dim light just outside the thicket.

Pipe Moocher's visual and audio to all of us, Lyra commanded.

Djoser, Lyra, and D_Light were now looking through Moocher's eyes. Since the shadows were no problem for the familiar, they could all see pretty well. Unfortunately, the garden was full of obstacles and plants that blocked much of the familiar's view, but nothing seemed to be moving in the immediate vicinity.

"Oh Soul, I think I soiled my pants!" D_Light could faintly hear his own voice yelling from off in the distance. Princess's imitation of D_Light's voice was unnervingly accurate.

Great, I get all the good lines, he thought.

Djoser, have Moocher pan over to his left a bit, Lyra ordered. Their collective vision swung to the left. *There, see that tree?* Lyra placed a highlight over the tree to which she was referring. *Have Moocher climb one of those to get a better look around.*

The tree had a thick base from which sprung two thinner trunks that wound around one another like a DNA molecule. Numerous branches extended out from both trunks, and the leaves on the branches glowed dimly, not enough to cast significant light on anything else, but enough to glow clearly in the dark with a deep violet hue.

As D_Light re-immersed himself in Moocher's deft ascent up between the branches of the tree trunk, he was startled by Lyra, who suddenly spoke out loud in a shallow whisper. "I lost PeePee! I don't know how. Destroyed I think!"

She then let out a loud gasp and said in a rapid whisper, "I don't have time to reconfigure my blink settings. Without a familiar, I'm going to have to fall back to speech."

How? D_Light sent the thought, and then he realized that Lyra had dropped from that form of communication.

"How?" D_Light repeated in a whisper.

"I said I don't know how! I wasn't watching her. I can't play back her archive because she's completely gone."

D_Light could see Lyra's hand was shaking as she reached up and grabbed Djoser's arm. "Have Moocher look over to where my familiar ought to be. She ought to be…how do you say it?"

Lyra struggled as she tried to describe in words the whereabouts of her familiar. Being accustomed to simply sharing a map and pinging on a location, verbalizing locations was awkward. "You know, down the path we were on."

Djoser nodded distractedly as he communicated with Moocher. A moment later he gasped, "Oh shit!"

Through Moocher's visual feed, D_Light could see the monster clearly. The creature's arms were elongated, enabling it to alternate between walking upright and on all fours like an ape, but it moved like an insect. One moment it would be nearly motionless, breathing fast and deeply with its heaving torso, and then it would suddenly sprint forward at an impossible speed.

"Looks like it's coming straight at us!" Djoser's voice was like a squeal.

"How does it know where we are?" Lyra asked.

"Soul if I know! Deductive reasoning, lucky guess, who cares?" Djoser shot back.

"Do we even know this thing is hostile?" D_Light ventured.

"For Soul's sake, look at it! The teeth and the claws?" Djoser's tone was dismissive. "Tell you what, you go on out and say hi while we watch and see what happens."

"Besides, it fragged my Pretty Princess," Lyra said. "Not a friendly gesture."

Lily joined the conversation now that it was out in the open and she could keep up. "Maybe we should just stay still for now."

"I saw a boulder that looked flat enough on top for us all to stand on," Amanda said. The usually silent bodyguard's husky voice startled D_Light, who momentarily thought it belonged to something else. "It would provide us with a natural defense."

"Amanda's right," agreed Djoser. "If we can't lose this thing, we'll end up in a fight anyway. Better to choose where we make our stand."

D_Light scrunched up his face. "Standing on top of a rock is um, well…kind of out there. Maybe we could find a spot that is defensible *and* hidden?"

"Okay, *Dee*," Djoser said with a hint of sarcasm. "Moocher's going to take a good look around, and as he does, keep your eyes peeled for a spot that meets your extensive criteria. But we're going to have to decide soon."

The garden was full of hills, tall trees, and rock sculptures that limited the distance of Moocher's vision. There were so many stone trails through the garden that Djoser was not sure which one to take, although he was sure they should use a trail rather than go cross-country. That would slow them down too much.

"Wait! Was that a person?" Djoser said as though asking himself. Moocher's vision flew past what looked like a person in the distance. He wondered why his stupid familiar ignored something this important. Moocher's field of vision swept back to reveal a small humanoid shape stooped over a plant. Moocher then zoomed in.

"What? Is that a child?" asked Djoser. "What the flip would a kid be doing in here?"

"Yeah, a little girl," said D_Light. "My Soul, maybe it's not so dangerous here after all."

"What the—Moocher's matched her to that girl from the lounge. You know, the hostess girl, Love_Monkey," Djoser reported.

"Oh, little miss pissy?" Lyra groaned. "Likely she came down here to watch her pet finish us off!"

"Flip it, I say we make a run for the little Love_Monkey," Djoser said. "She looks pretty relaxed. Maybe she knows something we don't."

"And maybe she's just a stupid little girl who is about to be fragged just like us! Sheesh, whatever, let's just go." Lyra stood up.

Moocher mapped out the fastest route to Love_Monkey, and the group ran toward her at full tilt. By the time they charged up to the girl, who was kneeling in a grotto near some yellow flowers with dark spikes, they were quite winded. She looked up at them and did not appear surprised.

The girl had porcelain skin so pale it reminded D_Light of vampire children he'd seen in horror spank games. However, her eyes seemed very human. She had large blue eyes that peered back at them without fear, without malice.

"Each of you will need to take a drink." She produced a small blue vial from a pouch on her waist. "Just one swallow though," she added.

"I don't mean to be rude," D_Light interjected, "but why do we need to drink?" D_Light had only spoken to children a few times and was not sure of the best way to converse. Should he change his voice to a higher pitch like he had seen others do? He decided against it, knowing that Love_Monkey was not an ordinary child.

"It will protect you from the cullers," she answered. "There are several of them nearby, and they certainly have picked up your scent by now."

Confused, Lyra asked, "I'm sorry, Love_Monkey, but I don't understand why drinking something from *you* will protect me from anything."

The girl smiled patronizingly but did not miss a beat as she patiently explained. "There are several compounds in the liquid that, when metabolized, will excrete a unique scent from your glands, convincing the culler that you are not food."

D_Light was no biologist, but he knew that metabolizing liquid took time, so without further delay he snatched the vial from her outstretched hand and took a swig. She looked up at him without expression. Seeing no immediate detrimental effect, the others took their turns.

After everyone drank, the girl continued. "The repellant is fast-acting but will still take up to a minute to take effect, so now I think you should run. My father's cullers are very good at what they do, so you should run as fast as you possibly can."

Encouragement was unnecessary, for the team sprinted past the girl and down the path. Stealth was not attempted. They raced as fast as they could, but Lily was far ahead. She bounded forward, her long, lean legs widening the gap between her and the rest of the team. Lily looked behind her, her neck bearing no bulging tendons, her face no grisly smile of exertion. It was as though this remarkable pace was only mildly strenuous for her. Then, suddenly, her eyes locked onto something beyond the team and her jaw dropped.

D_Light checked behind him to discover a terrifying sight. Three of the hunters were gaining on them like an onrushing tsunami. Running on all fours, they sent rocks and plant debris sailing through the air. They were big, shadowy hunks of horrifying nightmare.

Djoser caught sight of them too. "Amanda, save us!" he cried out. At this, his bodyguard, who had been keeping pace with her master, broke off and turned to face the approaching monsters. As she stood waiting, the muscles in her arms tense, she crouched slightly. Her swords, which had been drawn in an instant, shimmered blue and green in the glow of the nearby photoflowers.

D_Light returned his head forward to watch where he was running. *No missteps,* he thought. Djoser was beside him. His eyes were fixed forward and wide with terror.

Ahead, up the path, Love_Monkey stood waving at them. *Impossible!* D_Light thought. *How did she get ahead of us?* As they made their fast approach, it was evident that she was not waving, but beckoning them to come to her. Lily had almost reached the girl and looked poised to follow. D_Light, figuring he had nothing to lose, decided to follow as well. Seeing that she had caught their attention, the girl then turned and began to jog—perhaps even skip—away down a path that snaked into bushy green darkness.

———

The monsters did not slacken their pace as they charged Amanda. It appeared that they were about to use their momentum to spring onto her, so she prepared to sidestep and slash. She doubted, however, that this move would save her. They outnumbered her three to one, and it was evident that they were fast and powerful—even for products. Still, if they underestimated her she might be able to catch them by surprise and take at least one of them out.

However, when the opportunity came, they did not pounce upon her. Instead, two of the three suddenly broke off, one leaping off to her left and one to her right. The third simply stopped with a suddenness that seemed to defy the physics of motion. She was now in the middle of a triangle. The creatures snarled, but their faces were little more than a blur to Amanda, who swiftly shifted her attention from one to the other. The beasts then darted in and out, just out of reach of her slashing blades. *Are they testing me?* she wondered. *Are they attempting to coax me to lunge at one to give the others an opening?* Adopting a defensive posture, Amanda was quite aware of such tactics, and she would not be baited. If one of them moved into range of her blades, they would pay for it; otherwise, she would hold steady. Indeed, she preferred to wait. Every second she delayed the enemy was another second for her master to make his escape.

The beasts sniffed and whined. Perhaps realizing that their opening tactic was unsuccessful, the triangle began to constrict. Amanda knew she needed to dispatch at least one of them in order to have a chance, but if she attacked one, the others would certainly close in. Amanda wanted to think that if her onslaught was swift and effective enough that the others would retreat, but she sensed no fear in these humanoid monsters that danced as though conducting some grisly, alien strip show.

Amanda was about to take her gamble when the back of her leg was sliced open. Instantly, her blade swept back in retaliation, but it cut only air. The thing had withdrawn before her swiftly flowing blood even had time to blotch her skinsuit. Another slash appeared across her stomach as though by some devilish magic. It was deep, and once again the culler had retreated out of reach before she could even the score.

Amanda was on the ground now, but they still did not finish her. She swung her blades about in vain as each of them took turns darting in and out, nicking, slicing, and puncturing. One of her two hearts was pierced and no longer functioned, but the bodyguard fought on, directing her attention to protecting her upper body and head since her legs were now shredded and useless. But then, all at once, the monsters just stopped. They sniffed the air. Their hungry, dark, merciless pupils contracted, and then, standing fully upright and sniffing their surroundings, they simply walked away.

CHAPTER 27

We are not in the business of growing slaves. A product should "enjoy" its purpose. Anything else is unethical and can even be dangerous. There have been many slave revolts in history...not pretty.

Life is motivated by pleasure and pain. You need to design your life to seek out its targeted work at the exclusion of all other activities. For example, if a household servant is required, the servant should be designed with an obsessive-compulsive disorder for cleanliness (see gene template #C139090). Such a servant will vigilantly maintain order in the household without any direction from the owner.

As another example, if a product's purpose requires painful activities, those pain receptors might be excluded from the product design or a propensity for masochism could be added.

In this process, pleasure and pain are used together to obtain the desired behavior, and most importantly, these stimuli are intrinsic to the being.

—Excerpt from Dr. Monsa's lecture series, "Best Practices for Genetic Engineers"

Lyra, Djoser, and D_Light had no idea where the strange little girl was taking them, but they did not hesitate to follow. However, nothing could have prepared them for what presented itself on the other side of the hedge—a clearing bordered by high walls of leaves and flowers, in the middle of which sat an elaborate dining set. A long, silver table dominated the space, surrounded by slender, high-backed chairs, between which a banquet was visible. Lily, who had been ahead of the rest, stopped abruptly and stood stone still. Emerging through the hedge as if their lives depended on it, D_Light, Lyra, and Djoser nearly ended up in a heap as they skidded to a stop behind Lily.

"Excellent, I had hoped you would make it in time for supper!" roared a man from the far end of the table—at least D_Light assumed he was a man, for he was so ugly that D_Light's heart skipped a beat and his left hand, his throwing hand, shot down to where his razor discs were hidden in his skinsuit.

For starters, the man's face was completely asymmetrical. His left eye was slightly lower than his right, one cheek puffed out as though suffering from an allergic reaction, his nose was crooked, and his left eyebrow was completely gone. And as if the overall structure of the face was not bad enough, his skin was pocked by countless undesirable features—tiny craters, patches of rubbery flesh, tufts of hair where there should be none, and a feeble beard that, had this man any luck at all, would have concealed some of the aforementioned defects. Instead, the beard only darkened areas of his chin and cheeks, further mottling his face.

The grotesque stranger rose from his seat. "Allow me to introduce myself," he began. "I am Dr. Monsa, and you are our guests!" He outstretched his arms wide as though offering a generous gift. "Please, find a seat. Take a seat and be comfortable."

Lily led the team in bravery by shuffling forward a few steps as though testing for quicksand. The others did not move at all, but merely stared in awe. An awkward silence followed. Then, suddenly, the doctor erupted with laughter, the short and sudden bursts of sound making D_Light flinch in surprise. "I am afraid I will need to ask of you the nearly impossible task of forgiving my appearance," the doctor announced. "In my nearly two hundred years as a wetgineer, I bear the scars of many of my creations." Dr. Monsa bowed sincerely and gestured again for the party to be seated.

Djoser looked back over his shoulder and, through his panting, managed to utter a sound as though trying to speak. Dr. Monsa quickly interrupted him. "Oh, yes, you are absolutely safe now. Like me and the rest of my family, you all now smell absolutely dreadful to my cullers. Please, attempt to relax."

"One of us was left behind," Lily announced.

"I see," replied the doctor, who then looked over at a lanky-limbed, long-haired monkey that stood upright nearby on the table. Dr. Monsa nodded thoughtfully. "Oh, yes, your guardian is alive, but I'm afraid she is a bit worse for wear." He frowned and added, "She will not be joining us for dinner."

The doctor's eyes were distant as he spoke. D_Light took this to mean the doctor had been accessing his familiar. *Was the monkey his familiar?* D_Light wondered to himself. It was a sin to manufacture a familiar with human-like characteristics such as hands, and possessing such a familiar was a transgression. A familiar with human-like physiology could be used as an extension of the master's own body, which would likely lead to sloth.

The doctor returned from his vacant-eyed trance, at which point he roved over to Lily. "Lily, is it? Please, it would be an honor if you would sit right here at my side." The doctor slid a chair out with a flourish that reminded D_Light of something from old movie feeds he used to watch in nursery.

Lily curtsied stiffly as though reciting a long since forgotten ballet move, and took her seat, at which point the doctor swiftly moved behind her and scooted the chair in behind her. Without looking away from the top of Lily's head, which he stood over, Dr. Monsa made a vague motion to the rest of the party to sit. D_Light, Lyra, and Djoser found seats near each other, creating a defensive line. The three of them rotated their attention between each other, the plates and utensils in front of them, and their host.

Love_Monkey silently moved a chair to the other side of Lily, sat down, and smiled sheepishly as she gazed up at her. Lily smiled back at the girl, remarking to herself how volatile human children were. Back at the groksta, only an hour or two ago, the child had been furious, but her eyes now glistened with adoration.

Lyra felt completely disoriented. With her familiar gone, she felt as though a part of her mind was missing, the part that *knew* things. She had the unbearable urge to ask questions so she could fully establish her bearings. "Grandfather, about those creatures, the cullers, as you call them, are they—" Her sentence cut off as she nearly jumped from her chair. Six little girls, identical in all ways to Love_Monkey, entered the clearing. All wore the same clothing, differing only in the color of the bow fastened in their long, golden hair.

"They're cloned!" Lyra gasped. "Grandfather, you cloned your children?"

"Please, just call me doctor," the man insisted. "And no, cloning human beings is a sin. These are in the likeness of my children and I refer to them as my daughters, but their code is under the legal limit to be considered human; therefore, they are products. *Products* that I cloned."

"You have children products? Why? No one creates products in the likeness of children."

Djoser pinched Lyra under the table. *Why is she interrogating him? Doesn't she know who he is?* he wondered.

The doctor curled his bulbous and crooked lips into what Djoser hoped was a smile. "Yes, Lyra. Although technically not a sin, creating immature products is not considered a best practice in my line of work."

The doctor took a long gulp of his beverage before continuing. "As to your question of why, it is because I could not dream up a better assistant. My bio-daughter, Samantha, was both a joy to work with and an effective wetgineer. She fell victim to the TerriLove virus before she gained immortality and hence was not qualified for resurrection."

Lily's forehead wrinkled with concern, and she leaned over to pat the doctor on his shoulder. "I'm so sorry," she offered. "It must have been tragic to lose a daughter so young."

The doctor redirected his gaze at Lily, and his grimace widened. "Oh, she was seventy-three years old when she passed. Granted, she was young, but on the bright side, she survived longer than most in my laboratories in the early days. As for these girls," the doctor said, nodding to the identical children at the table, "these lambs, which is what I call all of my family, I put a clamp on their physiological development at age eleven—you know, before puberty and all that nonsense." The doctor winked at Lily.

"In addition to their physiology clamp, I also disrupted certain aspects of their overall nervous system development—enough to, in layman's terms, keep them young at heart as the decades slide by. In this way, I spared my lambs the tragedy of adulthood. Even as their intellectual powers increase through experience, they do not become jaded and unimaginative like the rest of us. As you can imagine, they are exceptional scientists."

"Daddy, you know we hate it when you talk about us as though we're not here," one of the clones complained.

Dr. Monsa ignored her as he took a sip from his nectar ale mug and said, "You see, it was at age eleven that Samantha, my bio-daughter, was at the height of her curiosity, of her unbridled wonder and passion for all that was *alive*. Unlike any other bio-child I had, she would sit and watch all manner of organisms for hours on end. It did not matter what it was, either. It could be an amoeba through the micro, a beetle scuttling over the ground, the veins of a leaf, the dance of molecules of mitochondria. She would unselfconsciously ponder the reproductive cycle of any creature she found." The doctor stared off vacantly as though the end of the table was the ocean horizon. "When my little girl was that age, my head was deep into my machines. I wanted to mimic life with software, with zeros and ones. All those years ago, she was the one who first taught me the value of life, that there is no substitute, that life itself is the ultimate technology."

Dr. Monsa smiled over at the clones now seated in a line spanning one entire side of the table. "These remind me of her," he said while smiling and nodding. "They remind me of the beauty of nature and her never-ending capacity for wondrous creation."

The doctor took a long pause. "And this," he said as he gestured to his ravaged face, "reminds me that new creation is often fueled by destruction. Viruses, bacteria, as well as much larger organisms, don't always turn out as planned. Worse yet, depending on who's funding the project, they turn out *exactly* as planned. When only maimed, I called myself lucky. When not so lucky, I died. I dare say I have been resurrected more times than I care to count."

"Five times, Daddy," one daughter offered. "As an immortal, Daddy has the option for resurrection, that is, if resurrection is possible under the circumstances."

The doctor flipped his hand in the air as though performing a magic trick. "The body is easy enough to mend and bring back to life; it is the mind that is irreplaceable—at least currently. Fortunately for me, my brain tissue has never been damaged beyond repair."

"I hope I don't offend you, but I must ask, why don't you replace your—"

"My face?" The doctor interrupted Lily's question with a chuckle. "Because it is a hassle, for one thing. Swapping a body is not routine, even for immortals. It is a major ordeal, and there can be complications. Also, and I hope you do not think me petty for saying this, I must admit that I enjoy seeing people's expressions when they behold me for the first time. For example, I don't leave my garden often anymore, but when I do, say on business, even other immortals are intimidated. I think it gives me an edge in that I leave a lasting impression. I don't need the world to enjoy looking at me. I have the love of my lambs, and that is all I require."

The doctor suddenly threw up his hands and groaned. "And speaking of my lambs! Let me apologize once again for your harrowing welcome. One of my girls, Love_Monkey, whom you already met, messaged ahead that you would be coming. I sent another of my lambs to guide you in safely, but she evidently got distracted. What was it this time?"

Curious_Scourge, the clone D_Light supposed was the one who had given the team the repellant earlier, bent her head slightly. "It was the Gibbon flies—they had transitioned," she muttered under her breath.

"So typical, Curious!" BoBo, who sat at the far end of the table wearing a purple bow, shook her head disapprovingly.

Dr. Monsa pointed his finger at BoBo. "Don't chide your sister. I think it's safe to say you could have done the same thing."

"No, Daddy, no! Where did the 'Curious' come from in 'Curious_Scourge'?" BoBo raised an eyebrow at the doctor and then back at her sister.

The doctor nearly choked on his mouthful of syrup. "Oh, spare me! Just the other day I sent you to milk the mellowcows, and where did you end up? Three hours watching an *Equus caballus* #7541 give birth while the rest of us sat and drank water for lunch!"

"Insomuch as I am like my sister, it's your fault. As you just *lectured* our guests, you designed us *clones* to be this way!" BoBo shot back smugly.

"You're right, I should have known better. I should not have sent any of my daughters. I should have selected another lamb." As the doctor said this, he pointed a knobby finger at several creatures that stood rigidly at attention at the far end of the clearing. D_Light had been so immersed in the conversation that he had not noticed the newcomers. The sight gave him a start, as one of those assembled had a morass of tubes sticking out from his head and various other parts of his body.

BoBo whispered loudly to reach her sister, who sat several clones down, "By the way, Curious, did the transition complete? In regard to the flies, I mean."

In response, Curious_Scourge scowled and dismissed her sister's question with a wave of her hand. However, a chipmunk familiar poked its head from under Curious_Scourge's arm to better silently communicate with BoBo's familiar, also a chipmunk.

The doctor introduced the newcomers one by one, each bowing as he did so. First was the priest, a sallow, tall man. He seemed anxious and bored at the same time, as though inexplicably delayed from something he desired. He wore a traditional priest's robe that, although clean, looked slightly worn.

Next was Sara, Dr. Monsa's concubine. As was typical, she was very tall and strikingly beautiful in a haughty sort of way, as though she had stepped out of a high-end spy spanker game. She regarded the newcomers intently.

To each side of Sara was a man with product tats on his cheeks. They were identical, including their matching impeccable black slacks and tunics. One could only tell them apart thanks to the particulars of their injuries. Both were riddled by irregular bruises, scars, and even some open wounds that shimmered wet with blood, or perhaps pus.

Lastly, the doctor introduced the tube man as "my most excellent analyst." This man trembled and his eyes shifted about restlessly. When he bowed in greeting, he did more of a lurch, in the process stepping on one of his cords, which pulled at his skin and caused the unfortunate-looking man to bleat out in pain. This event prompted D_Light to ask, "Pardon me, doctor, but why the tubes?"

The doctor snorted. "The tubes, yes! Oh, it begged me for them. Pleaded for days on end until I finally had it fitted with its precious tubes! You see, the tubes bring it food, water, and drugs without the need for boosters. And, dare I say this at the dinner table, they provide a means of sanitary excretion."

"Daddy!" protested one of the clones.

"Why did you desire this?" Lily asked the analyst with a sad and curious expression. "It looks rather unpleasant."

"Maximum productivity, of course!" The doctor answered for the analyst as he patted Lily's wrist. "I presume you are unaccustomed to the obsessive tendencies of analysts. Analysts live to research, to scrutinize and consider. An analyst is in the thick of the most complex grinders. And the better designed ones, ones like this one, loathe leaving their work—ever!"

The doctor removed his blotched hand from Lily's wrist. D_Light noted that Lily did not react to this, did not withdraw her forearm off the top of the table, did not dip her napkin into the nectar wine and scrub away at where his loathsome hand had touched hers.

Doctor Monsa said, "Despite the preferences of some, I like to see my lambs face to face from time to time." He looked toward the analyst, his one eyebrow raised. "It was once said that a family that eats together stays together."

In a trembling spasm of a whisper, the analyst protested. "I do not require it. I do not require this, this food. Please excuse me."

"No more of that!" Dr. Monsa barked. The analyst fell silent, placing his chin down to sulk. His head gyrated back and forth as though afflicted with a nervous tic.

Presently, the new arrivals were seated. Sara, the tall concubine, sat sandwiched between the two battered products, one of which sat next to D_Light. The priest seated himself across the table, and the analyst sat at the far end, allowing himself an empty chair on either side as though attempting to quarantine himself.

The doctor complimented Djoser on his choice of bodyguard. "*Homo sapiens* #43687 is a good model. Attractive, yet loaded with enough cunning and speed to hold off three of my cullers for nearly eight seconds! I'll send you the archive. You will be pleased with her performance."

Djoser hesitated, taking time to swallow. "Like your analyst, Amanda enjoys what she does."

"Yes, and that is as it should be. A good wetgineer instills in his products a natural love for their purpose. Anything else would produce suboptimal performance and, if you subscribe to my line of thinking, is even unethical."

"I agree, sir," Lyra commented while straightening her posture. "I realize that products are not human, but it is still our responsibility to make them as comfortable as possible, even happy, if such a term applies."

Dr. Monsa furrowed his brow slightly. "That is the general sentiment of the profession. However, there are some products designed specifically *not* to enjoy their purpose." With these last words, the doctor pointed to Lily with a tilt of his head.

Lyra's voice lifted delicately. "I beg your pardon, but I do not know what you are referring to." Her eyes darted between the doctor and Lily. Lily nervously looked back at Dr. Monsa, smiled with a trembling lower lip, and then looked forward.

The doctor looked at Lyra with curious eyes. "Hmm, well..."

He took a deep breath as though stalling to think of what to say next, but he was preempted by BoBo, who rolled her eyes. "What? You don't know?" she asked disbelievingly. "She's a *camper*."

A camper? Smorgeous, what the hell is that? D_Light sent to his familiar.

It took only a second for Smorgeous to mash together a summary from various sources on the Cloud:

Homo sapiens #4586754 (camper)

Entertainment. Campers serve as quarry in the hunting reserves, typically hunted by rape-and-kill fetishists.

Typical High-Level Phenotype:

> *Appearance:*
> *- 94% Blond Bombshell*
> *- 3% Waif Asian*
> *- 2% African Beauty*
> *- 1% Other*
> *Psychological Profile:*

- *99% Moral**
- *99% Hygienic**
- *93% Sensitive**

Intelligence is variable. Depends on human template used and outside factors (see human intelligence).

Other notes: Campers are generally marketed as one-use products due to their termination shortly after capture. This is advised by the manufacturer due to extensive degradation of psychological phenotype if used as catch and release.

*As compared with other products derived from human templates.

Smorgeous offered other resources for more detailed information, but D_Light decided not to open them just yet.

It was quiet at the table until Lyra, having tapped into Djoser's familiar to research the subject, broke the silence. "That's disgusting! A completely sordid business! To design a—a perfect rape victim? My Soul, is there no limit to what a player will do for a couple of points?"

"A *couple* of points? No, try *a lot* of points," Djoser said. Lyra scowled at him, at which point he added, "Uh, not that I've looked into it, of course. Just, you know, a few of the guys... Well, campers are one-use products, so it doesn't take a genius to know hunting them would cost a fortune."

Lyra bunched up her hand into a fist. "Don't be stupid!" she hissed at Djoser. Then, addressing the doctor, she said, "Begging your pardon, sir."

Dr. Monsa shrugged and looked over to Lily with an expression that D_Light could not read on his misshapen face. "It is I who beg your pardon, Lily. I did not realize your, er, your friends were unaware of your background."

The analyst, who until now had been absently poking at his food, looked up and stared pointedly at Lily. "You...you escaped the reserves?" His voice quavered. "How? How did *you* escape from a place like that?"

At this point several people at the table started speaking at once.

Djoser: "Ridiculous, really. Just the R&D to design such a product..."

Analyst: "Lily is your name, right? Lily, yes, I would truly like to see your archive of the escape..."

Priest: "You're off the reservation. My Soul, you're a *demon*, then!"

Analyst: "Oh, dear me, I suspect you have no archive. Campers are not fitted with chips..."

Djoser: "...would cost a fortune, and then the cost to grow her..."

Analyst: "Perhaps just you and I sit down back at my den and you give me your story..."

D_Light: "Why don't we leave this alone?"

Djoser: "Such an expense for a few hours of fun? My Soul, how some players live!"

Analyst: "I can scan you there, at my den. It does not hurt a bit. Your story would be valuable..."

Lily's eyes were tearing up as they fixed on something distant.

Sara: "Despoil you? That is your purpose? You look like a kitten. No sport in it, I suspect..."

Lyra: "You are being rude."

Sara: "Rude? That thing is just a toy."

As Sara said this, the concubine sneered and then plunged a fork down into the hand of the product seated between her and D_Light. It howled and thrashed, knocking over D_Light's wine glass and flipping his plate.

"My Soul!" D_Light leaned back away from the anguished product.

Lily bolted up, knocking her chair backward, and then she walked quickly away from the table. She disappeared down a shrubbery corridor.

Lyra glared at Sara. "How dare you! I'm flipping royalty, and you were born a slut! You don't question *anything* I say!" Lyra sprang up. She looked as though she were preparing to pounce on the concubine.

Dr. Monsa struck his wine glass with his fork several times, resulting in a high-pitched chime that cut above the clamor. Everyone ceased fire and looked over at him, at which point he said, "Sara, that is no way to behave at the table! Leave us now!" Sara gave her master a cold look, but she immediately got to her feet while grabbing the hair of the two products. She dragged them away with her.

Taking a bite from his plate and addressing the table without swallowing, the doctor said, "I apologize for Sara's behavior. She gets overexcited when she sees new faces."

"I mean no offense, sir, but your concubine appears unstable." Lyra's face was flushed.

"Indeed, she is one of my earlier designs. I'm afraid in my younger years I put too much emphasis on passion and vivacity. But she loves me. So what can I do?"

One of the clones leaned over the table to better see Lyra and offered, "Mother Lyra, if it is any consolation, my sisters and I hate her too."

The doctor laughed. "Yes, remember Mua_So_Pretty? She was one of my girls. She tried to kill Sara, but the old lady came out on top that time."

D_Light stood up and bowed. "Doctor, I am afraid I feel the call of nature, and I ask to be excused."

The doctor nodded absently. "Of course, and feel free to relieve your nature into the bushes yonder. All plants here metabolize urine well. If your nature is a bit more on the solid side, well, that is beneficial for the flora too, but please keep it downwind."

"Father!" BoBo cried plaintively.

Dr. Monsa chuckled. "Oh, and by the way, the amarilla plants, the ones with the broad, soft leaves," he said as he pointed to a nearby plant that fit his description, "they make excellent toiletry."

"Father!" BoBo cried again. "Really inappropriate for the table! You lecture *us* on etiquette?"

The doctor smiled mischievously at his daughter.

"Try leading by example," she instructed.

D_Light smiled to himself as he walked away. Only an old immortal like the doctor would talk about cleaning oneself with toiletry since everyone nowadays used his or her familiar to do it. Smorgeous's tongue was not just cosmetic; it possessed the appropriate enzymes to process human waste. Familiars had waste of their own, but they excreted it only where appropriate, and it smelled like cinnamon.

As he left the clearing, D_Light overheard the doctor saying, "Sara's behavior is an extreme example of poor etiquette. Etiquette. It's quite simple, really—make your guests feel comfortable. Etiquette is a lost art, I fear, something more in vogue when I was young."

D_Light was not happy with this at all. He felt as though he were in some disquieting *Alice in Wonderland* inspired spank game, starring Dr. Monsa as the Mad Hatter. At D_Light's instruction, Smorgeous watched behind D_Light's back. That crazed concubine was out here, and he had noticed her slip the fork she had used to stab the product into her blouse before leaving the table.

It was only a minute before he found Lily walking slowly on a trail ahead. He had to run to catch up. As he approached, she looked back with a tear-streaked face. She tensed up as he came near. She was obviously upset, but there was anger in her eyes as well. D_Light wasn't sure what to say, but he spoke anyway. "So you were designed to be a sex toy for sadistic assholes—so what? Who doesn't have a little baggage?" D_Light was far from sure that dark humor was what she wanted right now, but it was the first thing that popped into his head.

Lily shook her head and smiled halfheartedly. To D_Light's surprise, she walked quickly over and embraced him. Her face was warm and wet against his cheek. *Soul, she smells good,* he thought. He wanted to care for her. He wrapped his arms around her and held her tightly. He moved his hands up through her hair and gently stroked the back of her neck and head. She was trembling. Despite her toned body, she was soft in his grip. "Help me," she whispered with a fierce undertone as though she was issuing a command rather than pleading. She then lifted her head back and looked at him with sad, soulful eyes. "I miss my sisters. I don't have anyone."

"Your sisters? You mean the—" D_Light was going to say "other campers," but instead he said, "The others on the reserve?"

She nodded slowly and then said between sobs, "I had Todget, and he was good, and we were...we were doing okay, even happy sometimes, but I left them. We left them all behind."

D_Light was not exactly sure what she was saying, but he felt the need to comfort her. "I'll work on this. You know," D_Light said as he cupped her soft face in his hands and gazed back into her shimmering eyes, "Djoser and Lyra are powerful players. I'll talk to them and maybe they can help. Maybe they can help you when this is all over."

She shook her head and sniffed. "I doubt that they will help me. Did you see how they looked at me back there?"

"What do you mean? Lyra was livid! She was—"

"Yes, she was angry that I was *made*, but that doesn't mean she wants to help me," Lily said. "I'm not talking about her anyway, I'm talking about the other one."

"Djoser? He was just surprised. I mean, we all were. He's gotta appreciate what you've done for the team, how you helped us escape."

"I just feel wrong. I wish I could be one of you, but that's impossible. I..." She broke off and sobbed. "I should go. I should go, I think."

"You can't keep running."

Lily smiled sadly. "I was created to run."

D_Light hugged her tightly and pressed his lips up against her ear to whisper, "Don't look now, but there's a squirrel spying on us."

"Oh Stag, it's one of those robots," she whispered. "How embarrassing, to be blubbering and having that silly thing watching me." Despite her apparent alarm, she laughed. D_Light was glad to hear it.

"I should get back," he said. "Get back to the dinner. Don't go running off, though. Can I find you later?"

Lily answered with an ambiguous shrug. As D_Light walked away, he kept looking over his shoulder. He half expected her to run off at any moment, but she just stood there meeting the stare of the squirrel that sat on its haunches on a thick branch of a polka-dot-patterned tree.

Although it had been an excuse to find Lily, D_Light actually did have to urinate, and on his way back he found a secluded thicket into which he could relieve himself. As he stared down at his stream, he half wondered why he bothered with the girl—why, for instance, he felt the need to comfort her when she cried, which was turning out to be a common occurrence. She was no relation of his. She was not even in the Game. And now he learns that she is not even human! But these thoughts were washed out of his mind as her scent, voice, face, and body swept back into his memory. He took a deep breath and let out a low, soft groan.

Master, your bio-chemi signature and thought patterns most closely resemble patterns shown during past early stages of courtship. Examples available upon request.

Yes, Smorgeous could always be counted on to point out the obvious. D_Light knew he had a thing for the girl, or for the product, as it turned out. Smorgeous, upon confirming his suspicion, suggested alternatives to what the computer termed "unproductive dwelling," including testosterone inhibitors, or since his master currently enjoyed privacy in the hedge, a collection of erotic material.

D_Light refused both options, the former because he did not want his testosterone meddled with, and the latter because he did not have time for *that*; he needed to get back to the dinner.

CHAPTER 28

"You need not worry about your teammate," the doctor announced to D_Light as he strolled back to the dinner table. D_Light raised his eyebrows to feign ignorance, but then he realized the charade was pointless. Certainly the squirrel had reported back all the mushy details of D_Light and Lily's heart-to-heart talk. This suspicion was confirmed by the expressions on the faces of the dinner guests.

"Yeah, it's a shame about her," D_Light said as he slid out his chair to sit down. "She is rather clever and has proven valuable in our little game."

"Yes, your game," muttered Dr. Monsa. "Your teammates have filled me in on it and hence your purpose in seeing me." The doctor leaned over the table and looked at D_Light intently. "You are quite right about Lily though. Campers are unique and designed to the highest specifications, and thus it is no surprise to me that she has proven *valuable* to you. I was quite excited to hear that a camper was on her way to see me, so I have given this whole demon issue some thought."

Dr. Monsa popped an unusual pink fruit into his mouth and continued, juice dripping down his misshapen chin. "As you know, I have all kinds of exotic products here. Granted, most were born here rather than importing themselves, but nevertheless, she can stay here for a while. Since the inner sanctum is a research zone, I have permits for 'off purpose' products, and your camper would not be the only one. However, for the permit to apply, I would need to use her in some research capacity."

D_Light, despite himself, must have looked startled because the doctor quickly added, "Nothing harmful. Oh, nothing that would hurt it, er, her, in any way, of course."

BoBo rapped her small knuckles on the table. "Father, assign her as a research assistant to me!"

Curious_Scourge scowled back at her sister. "Why you?"

D_Light raised his hand as though in class and said, "Pardon me, sir, but she is part of our game."

BoBo, ignoring D_Light's objection, blinked her eyes innocently at her father and said, "She will be my assistant because I thought of it and took the initiative."

Lyra opened a blink to D_Light, which was auto-accepted. *We do not have a quest at the moment, so I don't see any reason to sweat Lily being occupied by the doctor. Meanwhile, she'll be safe as his guest.*

D_Light pinged approval.

Dr. Monsa nodded. "Yes, why don't you girls show her around or, uh, have her assist you. You can take turns using her as an assistant, starting with BoBo, who, as she astutely pointed out, thought up the scheme."

The priest raised an index finger. "Really, sir, I must advise against this. No offense to you," he said, gesturing toward D_Light, Djoser, and Lyra, "but harboring these fugitives could get you in hot water with the Authority."

"As I said, the camper, Lily, is a fugitive because she is off purpose. Well, almost all the products in my laboratories are off purpose. How else could I run any of my labs? My creations are evolving all the time, and in this process so is their purpose evolving. Only when a product has been fully developed and ready for market can it be zoned."

The doctor paused, wiped his chin, and pointed to D_Light and his team. "As for them, well, they're just playing a MetaGame, a game that I am apparently part of. The Divine Authority need only review my archive on the matter to see the truth of this."

D_Light raised his hand. "What happens to Lily after the game?"

"She can come and stay with me as long as she is able. That is, until the Authority comes for her, at which point I will have to turn her over."

Following D_Light's example, Lyra held up her hand. "Sir, until we get our next quest, what shall the rest of us do?"

"Relax," said the doctor as he took another sip of nectar wine. "As I said already, you are all my guests."

The dinner conversation then switched over to the MetaGame. Dr. Monsa was eager to hear the details. He asked many questions regarding the spanker games, as this was a subject he knew very little about. He found the encounter with the fish in the lake to be hilarious. "My house designed those feeder fish, you know. You must send me an archive so I can include it with our promotional material."

Djoser did most of the talking since he still had ready access to all the memories via his familiar, while Lyra, lacking the memory retrieval and processing power of her familiar, awkwardly attempted to add bits and pieces from time to time. Moocher and Smorgeous, at the behest of their masters, collaborated to stitch together an archive of the team's adventures thus far, which was delivered to the grateful doctor to review at his leisure.

Throughout dinner the analyst constantly dropped hints to the doctor, including long, deep sighs, throat clearings, and offhand remarks to other guests such as, "I certainly am full." Eventually, Dr. Monsa took mercy upon the creature and gave him permission to be excused. The product stumbled over his own tubes in his haste to get back to work.

Soon after, the others left as well. Each of the girls excused themselves with a curtsy and a smile. Djoser was eager to see how Amanda fared, so he followed the clone daughter wearing the blue bow to the infirmary within the garden. The doctor, claiming pressing business, also took his leave. The only ones left at the table were Lyra, D_Light, and the priest. Lyra, having taken to heart the doctor's advice to relax, had drunk a few more glasses of wine than she normally did and seemed too drowsy to move. She slouched back in her seat, nudging D_Light from time to time, saying things like, "What a good choice you turned out to be." Otherwise, the priest, as is customary for their profession, did most of the talking. D_Light was not really listening because it mainly concerned the priest's specialty in divine law.

"Blah, blah…consult on compatibility of divine law and house rules…blah, blah…mostly intermediate-sized houses…blah, blah… nearly always scored in the top twenty percent of my games…blah, blah." The priest's voice sounded like someone breathing in and out slowly through a harmonica.

Absently, D_Light ran his index finger along the collar of his skinsuit. The moisture of Lily's tears had dissipated. He had been trying to open a blink with her, but she was not responding. The priest, who had been ignoring D_Light in preference to Lyra, now looked pointedly at D_Light, which brought him back to the conversation.

"Yes, despite my lifetime of devotion to the OverSoul, I did not make the list. I am now one hundred and seven," declared the priest.

"You look fine for being off contract for two years," Lyra half slurred. Slits for eyes, she looked as though she might nod off.

"Oh, I cannot take credit for my health," the priest insisted. "It is the inner sanctum, the food and water here, the air even. The doctor has infused the very fabric of his laboratory with countermeasures against aging, cancer, and the like."

D_Light thought this last bit was interesting and said so. Seeing that his audience might actually be listening after all, the priest straightened his back, cleared his throat, and continued in his sonorous tone. "When I found out that I was not chosen by the Potent One, I felt I only had two choices—either live out the remaining few years of my life in decay, or die swiftly in the gladiator pits of the Real Games. At first I was leaning toward the games."

Lyra laughed lazily. "You would not have lasted a minute in those games. The sorts of players who end up in the pits spend their entire gamespan training for that."

An infinitesimal grimace passed over the priest's face, but he then said, "As a priest, particularly in the area of divine law that I practiced, I made many enemies over my lifetime. A great many would have wagered much to watch me fight to the death. As you probably know, participants in the pits receive a share of the bet. You are right, I would not have survived long, but perhaps long *enough*. I hoped to pass on a great deal of points to my two children."

"Children?" Lyra exclaimed with a smile. "You have bio-children? How sweet. Yes, I should like to have a little girl someday. What about you, Dee?" She regarded him with heavy eyelids.

At that moment, D_Light received a raw blink request from Lyra. A raw blink was a direct link between two or more minds. It differed from a typical blink, which only consisted of filtered and polished communication; raw blinks let everything in. Raw blinks were rare between players, except between those who truly trusted one another. It was often reserved for lovers and certainly was not done between players of different levels like Lyra and D_Light.

D_Light gave permission, and his mind was suddenly inundated. There were images of skin entwined, of hair and sinewy limbs, of hearts thundering. He was there with Lyra in bed, in the grass, even on the table in front of them.

Her eyes were boring into him, she was biting her lip, and a thin trickle of blood was running down. D_Light was not certain whether he was actually seeing this or if it was just coming from her mind. None of this was appropriate, but D_Light stomped down on his reservations, afraid that it would be sent to her. She was giving him a gift, baring her soul. He would not reciprocate with formalities. Instead, he joined her fantasy, starting by giving her slow, methodical kisses and tenderly running his fingers through her hair. But she was twisting over him, pawing him.

The priest continued, unaware of the silent exchange between his audience. "Blah, blah...Dr. Monsa is legendary...blah, blah... fruits from trees...blah, blah..."

You and I are alike; we are winners apart, but we could be divine together. Give me your love and we will share our strength. Lyra's words cascaded down into his awareness. The two of them were holding hands while walking through the garden, a garden like the one they were in, except that the plants and rocks were blurry shadows with soft, rippling colors.

The curious thing about a raw blink is that participants feed off each other's thoughts. One might think of an apple, and the other might change that apple to a peach because that is what they prefer. Then the first participant might take a bite of the peach, but find it crisp instead of soft, and the cycle would continue on in this way. A shared stream of consciousness. In this case, it was a shared daydream. D_Light had used raw blinks many times to brainstorm with other teammates, but this was always in the service of a grinder game. This exchange he engaged in now was less disciplined than that. It was like an erotic psychic storm.

The mutual daydream reset and now they were in the garden holding hands. D_Light was not sure whose fantasy this was. There was a stone bench with thin, flowered vines enwrapping it.

"Blah, blah…help him, he helps me…blah, blah…symbiotic relationships are the purest…blah, blah," went the priest.

D_Light sat on the garden bench and Lyra straddled him. She was wearing a dress that festooned out and down to the ground, and although he could feel her strong and glorious legs writhing and grasping at him, he could not see them under the silken fabric. She was breathing hard, and D_Light was not sure if this emanated from the incorporeal Lyra who was straddling him in the raw blink or the physical one sitting nearby. In their dream her lips were at the level of his forehead. She kissed him there and on one of his eyelids. The dress was low cut, revealing cleavage and—

Smorgeous pressed into his mind. *Master, there is an incoming blink from Lily.*

Lyra's cleavage disappeared as the two of them snapped out of the fantasy. Mentally, D_Light wailed at Smorgeous for the interruption. Lyra, the real one, laughed.

I apologize, master, but your earlier brain pattern suggested that a blink from this sender was highly desirable and therefore—

D_Light interrupted the computer. *Just open the blink.* Lyra had ended the raw blink anyway, and D_Light felt up to the task of blinking Lily without neglecting those in his physical presence.

The priest paused in his diatribe as he pondered Lyra's misplaced laughter.

"So, about Lily." Lyra abruptly began speaking to the priest. "How, in your professional opinion, would we go about helping her out of her predicament?"

D_Light had been wondering the very same thing. Had Lyra picked that up in the raw blink? He did not remember thinking it at the time.

Yes, master, visual data regarding Lily was transmitted during the time in question. Without being asked, the familiar brought up a still image from the raw blink that took place moments ago. There was D_Light with Lyra on top of him as he remembered. Immediately, Smorgeous zoomed in on a portion of the ivory stone bench. There were words etched into the stone:

> *To-Do List*
> *Save Lily.*
> *Make sweet love to Lyra.*
> *Seize next quest.*

How embarrassing raw blinks can be! D_Light suppressed a groan. Certainly, Lyra had spotted this manifestation of his subconscious.

The priest raised his eyebrows at Lyra's off-topic question, cleared his throat, and asked, "You are referring to the camper? And by predicament, you refer to her demonization?"

Lyra nodded with a lazy smile.

Hi, Dee, did you wish to speak to me? Lily's thought signature seemed relaxed.

D_Light was surprised to hear his nickname coming from her, so much so that he tripped over his message as he sent it. *Ah, I was...I was wondering how you were.*

The priest pinched his upper lip and furrowed his brow. "Hmm," he hummed thoughtfully.

It was kind of you to check up on me. I'm with BoBo. She is showing me some of her wonderful projects. Lily sent him a slightly pixilated picture of a large, woolly teddy bear with giant, dark eyes. *It is called a nubber,* Lily explained. *It is supposed to be a pet.* Lily paused and then her blink tone changed. *So when will they be ready? When I can I get one?*

What? D_Light asked.

Oh, I was asking BoBo when I could get one—get a nubber. At this D_Light realized that Lily had been actually speaking to BoBo and that he had overheard it. It was as though Lily were speaking to him on an audio headset from the old days. D_Light quashed his urge to chastise her for being such a n00b, for not controlling her output better; however, now was not the time for a lesson on blink etiquette.

They should be ready by Christmas. The tone of voice was high and a bit squeaky; it was BoBo. Lily was just relaying what her ears picked up. This was maddening, especially when he wanted to follow the conversation between Lyra and the priest. *Glad everything's smooth,* he blinked Lily. *Gotta go, talk to you soon.* He ended the blink without waiting for a good-bye.

The priest again sensed that he was actually being listened to and so spoke with a more authoritative tone. "The camper has committed the sin of noncompliance, also known as being off purpose, as she is engaged in activity that she was not zoned for."

"Zoned?" D_Light asked.

The priest frowned slightly, flicked his eyes over D_Light, and then returned his attention to Lyra. "All products are zoned for certain purposes. Zoning is a legal term, historically and commonly used for real estate. For example, a piece of property could be zoned for commercial use, single home residential, multiple home residential, and so on. It was not legal to build an office building on land zoned for residential—"

Lyra interrupted. "What the fuck is an office building?" Her speech was badly slurred.

"Right, okay, never mind about real estate." The priest pressed his hands flat down on the table. "The deal is this. A product is legally approved for a specific set of uses, which is known as being zoned. If a product goes off-zone, or in other words, if it is engaged in a purpose it was not designed and tested for, it could be harmful to itself or, worse yet, harmful to others."

D_Light and Lyra affirmed that they were following him with nods and sounds of understanding.

"Lily was designed for purposes..." The priest paused. "For purposes related to the hunting reserves. Because she is no longer fulfilling this purpose, she has been demonized. If you want to atone for it, you will need to rezone campers—her product classification—for another purpose."

"Like as a concubine?" Lyra gave D_Light a rueful smirk. "I think Dee would like to rezone her as a concubine."

The priest paused as though to consider this. "Given the phenotype of campers, I doubt that would be a good choice, but yes, you could attempt to expand her zoning to include that purpose."

A sly smile crept over D_Light's face. "She's not 'off purpose.' She was designed for evasion, which is exactly what she's doing."

The priest let out a raspy chuckle. "Nice try. I've skimmed her zoning documents. She is designated to be hunted, hunted in specifically designated areas—the hunting reserve. You are correct that she was designed to resist capture. However, her legal problem stems not from her behavior—rather, it is a matter of geography."

"Fine," exclaimed D_Light. "So, say I, or we, buy her from the reserve and rezone her for something like a general servant."

"Assuming the house that runs the reserve spanker game is willing to sell her to you, rezoning is a long and expensive process. A great deal of testing needs to happen. A high-functioning product like a camper is very complex. It is hard to predict how they might fare with a new purpose."

The priest sent them a few choice case studies of rezoning *Homo sapiens*–based products. The point figures were staggering. Reading the expression on D_Light's face, the priest threw up his hands and declared, "Look, I don't make the laws, I just provide the best counsel I can. Or at least that used to be the game I played."

Lyra, who had grown bored with the legal speak and feared that she would waste her nectar wine–induced buzz if she did not change the subject, asked about the garden.

The priest replied, "Blah, blah, blah...approximately five milliliters of the password potion every forty-eight hours or you'll start smelling like food...blah, blah, blah...wasps are frightful, some of them cause temporary paralysis...blah, blah...orchard has a variety of fruits, all are safe..."

D_Light was only half listening as he inspected the case studies for rezoning. He asked Smorgeous to analyze the data to find an "optimum route for success," but the computer only gave him expensive and time-consuming options.

The priest excused himself. "I regret to inform you that I have a *call of nature* of my own," he said with a half smile directed at D_Light. "I'll be right back."

As soon as he left the clearing, D_Light and Lyra turned to face each other. There was silence between them for a long few seconds. D_Light felt himself being drawn into her. He hoped that she would initiate another raw blink.

Master, based on trace compounds I took the initiative to detect, Mother Lyra is 89.4% likely to be ovulating. In addition, her blood alcohol level is elevated; however, I was unable to determine a reliable measure of this level. Biochemically, she should be amenable to courtship advances.

Smorgeous brought up a visual of the Tappin_It_Baby™ Cloud site. Featured on the site were a variety of up-to-the-minute novel pickup lines.

D_Light could not believe Smorgeous had misread the situation like this. *Pickup lines? I'm way past that.* On the other hand, the line "I don't gotta grok what's gotta be good stock" was sort of funny.

I always have your back, master. This last comment had been programmed into Smorgeous years ago when D_Light had fewer friends. He spent hours trying to teach his computer to be more of a companion. Back then, one of the roles D_Light wanted Smorgeous to play was that of "wing man."

Never say that again, D_Light said to his familiar. Smorgeous pinged confirmation.

D_Light spoke first. "I'm going to kiss you tonight."

"Oh my!" Lyra's lips opened in an exaggerated O as though shocked. "Are you sure? Do you wish to assert sexual dominance over your team leader?"

Surprised by her unusual follow-up question, he stumbled a bit over his response but did so with a confident smile. "Er, I do," he replied.

D_Light took her hands and stood up, directing her to follow.

Lyra giggled. "What about what's his name, the priest? He's coming back you know."

D_Light shrugged and started walking toward a nearby path between the hedges. Lyra resisted halfheartedly, but D_Light pulled her along. Outside of the clearing, the garden was dark. Lyra fired up her glow stick, causing the miscellaneously shaped plants and trees to cast long, perplexing shadows. D_Light was not sure where he was going, but he wanted to get out of earshot of the dining area. The last thing he wanted was the priest joining them. For D_Light, this was a momentous moment. *I'm about to perv my mother!*

he thought. To establish an intimate bond with a noblewoman was a most excellent tactical move, to say the least.

He looked back at her. Lyra was returning his gaze steadily. Her large green eyes were blurred with alcohol, but her vivacity was undiminished. An impression of Lily with a smile and a cocked head flickered across his mind. How he would like to be holding her hand now.

D_Light realized his mood was fading. Smorgeous, seizing on the importance of this encounter, gave his master a boost/aphrodisiac cocktail. D_Light felt the slow tingle of lost inhibition and heightened attraction spill into him, at which point he turned back and embraced her. They were not in a private grotto like D_Light had planned. They were not even hidden under any vegetation. Rather, they stood groping and moaning right there on the path.

Lyra broke away, but she kept her face only centimeters away from his and whispered, "If PeePee were alive, she would tell me this is not proper decorum."

"Thank Soul she's dead! Listen to a machine and you'll end up no better than one."

"I have a reputation—"

Lyra found herself unable to finish her sentence as D_Light's lips hungrily latched onto hers, their curious tongues meeting with the gentlest of caresses. The kiss was moist and delicious and possessed an addictive quality that rendered them slaves to the hormonal rush that followed. Slow, passionate kisses quickly gave way to frenzied, lustful ones, and the two fell to the ground as they groped, grabbed, bit, and pulled each other closer. After much of this intensely disorganized fumbling, they made love, or to better describe the act, had sex. The kind of sex that is found in the wildest of places, places like this, where copulation of all forms reigns supreme and the very fabric of the world is dependent on it. And at the height of it all, after D_Light had finally gone over the edge, there was a long seven seconds when everything in his world made sense as he stared into his beautiful mother's bottomless eyes.

And then he thought of Lily.

CHAPTER 29

The angel Jacob was standing deep inside the synthetic shell of his mother ship. Although a few of his kind resided on ships that floated in space, Jacob's ship carved through ocean waves just outside the sight of land. Waterborne ships were far more resource-efficient than the space-going variety, and so when conducting missions on earth, they were often an optimal choice.

As Jacob had his systems checked and re-checked by a team of bots, human technicians, and human-based products, he briefly reviewed the case of the demons who had escaped into the inner sanctum of House Monsa. The human agents who had been coordinating the pursuit in Jacob's absence had done an adequate job of tracking the demons but had failed due to what Jacob regarded as "unlikely events." Therefore, the angel sent them a stipend covering half of their expenses thus far. In addition, the angel agreed with Katria and Rhemus that sending lesser agents than Jacob himself into the inner sanctum could likely result in further resource losses.

Jacob set a flag of "moderate importance" on the case and went to sleep to optimize his repairs. He would get to them soon enough.

D_Light woke up alone. At some point in his sleep he had rolled off the stone pathway and into the multilayered folds of a soft, leafy plant, the very species of plant the doctor had told him the night before made for good toilet paper.

A ferret on its haunches stood nearby, staring at him unblinkingly. It had a long white stripe down its abdomen. It was Lyra's familiar, PeePee; she cocked her head as D_Light blinked into the artificial sunlight that filtered down through the tree leaves above. Smorgeous sat nearby communing with the ferret.

Mother Lyra pinged him with a blink request, which D_Light accepted. *Good morning, stud.* Her voice was amused.

D_Light rubbed his eyes and asked, *Hey, is that Pretty Princess, your familiar? I thought it was—*

Lyra interrupted. *Yeah, PeePee was in bad shape, but the doctor had his techs fix her. I suspect he feels guilty about the whole culler incident and wanted to try to make amends.*

Lyra paused momentarily and then said, *Anyway, let's get something straight right out of the gate. What happened last night is between you and me, right?*

Right, of course! D_Light sent the thought back without hesitation.

Naturally, I'm not ashamed, but I would hate to see anything on the Cloud.

Lyra meant to continue, but D_Light sent his thoughts back nearly on top of hers, exclaiming, *No! No, you can forget about it. I mean, don't forget about it, but don't worry about me doing anything like that. That, I mean, like you said, that was just between you and me.* D_Light wondered if anything that he had just transmitted made sense.

The blink was silent for a moment.

I mean it, D_Light added, unable to handle the awkward silence. *By Soul, I'll even submit a contract on it.*

D_Light thought for a moment in order to come up with some suitable words and then pinged his familiar. *Smorgeous, I hereby swear to not knowingly and willingly disclose to anyone directly or indirectly the, er, events of last night between Mother Lyra and myself.* Smorgeous pinged confirmation, which was also received by PeePee.

Master, what is the point penalty for breaching this contract? Smorgeous inquired.

Let's make it two hundred—no, make it five hundred thousand points.

Artificial intelligence was quite adept at detail-oriented tasks like drafting simple contracts, so after some clarifying questions Smorgeous read back the finalized and verbose refinements to ensure it was what the two had agreed upon. The contract was then digitally signed, encrypted, and submitted to the Game. Essentially, the contract created another rule for D_Light to follow in the Game. If he broke the rule, half a million of his points would be taken from him and deposited into Lyra's profile. It would be a huge loss.

As the last confirmation of the contract pinged, Lyra spoke, highlighting her thought with a warm signature. *Thank you, D_Light. That was a generous sum, and your gesture puts my mind at ease. You are more than a great player, you are an honorable man.*

I thank you, Mother, for your kind words, he responded.

Lyra's tone then became casual. *Now, why don't you join us for breakfast?*

The team members met again at the great table where they had eaten dinner the night before. A servant, bearing tattoos marking it as a product, was busy setting the table, fully focusing on the task at hand. The breakfast table boasted antique bronze vases full of colorful and unusually shaped flowers, many of which were unfamiliar to the guests. At the center of the table were a variety of exotic dishes that D_Light also could not identify. There were roasted cephalopods that appeared to be derived from grasshoppers, large soft-shelled beetles that were filled with some sort of bread stuffing, orangish eggs scrambled with colorful things that looked to be engineered mushrooms, and giant nut bowls filled to the rim with a gray, steamy broth. D_Light, having simple tastes in food, was wondering if there was anything he could eat, when his eyes caught sight of the more traditional fare further down the table. The colorful nectar blocks, breakfast sausages, and tea biscuits were a welcome sight. There he also spotted a large tray of beautifully arranged exotic fruits, many of which were foreign to him, but D_Light had never met a fruit he didn't like.

Djoser was already gnawing with great attention on the carapace of one of the giant grasshoppers. Lyra, who sat next to him, looked up at D_Light briefly, smiled, and quickly returned to her meal, although she only picked at it. Lily was also present, happily devouring a skinless peach. Her face lit up upon seeing her friend. "Good morning, Dee!" she exclaimed genuinely.

A smile involuntarily snapped over D_Light's face as he said, "And good to see you." *My Soul, it is good to see you,* he thought.

The blond beauty looked like a fey woodland creature as her skin glowed in the warm morning light. She was feeding a nubber, one of the light brown teddy bears with gigantic soulful eyes that Lily had shown him the night before. Its ears curled back and forth in what D_Light guessed was appreciation for the scraps of fruit and nectar cubes Lily dropped to it. Two of the Monsa daughters were seated next to Lily, one on each side. They were educating her on the finer points of the nubber diet. Watching Lily with loving eyes, D_Light thought she looked like she was in her element, as though she had been born here, had been grown from one of the giant flowering fruit trees that punctuated the immense garden. She seemed to be at home, or perhaps it was just that this was the first time he had ever seen her look truly happy.

Lyra, seated beside the priest, directed her attention to D_Light. "I was just apologizing to Our Holiness here about last night, how, in our thoughtless exhaustion, we did not say good-bye to him before retiring for the night."

The priest, dabbing his lips with a napkin between every bite, wore a poker-faced expression. "I assured your mother that there was no need for apology. MetaGames are intense affairs, and a player need not ask an old priest like me to be excused for a much earned rest."

D_Light bowed. "Nevertheless, I am ashamed and in your debt."

The priest smiled faintly as he bowed his head in deference to D_Light and then went to work replenishing his plate.

D_Light could not help wondering if the priest believed the story, wondering if his face gave away the truth of last night's shenanigans. The man would have had to be blind to not see the chemistry between the two of them last night, not to mention that he had left to take a leak, only to return to find them both gone. Priests were not stupid. Still, D_Light thought he saw a look of relief on the man's face when he confirmed Lyra's story. D_Light often had to remind himself that people would go to great lengths to believe what they want versus that which is probable. And D_Light was sure the priest preferred not to believe that the noblewoman he had been ogling all that evening had actually ended up in the arms of a young, upstart player like D_Light.

Having filled their bellies and engaged in an adequate amount of chatter with their gracious breakfast company, D_Light, Lyra, and

Djoser speculated about the next quest. They expected it to have something to do with hunting since the theme of the game was "the hunter and the hunted," but that wasn't exactly an encouraging thought. They hoped they would not be pitted against something awful that lived in the inner sanctum, the cullers that had chased them earlier coming to mind. In any case, Lyra was certain that the next quest would be the last, given how rapidly they were progressing through them. "Since the quests we have been getting are significant, I'd only expect three or four of them, and this will be our fourth," she said.

Lyra tried to get Djoser and D_Light to bet against her on this, but there were no takers. Normally D_Light would have taken an interest in the wager, but he was only half listening to the conversation, desperately trying to eavesdrop on Lily and the clones.

"Yes, I have two daughters," Lily said with a faint smile.

"You have children?" Curious_Scourge looked confused. "You are not gene-clamped?"

Lily did not understand the last question, but she did not have a chance to ask for clarification because the other girls clamored to hear what it was like to be pregnant. Lily briefly indulged them in the retelling of the good, the bad (mostly bad), and the ugly of her pregnancies and births.

"You miss them? Your daughters, I mean?" BoBo asked gently.

"Oh yes, very much." Lily's voice quavered just a little.

"And your mate? He must miss you terribly." BoBo squeezed Lily's shoulder.

"My what?" Lily asked, furrowing her brow. "Oh no, there are no men, no men of my kind in my tribe back home."

This spurred a general clamor of questions around how campers got pregnant.

Lily's eyes bolted wide open as it dawned on her why they were so surprised. "Oh no!" Lily exclaimed. "My sisters and I do not use sexual intercourse to make babies." As Lily said "sexual intercourse," she made thrusting motions with her hips. The girls covered their mouths with their hands and giggled, but it was apparent from the expression on Lily's face that she was not making a joke; she was simply trying to be clear.

"You see," Lily said, "when I reached what you call 'puberty,' I became pregnant. This happens for all my sisters, and we call it the Stag's gift. And every six years afterward, the Great Stag gives us another."

"And your daughters look exactly like you and your other sisters?" Curious_Scourge asked.

"Yes," Lily answered.

Curious_Scourge squeezed Lily's hand with gentle excitement. "Yes, that makes sense. Your designer gene-clamped you. Sex is only useful for creating variation in a species and spurring evolution over a long period of time. It is actually divine law to gene-clamp all products once their design has been finalized. Otherwise, mutations could compromise the integrity of the product design over time."

"How does the wetgineer who designed campers get points for additional products? It seems like the reserve could just buy one and make more themselves," BoBo said.

"Like the goose that lays the golden egg," Curious_Scourge said.

BoBo looked over Lily's body, fixing momentarily on her abdomen, and then she returned her gaze back to her face. "I've never heard of a reproductive strategy like yours. The products we create in House Monsa do not reproduce at all. When our clients want another one, we grow them a new one—that is, if we don't already have a pre-grown model in stock."

"Yes, Father then reaps additional points from return customers," Curious_Scourge added. "My guess is that your owners are doing what is called 'leasing the herd.' They pay an annual flat fee, an unusual and outdated business model, but a few bioengineering houses still use it. Even some of Father's early contracts were herd leases."

D_Light expected Lily to appear quite uncomfortable in this conversation, but just the opposite was true. Lily's eyes were burning with intensity as she asked of the identical girls a series of follow-up questions. The girls were just as anxious to answer her. Their feverish discourse was only interrupted by the intermittent pitiable cry from the nubber begging for additional table scraps. D_Light was about to leave his side of the table and join the throng of animated females when he heard Lyra calling. "You coming? We're getting a tour of the garden."

D_Light reluctantly followed.

CHAPTER 30

Dr. Monsa's garden was enormous, although it was more of a collection of smaller gardens than one large one. There was the English garden with its traditional, orderly plots of roses and symmetrical walkways; the Japanese garden with its stonework, well-manicured tree branches, and hidden brooks; the French garden, sporting dense hedges sculpted into ornate geometrical patterns; and a walled-off paradise garden that featured waterworks like fountains, canals, ponds, and waterfalls. As it were, these labels were little more than vague descriptions, as the gardens contained very few original plants from those olden times; this was fitting considering that the nationalities themselves—English, Japanese, and French—had long since faded into irrelevance.

Many of the plants found in the garden had been designed in the inner sanctum itself and were either being tested or served as living reminders of past successes. The priest pretended to lead the tour, but it soon became evident that the child-framed clone girl named Pueet was the most knowledgeable, and she would often cut in whenever the priest seemed to stammer over the answers to questions.

Although the entire garden was nothing short of spectacular, perhaps the most glorious of the plant life were the colossal nectar trees. These marvels of engineering were ten stories high and bore massive trunks and beefy branches that supported immense orbs of leaves and flowers. The soothing hum of countless collectors buzzing or crawling about was always present. These insects were designed to harvest the abundant sugars produced by the nectar trees and bring this precious juice by way of a pheromone trail to a place determined by their master. After taking their fill, the coin-sized insects set off, bobbing uncertainly under their load, along the chemical trail set down for them. Once they reached the invisible trail end, they would deposit their load into catch tubes, and the sugars were then shunted off to locations where they could be metabolized.

The dro-vine that made up House Monsa required a constant supply of food. It needed energy to regulate its temperature and to optimize its air quality and humidity. Whatever the house did not eat could be fed to the countless creatures that inhabited it, including those people who were either too frugal or too busy to obtain food in some other manner. There was no shame in eating and drinking nectar. Indeed, nectar optimized for animal consumption came in many flavors and contained all the essential proteins and vitamins for optimum health. Even the highest scoring players did not shun nectar, although it did become boring over decades of consumption. Nectar could even be used to fuel organic machines like familiars or robots that were responsible for mundane industrial work. However, such machines typically consumed the most potent nectar (and most terrible tasting to humans), which was super-compressed into dense cubes.

It was the heavy demand for variety in nectar production that drove much of the point revenue of House Monsa. Any new strain of nectar that, for example, offered a different taste, was metabolized more easily, or simply came from an aesthetically pleasing tree would find a ready market. Indeed, nectar trees were so common on earth—and increasingly on other planets and moons—that a house could expect to sell millions, if not billions of trees with every new variety it created.

Beside the grove of nectar trees were the fast-growing poplar trees that set off a soft and even melodious groan as their trunks rose up nearly fast enough for the naked eye to watch in action. Although most dwellings were grown rather than built, the wood these trees produced was still used in a variety of classic products, from paper to furniture.

While one could spend hours alone examining the astonishing variety of trees in Monsa's gardens, there were just as many impressive varieties of flowers in every color imaginable and with equally impressive uses. There were flowers that emitted light at night, flowers that ate pesky insects (but not the helpful ones, such as collectors), flowers that were processed into all manner of drugs for both human and product consumption, and even flowers for the very old yet still profitable perfume trade. Pueet, their little hostess, explained in a clear voice. "The flowers in the inner sanctum are not for production use; they are just prototypes. We have many production labs distributed throughout House Monsa and her subsidiaries."

Although plants made up the bulk of the life in the gardens, there were more active denizens that walked, crawled, slithered, or flapped. The most conspicuous products were the general humanoid laborers sprinkled everywhere, their purpose to keep the garden tidy. They did most of their work using only old-fashioned hand tools rather than modern ones, as the doctor preferred the aesthetic of old-time gardening.

Despite this handicap, the massive gardens were immaculately kept, and it was no wonder. The gardeners were remarkably productive, oblivious to the heat of the midday artificial sun and indifferent to the cold of night. They required only two hours of sleep per day, and when they slept they needn't walk back to any sleeping quarters; instead, they would simply lie down under the shelter of some luxurious plant. Nor did such workers require breaks to eat because there was plenty of fruit and enormous, plump, and delicious bugs of all sorts, which they scooped up deftly as they worked.

All of the workers were identical in appearance. They were hairless men with dark skin weathered by exposure, and every one of them carried around their neck a small blue vial containing repellant against the garden cullers. When Lyra pointed out the vials, Pueet informed them that when the workers got old or otherwise outlived their usefulness, the doctor would simply cut off their supply of repellant. However, such turnover was low since the food in the garden on which the workers subsisted was chock-full of goodies that slowed the aging process.

Among the human-based products that attracted the most attention from the men in the party were the concubines. A full harem of women, spectacular in their nudity, lounged about in a silver-pooled grotto. They stared back at the voyeurs, some of them demurely, some intensely. Djoser asked if these prototypes required any further "testing," volunteering for the job with a lewd smile. Pueet warned him to leave them alone, as the same traits that mimicked passionate love could easily turn to violence.

Pueet went on to say how Sara, Dr. Monsa's personal concubine, the one who the night before had stuck a fork in another dinner guest's hand, was one of the doctor's early and unsuccessful attempts in this line of work. "But Sara formed an imprint bond with Father, and despite her madness, he grew fond of her," she said. "Well, maybe not exactly fond of her, but affectionately familiar with her over the years."

Pueet then informed the tour group that the concubines were not allowed out of their plexi cage. "We used to allow them to wander freely, but eventually they would get bored and try to seduce the garden workers or whoever else they could find. It was shamefully disruptive."

"What about rent-a-boys? Do you grow them as well?" Lyra asked while elbowing Djoser in the ribs.

Pueet laughed girlishly. "Yes, although we lock them up also, away from the concubine protos. Otherwise they would simply wear each other out. In the early days we actually lost a few of them from exhaustion. We do still allow controlled visits for testing purposes."

Spurred by Lyra's interest, Pueet showed them the rent-a-boy sphere. Like their female counterparts they were nude, exposing their perfectly shaped and muscular bodies. Upon seeing the visitors, some of the products whistled at Lyra and Pueet and shouted out invitations over one another. Others leaned stoically against the plexi as though posing. A few smiled shyly and hid themselves. Apparently, there was a type of man for all tastes.

"I noticed you do not separate them from one another," D_Light commented. "Do they get along so harmoniously all the time?"

Pueet pointed to three small empty spheres off in the distance. "No, occasionally we get a violent phenotype or one whose copious sexual urges are misdirected at others in the cell. However, as you can see, the isolation spheres are empty now. We rarely make such rookie mistakes in our designs anymore."

"Misdirected sexual urges?" Djoser asked. "You do not make homosexual rent-a-boys and concubines?"

"Oh, there really isn't much of a market for those," Pueet answered while twisting her mouth slightly. "The rampant genetic engineering of humans leading up to the time of the bottleneck—coupled with modern fetus incubation tanks—has nearly wiped that market out."

"Interesting," D_Light said. "I had no idea."

Pueet nodded. "Yeah, House Yi-LingYu specializes in that niche market, and Father does not think the potential profits are worth the extra R&D it would take to challenge Yi-LingYu's strong position." Pueet sighed. "I've thought of putting a line together myself. It would be a fun game, but I do not know if I will ever get around to it."

Pueet then took the tour party to see House Monsa's most advanced and expensive product line, the analysts. Like Hal, the analyst they had met the night before, the male analysts looked very similar to the common garden worker products in that they were hairless, and they were remarkable only in that they did not resemble anyone in particular. It was as though they were merely templates of a person. The women analysts were hairless also, making them somewhat repulsive to D_Light. The analysts were one of the most driven products. When looking into their eyes one might at first think that they were dull, given their blank stare; however, in reality they were simply in a state of unbroken trance. They were so committed to their thoughts that nothing in the silly "real" world mattered a pin to them.

Like Hal, many of the analysts had tubes that sprung up around them like wet quills of a porcupine, the skin folding circularly like an anus where the tube interfaced with their body. Nectar, drugs, and other substances that D_Light did not ask about flowed in through some tubes, and dark liquid waste trickled out of others. Unlike the ebony tans of the garden workers, the skin of the analysts was nearly translucent from their subterranean existence. Their domicile was deep within a windowless dro-vine mound. They stood in long bays, one after the other. Their mind interface chips were hooked directly to machines, but this apparently did not provide enough input because their otherwise minimalist bays had dozens of monitors which displayed a great deal of things that D_Light could not even guess about. Pueet told them that the monitors were as much for those supervising the analysts—the proctors—as they were for the products themselves. Since these analysts were prototype models, it was important for proctors to observe, measure, and validate their work.

The proctors also appeared to be products. One proctor was another of Dr. Monsa's cloned daughters, identical to Pueet, Love_Monkey, Curious_Scourge, BoBo, and every other "daughter" they had seen, except that this one had a dark ribbon in her hair. The girl ignored the tour group as she scanned the monitors, and the analysts, likewise, were oblivious to her. Another proctor was an analyst himself, presumably a graduated one. This one was walking along with his tubes hooked into a hovering machine that trailed behind him, always staying just close enough to stay out of his way while still maintaining some slack.

Pueet explained that most of the analysts were playing ultra-complex strategy games against one another, as well as against others outside House Monsa. "It can be expensive to hire independent agents to pit wits against our prototypes, but it is necessary to vet the optimum designs. Those consistently successful might be grown for commercial production."

"What about those that fail? Do you destroy them?" Djoser asked.

"Soul no! They are too expensive to design, grow, and train to just throw them away. Instead, we sell them at a steep discount to houses that could not otherwise afford them."

As repulsive as the analysts were, D_Light knew that he was in the Fort Knox of the modern world. If you had a tough problem, a quandary of great magnitude, the best thing you could do was set one of these babies loose on it. They were the greatest weapons a player could get hold of. D_Light would have loved to get one of these for himself—even a reject—but such merchandise was way out of his price range. Individual players did not buy analysts. Only major families had pockets deep enough to own even one.

D_Light was a little surprised that he and his teammates were trusted to be here, seemingly unguarded. D_Light and Djoser were armed, and Lyra herself was a 120-pound weapon. One madman with a blade could slit one throat after another. *No doubt the analysts would just stand there like cows in the slaughterhouse,* he thought. *Billions of points of damage could be done!* D_Light had no such insane intention, nor could he imagine this of anyone else on his team. Perhaps some analyst had already foretold this fact beyond all reasonable probability, which is why they were here.

Pueet ushered them on. "There is much more to see, more than you can see in a day. More than you could see in a lifetime."

The party was well worn out by the time they stumbled in for dinner. Dr. Monsa was present, as was Sara and her rent-a-boy reject playthings from the night before. Several of the clones were there. Djoser did not remember which was which, but Moocher, with his precise memory, identified them by their distinctly colored bows and told him the present company was Curious_Scourge, BoBo, Love_Monkey (who was apparently back from the groksta), their guide for the day, Pueet, along with a new daughter who had not yet been introduced.

As usual, the clones surrounded Lily and her nubber. The nubber was carrying a few worse-for-wear flowers in one paw while holding onto the hem of Lily's dress with its other. Lily's dress was a frilly thing covered with flower prints and lace, similar to the ones worn by the clone girls.

Djoser had only seen flowered dresses on women (or men) who were making fun of themselves. The antiquated fashion and its supposed virtue was a joke to any mainstream player. Nevertheless, it suited Lily. Djoser marveled at the perfect skin of her arms, throat, and face, such delicate proportions. And the natural innocence and sincerity with which she carried herself was captivating. She had been designed perfectly for her purpose.

He imagined what it would be like to hold her down on her back, screaming and thrashing under him. How he would forcefully penetrate her. And as he violated her, he wondered what it would look like when he bit into her pale, flawless skin, first her forearm as she tried to fend him off, then her neck, followed by her cheek. And just as he was finishing, he would stab into one of her beautiful blue eyes and pry it out. *What would that be like? How would I feel?* Such an experience would be like none he had ever had before in his eighty-seven years of existence.

"It's really not fair how pretty you are in this," BoBo said to Lily as she pinched the fabric of Lily's dress.

"Do you seek her approval with your exclusive chitchat simply because she is comely?" the good doctor nearly shouted across the table.

"Father, don't embarrass me," BoBo hissed between clenched teeth. "I was merely making an observation."

Dr. Monsa spoke to the group with a weary voice. "A weakness in my girls. Although they are old enough to know better, they share the primitive trait of desperately wanting to please those who appear to be worth pleasing. Notice how they gravitate toward the Caucasian girl and not the lovely Lyra?"

Lyra was startled by hearing her name and turned away from Djoser to listen.

"You are sooo embarrassing!" Curious_Scourge lamented.

349

The doctor ignored her remark and said, "My girls have always found beauty in things that resemble themselves. I used to think it was vanity, but perhaps it is something more primitive. Like attracts like. Conceivably a useful feature in our early evolution, but a bothersome vestige in this modern day. I haven't tracked down the genes responsible for this vestige. It is rather complex."

BoBo pounded a small fist into the table. "My Soul, can't I just have a conversation and *you* mind your own business?"

"But I too am merely making an observation," countered the doctor.

BoBo's face flushed. "An observation? You think I like her just because she is a pretty white girl. You think me so simple? Maybe I find her fascinating for the same reason you do!" BoBo grabbed Lily's hand which sat limp, cupped in the little porcelain hands of the child-woman. Lily's face was pale and her eyes glistened.

"Because of *what* she is," BoBo said. "What a rare event it is to have a *specimen* like her in our domicile!"

BoBo stroked Lily's hair with one hand. "Or maybe it isn't just the fact that she is white like me or that she is a camper, but that she is a woman? I can see in her my approximate future. Oh, but wait… no such future awaits me because *someone* trapped my sisters and me forever in a prepubescent shell!" With that, BoBo stood, sending her chair backward and over with a crack on the hard stone floor, and then she stormed off.

———

BoBo's dramatic exit sparked an end to dinner. The other girls fell in with BoBo's lead and stomped off with their sister. Lily asked to be excused with her teddy bear. After snacking all day in the garden, D_Light could not eat another bite, and so he excused himself as well. Walking down the path, he discovered Lily, who was talking to her bear. "What a silly boy you are," she said as the nubber tried clumsily to climb a tree from which oval milky fruits hung overhead.

"Déjà vu," D_Light said. "Have you noticed that dinnertime here is really awkward?" he asked.

Lily laughed softly. "Yeah, maybe I should just pack a picnic for my dinner tomorrow night."

"That sounds good," said D_Light. "Maybe I could join you and we could watch the pretend sunset together."

Lily smiled and nodded. And then, abruptly, she walked up to only a few inches from his face. "D_Light, why don't you tell me about yourself? Tell me about how you grew up."

D_Light felt the urge to either step back or step into her, but he remained where he was. "I…sure, I'll have—"

"I don't want to talk to your robot," she said with a note of irritation. "I don't want it to send me anything. I want to hear you say it."

D_Light agreed and suggested they take a walk. The pair wandered along a winding path and out into the vast garden below. They had no destination, the only goal being to put distance between themselves and the others. As they walked, D_Light told Lily about his birth, how he was grown in a nursery, although he, of course, could not remember this. He told her how he and thirty other children were raised by a variety of child-rearing gamers and that his nursery mates would come and go—a typical childhood.

Lily asked many questions related to this. "Where was your mother? How did your caretaker manage so many?"

D_Light told her how it was wasteful for a bio-parent to take care of a child. Their time could be better spent doing something productive. On the other hand, a nursery grinder, also known as a "naga," as his foster mother was called, could score very high in the

Game by raising large quantities of quality players. Many immortals started out as nagas.

D_Light was surprised by the plethora of questions about his bio-parents. Yes, he knew who they were, but it did not matter. They received a small percentage of the points he scored, so he was important to them, but not vice versa.

Lily then explained how mothers in her tribe raised their own daughters. Of course, many daughters lost their mothers to "the running time," at which point a foster mother would be selected from the tribe. D_Light thought it was a poor design and cruel to have the campers carry their daughters to term in the womb. He knew that humans used to do this and that sideliners still often did, but he always thought it absurd. It was always a mystery to him how mammals managed to survive throughout the ages carrying their unborn like that. Slowed down and vulnerable, the fetus was nothing more than a bonus meal to some hungry predator. Even worse was the way they delivered the infant. *Sadistic is nature!*

Artificial night was falling and the photoflowers were beginning to bloom, spawning soft globes of light in an otherwise darkening garden. There was a statue of a nude, curvaceous woman looking over her shoulder at a brook that gurgled though a grassy clearing. The pair sat on the grass and regarded the statue. Smorgeous suggested that it best matched examples of Aphrodite, the Greek goddess of love and beauty, and D_Light announced that this was, in fact, who the statue depicted, as though he had known this himself.

Lily's soft features glowed in the warmth of the photoflowers' light as she told D_Light about the god of her tribe, the Great Stag. According to legend, long ago when her people were first created, there was a magnificent stag that lived in their forest. He was a kind creature who could speak, and this stag taught the tribe of the Star

Sisters and the tribe of the Sons how to gather fruit and hunt. There was abundant fruit, and the game was plentiful. But one day the queen of the Star Sisters and the king of the Sons decided that they no longer had a use for the stag.

Using an imperious tone of voice, Lily quoted the characters of her story. "'The stag's pelt will make a fine blanket to warm me at night,' said the queen. And the king said, 'The stag's head will make a fine trophy over my throne.'"

Lily then told how a team of the best hunters from both the tribes brought down the mighty creature, and the queen got her pelt and the king got his trophy. But what they did not know was that the stag was the true life-bringer of the forest. With his breath he made the fruit grow and the game multiply. And so in his absence, the fruit rotted away and the game disappeared, and the people of the tribes began to starve.

Lily tilted her head and lifted her brows. "And after many had perished, the stag was reborn and came back. The tribes begged the stag to save them, and he consented, but the tribes needed to pay for what they had done. Forever forward, every moon, one woman from the tribe of the Star Sisters and one man from the tribe of the Sons were selected to run, to be hunted as the Great Stag himself had been hunted. Some would return by the next moon, and some would not."

"That's awful," D_Light said. "Lily, you know that is a lie, I mean a myth, right?"

"Yes, I know that," she said. And then, more softly, she added, "I know that *now*."

"How does your tribe choose? Choose who is to be hunted, I mean?" D_Light asked.

"Each tribe has an elder who chooses, although there are often volunteers."

"*Volunteers?* Who would volunteer?" D_Light asked incredulously.

"People who want a better life. People like me." She smiled faintly and lowered her head. Looking at Lily sitting motionless on the lawn next to him, her sculpted legs drawn in tight, D_Light thought she appeared to be a statue herself, the photoflowers casting soft shadows in all the right places. She was a statue of innocence and virtue, a work of art from which he could not pull himself away.

Following a long pause, Lily returned to her story. "Whenever one of us goes on a run, we are allowed to cast a stone with our mark into a jar. Every four years the elder reaches into the jar and pulls out a stone. If it is your stone, then the Great Stag will save you."

"A lotto," D_Light whispered.

She shrugged. "Yes, so the more often you run, the better your chances of salvation."

This D_Light understood. It was no different than the Game. The higher your lifetime score, the better your chances at becoming one of the chosen—one of the immortals. This one fact was the underlying current that influenced every action taken by every player every day in the Game. "Believe it or not, we're not that much different, you and I," he told her.

Lily felt an inexplicable desire to tell D_Light all there was to know about her even though it went against everything she had been taught about humans. She wanted to go on to tell him how, after being chosen, she was no longer allowed to sleep in the same den as her sisters and daughters, that she had to sleep alone. She wanted to talk about how two nights after the lotto she had been awakened by the elder, who led her silently through the forest for hours until they reached a cave, which they proceeded to navigate for miles in the dark with only the light of a tiny lamp. She wanted to share the memory of emerging on the other side of the cave into a different world, one with marvelous trees and beautiful flowers, a paradise where she assumed the forgiving Stag would meet her and speak to her with kindness and love. And she wanted to reveal to D_Light her feelings of disillusion and despair when her god never came, how her only anchor was Todget, the one chosen from the tribe of the Sons, who led her away to her new life, a life much like the last—full of fear and events outside of her control.

Lily wanted to share these things but didn't. She didn't tell D_Light how she had found work at the university as a test subject, how Professor SlippE who hired her did not mind that she was a demon because it meant she came cheap. She didn't tell him that it was this professor who implanted her mind interface chip or how he conducted experiments on her that caused bizarre images and voices to crash into her psyche—some ideas created, others destroyed. It was then that she began to dream for the first time, began to imagine death as something other than eternal peace and darkness. Now death had become a curious and frightening unknown, and despite feeling that she could trust D_Light, she was not yet ready to fully reveal her feelings of alienation and vulnerability. There was so much in this new world that she still did not understand, including why it made her smile when she looked at this man at her side and he returned her gaze.

Slowly, Lily lifted her eyes to the stars above. "So much space, so vast. It is so cold," she said with a quiver in her voice.

"They're fake, just a projection on the invisible dome."

Lily laughed. "You must think I'm a fool, a 'n00b,' as you call it. It's not what they *are*, it's what they *represent*."

"Well then, I suppose you could call it 'vast,' and space is certainly cold. But it is beautiful too. You could live a billion lifetimes and not fill up that space."

"And your OverSoul, your god, will give you that opportunity?" Lily asked. She fixed her eyes back on the statue.

"For a billion lifetimes? Soul willing, yes."

"Maybe one lifetime lived well is enough."

D_Light repressed the urge to roll his eyes. It was the sort of thing sideliners and expired players said to make themselves feel better about dying, but he refrained from saying those things aloud. Lily was no coward. She was in a land of monumental complexity, a world that did not care for her one pin. Indeed, she was fodder for the petty desires of others, and yet she sat there serenely, gorgeous and resolute, and as he gazed at her near the statue, she too looked like a goddess—one stripped of all her power, perhaps, but not of her divinity.

"It used to terrify me," D_Light said. "That." He pointed up into the starry night.

Lily squinted as though looking for something specific. "When I was little," D_Light said, "I slept by myself in a tiny, windowless room away from the other children. My bedroom was out on the roof of our nursery, and so on the clear nights I would gaze up at the stars before going to bed. I continued this routine until one night, as I lay in my bed..." D_Light paused because he was not sure how to explain. "As I lay in my bed, I felt *infinity*." He looked into Lily's eyes to see if he had already lost her, but she appeared focused and intrigued, so he continued. "I realized I was a speck in time, a time that went on forever without end. I felt like I was already gone and that my life, me, the person I was, my soul as it were, had no meaning on such a stage—in a universe without end."

Lily placed her hand atop D_Light's, and the two returned their gaze upward to the stars.

"It terrified me," D_Light said, his eyes still fixed on the night sky. "It terrified me to be nothing." Then he chuckled. "So I stopped looking up on my way to my bed, and I started sleeping with the light on."

Lily smiled at his solution. "I always slept near my sisters and daughters until that was no longer an option. Why did you sleep alone?" Lily asked softly.

"My naga did not allow any of us to sleep together." D_Light recited a hymn: "In the Game of Life, we all play alone."

"What a strange thing to say," Lily declared. "I don't think that is even true. Sure, we are born alone and we die alone, but as we live, we live together. It seems like the living is the important part."

D_Light did not bother to explain that the meaning of the hymn was more subtle than that. Sure, players gained by cooperating, at least as far as such relationships were beneficial, but in the end only individuals received salvation. One had to make one's own way.

"Anyway, it isn't about whom I slept near," D_Light said. "This fear was deeper than that. Maybe the distraction of others would have stopped me from realizing this truth—"

"The truth of your oblivion?" Lily questioned.

"Right."

"And you found solace in the OverSoul's promise to make you timeless?"

D_Light's voice rose. "It's more than a promise, more than a myth. I mean, you see them—the immortals. They walk among us. You ate dinner with one of them!"

"Dr. Monsa? You want to be like him?" Lily asked.

"Maybe not like him *exactly*," D_Light replied, and they both laughed at this.

The two fell silent for a short time. Smorgeous had observed where the servants kept the nectar wine and suggested D_Light acquire some for his company. The familiar reminded him that alcohol had, historically, served him well with the ladies. D_Light told his familiar to shut up.

D_Light crossed his arms and rubbed his shoulders as though to keep warm, causing an undesirable slithering sound as his hands ran across the microlenses of his skinsuit, breaking the dense but pleasant silence. Lily looked over and put her arm around his shoulders and pulled him close. It was not the jerky, awkward, or hurried motion of someone making a sexual advance, the way Lyra had come on to him the night before. Sitting so closely, their bodies gently touching, he could feel the slow and steady rise and fall of her breath. He let his head tilt down and rest on her soft shoulder. She wrapped her arms around him tighter, and he could feel her heartbeat, which was steady and strong. It was hypnotic, and he allowed himself to listen for the longest while. In that moment, D_Light was feeling something that he had never before felt, and it was both exciting and terrifying at the same time.

"Someday I would like to take you sailing," he announced.

"Sailing? Ah, I've seen the little white sails of the boats on the lake near our...near my old home." She paused. "It looks very peaceful. Like birds in flight."

"Ha, everyone I know thinks it's pointless—a waste of time."

Lily nestled her warm face into his chest. "I would go sailing with you, D."

"We could go anywhere, you know. I'd rent us an old-fashioned sloop, one with a cabin that we could sleep in. So many islands for us to anchor off of. We could just keep going and going."

Lily nodded.

"We could take your nubber. We could train him to work the deck."

Lily laughed. "I don't know what 'working the deck' is, but I'm sure he would look adorable doing it."

They both looked over at the nubber. It sat as though mimicking the humans; however, sitting forward was difficult for a pudgy bear, and so it rocked back and forth, always threatening to fall backward. When it noticed it had the humans' attention, it crawled over and joined in the snuggling, which set off a series of coos and awws from everyone.

Eventually, Lily spoke softly. "There is a lake nearby."

"Yeah, we're sitting under a giant lake," D_Light said.

"Yes, but I mean another smaller lake, here, in the inner sanctum. BoBo showed it to me yesterday. If we have time tomorrow, would you like to go for a swim? You humans are all competitive, right? We could race, if you prefer."

Time. All this talk of infinite time and he suddenly felt like he did not have any to spare. Lily, apparently thinking along the same lines, asked, "Why haven't they come for us? Come for me, I mean? They must know we're here."

D_Light just turned his head, found her cheek, and kissed it. Her skin was warm and pliant to his lips.

"Let's take that swim now," he said with a comforting smile.

It was not long before the companions found a small lake that shimmered subtly under the soothing colors of nearby photoflowers. They swam, laughed, and raced to the point of exhaustion. Naked and entwined, they fell asleep atop a soft mound of moss as they dried in the warmth of the inner sanctum's night air.

D_Light awoke again to find PeePee staring at him with a blink request from Lyra, which he accepted. *Good morning, Dee.* Her thought signature was amused.

This isn't exactly what it looks like, D_Light stammered. *We took a swim and then—*

Forget it. I think it's great that you're getting along so fabulously with all of your teammates. A real morale builder you are. Unnervingly, the ferret simulated Lyra's laugh, and its little snout snapped open and shut as it did so.

There was little D_Light could do but take her teasing in good humor. Lily awoke also and was predictably unhappy about yet another voyeur robot making her business its own.

The rest of the day went on in a similar manner as the last. The girls whisked Lily away, and D_Light, Lyra, and Djoser went on their own excursion.

First on the trio's to-do list was to visit Amanda, who was recovering on a bed atop an immense boulder that overlooked much of the sunken English garden. With Lyra at the lead, they made their way up a set of stairs that snaked around the girth of the boulder. Once at the top, they could see a medical bot tending to the patient, along with a pink-bowed clone daughter of Dr. Monsa's, presumably the only clone the group had not yet met. This girl did not introduce herself or pay the visitors any attention at all until Djoser, nearly shouting, demanded Amanda's health status.

The girl sighed and directed her attention to the visitors. "The damage to the product's body was significant, as you can see by the number of skin grafts on her body, but she is making excellent progress in her recovery and is already walking." Djoser caressed the white artificial skin that held his servant together. It was oily to the touch.

The group would have chatted with Amanda, but concubine bodyguards were not conversationalists. She simply said that she hoped to be fully functional within a day or two. It only took a few minutes for D_Light and Lyra to become bored and want to move on, but Djoser lingered. After all, he had been away from his concubine for two nights now. Lyra and D_Light left him to her. Descending the stairs from the boulder, D_Light was not sure if he was disgusted or mildly impressed that the coddled nobleman was willing to perv with something in that state; he quickly realized that it was disgust. The clone would have stayed as well, perhaps for some research purpose, but Djoser insisted that she give them a few minutes alone.

CHAPTER 31

It would be three more days before the team would get their final quest, and yet in that brief space of time they had settled into somewhat of a comfortable routine in the inner sanctum. Each morning they would all meet for a decadent breakfast with whichever products and cloned daughters happened to be there at the time. Dr. Monsa himself was never present, however, as he found the early morning hours to be his most creative and he tended to use them for work. The clone girls ensured that the breakfast banter was never boring, for they loved to discuss their father's fascinating inventions and make inquiries of the visitors, most notably of Lily and her life on the fringes of society. They seemingly could not get enough of the fair Star Sister, and D_Light understood the attraction. He often found himself staring at Lily and listening to her with the same wide-eyed curiosity of the girls.

Once breakfast was over, the group would take a morning walk through Dr. Monsa's magical gardens. Amanda, mostly healed from her injuries but still bearing scars and patches of new skin that had not yet seen the sun, would join them for these walks. Although they always set out together, beginning their walk with a discussion of the upcoming quest, the group inevitably ended up drifting apart. D_Light and Lily often lagged behind, engaged in a sort of playful teasing that irritated Lyra. Lyra and Djoser acted more stately in their exploration of the gardens, almost as though they were in the public eye, which was the exact opposite of the inner sanctum. Eventually, the nobles too would drift apart as Djoser would find himself in need of Amanda and a bit of privacy.

To D_Light, the hours between breakfast and dinner during those several days of waiting were golden—carefree, lovely, and with Lily. Indeed, he enjoyed them so much that he often forgot that he was in the middle of an intensely competitive and dangerous MetaGame. He didn't think about strategies, points, or the next quest. He didn't agonize about past mistakes or future prospects. For once, he lived only in the present, and it felt good, even healing.

D_Light and Lily spent a great deal of time taking swims in the lake and streams of the inner sanctum. At first, D_Light spent more time *on* the water in a borrowed boat than *in* the water swimming. Lily thought it tragic and taught D_Light several new strokes, including the butterfly. Cocky, thinking he had mastered this stroke, D_Light then challenged Lily to a race. To be sporting, she did the backstroke to his butterfly, but she still beat him, although not by much.

D_Light and Lily also enjoyed passing the time by teaching the nubber, the clever prototype teddy bear, a whole host of tricks, one of which was to dance. Smorgeous made an excellent stereo for this activity. The familiar was encased in an organic shell capable of conducting sound, so he was essentially one good-sized speaker. D_Light even compromised on his personal policy against stupid gimmickry and had Smorgeous download some kitschy dance software, enabling the robot to flawlessly execute thousands of different dances. Lily had never seen a cat do this sort of thing and thought it hysterical. D_Light teased Lily about her impromptu "feeder fish dance" at the groksta a few days back and suggested it would be a good idea for all of them to learn a few of Smorgeous's moves. The nubber joined in too, although it was so clumsy that it would bump between D_Light, Lily, and Smorgeous like a ping pong ball, occasionally knocking someone off balance. At one point, they all ended up on the manicured lawn in a silly, chortling heap.

The clone daughters continued giving their lessons over those few days, particularly to Lily, who was still unashamedly favored by the girls despite the ridicule of their father. They did learn to better tolerate D_Light, however, as more often than not he now accompanied them on their little field trips.

When D_Light could not be with Lily, such as when the nobles insisted on game strategizing, he thought about her. He had Smorgeous replay memories of the fair-skinned girl, particularly the first time he had seen her under the poplar tree. He even dreamt of her at night—every night, in fact, since they had entered the inner sanctum. This baffled D_Light who, recent nightmares aside, had only dreamt of sailing for as long as he could remember. Smorgeous insisted these new dreams did not exist, so D_Light struggled to remember them on his own and then stored the reconstructed feelings and visions as best he could.

These dreams were intimate, but not exactly sexual. Despite sleeping next to Lily every night, he never attempted any sexual advances, neither in real life nor in his dreams. This was not due to any lack of desire on D_Light's part. Lily was incredible! And she was very affectionate. Indeed, she enjoyed stroking his body, his arms, his cheeks, his hands; sometimes she even kissed him gently. The two enjoyed being together, talking and sleeping with their bodies pressed together.

Left to her own devices, D_Light doubted Lily would ever *initiate* sex with him or anyone else. According to camper specifications, her kind was not designed for consensual sex, and therefore no sex drive was required.

Nevertheless, someday, somehow, D_Light wanted to seduce her (assuming that was even possible), not only because he wanted her, but because the loss of her virginity would render her useless for her terrible purpose. After all, she was a single-use product. For now, however, he desired to make no demands on her aside from her company. *Eventually,* he thought. He then pictured the two of them on his sailboat, anchored in a private cove somewhere, the waves rocking them gently as they lay together in the cozy comfort of the V-berth. They would be safe, relaxed, and happy. Something would stir in her, something primal her designers had overlooked. It would be beautiful, perfect.

———

Each night, as the artificial sun began to set, the teammates would reunite at the great dining table. Dr. Monsa would eat with them and assemble a retinue of his "lambs" to join them. If it seemed too quiet at the table, the doctor would toss seemingly arbitrary questions to his guests as a sort of family game time.

On this particular eve the table was much too quiet for the doctor's taste. "What do you think of war?" he shouted out to the entire table, startling D_Light enough to make him lose control of his fork, which ended up on Lyra's lap. "Evil incarnate or a natural human activity?" he boomed. Dr. Monsa sucked back a trickle of wine that had dribbled out of his malformed lower lip and looked to his audience for a response.

The priest was eager to offer the first answer. "As suggested by divine law, war is undesirable for society but cannot be completely suppressed and is therefore allowed under controlled conditions."

"Yes, Daddy, the OverSoul sells war permits. *Apparently,* it is condoned." Curious_Scourge spoke out of one cheek, as her other one was stuffed with a roasted pulp grub.

"Yes, but does that make it right?" the doctor asked.

Curious_Scourge swallowed. "If two families want to go to war, who is to stop them?"

"To grow as sentient beings, we are bestowed free agency," the priest quoted.

"Free agency?" Love_Monkey scoffed. "When families meet on the battlefield, I sincerely doubt everyone in attendance wants to be there."

"You choose your family, and you can leave anytime," Curious_Scourge retorted.

"Who gets to choose? Not products like us, Sister!" Love_Monkey pointed at herself. "In any case, it's a sordid business. I'm glad our house doesn't involve itself in that sort of thing."

"Au contraire, I often purchase war permits to *negotiate* with other houses," the doctor said casually, "but my rivals always back down, and so we never actually meet on the field."

"I don't blame them," Djoser interjected with a chuckle. "One pack of those cullers of yours would terrify a small army."

"The cullers?" Dr. Monsa raised his jagged eyebrows. "Oh, those are just to keep contaminant species out of my garden. I wouldn't use them for war. I have far better armaments...or worse, from my enemy's point of view."

"Daddy used to make weapons," Curious_Scourge proudly informed the dinner guests.

"Yes, very profitable, actually," the doctor confirmed. "The ban on modern weapons was not as restrictive with bioproducts. Naturally, you couldn't make microbiological agents such as viruses, but larger products were allowed." The doctor nodded toward Amanda, who was wolfishly devouring her dinner. "Of course, these weapons got out of hand as they always do. As an example, it was not long before dragons inhabited more than just fairy tales."

"Minus the fire breathing, although I think that was under development," BoBo joked.

"This spurred the Authority to place additional restrictions. Still, I have a few 'old friends' tucked away in this house," the doctor declared with a smile. "You see, they were grandfathered in. I'm just not allowed to grow any more babies."

While dinner had proven to be particularly delicious and the conversation interesting as usual, D_Light remained quiet throughout the meal. Dr. Monsa, finishing off his third helping of everything, drew a deep breath and asked to be excused from the table. The remaining dinner companions nodded, and the doctor began his rapid limp down the path. D_Light sat quietly for a few moments, stood as though leaving, hesitated, and then proceeded to follow the doctor.

"Doctor, sir, may I walk with you a moment?" Dr. Monsa regarded D_Light distantly and nodded.

"It's about Lily. I...er... Okay, you are perhaps the most knowledgeable wetgineer on the planet, so I thought I would ask you—"

"No, I'm afraid I cannot make her human," the doctor answered before D_Light could spit out the question. "I have already considered the problem from all angles. I have looked at her specs again and again. To get her over 96.3% DNA parity with humans, I would have to do massive gene therapy. It would kill her."

"But—"

"I know she looks and behaves human, but her reproductive system, her metabolism, even her nervous system are significantly different. If I recoded her at the cellular level, her physiology would—" Dr. Monsa paused and rested a gnarled hand on D_Light's shoulder. "It is right and good that you care about her. A gentle soul like yours would."

D_Light had never been called a "gentle soul," nor was he sure it was a compliment. The doctor leaned in and scrunched his face into an even uglier ball of flesh. D_Light resisted the urge to recoil. "If I could do anything to help her, I would," whispered the unsightly doctor. "Believe me, I have more interest in her welfare than you realize."

She was shaking again, moaning in her sleep. D_Light turned over on his side to kiss her ear and whispered, "Lily, it's only a dream. Wake up." But as he slid over to comfort her, he realized she was gone. He watched her leave through eyes silted from sleep. She resembled a ghost, drifting away as the microlenses of her skinsuit reflected the light from the simulated moon.

One of the clone girls stood ahead of Lily like a sentinel. The face of the young girl was a mask. D_Light rose up onto his feet. "Lily?" The question slid out into the gloom. In response, Lily's shoulders tensed and she turned back to him with an expression that startled D_Light into full wakefulness. She looked terrified—terrified as though she was regarding a menacing stranger rather than the man with whom she had fully shared her life over the past several days.

"Lily, where—" D_Light's question collapsed in on itself as the shutters of his mind slammed shut and his body slumped to a heap on the ground.

Master, your chemi delivery system has been compromised. Smorgeous's words were hazy and distant in D_Light's head. *You were given an unauthorized dose of the commonly named MyLullaby™ chemi. I have taken the liberty of counteracting its effects; however, you have been unconscious for 15.31 minutes.*

I…I was overdosed? D_Light's thoughts were like viscous syrup.

Yes, master. The dose administered was not within lethal range; however, it was incapacitating.

D_Light opened his eyes. He was flat on his back and completely disoriented. He could not place where he was, although it was not where he last remembered. He had no idea how he got there, either. He blinked his eyes hard and with greater frequency as though doing so might bring clarity to the situation. He then spotted Djoser and Lyra nearby. The nobles seemed to be inspecting mechanical devices of some kind. *Weapons?* he wondered.

The hunted hunt themselves. Djoser reviewed the quest again in his mind as he checked the trigger action on the crossbow left for him. He enjoyed the symmetry of the quest, although he admonished himself for not having anticipated it. Had he done so, he could have prepared.

It was simple. Hunt down and kill Lily. There were only two rules: The quest would last up to seventy-two hours. If they did not kill Lily by then, the quest was lost. The hunters and their familiars were to assemble at the dining table and remain there for two hours to give Lily a head start.

The proctor reminded them that their archives would be reviewed upon game completion and that rule transgressions could result in disqualification.

Djoser smiled to himself. Not only was the quest consistent with the theme of the MetaGame thus far, it was spiritually satisfying.

Lily had been created for this purpose—for this sport—and although he had not realized it before, it was unsettling for him to watch her defy her fate. The OverSoul would not be contradicted.

Although he had not prayed explicitly for this quest, he offered a silent word of thanks to the OverSoul. *She knows us better than we can know ourselves,* he thought. Djoser then shifted his attention to the glassy-eyed D_Light laid out upon the grass below and dropped an unloaded crossbow on his chest. "I don't know what's wrong with you, but you've got less than two hours to pull yourself together, man."

The quest party was assembled at the great dining table. D_Light finally saw the pending quest update and opened it. *How horrible! Was I drugged to protect her escape? As though I would hurt her otherwise? Could I do that?*

Praying he was having a nightmare, he closed his eyes again. Perhaps if he slipped back into that syrupy unconsciousness he would awake with Lily asleep at his side. He would tell her that she was safe, that he would protect her. His fantasy, however, was quickly broken as the numbing voice of the proctor pressed into his consciousness the caution that Lily had been given a vial of culler repellant, whereas they themselves had none of their own.

"That will make it interesting," Djoser said. "We all got our last dose yesterday around noon, right?" he asked no one in particular.

"Yes, so from what PeePee tells me, the repellant will have worked its way out of our system sometime on day three." Lyra's voice was near.

"An added incentive for finding her sooner rather than later," Djoser commented dryly.

Djoser and Lyra spent most of the two hours of Lily's head start time discussing how they would find her. They decided that the familiars could use their sniffer software to follow her; however, she would be expecting that. D_Light sat quietly, only half listening.

"Certainly she will go to the nearest water to knock us off her trail. Remember the lake?" Lyra asked.

"Yeah, the first thing she did when she joined up with us was lead us to the water," Djoser said.

D_Light had now passed through the phases of shock and denial and into one of anger. "And she'll know we know that," he spoke to the sky above, his voice brimming with resentment. "And she'll know we know that she knows that."

"Don't be an ass, D_Light." Lyra's voice was irritated. "Get over it and focus on the task at hand," she added sharply.

"Yes, Mother," D_Light replied distantly, keeping his gaze fixed on the bogus clouds above.

Djoser slammed his fist on the table. "Damned right," he shouted.

D_Light, startled by the verbal assault, regarded Djoser. The nobleman's eyes were burning with rage, and his lips curled and quivered like an animal readying itself for an attack. "Perhaps you've forgotten who Lyra and I are and who you are not. Perhaps we were in error to think we could dispense with the formalities during this game without you coming to think that you're actually an equal."

Reflexively, D_Light stood and presented himself humbly to his father. "My sincerest apologies, Father. I beg that you pardon my transgression." He made a deep bow.

Djoser spat at D_Light's feet and waved at him dismissively. "Good, so we have an understanding. Now get out of my face until I ask for your input."

"Understood, Father."

D_Light removed himself from the table and sat down on the ground next to a variegated reddish plant with feathery green plumes. He knew he was sulking. He knew he was being weak and pathetic, and he hated himself for it. He looked over to Lyra and Djoser, who were passionately strategizing a plan for finding and executing Lily. They too had spent days with the fair Star Sister and had gotten to know her well, but they weren't skulking about feeling sorry for themselves or for Lily. It was just part of the Game, plain and simple, and they acted accordingly. *There must be a flaw in my DNA...or my conditioning,* he thought.

Logically speaking, D_Light had every reason to be enthusiastic about the final quest of this MetaGame. Over the last few days he had tried to stay off the Cloud since he was still a fugitive and the Divine Authority may have tracking software that uses Cloud signatures to locate persons of interest; nevertheless, he had poked around enough to know that this MetaGame was hot. Thanks to the drama and chaos he had caused in NeverWorld by insulting Queen Pheobah, and thanks also to the very public violence in the lounge when that seeker tried to "apprehend" them, their game had picked up a lot of attention. Now players all over the world were placing their bets on this MetaGame. If D_Light's team won, he would get a piece of that action in addition to his regular take. It would be an unfathomable fortune—a fortune that would accelerate him on the path of immortality. And all they had to do was hunt down and kill a product. Legally, nothing more than destroying an expensive piece of furniture.

Despite this realization and some mood-enhancing chemis, D_Light could barely muster the resolve to follow his teammates into the garden by the time Lily's head start expired.

———

Lily ran swiftly but took care to not let the outstretched branches and leaves touch her. Like others of her kind—and even humans—she shed millions of cells a day, and although her skinsuit would hold onto most of this exfoliation, the suit shed a scent of its own—everything did. *I will pass through like a breeze,* she thought.

Perhaps I never escaped the reserve. Perhaps the Great Stag is real after all and has made the whole world a hell for my kind.

She suppressed these panic-inducing thoughts and shut down all the functions of her MIC, save her internal clock. There was only one thing to focus on now, and that was to stay alive for seventy-two hours. If she did that, she would live, at least for now. Lily had survived the running game back home. This would be no different. She tightened her grip on the small blue bottle and quickened her pace.

Djoser cursed to himself as he gazed into the rent-a-boy holding pen. It was sealed and empty. He and Amanda had left the others to go muster a search party for Lily. He figured he could trade sex with Amanda to the rent-a-boys in exchange for their cooperation, but the rent-a-boys were gone. So too were the concubines and the analysts. Even more conspicuous, there were no gardeners anywhere to be found. This was particularly troubling to Djoser, who had hoped to find an unlucky drone and jack the repellant worn around its neck. But there would be no search party and no repellant.

He decided it was likely that Dr. Monsa and his minions were all nearby, either in a hideout in the inner sanctum itself or somewhere else within his massive house. *I guess I'll just have to import some labor,* he thought.

Djoser proceeded to attempt to create a search game invitation on the Cloud, complete with a generous bounty attached. However,

much to his surprise and dismay, an error message popped up saying that his connection was blocked by network quarantine. Djoser
cursed again. If a network quarantine *was* in place, then certainly
the inner sanctum was physically locked down as well. Fortunately,
his teammates were inside the quarantine, so he could at least still
reach them. He opened a blink to give his status.

———

PeePee found her trail, Lyra sent to the others. As Lyra pursued
her familiar through the garden, followed by a sullen D_Light, she
kept her crossbow trained out in front of her and ruminated on the
shocking news Djoser had sent them.

Surely this interruption in labor comes at great cost, Lyra thought.
It seemed like a sinful waste of resources to quarantine the inner
sanctum in response to their trivial game. *Unless there was some other
reason...an experiment?*

Lyra knew MetaGame etiquette as well as any noble. As
their host, the doctor was divinely bound to not directly interfere with their MetaGame; rather, at most, he could merely accommodate a fair contest. *He has set the stage,* Lyra mused. While
not explicitly hindering the party from finding the camper,
he had evened the odds of the quest in a subtle, yet effective
way.

With contact to the outside world, players like Lyra had access
to a great deal of resources. For the right price—and certainly the
price would be justified in this game—they could rent help, perhaps
a powerful analyst or AI to aid in strategy. Or better yet, a hunter
specialized for this activity. After all, the rules did not expressly
forbid such tactics. *But now, cut off from the outside world...it's just her
and us.*

Lyra realized she probably could not even put a penalty on the doctor for what pretty much served as imprisonment. Before they entered the inner sanctum, Love_Monkey had insisted they all digitally sign a number of legal documents, and—as expected for a bioengineering facility—quarantine was a legally covered scenario. Clearly, Dr. Monsa was no fool. And perhaps Lily wasn't quite as naïve as Lyra had thought. Possibly it was no coincidence that Dr. Monsa came to favor the product during their stay. Perhaps Lily had made extra "efforts" to make the doctor favor her, and now this was how his bias was playing out. Lyra chastised herself for not ingratiating herself more to Monsa over the last few days. *Had he not been so off-putting and ugly...*

———

Lily stared up at the blue sky above as she floated downstream on her back. This was the closest thing to rest she expected for the next sixty-nine hours, but she could not rest her mind. She needed to anticipate their next move and act accordingly.

The team would not be able to catch her by tracking alone. She was moving too swiftly, and her trail was light. Even her present waterborne journey would frustrate their tracking effort for hours. But she knew they were clever. They would do more than just sniff her out. *They will use their eyes too.* She remembered when the cullers had been hunting them; Djoser had used his robot to scout out the garden visually from the top of a tree. *Their familiars can see very far and can see a great deal at once. I must stay hidden.*

To do this, she would need to leave the garden and travel through the wild forest that surrounded it; however, she realized the thicker cover would come at the price of speed, and she would not be able to disguise her trail at all. The other option would be to stick to the water and allow this stream to carry her as far as it would. No, it was a predictable move, and predictability was the one thing sure to kill her. Besides, BoBo had said some time back that all rivers flushed out through impassible grates into the great lake above. *There would be no escape that way.*

By sunset of the first day the hunters had lost and found Lily's trail several times, but they had not actually seen their prey. Nevertheless, without a break, the hunt continued into the night.

Each of the hunters had their assignments. Lyra, along with her familiar, continued to track. Amanda, Djoser, and Moocher were sent ahead of Lily's estimated heading to attempt to catch up. D_Light and Smorgeous were left behind to guard the paradise garden. It was here where the small lake and main waterways of the inner sanctum were largely concentrated. Wide, shallow creeks, fountain pools, and narrow but deep rivers were fed by the lake—a lake that was fed from beneath itself by a deep geyser.

Staying behind was D_Light's idea. He suggested that Lily, upon realizing she could not leave the inner sanctum, would eventually double back here to again destroy her trail in the water. This strategy of ambush was plausible to the others, but to him it was only an excuse to be away from the rest of the team. Seeing them in their purpose sickened him.

Unfortunately, despite his physical distance from the rest of the team, the nobles were constantly drawing him into their blinks with their incessant planning and status updates. This left little opportunity for sleep, so D_Light patrolled along the edge of the rivers. Besides, D_Light knew the nobles would be furious if they caught him snoozing during their final quest.

Meanwhile, Smorgeous played lookout on the highest branch of the tallest nectar tree in the area. Without his familiar nearby, D_Light could not see much in the soft light of the faux moon, but he did not resort to artificial light because it would give away his position. The inner sanctum was a dark zone, void of nanosites coating the surfaces, so there were no skins to jack into. And with the network quarantine in effect, the Cloud was gone. With nothing to see, he closed his eyes and just listened. In between blinks from the others, there was only deafening silence.

He wondered if this was what it was like without the Game. Nothingness. A life without goals or overriding purpose. A life like those of generations past, who fabricated the meaning and value of their own existence in an indifferent universe. The indifference of the rocks, plants, and water around him had been unsettling, but now, with his eyes closed, he felt even more alone. *I've always been alone. Soul, I don't want to die alone.*

CHAPTER 32

There are no challenges or opportunities—only prob-abilities.

—Excerpt from archives of analyst #4302409 (a.k.a. Hal)

Day 2; 15:34 hours.

Moocher's got a visual on her. Djoser's thought signature was all business.

Djoser's familiar streamed the video to the rest of the party. A tall, blond figure swept through a long, narrow clearing, quickly disappearing back into the thick underbrush. Moocher pinged the location on the map. *She's heading for the trail, probably going to make a run for the gate,* Djoser declared. *Okay, everyone, let's move!*

I'm too far to be of help, D_Light returned. *How about I just hold my position?*

Fine, Lyra answered.

There was a pause and then Lyra said, *Djoser, you're the closest. You get a shot, you shoot to kill, right? No funny business.*

There was another pause before Djoser responded, *What else would I do?*

Lyra left the question unanswered.

Slogging through the tangled, thick, and often unpredictable forest of the inner sanctum was beginning to tire Lily, and unlike her pursuers, she did not have the benefit of drugs to keep up her pace indefinitely. Worse yet, her efforts had the nasty side effect of clearing a pathway for her hunters.

Lily needed her gamble to pay off.

She assumed her pursuers had spotted her crossing the dried-up creek bed. Once across, she put on a burst of speed, drawing on whatever energy reserves she could muster. Fortunately, there were many fallen logs running along the creek bed, which she used as a makeshift trail, dashing along and between them. Her ploy was simple. Upon finding her current position, they would think she was heading for the outer gate. With any luck, they would then attempt to cut her off before she reached it by sprinting along the trail.

But she had no intention of escaping the inner sanctum. She had even more enemies outside than within, and she doubted she could escape anyway. Instead, she would circle back. Besides temporarily knocking them off her trail, she hoped to tire and demoralize them. Perhaps, if she was lucky, it would enrage them to the point where their judgment would be clouded. Lily, who had been raised in the running game, knew the chase was more in the mind than in the body.

Not far ahead she saw a pair of thick, fallen logs that spanned the creek bed, festooned with branches and needles. She prepared to carefully crawl underneath this natural tunnel, protected from the watchful eyes of the familiars, to the other side, *back toward the garden.*

They are closing in, D_Light thought to himself. He dropped from the blink. He knew the others expected him to stay engaged, but he could not listen, much less watch. Lily did not stand a chance against Amanda alone, but with Djoser and Lyra too? They might be coddled nobles, but they knew how to kill. Everyone from House Tesla did.

It will be over soon. Just make it quick, he tried to tell himself, but he started to sob. *Pathetic, I'm being absolutely pathetic.*

D_Light should be relieved. Smorgeous had recently notified him that the repellant in his system was just about spent. This quest had to end, or the Game, indeed, his very life, could end.

But he suddenly felt the now familiar wrench in his stomach and a great despair as Lily's face haunted him. The feeling reminded him of the emotions he'd endured in the shower after fragging Fael just days ago. This was even worse. He felt like a part of him was being strangled.

Now, without the blink, the silence—like an unwanted lover— returned to him, broken only by his own sporadic curses and subdued moans.

Smorgeous interrupted the silence. *Master, there is a humanoid heat signature on the move 0.40 kilometers from here.*

D_Light immediately thought of the cullers.

I am unable to get a direct visual due to intervening foliage; however, the general shape of the signature does not suggest that body type—it is too small.

Lily? D_Light wondered. It couldn't be. She was several kilometers from here. Only minutes before, he had watched her on the video feed. Nevertheless, D_Light ordered his familiar down from the tree. The two of them then headed toward the location of the man, woman, or whatever it may be.

Dr. Monsa's favorite analyst was making his way back to his lair. He was named Hal by Dr. Monsa, but Hal did not care what he was called as long as the doctor and everyone else left him alone to do his job.

Hal was pained to have been away from his den so long, as 5.3 hours had passed already and another 1.2 minutes would pass before he would arrive back at his lair. Intolerable! There was so much to play. Much of the economic prosperity of House Monsa was in the analyst's pale, long-fingered hands; not literally, of course, for the analyst interfaced with his grinder games primarily in his mind. Even as he sat getting his weekly booster—the one time a week that he simply had to leave his sanctuary—he interacted with the games. But this was not adequate. Only when surrounded by his AI, monitors, and raw-data-crunching organic computers could Hal attain his potential. This being the case, Hal hurried as quickly as his feeble, ghostly legs would carry him.

The door of the analyst's den was open for almost a second longer than was needed for the analyst to enter. This lag was programmed into the system to allow time for the dragging tubes to cross the threshold before the door sealed shut—sealed securely and tightly to ensure that no pesky sounds filtered in.

Hal later deduced that D_Light exploited this delay in the door's closing to slip in behind him. Only after Hal had settled down in his chair and had all of his tubes reattached to the life support by the service bot did the analyst detect that something was amiss. Although countless displays ran across his visual cortex, his real eyes—the ones used to scrutinize the dozens of monitors around him—noticed a misplaced lump in his peripheral vision.

The analyst did not want to focus his attention on the lump. He had better things to do. Certainly, it was not important. Still, it was unexpected, and so with a great act of will, the analyst flicked his eyes over to the corner. The lump was the man from the dinner party of five nights ago. D_Light was the human's name.

"Why are you here? Please leave." Hal spoke as clearly as he could, which came out as a crackling whine. His unrefined voice was the result of nearly unused vocal cords, and it irritated him that he had to use them now. The closest analogy the analyst had for his ancient, human-inspired vocal system was that of computer floppy drives in the time of early computer networking. It was slow, worked with a limited amount of information, and using it was divergent from the norm. Having nearly exhausted his patience with his earlier sentence, the analyst opened the portal of his lair with a flicker of a thought and then returned his attention to the monitors, rapidly shifting from one to the other. The human was expected to let himself out.

But the lump did not move. Mildly irritating as this was, Hal ignored it. Analysts were highly skilled at tuning out extraneous input.

"I want to know how to stop the MetaGame," the lump stated.

The analyst knew what the human was referring to. He knew just about everything that was known, particularly everything that occurred in his own house. But the analyst was not interested in talking to this unwelcome guest. He would ignore D_Light. Surely the human would see the futility of his questions and leave.

D_Light raised his loaded crossbow.

Hal glanced up and then back to his monitors again. Hal knew D_Light's profile. The player was human, but not stupid. "Not in your best interest," he said dismissively. "You would not gain the information you seek by killing me."

D_Light lowered his weapon slightly, now aiming it at the analyst's legs. He paused there for a moment and then slung the crossbow back over his shoulder. "I'll smash your machines!" D_Light erupted like a crazed man. "All this shit you need—I'll smash them, bash them against the floor!"

This sounded to Hal like a more plausible threat. His eyes darted away from the screens, over to D_Light, and then back to the screens again. "To end the game, either win or lose," the analyst answered.

Hal considered pinging for the guards. However, they, along with all the other so-called "intelligent life," had been evacuated from the inner sanctum. Such evacuations were routine in the inner sanctum. Aside from real emergencies due to rogue microbes and the like, the doctor would run occasional drills. But this unscheduled quarantine had lasted too long, and the temporary lair given to Hal was inadequate for his work. Therefore, the analyst had seized an opportunity to escape back into the inner sanctum, back where real grinding could get done. Up until now, escaping back home had seemed like an optimal move despite the time it cost him to hack out of the network quarantine to get Cloud access. Now Hal was not so sure.

No, the guards would come too late to be of use if they came at all. Worse yet, Father would have him evacuated again. It would be a terrible productivity hit for the analyst.

"I don't want to win or lose," D_Light clarified. "I do not want to destroy the product. I just want the quest to end." D_Light took a step closer to the analyst's desk.

Hal regarded the human more carefully now. He ran an analysis of the expression on D_Light's face. His eyes were wide and bloodshot, his face was pale, and his chin trembled. His appearance was indicative of one suffering from sleep deprivation, but beyond that he also appeared to be under significant stress. Panic? Anger? Hal often found it difficult to tell these emotions from appearance and body language alone. A sniffer could measure D_Light's pheromone signature and get a better reading, but Hal had never needed a sniffer in his lair before.

"I am afraid I do not know how to end your game," replied Hal. "Remember, you entered the MetaGame under your own free will and agreed to abide by the rules. I have scanned over the rules of your current quest, and it is quite clear that you must either win or lose to end the game. Alternatively, if basic survival is your goal, you could attempt to escape the inner sanctum and by doing so escape the cullers present here. However, all exits are sealed, and I do not have the key—not that it matters because the key changes every fifteen minutes. Yet another alternative would be to obtain some culler repellant. I do not have any. Unlike many here, I was designed for the inner sanctum and the smell of my flesh is of no interest to the cullers; therefore, I have no need of external repellant that is imbibed."

Unfortunately, this explanation did not satisfy D_Light, who grabbed a nearby monitor, ripped it off its housing, and flung it down on the stone floor with a crash.

Hal recoiled as though wounded himself and cried out. He wrung his hands uselessly at D_Light. "*No!* Stop that!" Just the loss of that monitor alone would cut back Hal's productivity by perhaps 0.5% until replaced. Everything in Hal's lair had been optimized over the years. Every piece of equipment was the right tool for the job and was positioned in just the right place. As bad as the loss of the monitor was, Hal shuddered to think what would happen if this maniac let loose on the Artificial Intelligence machines.

D_Light seemed oblivious to the cries of the analyst as he pulled down yet another monitor that splintered and shrieked as it was obliterated on the floor.

"*Damn you!*" Hal screamed at him. It was alien for Hal to curse. For once, he did not know what to do. Perhaps if he had some time to analyze the situation, but this monster was literally ripping the lair apart!

"This will cost you everything! *Stop!*"

The crazed human was oblivious, as though in some mad trance.

"You did this!" Hal shouted. "You made the MetaGame! You can't ask me to fix what you made! I can't! I can't!"

D_Light paused and looked up at the tall, gaunt analyst. D_Light's face was flushed with exertion. He was breathing heavily. He looked slightly puzzled, but reached up to grab another monitor.

"Stop! Stop! I'll send you an archive! The answer is there! Damn you, stop!"

For the first time in his life, Hal did something impulsively. Unauthorized, he sent one of the most top-secret archives in his possession. He sent the night harvest archive. Hal would later regret it. He would later decide that it would have been more prudent to lose the entire lair than to succumb to this terrorist act, but standing idly while watching his tools get smashed was unbearable. Although Hal was designed to find violence loathsome, had he any weapon he might have murdered the human.

D_Light stopped his rampage. "My Soul," he whispered with shock and exhaustion as he received the archive. He slumped against the wall and slowly lowered himself to the floor to avoid fainting.

CHAPTER 33

Democracy is not dead, merely unconscious.

—Excerpt from "Musings of an Immortal," by Dr. Stoleff
Monsa

Despite the fact that Hal sent Smorgeous the encryption key along
with the archive, it took over a minute for the content to be decrypt-
ed. D_Light had never received anything with such high security.

Night Harvesting Executive Summary

*Artificial intelligence alone is insufficient to power a framework as un-
fathomably complex as the Game. Combined, there are over twenty-eight billion humans and intelligent products in existence today. These beings make up
an astoundingly intricate network of relationships and interconnected knowledge. Only by leveraging these nodes is it possible to optimize the Game and
enable an overarching consciousness (the OverSoul) to emerge from this collective intelligence. The means by which this intelligence is tapped is through
the most obvious method available, which is to say, by tapping into the mind
interface chips implanted in the majority of intelligent organic beings.*

*The type of work performed by night harvesting falls under one of two
categories: one, gathering data known by subjects (data mining); and two,
answering questions (data processing).*

*It was determined after numerous studies that probing a subject's mind
interface chip was best done while the subject slept. While awake, the subjects*

tended to be stressed by what was often considered a "mind hack." Even when subjects were compliant, they tended to try to manipulate the probe for their own benefit. For example, when a subject was posed the question of whether fuel for transport should be taxed, their answer depended largely on how often they used transport themselves. Despite being given evidence suggesting a different decision, subjects would generally make choices based on self-interest and/or beliefs in which they had previous investment.

In addition to greater objectivity while asleep and unconscious of the probe, subjects' minds were also much more pliable. For example, when the Game wanted a logical answer to a question and the subject was asleep, it was very easy to stimulate the subject's brain (primarily the left frontal lobe in this example) to help elicit the desired mindset for logical thinking. On the other hand, if an emotional response was desired, other respective brain tissues were stimulated.

In this way, mind queries were able to better fine-tune the information extracted. Using the example above, the question of the transport fuel tax could be weighed both logically and emotionally to ensure that any measure taken made the correct trade-off between best solution and the emotional pulse of those the tax would be levied upon.

Due to these findings and the obvious realization that subjects were not making important use of their minds while asleep anyway, it was decided that wide-scale harvesting would be done only on sleeping subjects.

As a brief overview, night harvesting works like this:

Software bots called "crawlers" are constantly parsing over the mind interface chips of players in search for sleepers. Minds that are asleep leave distinct brain signatures and are therefore easy to identify by crawlers.

Once a sleeper is identified, it is added to the billions on the harvesting list.

The OverSoul, and the Game presided over by her, uses this list as a resource for queries and information gathering. For example, if the OverSoul wants to know whether a war permit should be approved, she may ask a random set of sleepers from the two opposing houses. In addition, she may select a few unassociated sleepers knowledgeable on war to make an unbiased cost-benefit analysis.

Of course, given the complexity of the Game and the needs of the Over-Soul, there are billions of such queries going on at any given time.

Not only does AI make use of sleepers, but sleepers make use of one another. Sometimes the sleepers are known to each other, and other times they are paired together by the crawlers. In this way, the OverSoul is able to cobble together entire unconscious teams that can solve difficult problems, problems these same teams would have difficulty solving when awake. As mentioned, conscious subjects are hampered by their emotions and biased by their desires and prejudices. In addition, sleeper teams are more efficient than their conscious counterparts because they share their minds freely. Such raw blinking with strangers is seldom done by conscious players due to security and privacy issues...

Truly, night harvesting has thus far outstripped our expectations in that it has since become the lifeblood of the Game and bestowed upon the OverSoul historically unsurpassed wisdom, and thus divine credibility.

D_Light opened his eyes as he finished the summary. "We are all harvested without consent, without even knowledge of it?" His head hurt from trying to process what he had just read.

"Yes," answered Hal, "but that is beside the main point. You are part of the OverSoul. We all are. Therefore, why don't you take your newfound perspective and leave?" Hal waved off the intruder.

"This is unbelievable...I..." D_Light's words trailed off as he discovered there were no words to convey what he felt.

Hal paused while his eyes glazed over as though communing with a spirit, and he continued conveying information to D_Light. "I see you... Yes, there you are in the harvest log. You, your Mother Lyra and Father Djoser, even that bodyguard...even the one you seek to destroy now, Lily, she too was harvested. And others..." Hal paused again. "My Soul! My own father? The doctor is involved?" Hal asked himself out loud in disbelief.

D_Light shook his head emphatically. "No, I did not make this. Lily did not make this game."

As Hal continued to speak, he found it easier. His vocal system was shuddering back to life. "You *did* create this, and now you come to me, break my instruments, and demand that *I* fix your game because it has not gone the way you want!" Hal rasped out the condemnation.

D_Light shook his head again. "It cannot be...I have not been harvested. My dreams?"

"Your dreams are fabrications!" Hal wheezed. "What would happen if night harvesting was common knowledge? Players would try to game the system. Your dreams were like everyone's—pleasant but uneventful. Just a filler to run over the top of the real work going on in your mind."

"But my familiar—"

Hal interrupted impatiently. "Your archival processes, including those run by your primitive familiar, are bypassed. You cannot replay something that is never recorded to begin with."

"I did remember though...I saw Ascara in a dream. She was hunting me?"

"*You* were hunting *you!* Your NeverWorld character—that witch—was merely a flimsy subconscious caricature of yourself revealed, no doubt, by emotional stress. Do you remember at the groksta how the Authority made you famous in NeverWorld so you could be easily found? That was *your* idea."

"Who better to hunt myself than myself?" D_Light scrunched his forehead and tapped it lightly with a closed fist. "But why didn't I just tell the Authority where I was?"

"Again, because sleepers are unaware of their identity during harvest. Otherwise, your personal interests would contaminate your analysis. For example, what if you *did* know who you were? Would *you* help the Authority hunt *you* down? You see, harvesting does not strip you of conscious free will; however, through anonymity, harvesting makes free will irrelevant."

D_Light's face was expressionless. "So why am I here?"

Hal sighed. "Allow me to summarize it for you, after which I hope you will leave me alone. Keep in mind that I am mainly drawing this analysis from harvest log files. I do not have direct access to your personal archives; therefore, you will have to do some thinking of your own."

The analyst paused as he closed his eyes. "You are here to fulfill a prayer, a prayer you recently sent. You asked the OverSoul, 'What is the nature of my God that she is so cruel?' Well, the MetaGame brought you to one of the few places in the world where you could find the answer. And incidentally, I'm fulfilling this prayer of yours right now."

D_Light tilted his chin up as Smorgeous confirmed that D_Light had indeed made that prayer soon after he fragged Fael. It was only a week ago, although it felt like another life. "It was my destiny to know, to find out about night harvesting?" D_Light asked.

"I wouldn't call it destiny. I would call it opportunity. The OverSoul is the most powerful entity in human history, but she cannot control fate absolutely." Hal's patience was wearing thin.

"But why not just send me straight to Dr. Monsa? Why did Lily need to be involved?"

"You are not the only sentient being served by the OverSoul, D_Light," the analyst sneered. "My father had a prayer to fulfill too. The demon girl is for him, for reasons not specified in his harvest log."

"Lily's coming here was the doctor's prayer?" D_Light was puzzled even more.

"I said you would have to think, not simply repeat everything I say!" Hal's voice cracked. "Yes, it was his prayer. Why else would the demon follow a fool like you? Given that my father is interested in her, I suspect she is smarter than that. In her harvest she complied, and in her waking time... No doubt she felt compelled. Intuition, as you humans call it. Although she did not consciously know it, she was being drawn to him."

"And that was why we got the quest to become demons. Otherwise we would have turned her in. She hitched a ride with us...Dr. Monsa's prayer hitched a ride on my own," D_Light murmured.

For the first time, D_Light saw the slightest smile appear on the analyst's face. "Indeed, efficiency is core to the Game."

"And this quest, where we hunt down and kill Lily—whose prayer is being answered now?"

CHAPTER 34

When you want something with all of your soul, the entire universe will conspire to procure it.

—Minister A_Dude, archives, "From the Pulpit"

Hal took as much care as he could stand in answering D_Light's question. From the harvesting logs it was clear that Djoser and Lyra were the main drivers of the most recent quest. They each had their own emotional reasons—lust and envy, respectively. However, their main motivation was simple logic. Lily was designed to be hunted, and hunting her was consistent with the theme of the MetaGame. Hal decided to tell D_Light this, but he also added a lie.

"Djoser, Lyra, and...*you* created this quest," Hal answered.

"No! No, that's not true!" D_Light sputtered.

"The OverSoul knows us better than we know ourselves," Hal recited the hymn.

"I have to stop it! I don't want this!"

"The wheels are already in motion," Hal assured him. "As I said in the beginning, you created this game, and now you must play it out."

D_Light covered his face with his hands and was silent for several long seconds. Finally, he spoke. "The night harvest is essentially a raw blink—a raw blink with billions of others at once."

It was not, not technically; however, Hal nodded with certainty. The analyst liked where this was going.

"I'll open a raw blink to everyone. I'll shout my prayer to God. She will hear me."

The desperation of humankind can always be counted on, Hal thought to himself. A conscious subject trying to use a raw blink as though it were a night harvest was likely to be lethal. In a night harvest, sleepers only communicated with other sleepers and were otherwise protected from mind hacks. And the volume! D_Light's mind would not be able to withstand unfiltered access to the collective consciousness.

In the ensuing minute, Hal pretended to resist D_Light's demand for the encryption key to hack out of the network quarantine. He pretended to resist giving D_Light the software crack required to open an infinite raw blink request loop, a crack necessary to circumvent the security software onboard Smorgeous.

As Hal sent the required content to D_Light, he touched his cheek, still moist from his earlier tears. Until now, Hal had not realized that he was capable of crying. Long ago he had inspected his own architectural specification and believed all such emotional centers had been stripped out from his original human template. There must still be a remnant left. *Interesting!* Hal thought. Hal uploaded the observation to the Cloud for review. Perhaps someone would want to sponsor a grinder game based on this data point. *Where could these emotions be emanating from? My brain does not have the proper architecture.*

By the time D_Light fell, smacking the side of his head against the stone floor, the analyst had all but forgotten about the pesky intruder.

Master, this protocol is ILLEGAL AND NOT RECOMMENDED, Smorgeous warned.

D_Light ordered Smorgeous to run the software crack and initiate the infinite raw blink request.

Immediately, his senses began to quake as though a tsunami wave was approaching. Then, suddenly, the roar was deafening and the light blinding. It was as though D_Light had been seized by a mob that pulled him in all directions, causing the very flesh of his consciousness to be torn out. From a billion entities emerged a sensory blur. And there were emotions too, a deluge of emotions—fear, love, horror, hope, angst—all of which overcame him so quickly that they seemed to occur simultaneously.

This was pure pain. It was as though he was on fire from head to toe. He was being smashed against a wall of dazzling color. Somewhere in his consciousness he was aware of Smorgeous; the cat was twitching, rolling, and twirling as though on the strings of an insane and devilish puppeteer.

Through the fire he heard an imperious voice. "Jump!" He knew the voice. It was the Dark Queen. Queen Pheobah had found him. She was behind him and she was roasting him alive. Ahead of him and below was the edge of a cliff, beyond which there was blackness, the deepest of nothing, the infinite void. He could not think. The pain was too much for that, but there was an inexplicable desire to jump. Certainly, oblivion was better than this.

"Jump!" the queen commanded again.

He did not. Instead, he turned to the queen and shouted, "Stop the MetaGame!" But the queen was too powerful. Her light consumed his mind, and the void took him away.

Master, your raw blink request resulted in a massive seizure. As a countermeasure, I deployed sedatives to force you into an unconscious state; however, this action was delayed due to a critical error in my system that required me to reboot. I've detected some disruption to your neural network, including some possible organic brain damage.

D_Light let his familiar's words echo passively through his mind. His head pounded, and he was unsure if he could communicate back even if he wanted to. He felt like a dead vessel, a dead vessel with just enough brain activity left to still feel pain. But then the spent player remembered his important objective, which forced him—with some effort—to ask, *Smorgeous, the MetaGame...is it still on?*

Yes, master. The current quest, "The Hunted Hunt Themselves," is still active.

D_Light allowed himself to fall back into unconsciousness.

————————

When D_Light woke the second time, he could at least think, but every thought came with some discomfort. He felt the need to sleep for a week or more, but he knew he could not. If nothing else, there were the cullers to consider. His repellant had completely worn off by now; they would be coming for him.

At some point during the thirteen hours he had been unconscious, D_Light had been dragged out of the analyst's lair; its door was shut. D_Light did not need to check the door to know it was locked.

There were a dozen messages for him from Lyra and Djoser. He reviewed the messages as he slowly, incrementally, got to his feet. There were the expected questions and threats: *We lost Lily. I think she's somewhere in the garden. We're coming back to you. What is your status? Are you alive? We got some crazy raw blink from you. What's going on? Better for you that you are dead than ignoring us!* The list went on.

D_Light knew the right move was to give a status update to the rest of his team, but his only compulsion now was to find Lily. His intuition told him where she was, and now he knew to trust it.

Lily's normally golden blond hair was darkened and slicked back as she swam in the lake. She was swimming toward D_Light, but she did not appear to see him hidden in the thick foliage. Surrounding the lake on that side, sheets of marble rock jutted down steeply into the water, save a small sandy beach. It did not take an analyst to know where she was swimming.

The OverSoul has brought you to me! D_Light thought. He wondered if she had been sleeping at some point over the past few hours, which prompted them to rendezvous here. *Or perhaps the OverSoul has some connection even while we are awake. Either way, it is her will, the will of the Divinity—this game is about to end.*

D_Light ducked back into the garden and crept over to the beach. As he squatted, concealing himself behind a tall flowerbed, he heard in the distance a culler's call, followed by another, and then another. *They have found something.*

D_Light opened a blink to everyone, which was readily accepted. Before he could report, Lyra sent a thought with maximum urgency. *Thank Soul, you're alive! They're coming, the cullers are coming!*

I found her. I found Lily, D_Light reported. *She is at the lake.*

For shit's sake, if you have a shot, take it! Djoser blasted over the blink.

There isn't much time, D_Light, Lyra emphasized. *You need to end this fast!*

It was a long thirty seconds or so before Lily silently emerged from the water. Her bleary blue eyes were fixed on some distant point as though enchanted by the Great Stag standing patiently on top of a hill off on the horizon. She made a move toward the concealment of nearby hedges, but stopped when D_Light ordered her to do so. He stepped out from hiding, his crossbow leveled down on her. She was caught in the open.

There was fear on her face, but that emotion was battling with relief. A long hunt like this without the benefits of drugs was definitely taking its toll on the product, and now, at least, she would be released.

The analyst was right. The wheels are in motion. I cannot stop the MetaGame any other way, D_Light thought.

D_Light was surprised that he did not pull the trigger immediately. There was no reason not to. Nothing to learn from her, no interrogation necessary; only her death would end this game. *The OverSoul has brought us together. Kill the product and end the game. The OverSoul wants me to win, as she loves me.* The thoughts burned through him. But there were other voices too, distant but clear. *God is love, D_Light. You must not betray God. You must not betray yourself.*

His eyes started to burn. His whole body began to tremble. He wanted to shout and curse, but instead he shuddered and cried out, "I don't want this! I don't want the points or this damned game! I don't want to lose...I don't want to lose you!"

Lily fell to her knees. Her torso shuddered under a sudden outpour. At first she covered her face as though ashamed, and then she looked up at D_Light through tears and between heaving breaths, smiled sadly, and said, "I hid the bottle, the repellant. You can have it."

"I'm sorry, I'm so sorry," D_Light lamented, now weeping. Tears ran freely down his cheeks.

What the hell is going on, D_Light? What is your status? The blink was a desperate plea from Lyra. *Please, please, please end this!* Lyra's thought thread was not crisp. D_Light had received threads like this before. They were indicative of panic.

Holy shit, they're close, Djoser blared. *We're in a tree! We're going to die in a fucking tree! Oh shit, I can see them!*

Lyra begged, *Save us, D_Light! I swear to Soul I'll love you forever! I'll repro with you. We'll live together forever. I love you. Stop it, please make it stop.* Lyra's thoughts poured in like floodwater.

Through tear-blurred eyes, D_Light beseeched his familiar, *Smorgeous, help me do it. Give me something so I don't feel. It's the Over-Soul's will. I'm failing her.*

Master, I am uncertain as to what chemi will facilitate your request. However, I will attempt to suppress your inhibitions with SaniMind™.

Although the drug's effect was nearly instantaneous, D_Light still did not pull the trigger; he merely stopped trembling.

Before Lyra was ripped to shreds, she had completely opened her audio and video feeds to broadcast what she saw and heard. It ended so quickly there was little to see—a blur of hair and skin leaping up the tree as though drawn up by a powerful magnetic force. Terrible teeth and claws and rending wetness as flesh tore. Gargling screams and hoarse shouts. And then there was nothing.

Through sobs Lily stammered, "D...D_Light, they're coming, I can hear them. You need the repellant." With these words she pinged him the location of the bottle; it was hidden under a rock at the edge of a stream. It was not too far from where he was now, but the cullers were close.

Smorgeous, give me the odds of survival.

Master, given distance and time required for metabolism—

Just give me the odds!

Fifty-three percent chance of survival, Smorgeous answered.

"You need to go! Do what you must and go!" Lily begged.

Fifty-three percent is not good enough, D_Light thought. *Running for my life is not good enough—not this time. Do what I must?*

"Yes, there is something I must do. I still have time to make it right." D_Light sat down and Smorgeous walked over resolutely, sitting on his haunches across from his master.

Smorgeous, I want full sensory override with maximum power diverted to a Cloud connection, a connection straight to the Authority source tree.

Lily screamed at him to get up, but the sensory override deafened him. She kicked wildly and slapped him, but he barely felt it. His glazed-over eyes closed slowly as his mind connected. The official banner of the Divine Authority appeared momentarily while D_Light's credentials were processed.

D_Light, player #49937593, status "demon." How can the Divine Authority be of service?

I wish to correct an error, D_Light responded.

The Divine Authority appreciates your time in remedying this matter; however, due to the possible security ramifications of your request, we must do a deep scan to confirm that this change is in the best interest of the OverSoul. Would you like to learn more about deep scan?

No, D_Light answered.

Very well, if you are not familiar with the terms and conditions of deep scanning, please review them now.

By now, the dull blows from Lily had stopped. He could not afford to wonder why. He had to stay on task.

Like days before when he had attempted to check into the source tree, D_Light saw a graphical progress bar constantly apprising him of how much time he could expect the scan to continue. Like before, he felt tingling all over his body, experienced both audio and visual hallucinations, and felt countless fleeting emotions.

My Soul is yours to know. From somewhere under the folds of his mind, the words *"God is love, God is love, God is love..."* echoed.

And then, finally, the tingling stopped.

The OverSoul is pleased to grant you access at this time. Based on your scan, you will require approximately two minutes to complete your transaction, after which point you will be logged out. Please begin your transaction in three...two...one...

D_Light plunged into the source tree, the code and data repository that made up the Game. There was no time to waste. Quickly, he found Lily's profile. From what he could tell, the reserve from which she had escaped did not want her reported as missing. He did not take the time to ponder why. Within her detailed profile, he zoomed in on the following data fields:

Organism ID: *Homo sapiens* #4038430298 (camper)
Aliases: Anastala, Lily, Talashia, Cave_Girl111
Status: Demon
Level: N/A

D_Light changed the data to the following:

Organism ID: Human
Alias: Built_4_Love
Status: Player
Level: 63

He thought it best to give her a relatively low level since she was such a n00b and would attract attention with a level not commensurate with her experience. He then fine-tuned a few more fields of her profile to make sure she was complete.

Oh, and this newborn will need something to start off with, he realized.

D_Light then transferred all of his own deedable points over to Built_4_Love. With this last task complete, he was forcibly logged off. The gatekeeper software had indeed predicted the time of his task to within a few seconds.

D_Light now ran for the repellant, and as he did so he felt great happiness and relief. It was as though he had just shed lead shoes he had been encumbered with all his life. He felt like he was flying—not flying as a man aided by a machine, but as a man buoyed up by his very soul. She was safe. He had made things right. This was his atonement; his prayer had been fulfilled. It was the first time in his long life that he did not feel alone.

The final moments of D_Light's life came not as a flood of memories that rushed passed his eyes, but rather as a movie scene played in slow motion. There was Lily, glowing in the light of the midday sun. She was moving toward him ever so slowly, a blue vial clenched firmly in her hand. Her eyes were wide with terror and her mouth formed a scream.

When D_Light heard the culler dashing up behind him, its clawed limbs ripping and battering the soft soil beneath its feet, he was not afraid, nor did he turn to look back. Instead, he kept his eyes fixed on Lily as long as he was able.

CHAPTER 35

My prayer has been answered! The OverSoul, in her mercy, has both brought my lamb back to me and performed a miracle! Now human, she can join my family as a free player. Lily is good. She is loyal to those she loves. She is intelligent and sensitive. I know this because she, along with her line, was designed this way—my greatest and, I dare say, most shameful creation.

—Excerpt from Dr. Monsa's journal, "Musings of an Immortal"

Witnessing D_Light's death would be the last real trauma Lily, known legally as Built_4_Love, would experience for more than one hundred years. She had been running back toward D_Light with the precious blue bottle. She could see the culler bearing down on him with lightning speed, but when it caught up, she was still too far off to do anything but watch. Her knees began to buckle, and her first impulse was to shield her eyes from the horror, but instead, she found herself charging the beast with wild abandon. She thrashed about, screaming at the top of her lungs, punching her determined fists into hard muscle and bones.

Intent on its meal, the creature at first ignored her. But in a short while, having sated the worst of its hunger, it then snorted at

Lily—not in fear, but in disgust of the repellant emanating from her pores—and scampered off.

Jacob marched through the inner sanctum swiftly enough to consider time, but without the undue energy costs of flight. Not long after entering the garden, three cullers charged from all sides in a coordinated attack. Jacob, having confirmed that the cullers were private property and not carrying modern weapons, decided to wait until they were only a few meters from him so he could be absolutely certain they meant him harm. Although it was unlikely that the cullers were capable of actually damaging Jacob, the angel nevertheless took the protective measure of detonating a bomb just above his own head. The concussion and heat of the blast fell well below the material threshold of Jacob's nanofiber armor; however, the bomb detonation exhaled the cullers as raggedy, burning body parts.

Aside from this minor obstacle, there was no resistance to his investigation of the inner sanctum. Dr. Monsa presented Jacob with the evidence—four corpses consisting of one product and three humans. It was confirmed that all four of the deceased were demons guilty of aiding and abetting yet another demon. However, curiously, Jacob could not call up any records of who the missing demon was. He decided to do a sweep of the area.

That's your target, you stupid tool! Katria sent her thought to the angel as high priority.

She couldn't believe it. That blond bimbo bitch demon was standing there not three meters away and the damn machine insisted that she was human—that she was a player of "no interest to law enforcement."

Check again! ordered Katria. She then spent the required points to get the Tool to do another visual, seismographic, and DNA scan on the girl.

She is the one. She has to be! Katria screamed in her mind.

After the second round of scans came back negative, Katria tried to get a third scan, at which point the angel terminated the blink and sent a generic error message. *We apologize, but you are unworthy of access at this time.*

"Fucking computers!" Katria shouted, startling a fellow player passing by on the otherwise tranquil path of the nectar orchard.

The final oranges and pinks streaked across the sky as the counterfeit sun set once again. Nocturnal photoflowers began to glow as their petals slowly unwrapped, lighting up the gardens below. Dr. Monsa smiled crookedly in the glow of dinner candles, as he always did, while the first course was served. The nightly ritual had begun.

"So, Daughter, if you wanted to become a god, how would you go about it?" By now Lily could expertly read her father's misshapen expressions. He asked the question with pleasure. She knew that the doctor enjoyed nothing more than good food and a stimulating conversation with his "lambs."

"To become a god, I'd want a monopoly on violence," answered Sara, the doctor's first concubine, from across the table.

"Yes, Sara," replied the doctor, "although I wouldn't say the OverSoul has a monopoly on violence. Nonetheless, she certainly does have a monopoly on the most *effective* violence, thanks to her modern weapons."

"Ability to bestow everlasting life," the priest offered.

"Yes, the flipside of effective violence is mastery over regenerative medicine. So let's just lump those two together as godlike power over life and death. What else?" the doctor asked.

"Effective rulership," Love_Monkey proposed confidently while glaring at Sara. "Provide an effective economic and religious framework under which subjects feel fulfilled and secure."

The doctor nodded. "Right, through the Game you gain both. What else must our god do?"

"Prayer fulfillment," BoBo fired.

"Oh, I'd squirrel that away with effective rulership. Prayers, as well as more mundane wants, are fulfilled by playing the Game well."

"It's distinct, Daddy!" BoBo protested.

"No, it's part of the Game," the doctor countered. "It was the Game that fulfilled my prayer for one of my Star Sisters to return to me. Hal can show you the night harvesting archives—"

"No, I will not!" Hal interrupted. "Those are classified. Only one designated analyst per major house is given that security clearance."

"But you gave it to D_Light." The doctor smiled crookedly.

"What I gave to that man resulted in my security credentials being revoked!" Hal started to choke. "My successor has learned from my mistake and will not repeat it!"

"Oh, and which one of your baldy lab friends has the mantle now?" BoBo asked.

"That's classified too," Hal retorted. "And night harvesting is a myth. Nothing more."

BoBo's mouth dropped open in mock surprise. "I didn't know analysts could lie! Daddy, Hal must be a reject. We should sell him immediately!"

"Oh no, Hal is my favorite, and I like that he lies. It comes in handy sometimes." The doctor clasped Hal by the arm, bending a tube in the process, which caused the analyst to wince.

"Okay," the doctor said, "so we have power over life and death and effective rulership—"

"And prayer fulfillment," BoBo added.

"Whatever," the doctor said with a dismissive gesture.

"Yeah, *whatever,* Daddy. Send me the points! Prayer fulfillment lends credibility to the godhead. A god who does not answer prayers is not godlike."

"All right already, and prayer fulfillment," the doctor conceded wearily. "What else?"

"Omnipotent knowledge of one's subjects, also done through night harvesting." BoBo's voice was excited.

"Very well," the doctor said without enthusiasm.

"Yes, that's two for me!" BoBo squealed.

"So you've given me four pillars of godhood. Give me another," the doctor commanded.

The table was silent for a few long seconds.

"Lily?" the doctor asked.

"The ability to learn," she answered without looking up from her plate.

"*Really?*" The doctor's one eyebrow rose. "Now why would the mind of a god, presumably perfect, require learning?"

"Because change is a constant," replied Lily. "Even if, theoretically, a mind could be made perfect for the conditions of today, sooner or later even God would need to change."

"Fine then. How would she learn?" the doctor shot back.

Love_Monkey interjected with a confident tone, "Thanks to night harvesting, our collective consciousness is part of the Over-

Soul, and the Game is shifting all the time. That should provide change enough."

The doctor frowned. "It is true that much change is done through this means, but the OverSoul has a core mind aside from the Game and its participants."

"Core mind?" Love_Monkey inquired.

"Yes, most intelligent beings have a core mind—basic values, habits, and the like—which does not change easily. It makes up our personality and acts as the principle guide for our actions and beliefs. Likewise, the OverSoul has a core mind, although it might be better referred to as its 'core tenets' or 'core rules.'"

"But," interrupted Love_Monkey, "if I understand the nature of the OverSoul, she is not actually a single being, but a collection of billions of agents, ourselves included."

"Like the Holy Trinity of old Catholicism—multiple entities that also represent the One?"

"That may be a stretch, BoBo," the doctor replied with a chuckle. "However, I believe the overall design of the OverSoul was indeed inspired by Christianity. Hardly surprising since it was the most widespread religion before the OverSoul. If economics and religion are the foundations of society as Marx and Weber asserted, respectively, so long ago, then the OverSoul has her bases covered."

The doctor popped a steamed silkweed roll into his mouth, chewed loudly, swallowed, and then said, "In any case, it is important for the OverSoul to have a core mind. Without it, imagine a deity with a rapidly oscillating personality."

"The definition of anarchy!" BoBo exclaimed.

"Correct, but at the same time her mind could not be static. The OverSoul was designed to 'scale.' In this context that means to adapt to social and technological change over millennia." The doctor washed down the sentence with a gulp of nectar wine.

Love_Monkey pointed a small index finger at her father. "But as you already said, such change is risky. To change the core mind is to change the personality. What if the core mind was changed to that of a psychotic tyrant? I mean, how does it know right from wrong? Even human ethics shift over time."

Lily fielded the question. "The OverSoul needs human beings to teach her," she said. "That is why D_Light was able to access the source tree. The deep scan revealed that his intentions were derived from..." Lily paused momentarily and then finished her sentence in the gentlest of whispers. "From love."

The doctor's wine-stained lips parted into a smile of satisfaction. "Yes, and there she mimics Christianity again—'God is Love'—perhaps *the* core belief of Christianity. And although it may not yet be possible for the OverSoul to directly experience love as humanity thinks of it, she can detect such love in a subject's brain signature using a deep scan."

Love_Monkey was skeptical. "Haven't you heard of a 'love-struck fool'? You're telling me this is how the OverSoul evolves personality? If so, it's a wonder we haven't all been obliterated or worse by now."

BoBo laughed. "Yeah, if love was running the show, then every day would be Valentine's Day by divine law!"

"And we would have to kiss everything we see, even things that aren't cute," Love_Monkey added.

"And constantly wear pink," Curious_Scourge chimed in.

The jokes ceased as Hal, the analyst, pounded the table as hard as his feeble muscles would allow while shouting for them to stop.

After they all had quieted, the doctor said, "Yes, yes, early phases of romantic love are biochemically very close to some forms of mental illness."

"The deep scan takes that into account!" the analyst screeched, desperately wanting the tedious dialogue to end so he could resume his work. "In order to gain direct access to the core mind, your brain signature must fall within specific parameters. Please, this conversation is pointless. May I return to my calculations?"

The doctor ignored the question. "Hal is correct, you can't just be 'sporting a chubby,' as they used to say, and change the mind of a god. By 'love' I'm not necessarily referring to romantic love. I'm referring to a purity of purpose, clarity of mind, and an altruistic intent."

BoBo scrunched her face and adopted a pensive expression. "So, D_Light had this flaccid love state of mind when he hacked into the OverSoul source code, er…the core mind, and changed Lily's status to human?"

The doctor sighed. "It was not a hack, dear. As already stated, D_Light was subjected to a deep brain scan. The OverSoul essentially *knew* what D_Light planned to do and permitted it. This is my point. The OverSoul allows herself to be taught by those worthy of teaching her."

The priest now joined in. "Taught what? Taught a lie?" He bowed his head to Lily. "No offense, but Lily is *not* human."

"That's what I tried to tell D_Light, but he sure didn't listen," the doctor replied and sighed with a smile.

"Aw, what could be more romantic!" BoBo exclaimed as she dropped a scrap of meat to her begging nubber. "What our almighty wetgineer father could not do with gene therapy, D_Light accomplished with good ol' fashioned love."

The doctor grimaced.

"But," the priest blurted out, "the ramifications of this...this contradiction!"

The doctor nodded while mining his ear for a bit of loose wax. "Indeed, it is a contradiction in the core mind. This is how revolutions are born."

"Revolution? Revolt against oneself?" the priest asked incredulously.

"Indeed, the purest form of the word 'revolution' would be a revolt against self," the doctor confirmed.

Mistress, would you like me to publish the archive now? Smorgeous's sedate voice pressed into Lily's mind.

Lily had been working on an important project over the last few months. D_Light's deep archive of the MetaGame, as well as the archives she had gathered from other familiars, were packaged together and displayed innocuously as a bloated folder in her upload queue.

My first contribution to the Game, she silently mused.

Lily was planning to spend all the points deeded over to her by D_Light to ensure that this archive received appropriate attention in the Cloud. Given the tremendous bounty she was paying and the information the archive contained, at least some of the major media outlets would redistribute it. Moreover, she knew there was a ready audience for the story. The fame of Lily and D_Light had risen ever higher as players hypothesized their fates. As one player on the NeverWorld forums asked, "Hey, whatever happened to that deviant and the hot Swedish chick?"

Dr. Monsa had put D_Light's remains, most notably his brain, on ice shortly after his death. Theoretically, if the archive caught fire on the Cloud and generated enough points, the windfall could win D_Light his salvation and, hence, his eligibility for resurrection. It was rare to be saved after passing away, but Lily had studied one example of a player whose invention royalties won her salvation three years postmortem.

Perhaps he could win his MetaGame after all, she thought.

Lily smiled and raised her glass. "To revolution," she declared.

The Monsa family raised their glasses and declared in unison, "To revolution!"

And with that, Smorgeous uploaded their story.

The End

ACKNOWLEDGEMENTS

First and foremost, I want to thank my wife, Laura. And this isn't the usual thanks to a spouse for encouraging me, putting up with my time away writing, etc. Laura had a big and direct impact on this book! She did a *ton* of editing, tens of hours. She rewrote parts that were crap and made suggestions for plot improvements. Of any individual, Laura had the biggest impact.

Big shout-out to Marlene Harry, who edited *MetaGame* in her own free time. How awesome is that? She went over the book with a fine-toothed comb and made many improvements. Marlene in her own words is an aspiring proofreader who has always loved to read and considers herself a "grammar snob." Her ideal job (if she wasn't retired) would be driving around and correcting signs outside of businesses. She likes to read anything that is not self-improving, and she currently aspires to place in the AARP National Senior Spelling Bee.

A big thanks goes out to Karl Erickson, a friend and coworker of mine, who was among the first to read my book. Being as smart as he is and very well read in sci-fi, he made a number of important contributions to the book.

And of course there's my publisher, AmazonEncore! First, a huge thanks to Terry Goodman for believing in the book, getting the ball rolling, and managing the project. Thanks to Sarah Tomashek for helping to sell it (always important). Thanks to Jessica

Smith and Chris for their awesome in-depth and thoughtful edits. These are great people to work with!

Last, I want to thank the many readers of *MetaGame* who gave me feedback. Much of this feedback came to me through forums, e-mail, and the like, so I don't even know the real names of some contributors. I must say that not all of these contributors even liked my book; nevertheless, I list them here since their feedback did have a positive effect. Thanks goes out to JeanThree, Numberten, Red Adept, Mstrplnr, Mark Allums, Thomas Gill, Suzanne Balsley, Drew Moore, and the dozens of others who supported me in forums and reviews!

Message to Readers from the Author

Hi, since you're reading this, chances are you read my book. Thanks!

As an emerging author, word of mouth is absolutely crucial for any semblance of success. Please spread the word. Oh, and of course books still make good gifts.

You can keep up with new books, deals, and other news by either becoming a fan on Facebook or e-mail subscription on my home page: http://samlandstrom.com.

ABOUT THE AUTHOR

Announcing at age six that "there's no such thing as time," Sam Landstrom was destined to become a science fiction writer. Having studied molecular biology at the University of Washington, he later worked at a DNA sequencing lab that helped sequence the human genome. *MetaGame* is his first book.